THE GREEN HAT

The Green Hat is the quintessence of the Twenties: gay, stylish, mannered and bitter-sweet, a brilliant mixture of cynicism and sentiment. When it first appeared in 1924, it was (as Margaret Bellasis said in *The Dictionary of National Biography*), 'acclaimed, attacked, parodied and read, to the most fabulous degree of best-sellerdom . . . The character of the heroine, Iris Storm, that wanton of quality, "shameless, shameful lady", gallantly crashing to her death in her great yellow Hispano-Suiza—"for Purity"—set a new fashion in fatal charmers: and the pictures of London cafe society were exact as glossy photographs.' Michael Arlen himself was Armenian by birth, but he was educated in England and was both entirely at home in English society and yet distanced enough from it to write about it accurately and mockingly, with that brilliance and wit which the English are always supposed to permit to foreigners but to decry in their fellow countrymen. *The Green Hat* is above all a witty tragi-comedy of manners, that captures the spirit of the glittering, colourful yet slightly unreal world of London after the first World War.

Michael Arlen was born in 1895 in Bulgaria. He changed his name from Dikram Kouyoumdjian in 1922 when he became a naturalised British citizen, having already published novels and short stories under his new name. Following the success of *The Green Hat* he wrote a number of further novels, the last of which appeared in 1939. He died in New York in 1956.

THE GREEN HAT

A Romance for a Few People

Michael Arlen

THE BOYDELL PRESS

Copyright 1924 Michael Arlen

First published in BOOKMASTERS 1983
by The Boydell Press
an imprint of Boydell and Brewer Ltd
PO Box 9, Woodbridge, Suffolk, IP12 3DF

British Library Cataloguing in Publication Data

Arlen, Michael
The green hat
I. Title
823'.912[F]   PR6001.R7

ISBN 0-85115-210-4

Printed in Great Britain by
St Edmundsbury Press, Bury St Edmunds, Suffolk

CONTENTS

Chapter One	The Green Hat	1
Chapter Two	The Cavalier of Low Creatures	37
Chapter Three	For Purity!	52
Chapter Four	Aphrodite	76
Chapter Five	The Dark Letter	103
Chapter Six	The Red Lights	119
Chapter Seven	For Venice!	145
Chapter Eight	Piqûre du Cœur	164
Chapter Nine	Talking of Hats	175
Chapter Ten	The Fall of the Emerald	187
The Last Chapter	St George for England!	209

CHAPTER ONE   THE GREEN HAT

I

It has occurred to the writer to call this unimportant history
The Green Hat because a green hat was the first thing about
her that he saw: as also it was, in a way, the last thing about
her that he saw. It was bright green, of a sort of felt, and
bravely worn: being, no doubt, one of those that women who
have many hats affect *pour le sport*.

I saw it for the first time (writes the Author) on the eve of
my removal from one residence in London to another;
although when I say residence I mean that I was, by the
grace of God and at the impulse of my own temerity, remov-
ing to somewhat more habitable premises nearby from two
rooms and a bathroom above a mean lane in a place called
Shepherd's Market. Not that our lane hadn't attractions of
its own to offer. Our lane was one in which many improbable
things were wont to happen, but it somehow seemed inevitable that such things should happen there. But maybe I had
better select a few of these things, that you may know the
sort of lane ours was. I have seen men arrested there, and I
have seen a heavy constable worsted in a fight with a little
Jew pick-pocket, who was for some time responsible for a
rag-shop in our lane. I have seen two butlers fighting in our
lane. I have seen a very old nobleman woo a flower-girl in
our lane, but whether or not she ever favoured his suit our
lane had no means of telling. One night I fell over the body
of a woman lying in the blood of a broken head, and in our
lane by night policemen solace themselves by smoking
cigarettes into the crowns of their helmets, while cats, I must
tell you, will never cease to sport together all about it.

But it was by day that our lane attained to any real interest
for a student of such things, for then it was sacred to the
activities of a hearty-looking man in a brown bowler-hat,
who with one hand would write interminably in a small book,
while with the other he dealt with passing men in slips of
paper known to the law as 'betting-slips'. As partner to the
hearty-looking man—we are, I venture to say, already
embarked on our tale, for these gentlemen will make a faint

I

devil's chorus for more spacious happenings—was a tall, wizened man who wore a check cap and had hair growing out of his ears. This man would stand at one end of the lane and now and then say, 'Oi!' When he had said 'Oi!' he would light a cigarette, while the hearty-looking man would run heavily round our end of the lane, for 'Oi!' meant that the law was after him. When the law had gone he would come back wiping his mouth, and jokes were exchanged with the butcher and the fishmonger; but when the law really wanted him, say twice a year, a posse of policemen would simultaneously rush both ends of our lane, and the hearty-looking man was mulcted in a fine not exceeding so much and was back again the next morning within a yard of my door. Among his most persistent admirers was a little bent old man with blood-shot eyes and a twitching mouth, who was a window-cleaner without a Union, which meant that he would clean a window for threepence and want no tip. He liked me, and used to give me racing information, but I never won anything.

Now the first thing to do is to clear the ground as quickly as possible for the coming of the green hat, for Mr. H. G. Wells says that there is no money to be made out of any book that cannot bring a woman in within the first few thousand words. But in setting the scene in Shepherd's Market we have evaded the necessity for any 'writing-up' of atmosphere, for that place has an atmosphere quite impossible to convey in a book, unless, of course, you were to take the book to Shepherd's Market and leave it in our lane for a few days in nice warm weather. Shepherd's Market is, in fine, a collection of lively odours bounded on the north side by Curzon Street, on the south by Piccadilly, on the west by Hertford Street, and on the east by Half-Moon Street; and rejoices, therefore, in the polite direction of Mayfair, as you will see printed on the notepaper of any of its residents. A flower-shop which was opened in our lane lived for only six months, and that in spite of the gardenia gallantly affected by the old nobleman from Curzon Street every day. I, after having lived there for six years, was (by the grace of God) leaving on the morrow.

It is late, after midnight, when the tale begins.

I had been that evening to a party; for that is now the name that folks give to a dance—I am not sure why. In America, I believe, one doesn't even give a party, one just throws a party, but as to this party I am telling of, it had, with that infallible sense of direction peculiar to parties, whether given or thrown, taken a man by the nerves at the back of his head and had hurled him into a deep pit. And it was as one encompassed by that pit, deep as the playground of the seven devils, dark as the very dungeons of gaiety, that I found myself back in my flat above the mean lane. It would be the last night I would ever spend in that flat, and I was so glad. The bookshelves had already been taken away, and books littered the floor, books and pictures and what-nots crowded the gate-leg table, while the ottoman with its soiled Chinese yellow cover was a shambles of whatever you will find in a bachelor's flat if you begin to clean out the drawers. The bedroom, however, was still ordered for human habitation.

Now I had no sooner cast my hat on the bed than the bell rang. It was one of those infernal things you pull at, so that they may go on clanging for ever, and as it clanged I wondered, I am afraid ungraciously, who it could be. Could it, I wondered, be anyone for Gerald March, who lived in the flat above mine? But no one, I told myself, has called on Gerald March within the memory of man, for that man discourages callers, that man knows how to discourage callers.

I had no hope in pretending not to be at home, for my lights were plain to see from our lane. And in my mind's eye I saw the hearty face of the acquaintance at the door, and with my mind's ear I heard the hearty greeting that dropped from his parasitical and thirsty lips. He had seen my light, that man, as he went his way home from some party even more pestilential than the one which had sent me home stricken; and he would fain drink a glass with me, after the fashion of pests of the night, that are hearty with the weary and thirsty with the unwary.

I could, however, always order my privacy without seeming too unfriendly by looking down from my bedroom window, for whereas the windows of my sitting-room faced the public-bar of The Leather Butler and an angle of the offices of the Duke of Marlborough's fine house, from my bedroom window I had a clear prospect of our lane. Of pests, however, there was neither sight nor sign; nor of cats, nor of men, nor of any low and usual thing; only, under the lamp at the Sheep Street end of our lane, a long, low, yellow car which shone like a battle-chariot. It was empty.

Now I am of those who are affected by motor-cars: their lines thrill me, the harmony of their colour touches me, a gallant device wins my earnest admiration so that, walking along Piccadilly, I will distress my mind by being a partisan of this one, a despiser of that one. Nor am I to be won by any cheap thing, no matter how brave-seeming it may be to the eye, how admirable in endurance; but I am to be won only by the simple lines, the severe and menacing aspect, of the aces among motor-cars; for economy hath charms, but not to the eye. This car charmed the eye. Like a huge yellow insect that had dropped to earth from a butterfly civilisation, this car, gallant and suave, rested in the lowly silence of the Shepherd's Market night. Open as a yacht, it wore a great shining bonnet, and flying over the crest of this great bonnet, as though in proud flight over the heads of scores of phantom horses, was that silver stork by which the gentle may be pleased to know that they have just escaped death beneath the wheels of a Hispano-Suiza car, as supplied to His Most Catholic Majesty.

Downwards to my door I looked, and there was a green hat before my door. The light from the one lamp in Sheep Street fell about it, and that was how I saw that it was a green hat, of a sort of felt, and bravely worn: being, no doubt, one of those that women who have many hats affect *pour le sport*.

2

'Do you know if Mr. March is in?' asked the voice of the green hat. But I could not see her face for the shadow of the brim, for it was a piratical brim, such as might very possibly defy the burning suns of El Dorado.

I said I was not sure. I was very surprised—a caller for

4

Gerald March! 'If we look up,' I said, 'we can see by his lights if he is in.' And I stepped out into the lane, and the green hat and I stared up at the topmost windows of the grubby little house.

'There's no light *there*,' she said. 'I suppose the light below is yours. . . .'

'There is,' I said, 'but it's very faint. He's in all right.'

Still she looked up, thoughtfully. She was tall, not very tall, but as tall as becomes a woman. Her hair, in the shadow of her hat, may have been any colour, but I dared swear that there was a tawny whisper to it. And it seemed to dance, from beneath her hat, a very formal dance on her cheeks. One had, with her, a sense of the conventions; and that she had just been playing six sets of tennis.

'If I look surprised,' I said, 'that is because you are the first caller Gerald March has ever had.'

She seemed to smile, faintly, as one might in the way of politeness. Otherwise she did not seem to be given to smiling.

'He's my brother,' she said, as though explaining herself, the hour, everything. 'It's very nice of you to have opened the door. . . .'

I was listening, oh intently! One had to, to make out what she was saying. Then the voice suddenly expired and one was left standing there, listening to nothing, unprepared to say anything. It was, you can see, rather silly; but one got used to it.

'Oh,' I said, 'Gerald wouldn't open a door! He never opens doors. . . .'

She looked vaguely about our lane. I was proud of our lane at that moment, for it set off the colour of her hat so well. There was no doubt but that she was tired. Seven sets, possibly. Her eyes seemed at last to find the car of the flying silver stork.

'That car . . . I suppose it will be all right there?'

She seemed to me to lack a proper pride in her car. I said I thought it would be quite all right there, as though a Hispano-Suiza was a usual sight near my door; and I suggested that maybe I had better see her upstairs to her brother's flat, as it was the top flat and there were no lights on the stairs. But she appeared to be in no hurry. Thoughtful she was. She said dimly: 'You are very kind. . . .'

One somehow gathered from her voice that her face was very small.

'I've often wanted,' she murmured, looking about, 'to live in this place. You know, vaguely. . . .'

'Of course, vaguely,' I said.

She looked at me, seemed to see me for the first time, seemed faintly surprised to find herself talking to me. I was surprised, too. Maybe it was the way her hair danced formally on her cheeks that made it look such a small face, but it seemed to me no larger than a small size in ladies' handkerchiefs. That was why I was surprised. She stood carelessly, like the women in Georges Barbier's almanacks, *Falbalas et Fanfreluches*, who know how to stand carelessly. Her hands were thrust into the pockets of a light brown leather jacket—*pour le sport*—which shone quite definitely in the lamplight: it was wide open at the throat, and had a high collar of the fur of a few minks. I once had a friend who was a taxidermist, and that was how I knew that. One small red elephant marched across what I could see of her dress, which was dark and not *pour le sport*.

'Perhaps you are right,' she admitted doubtfully. Not that I had the faintest idea what she was talking about.

I went before her up the dark narrow stairs, sideways, lighting and dropping matches, after the custom of six years. There were three floors in the little house, but the first was untenanted except by mice. I wondered whether it would interest her if I told her I was leaving to-morrow, but I did not see why it should. She, after all, had probably just come back from foreign parts. About her, it was perfectly obvious, was the aura of many adventures. But I was looking on her in brotherly sort, interested in her because she was Gerald March's sister. For that was a most deficient man in every other respect. Fancy, I thought. She said: 'Oo, isn't it dark!'

'Of course,' I said, striking yet another match against the wall, 'I knew Gerald *had* a sister, but I had a vague idea, I don't know why, that she was still at school. . . .'

6

'I don't suppose,' she said helpfully—stumbled slightly, I helped her—'that anyone knows *everything*. Is that mice downstairs? Rats? Oo, really. . . . Gerald and I showed, once upon a time, a strong tendency to be twins, though there was a good hour between us, so I was told. I was at the tail end of the hour.' Slowly struggling up those dim, narrow, musty stairs, her green hat now and then flaming in the matchlight, she gave one worthless information in a slightly husky, impersonal voice. As we came up to my landing I asked her if she had seen Gerald lately.

'Not,' she said, whispered, 'for years and years. Nearly ten, I think. Do you think that comes, perhaps, of having been almost twins once upon a time?'

I did not say anything for I was thinking hard. Now I was Gerald's friend. This lady of the green hat was Gerald's sister, nay, his twin sister. Fancy, I thought. Where, I asked myself, did one stand? It was a matter for thought, for deep thought, and so I treated it, as she did not appear to be in any great hurry.

Now while these things were passing the lady and I were standing on my landing, which was four foot by three; she with one foot on the stair below, one leather shoulder against the wall. And one had again, with her, a sense of the conventions.

'You are thinking,' she accused me. 'I wonder what about. . . .'

The light that plunged through my half open sitting-room door fought a great fight with the shadow of her green hat and lit her face, mysteriously. She was fair. As they would say it in the England of long ago—she was fair. And she was grave, so grave. That is a sad lady, I thought. To be fair, to be sad . . . why, was she intelligent, too? And white she was, very white, and her painted mouth was purple in the dim light, and her eyes, which seemed set very wide apart, were cool, impersonal, sensible, and they were blazing blue. Even in that light they were blazing blue, like two spoonfuls of the Mediterranean in the early morning of a brilliant day. The sirens had eyes like that, without a doubt, when they sang of better dreams. But no siren, she! That was a sad lady, most grave. And always her hair would be dancing a tawny, formal dance about the small white cheeks.

She smiled, when it occurred to her that she was looking at me.

'I know what you are thinking,' she said.

'I wonder!'

'Yes. You like Gerald, don't you?' She thought about that. 'Well, what you are thinking is, whether it is fair to him to take me up there in case he is drunk. . . .'

'If only it was "in case,"' I said. 'You see?'

She closed her eyes.

'Poor Gerald!' she whispered. 'Isn't it a shame!'

'I'm afraid,' I said, 'there's nothing to be done. . . .'

'Oh, I know!' Oh, she seemed to know that from her heart. And I wondered why they had not seen each other for ten years. I couldn't imagine her disliking Gerald—childish, furious Gerald! Probably, I thought, he was to blame, and I wondered if there was anything in Gerald's life for which he was not to blame. Poor Gerald.

'You see,' the slightly husky voice was saying, 'I just came to-night on an Impulse. I am scarcely ever in England. . . .' The voice expired. We waited, and she acknowledged my patience with a jewel of a smile. 'And I suddenly thought I would like to see Gerald to-night. Please,' she suddenly begged, so seriously, 'won't you let me? I'd like just to *see* him . . . but if you think . . . ?'

'Oh,' I said, 'come on.'

She laughed, a little nervously, abruptly. Gerald's door was at the head of the next flight of stairs, and it was, as usual, wide open. She moved one step forward into the room, she stopped, her eyes on the ceiling, as fixed as lamps. Yes, those were very sensible eyes. She didn't look at Gerald.

'What is it?' she asked dimly.

'Whisky,' I said. It was so obvious.

'But more than that! There's certainly whisky, but . . .'

'Wet shoes. . . .'

'But that's too literary! Oh, of course! Old women in alms-houses. . . .'

She was talking, it was so easy to see, against her eyes. Now

8

she was here she didn't want to see Gerald. She was trying to put off the moment when her eyes must rest on Gerald. Still just within the dingy room, she looked everywhere but at Gerald.

'Lot of books,' she said.

I made to go, but the slightest hint of a start detained me. She suggested her gestures. That was a very quiet lady. She didn't, if you please, intrude her womanhood on the occasion. Women do that unconsciously. But she didn't do it, unconsciously. She met a man on his own ground. That was a gallant lady.

'Oh!' she said. 'Oh!'

'Might just as well come away,' I muttered. I was used to Gerald, but at the moment, at her sudden whisper, I would have liked to murder him. Here for sixteen months not a soul had come to see him—and now, before his sister, and his twin sister too, he was in this vile state. But she had insisted on seeing him. What could I do? I promised Gerald a pretty speech on the morrow. He would be more or less human to-morrow, for Gerald had those phenomenal recuperative powers that are peculiar to lean drunkards.

'The illness,' I told her, 'goes in periods of three days. On the first day he is thoughtful, on the second he is thoughtless, and on the third speechless.'

I could not see her face, her back was to me. The leather jacket, the brave green hat, the thoughtful poise. But I heard her whisper the name of the inert thing sprawling half on a broken Windsor chair and half across the littered table, and it was as though there was a smile in the whisper, and I thought to myself that these twins must have been great playmates once upon a time. 'Gerald!' she whispered. 'Gerald! Gerald!'

'Oh, go to hell!' muttered Gerald, and, without looking up, without waking up, twitched his head feverishly to one side, upsetting a tea-cup half-full of whisky.

'He thinks it's me,' I explained from the door, and suddenly I found her looking at me over her shoulder, so thoughtfully. I can see her now, the way she suddenly looked at me, half over her leather shoulder, thinking I knew

9

not what, and her right hand spread out on her brother's arm. There was a striking emerald on the third finger of her right hand, livid against the dark thing that was Gerald March.

'Only twenty-nine,' she told me gravely, 'Gerald and me. . . .'

'Oh,' I said. What could one say?

'Bad luck, I do think,' she murmured. I wondered, you know, whom she was talking to. Certainly not to me.

'He's a very good fellow,' I said.

'Heredity, you see,' she suddenly explained. 'Father almost died of it. Brandy, though. He liked brandy, Barty did. They said he would die if he had more than half-a-bottle a day, but he had a bottle to make sure, and then he died of pneumonia.'

Then, in her silence, she was so still that I grew very uncomfortable. What was she thinking about? She was staring down at the sprawling thing that was her twin brother, the emerald still livid against his arm.

'He wrote a very good book once,' I said, to say something.

'Yes. About Boy. . . .'

'Boy?' Gerald, you see, was no talker. He just swore, but automatically, it meant nothing.

'Didn't you know?' She looked at me again, but her eyes seemed to me masked. I was to know later why her eyes were masked just then. I said I knew nothing at all about Gerald.

She passed a finger over one of her eyebrows, and looked at it. 'Dirty,' she said.

'Years ago,' she said, 'before the war, Gerald had a very great friend. Gerald, you see, is a hero-worshipper. In spite of his air and everything, that is what Gerald is, a hero-worshipper. And no hero, no Gerald. And so, when his hero died, Gerald died too. Funny life is, isn't it? Then the war, and that, of course, buried him. And now . . .' Those absorbed, blazing blue eyes! The sea was in them, and the whisper of all open places: the magic of the sea was in her eyes, whipped with salt and winds.

'No friends?' she asked dimly. 'No women? Nothing?'

And just at that moment I had, for the first time, that

feeling of incapacity with her. I was to have it again, profoundly, but I remember vividly that it came for the first
time just then, in poor, furious Gerald's room. Dingy—that
is what I felt before this quiet, thoughtful woman with the
absorbed eyes. Dingy. I felt, I suppose, the immense dinginess of being a human being, for there is an immense, unalter-
able dinginess in being human, in the limitation of being
human. But why I should feel that particularly with her I
did not know then. She, too, was human, quiet, gentle, very
unaware. But, later, I was to know why.

It was with an effort that I told her about Gerald. That
feeling of self-dinginess came somehow to a point in just
feeling common. For I was what Gerald was not, what she
obviously was not. I could somehow 'cope with' my time
and generation, while they were of the breed destined to
failure. I was of the race that is surviving the England of
Horatio Bottomley, the England of lies, vulgarity, and unclean savagery; while they of the imperious nerves had
failed, they had died that slow white death which is reserved
for privilege in defeat.

Gerald, I told her, was a more solitary man than I had
ever known or thought to know. I supposed he had a small
income, for he seemed to manage to live. He was very shy,
absurdly shy, tortured shy. She nodded gravely, and I went
on to say that shyness was a cruel disease with Gerald: it was
a shyness, to strangers, without charm, for he never could
show his shyness, he must show everything but his shyness.
And so it was that he couldn't get on with people, and now
he had ceased to try, he just had drinks. Every Sunday afternoon he went to tea with his aunt Lady Eve Chalice in
Mount Street.

'It was Eve who really created my impulse,' she told me,
then: 'Oh, here!' and I found I had an empty cigarette-case
in my hand and that she was offering me hers. It was an
oblong white-jade case, and chained to it by a double chain
of gold was a hectagonal black onyx box which may or may
not have held powder. One corner of the hectagonal black
onyx was initialled in minute diamond letters: I.S.

'Iris,' she said. 'Iris Storm.' And she smiled, childishly,

formally, saying: 'You have been so nice, I had forgotten we didn't know each other.' I told her my name, in that embarrassed way one always does tell anyone one's name, and we smoked a while in silence. She inhaled her smoke with a faint hiss, and her teeth were a regiment of even bits of rice-paper standing at attention, very smart and sharp. Teeth always give one ideas. These were imperious, dangerous teeth. On a middle one was wedged a small string of tobacco: it lay coiled there like a brown maggot, and when I told her about that she removed it with the nail of her small finger, and regarded it. She had a great talent for looking at nothing in particular, and that was the only likeness I could see between the twins: thoughtful they both were. Suddenly, from the tousled dark head on the table came a jumble of inarticulate words. She listened intently. Gerald shivered, but his face remained buried in his crossed arms.

'He's dreaming,' I said. She looked at me, and I thought there were tears in her eyes. But as they never fell, I am not sure. Thoughtful she was, smoking. . . .

'Why does God do these things?' she asked in a suddenly strong, clear voice, a most surprising voice; but I said nothing, knowing nothing of God.

'Let us go,' she said.

'Shall I tell him you came?'

She thought about that, looking at me. 'Yes,' she said, 'will you? Please. Just that I came. You see, Gerald doesn't . . . well,' she smiled somewhere in those eyes, 'let us say he is against me. . . .'

We were in the doorway of the soiled room of the drunkard. I was going to switch out the light. Often I would come upstairs and switch out Gerald's light.

'Gerald,' she said suddenly, in that strong voice, and I thought of a prefect's voice at school, down the corridor of a dormitory. 'Good-bye to Gerald.'

'You see,' she said to me, 'Gerald and I are the last Marches, and we ought to stand together. Don't you think so?'

'Yes, you ought,' I said gravely. One hand, the hand of the great emerald, hung against her leather jacket. 'Cer-

12

tainly you ought,' I said, and raised the hand to my lips. Her hand smelt dimly of petrol and cigarettes, and a scent whose name I shall now never know.

'These defiant courtesies,' she said thoughtfully. 'They're very nice, I always say. . . .'

3

Slowly, she first, we went down the narrow stairs to my landing. In the sudden flare of my match there was revealed a threepenny-bit of flesh just above the heel of her left shoe, and I had occasion to rebuke myself on the depravity that is man. She said over her shoulder: 'Hilary Townshend has told me about you. . . .'

'But he has never told me about you!'

'Oh, he would if you provoked him!'

'And may I?'

But she did not seem to hear. Once Hilary had, I thought, said something about Gerald March having a sister, but I had not connected the vaguely heard name of Mrs. Storm with her. I don't know why, but I had always imagined Gerald's sister as a schoolgirl living somewhere in the country with a bankrupt old gentleman called Lord Portairley, Gerald's uncle.

We were on my small landing now, in the light that plunged out of the half-open door of my sitting-room: she with a foot on the stairs leading downwards, away.

'Good-bye,' she said. 'Really, I think you've been very kind. . . .'

She seemed to me very nice and gentle; yes, nice; and then it seemed to me that across her gentleness flamed a bar of fire. She walked, oh, impersonally, in the fires of herself. I was on another planet. Hilary tells me now that he also had that feeling with her; but Hilary must have struggled against it, whereas I am incapable of struggling against any feeling.

'Good-bye,' I said.

I was looking not at her but through the half-open door into my room. There lay the disorder of my life, the jumble, the lack of purpose, the silence, and the defeat of my life.

I wasn't, it seems almost an intrusion to say, very happy in those days; but that is by the way in the history of Gerald March and Iris Storm.

Now here is the difficult part of this history. Of the many gaps it will contain, this seems to me the most grave, the least excusable. One should write, if not well, at least plausibly, about the things that happen. And yet I cannot be plausible about this, because I do not know how it happened. I mean, how she came into my room and sat down. I did not ask her. Did she want to? Mrs. Storm was a lady who gave you a sense of the conventions. Mrs. Storm was a . . . and yet . . . I do not know anything about her.

I am trying, you can see, to realise her, to add her together; and, of course, failing. She showed you first one side of her and then another, and each side seemed to have no relation with any other, each side might have belonged to a different woman; indeed, since then I have found that each side did belong to a different woman. I have met a hundred pieces of Iris, quite vividly met them, since last I saw her. And sometimes I have thought of her—foolishly, of course, but shall a man be wise about a woman?—as someone who had by a mistake of the higher authorities strayed into our world from a land unknown to us, a land where lived a race of men and women who, the perfection of our imperfections, were awaiting their inheritance of this world of ours when we, with that marvellous indirectness of purpose which is called being human, shall have finally annihilated each other in our endless squabbles about honour, morality, nationality.

We have all of us a crude desire to 'place' our fellows in this or that category or class: we like to know more or less what they are, so that, maybe, we may know more or less what we shall be to them. But, even with the knowledge that she was Gerald's sister, that she was twenty-nine years old, that she was the niece of Lord Portairley, you could not, anyhow I couldn't, 'place' Mrs. Storm. You had a conviction, a rather despairing one, that she didn't fit in anywhere, to any class, nay, to any nationality. She wasn't that ghastly thing called 'Bohemian', she wasn't any of the

14

ghastly things called 'society', 'county', upper, middle, and lower-class. She was, you can see, some invention, ghastly or not, of her own. But she was so quiet about it, she didn't intrude it on you, she was just herself, and that was a very quiet self. You felt she had outlawed herself from somewhere, but where was that somewhere? You felt she was tremendously indifferent as to whether she was outlawed or not. In her eyes you saw the landscape of England, spacious and brave; but you felt unreasonably certain that she was as devoid of patriotism as Mary Stuart. She gave you a sense of the conventions; but she gave you—unaware always, impersonal always, and those cool, sensible eyes!—a much deeper sense that she was somehow outside the comic, squalid, sometimes almost fine laws by which we judge as to what is and what is not conventional. That was why, I am trying to show, I felt so profoundly incapable with her. It was not as though one was non-existent; it was as though, with her, one existed only in the most limited sense. And, I suppose, she affected me particularly in that way simply because I am a man of my time. For that is a limitation a man can't get beyond—to be of his time, completely. He may be successful, a man like that—indeed, should he not blow his brains out if he is not?—but he who is of his time may never rise above himself: he is the galley-slave working incessantly at the oars of his life, which reflects the lives of the multitude of his fellows. Yes, I am of my time. And so I had with this woman that profound sense of incapability, of defeat, which any limited man must feel with a woman whose limitations he cannot know. She was—in that phrase of Mr. Conrad's which can mean so little or so much—she was of all time. She was, when the first woman crawled out of the mud of the primeval world. She would be, when the last woman walks towards the unmentionable end.

'Good-bye,' I said, and then, as I looked from the disordered room and my disenchanted life at her, the eyes in the shadow of the green hat were brilliant with laughter, so that I was stunned. 'Why are you laughing?' I asked, or perhaps I did not ask that, perhaps she had not been laughing at all, for when I was recovered from my stupor her eyes were quite grave, and dark as in a crypt. I pushed open the door of my room.

'How I would like,' she said, that husky voice, 'a glass of cold water!' That was what she said, and so I let her go in alone into the sitting-room, whilst I turned on the tap in the bathroom. Fiercely and long I let the water run, pleased with the way it was filling the little house with its clean roar, pleased with the clean scent of the rushing water, which is always like the scent of cool sunlight. Then she said: 'You have had a quick bath,' and so we became friends.

She stood among the littered books on the floor, looking round at the disorder, like a tulip with a green head. She sipped the water, looking round wisely over the rim of the tumbler. I explained that I was leaving to-morrow, and therefore the disorder.

We talked.

In that disordered room, so littered with books that you might hardly take a step without stumbling over one, it was not difficult to talk. Indeed, it is never so easy to talk about books as when they are about the floor, so that you may turn them over with your foot, see what they are, pick them up and drop them anywhere with no precious nonsense as to where they should exactly go.

She waved her glass of water about, sipping it. A drop of water clung like a gem to the corner of her painted mouth. It was not fair.

Talking with her in that room was like talking with her as we walked on a windy heath: she threw out things, you caught all you could of them, you missed what you liked, and you threw something back. Now and then something would turn up in a voice which was suddenly strong and clear, and every time her voice was strong and clear you were so surprised that you did not hear so well as when she spoke inaudibly. She had none of the organised, agonised grimaces of the young lady of fashion. But one knew she was not a young lady of fashion, for she hadn't a sulky mouth.

Hers was that random, uninformed, but severely discriminating taste which maddens you: you try unsuccessfully to think that there is nothing at the back of it, nothing but a misty criterion of enjoyment. She used some words as though she had never heard anyone else using them. 'Nice', for instance, she used in a calmly immense sense. The word seemed turned topsy-turvy, and to turn everything else topsy-turvy. She used the word 'common', I think, to denote a thing attempted and achieved scratchily. Mr. Ernest Bramah was, for instance, not 'common'. But Miss Clemence Dane in *Legend* was. 'Oh, come!' I said, for to me *Legend* is an achievement in literature.

'All those women talking and dissecting and yearning together,' she said. 'Their breath smells of . . . oh, red hair!' She thought Miss Romer Wilson was among the greatest writers of the time: *The Grand Tour* particularly. She was loyal to girlish admirations for Mr. Locke, Mr. Temple Thurston, Oscar Wilde. D. H. Lawrence was 'nice'. 'Nice?' I said. 'Well, wonderful,' she said, with wide eyes, so that I was made to seem slow and stupid. M. Paul Morand was 'common', a 'stunt' writer.

'I detest the word "stunt",' I said.

'That is why,' she said, 'I used it about Monsieur Morand. He is an abbreviation, like nightie for nightshirt.' I did not agree with her. She did not like abbreviations, even lunch for luncheon. 'What,' she asked, 'is the hurry?' I could not tell her. She thought that perhaps English was not the language for abbreviations and diminutives. She deferred to my judgment about that, and I said what I said. One just didn't discuss Barrie: there he was. 'You can't laugh me out of him,' she smiled, 'by calling him whimsical.' She had once enjoyed a book by Mr. Compton Mackenzie, a garden catalogue called *Guy and Pauline*. There was Hergesheimer. She put up a gallant, insincere defence for the Imagistes but it turned out that she had never read any, and wasn't at all sure what they were. 'They're short for poetry,' I said coldly, 'like nightie for nightingale.' But perhaps the book she most profoundly liked was *The Passionate Friends*, with perhaps the last part of *Tono-Bungay*. 'And, of course,' she said, '*The Good Soldier*,' Mr. Ford Maddox Hueffer's amazing romance. From a table she picked up Joyce's *Ulysses*, looked at it vaguely, dropped it absently on the floor amongst the others.

17

I held a watching financial brief for it. One was to find later that she was completely without a sense of property, either her own or other people's.

'It's a funny thing,' she mused. . . .

'What's a funny thing?'

'Satirists. . . . They are all very plain men. Grubby, too. Why?'

'Why?' I said. 'But, really——'

She looked at me through the smoke of her cigarette. She was grave, intent. But one never knew what about. . . .

'Genius,' I said, 'has——'

'Of course, genius. But——'

'They are striving,' I said, 'for——'

'Yes, I know. But why are they always so ugly? I mean, these people called "satirists". One sees them abroad, at the Rotonde, or in Rome, Florence. . . .' I saw her among them, the small white face, the cool, sensible, huge eyes, very attentive, deferring. 'They marry plain, too. Always. Invariably. Why? And man and wife hang on to each other like grim death, despising everything hard. And they come out in spots. Why? One just wonders . . . It seems to need very ugly men with very unattractive wives to despise things, to show us our ugliness. Has ever any even fairly human-looking person ever been a 'satirist'? But I suppose if they weren't so plain they wouldn't have so much time to be obscene on paper. Or am I talking nonsense?'

'It's absurd,' I said, 'to make it a question of looks——'

'But it makes me furious!' she said in that suddenly strong clear voice. 'These despisers! These grubby clever men with their grubby genius. The heroes of the weekly reviews. Their impotent little obscenities. I've tried to find, in knowing them and reading them, a great, real contempt, something as fierce and clean as fire, a nightmare of contempt, so that from the pillars of burning smoke we can build beings of better shape than ourselves. I've read, watched, listened, wanting to know. . . .'

I said things, too. But who am I? For instance, I said: 'You don't allow to all men one common failing, which shows particularly when the men are satirical writers: they

18

must always write about women rather in the spirit of unclean-minded undergraduates who are very upset at not having physically enjoyed their first Woman as much as was to be expected. It is from such things that satirical genius is made. You should be more tolerant, Mrs. Storm. . . .'

We talked of vulgarity. She had once read a book of mine, and I complained bitterly of my vulgarity, saying, you know, that one didn't begin by being vulgar, 'but one began,' I suggested, 'by being just bumptious. The meeker you are, the more bumptious you probably are inside, but that does no harm. Not that I was ever really meek. And at the beginning there's a tremendous humility in you to yourself. You can't have any achievement without that humility, and yet you lose it later on because you find out all the wrong things about yourself. People are only too ready to show you the wrong things about yourself. They like doing it. They seem to think there is something wrong with conceit. It irritates fools, because they think it is unwarranted. How do they know if it is unwarranted, and what does it matter if it is or not? Or it irritates them because they too once had in themselves a humility to themselves, and then allowed it to be, according to that Bottomley - Kipling - John - Bull gospel, "knocked out of them". And so if a young man is not very strong he lets the mischievous fools take his conceit away from him, he turns his back on his real conceit, which is himself—he has it "knocked out of him", just as any taste for music was knocked out of him by his public-school—and goes out for one of the spurious conceits which are called "being as others are". Then he has put his feet on the endless and never-ending road of vulgarity, and there are very few turnings. . . .'

She sat in the deep wicker armchair, which had come with me from Chelsea six years before but would travel nevermore. It creaked madly as she sat down, and she glanced at it in surprise. 'Of course,' she said, 'it's contagious. . . .'

'You are quite wrong,' I said. 'The real sticky part seems to come from inside one. And there, you see, is where a writer has a sense of defeat—a writer, I mean, who must earn his living by writing, and so must always write. For it is more difficult for a second-rate writer not to be vulgar than for a camel to pass through a needle's eye. It uncoils from somewhere inside you, like a nasty, sticky snake. So slick it is, too. So helpful, often. And when you see it for the first time you stare at it transfixed, and you say, "But *I* am not vulgar!" But you get used to it later on. Very few people notice it. Most people like it. And, of course, it pays.'

'The golden snake,' she said. 'It's quite a good snake. It is silly to despise money.'

'Writers,' I said, and, I think, said rightly, 'love money, they adore money! Successful writers, I mean. The ones who have become venerable, the ones who have made great names by writing about the irony of life and the incapabilities of wealth, the writers of the people for the people. They worship money, they hoard money. One and all despise rich people, and are perfectly beastly about the upper-classes. You should ask any publisher about the business capacity of any great author who writes about the Irony of Life. They will argue about sixpence, kick up a row about sixpence-halfpenny, and if they have a mistress, as men who write about the irony of life should have, they will allow her about as much a year as a Jew gives to a schoolboy. To really intelligent men of the middle-classes, living in sin does not seem nearly so wicked as living in luxurious sin. I only know one successful author who has the decency to get drunk with his easily-earned money. One should keep a sense of proportion about money, and you can only do that by throwing it away. The Jews, for instance——'

'Jews,' she said, 'are charming. The rich ones, I mean, and preferably the fat shiny ones. They understand luxury and elegance, and elegance is an enchantment that the skin loves. But nowadays only Jews have an idea of enchantment, only Jews and Americans. Furs, jewels, spacious rooms, trellised terraces, all lovely baubles, silks of China, myrrh, frankincense, and motor-cars. The Jews are disenchanted, but at least they're brave enough to insist on having all the enchantments of disenchantment. Luxury, ease, splendour, spaciousness. You'll say they're florid. Well, they may be,

20

they are, but they're also the last towers of chivalry. Mr. Chesterton goes running after them shouting about beer and the Pope, but if you're going to leave chivalry to beer-drinkers and the Pope, God help enchantment. You'll say that the Americans' indulgent admiration for their wives almost borders on the *gaga*, but they fight for it very really, they don't just talk and indulge. They fight with money, they have the courage of their cheques, they dare tremendous duels, they get up at unearthly hours in the morning to dash towards the rendezvous, and they draw a cheque just as gallantly as any rather caddish cavalier ever drew a sword. . . .'

'Englishmen,' I said, '*respect* their women . . .'

'Maybe,' she said absently.

We were impersonal. Now and then the wicker armchair creaked beneath her, and she looked at it with faint surprise. Now and then a car screamed on Piccadilly, an electric-landau sounded its bells through Shepherd's Market towards its garage by Camelot House. Now and then her slightly husky voice expired. Then we waited a while. She stared deeply into the eyes of a mask which a Russian artist had once given me in exchange for a poker debt. It lay sideways against a corner of the fender. I waited for her to say something about that, for it was the mask of a Florentine gentleman that was a lecher. I had grown used to it, as one can grow used to anything, but people would remark on it adversely. The lady of the green hat said nothing, and that was how I knew that for her everything was inevitable. That is an important thing to know about a woman, for you know then that you will never know where you are.

We became personal. She said: 'Let us talk about our friends now.'

'To-night,' I said, 'I have been to a party at the Hallidays'.'

'Ah, the pitiless vulgarians! Surely, between us, we can do better than that!'

'There's Hilary. . . .'

'The sweet! Can you *not* love Hilary? But to-night,' she said very seriously, 'I have been dining with old Maurice Harpenden. How he would hate me to say old! I went out all the way to Sutton Marle to do that, because he expects it of me when I am in England. We are enemies, and we watch each other. He was very courtly. They are difficult to deal with, handsome old men who have known one since one was so high. You need to be a woman to know what I mean, but you must try to pretend for a minute. Thank you. Organically, of course, they are perfect. Good features and long legs and iron-grey hair. Character and clothes by Robert Hichens. They are very courtly, and then they touch one. Now, why do they do that? They pretend to do it in a friendly way, as any gentleman of the old school might to the daughter of another gentleman of the old school: but they make *opportunities*. . . .' The husky voice committed suicide, was buried, and in the third second rose from the dead. 'I do not understand men. I do not understand the "old school" type of man, nor what "old school" means, unless it means that you never did anything at school except win the Battle of Waterloo. Then as soon as you left school you were qualified by good-looks, a charm of manner, and a habit of becoming popular with elderly men which is peculiar to right-minded young Englishmen, to become Major-General Sir Maurice Harpenden, K.C.B., C.M.G., D.S.O., and to lead your troops in battle with that gallant inefficiency patented by English infantry-commanders who know a good horse when they see one. After which you can spend the rest of your life in *bantering*. You can see that I do not like Maurice. We dine, and we are enemies, and we watch each other.'

'The sire doesn't seem very like the son. Napier is a saint. . . .'

The chair creaked. She was looking at me from under her hat, gravely as a Red Indian. 'There were two roads leading from a certain tree, and when we were eighteen life said to me, "You go this way," and life said to Napier, "You go that way." And so we did that, and so it has been. . . .'

Now I was staring at her mouth, which was a silky red mouth engraved with I don't know how many deep downward lines, and my heart beat twice so loudly that I wondered if she had heard it, for she whispered sharply: 'Listen!' But

22

it was only a clock striking somewhere in London, and its striking was quickly done.

'I must go,' she said, but not even the armchair creaked, and her green hat was still crushed against the back of the chair, and her eyes were still staring profoundly over my shoulder. There was only the window there. The curtains were not drawn, and I thought I would draw them, but it seemed a pity to move. Her eyes glowed like an animal's. She was staring, absorbed, over my right shoulder, but there was only the window there. She was asleep. Then her eyes dilated into glowing points, and her lips said: '*On a envie.*'

Then she made a gesture of distaste.

She said: 'There are desires. . . .'

'Heavens, do you need to tell me that!'

'Oh, not those desires!' Expressionless, blazing eyes absorbed over my shoulder, she waved away 'those desires'. I was snubbed.

'They call it,' she said, 'the desire-for-I-know-not-what. They will find it one day when we are dead and all things that live now are dead. They will find it when everything is dead but the dreams we have no words for. It is not chocolate, it is not cigarettes, it is not cocaine, nor opium, nor sex. It is not eating, drinking, flying, fighting, loving. It is not love's delight, it is not bearing children, though in that there are moments like jewels. There is one taste in us that is un-satisfied. I don't know what that taste is, but I know it is there. Life's best gift, hasn't some one said, is the ability to dream of a better life. . . .'

The green hat crushed recklessly against the back of the chair, she stared, still and absorbed, at the names that friends of long-ago had written on the ceiling with smoke of candle-flame. Her eyes glowed, glowed like an animal's. The light of the reading-lamp on the littered table by my elbow kissed her lip, and the light kissed the faint, faint down on her lip into a few minutes of existence as a garden of gold dust. A sword lay in my mind, twisting and shining among the inner grotesqueries where we keep ourselves, in the real sense, to ourselves.

I forced my mind to a more legal aspect of her. There

23

were two rings on her wedding finger. A narrow circle of platinum, a narrow circle of gold. I wondered if she had been married twice. I tried to imagine her husbands. They would be tall, handsome men, and she would be passionately in love with them. She would, like all women in love with tall, handsome men, be worshipful as a dog. Physically they would be very courteous to her, but no more than courteous, and mentally they would, if I may say so, treat her rough. They would go to sleep quickly, and she would lie awake far into the night, pressing her breasts, because they hurt her. She would think. She would not think. Then one day, when she was between thinking and not thinking, she would be unfaithful, and the tall, handsome man who was her husband would apologise to her for not have understood her better. But she would say, with cold eyes: 'There is nothing to understand. *On a envie*.' Then he would say, 'Oh!' and instruct her lawyers to divorce him.

'I was trying,' I said, 'to imagine your husband. . . .'

The chair creaked, and from the shadow of the hat one blue eye looked at me like a blue stone worn by fire. 'Two,' she said. 'They are dead.'

I wondered what she saw, looking over my shoulder. She kept strange, invisible company, this lady. She walked in measureless wastes, making flames rush up from stones, making mole-hills out of mountains. Then suddenly the headlines of a penny paper of two years ago unrolled before my mind, stood livid against my memory, slashed with the name of Storm. I had not a doubt but that he had been her second husband. 'V.C. murdered. Sinn Feiners kill Captain Storm, V.C. Left on roadside with five bullet wounds. . . .'

She said suddenly: 'I am a house of men.'

'What!' I said. 'You surprise me.'

'A house of men. Of their desires and defeats and deaths. Of their desires, yes, of their deaths, yes and yes. It is, you can see, a great responsibility for me, and I have lodged complaints about it, but it is no use. I am a house of men. Ah me, ah me! Oh, dear! My friend, there is a curse, a quite visible curse. On us, the Marches. You will see it in my eyes one day, and you will be sorry for me.'

24

'You mustn't believe in curses,' I said. 'Good God, curses!'

'The Marches,' she said, 'are never let off anything. That is the curse.'

Her eyes were stronger than mine, even as wind is stronger than air, and always in them was the magic of wide open places. I looked down, and far below, like pearls in the dust, shone two ankles clasped in silk the colour of daylight. I thought of her fate and of her. I thought of corruption, of curses, of death, of life, of love, and of love's delight. I took hold of the sword in my mind with both hands, but was not strong enough to lift it. I though of the limbs of Aphrodite, of the sighs of Anaitis, of the sharp cries of love's delight. I thought how charming men would be if they could misbehave outwardly as prettily as they can in their minds. I said: 'And so the house of March, fatal and damned, can never avoid its destiny. . . .'

'Yes,' she said reasonably, 'it can avoid it. By not being weak enough to desire so strongly.'

'Oh, I see,' I said.

'I'm glad you see,' she said gravely. 'They listen to voices whispering dreams. While they listen, they do queer weak things. Of the soil sordid—there is your March. But there is another March, who listens to voices whispering dreams. My father Barty March was, I think, one of the most loved men of his time. Like Napier is now, but of course Napier behaves. A policeman found Barty early one morning on the doorstep of a house we had then in Cambridge Square. He used to say he was never drunk until he closed his eyes, but this time he had closed his eyes into pneumonia. He only opened them once again, to look at Gerald and me, sixteen years old apiece. He smiled, you know, because Barty couldn't help smiling. Besides, he was happy at last. 'Avoid dreams,' he said. 'Never stop to listen to the clouds passing overhead. You will be run over. Never sympathise with the moon when you can hear it, cold and lonely and blind, crooning to itself like a corpse singing a hymn. You will catch pneumonia. Never dream of a world in which men are men and women are women. You will go mad. . . .'

Her right hand hung limp over the arm of the chair. It was just faintly dirty, and the nails shone like pink ivory. The emerald on the third finger held my eyes enchanted for a long while. She smiled at my look, and as she lay her eyes swept falcon-like down to the stone. It made me rise out of myself, that falcon-like sweep of her clear eyes, and I thought of the pitiless misbehaviour of life, that had not let her stay within the sensible stability of marriage.

'It's a bit loose,' she was saying.

'I was wondering. It's such a beauty! Aren't you afraid of it falling?'

She shook her head, staring at me with a mischievous smile. Her childishness did not jar. She was always herself. 'Oo, no! I have a knuckle. I crook it. And lo, it doesn't fall. . . .'

'But this sounds like a plot!'

'It is a law,' she said. 'There are four laws, variously entitled a, b, c, d. The law (a) declares, against all formerly-held beliefs, that a flower is less beautiful because it is sure to die. That is a religious law, having to do with the unworth of perishable things, if you see what I mean. The law (b) has something to do with the fact that all men with long legs make poor lovers. That is a pagan law. You might write an essay on the long arm of coincidence and the short legs of co-respondents. It would be fun for you. The law (c) has something to do with exhorting a woman never to trust a man of honour, for he serves two mistresses. That is the law of good sense for amorous women, and will save them disappointment. The law (d) has to do with this ring, which is a bit loose, according to the directions of Jehovah.'

'You have mighty friends, Iris Storm!'

'Ah, I need them! Desire is a child with hungry eyes, and for him a dragon lies waiting. This ring is a charm against dragons.' The slightly husky voice dreamed. It was an hour for dreaming. She would mask unhappy things with passing talk. 'I called him Jehovah because the same was a jealous God. And I would mock him with that, saying that it was I who should be jealous of him, for doesn't a man of honour serve two mistresses, while it is well known of women of

26

dishonour, I would mock him, that they never serve but one god at a time. But he never was a worldly man, and so eaten by doubt that you would have laughed if he hadn't been such a pet. . . .'

'And so he gave you the emerald to be as a witness against you, and to testify against your frailty?'

'Now take,' dreamed the husky voice, the great eyes fixed on the ceiling; and there was a smile in them, like a distant wave of music; 'now take a night in Algeria. Take also a hill, and on the hill a garden. . . .'

'The Hotel St. George, Mustapha Supérieur, Algiers——'

'Ah, don't forget the American Bar!'

'And the Benares bowls——'

'And *calorifères* too hot or too cold——'

'And Arab carpets from Victoria Street——'

'And Americans with low heels——'

'And a passion for "mailing postals——"'

'Not to mention veal every day——'

'And a Soirée de Gala every Saturday——'

'And the best-dressed women——'

'Of Tunbridge Wells.'

'But take instead some red and purple flowers against a yellow wall, some oranges, a tangerine or two, three gazelles on a tennis-court, poppies tall as choir-boys, the cactus, the palm, and the pyramid cypress-tree. And watch, my friend, two shadows that walk in the wicked shadow of the pyramid cypress, that stands in the garden like a dark torch keeping watch over disillusion. It is night, or have I already told you that? Ah me, ah me, now will she who walks there ever forsake her love, will she ever be disloyal to her vows, that were made with so much pomp and circumstance in the Guards' Chapel at Westminster before a congregation notable for the absence of all her husband's relations? Why, her heart is confident, her heart is fragrant with the honey of that moon's passage, and she knows what she knows. And yet, and here is a most pitiful thing, there must be something in her, some fatal abandon, that sets men doubting, for he who walked with her in the wicked shadow of the pyramid cypress wore the silence of the destroyer, so that her heart

27

cried that he was misnamed, for the mortal disease of his heel was suspicion. Now I must tell you that it was Christmas Eve, and after a little desultory conversation he said: "Here is a present for you, sweet," and he gave me this emerald which you are kind enough to admire. "Alas," I said, "it is a little big for me! It may fall from my finger, don't you see?"

' "Yes, it may fall," said he. "But if you are careful, my sweet, if you curve your knuckle in time, it won't dream of falling, not it!" And then I cried miserably, knowing there was a catch in this somewhere, for at that time I was not yet broken in and was still fearful of suspicion. And I cried: "Hector Storm, what do you mean?"

' "I mean, Iris, that you are as that ring——"

' "Beautiful but loose, Hector? Ah, *timeo Danaos*!'

' "Iris, will you never be serious! Yes, you are as that ring, which you must always wear on the third finger of your right hand. And as that ring may fall, Iris, so you may fall, for that is the sort of woman you are. But as that ring may be kept from falling, so may you keep yourself from falling. Oh, God," he said, "my life is darkness without you, I love you so, and it's a perfect hell with you, I love you so!" And he said much more that is unmentionable, and I learnt something, for it is only by listening to their husbands in moments of intimacy that well-brought-up women can become acquainted with certain good old English words. And though I pleaded bitterly that he was unfair to me, saying I was chained to him as my wrist might be chained to a star, which was no more than the truth, he insisted that I could be constant only to inconstancy, and so I was tired and went to bed. But look! Oh, look! Please look! Ah, the discourtesy of time! Really I must go now!'

I drew my eyes from her eyes to see that the dawn had slyly thrown a grey handkerchief over the window. It was but the shape of the dawn creeping out into the night, it was but a ghostly breath in the night, but it was the dawn. And I did not know what to say, for can a man deny the dawn, that speaks good sense in its vast elemental language?

The chair creaked and creaked. She was going now, there was no doubt about it. The texture of her face was grave, she was busy with the angle of her green hat. I examined the sword in my mind. The chair creaked and creaked, and then it was as though snapped by silence, and our startled eyes joined over the emerald that lay on the floor like the echo of the kiss, which was an unfair kiss. She shivered faintly, and drew herself taut, and was very proud. She was remote as the evening star, and very proud. Her eyes were dark as in a crypt, and her eyes looked lost, as though she had strayed into a maze. I lit a cigarette, and found my throat dry and parched.

She found difficulty in speaking. I was amazed.

'No,' she said. She shook her head. 'Certainly not. My ring, please.'

Imperiously her finger pointed to the floor, but her eyes were as plaintive as a nun's who has strayed into one of the corridors of hell. That I might walk with her there I again made myself a Judas to her hand, and she shivered with her whole body as in a torment, and she seemed to bite her lip from within.

'It means nothing,' she said coldly.

'I know,' I said.

She breathed deeply, with a hand pressed to one breast, as though it hurt her. I think it must have hurt her very much. I was sorry. She shook her head, as though she was in a cage, and then she was as still as a cut flower. The whole brim of the green hat was between me and her face, we were both terribly alone. Her right hand drooped naked over the arm of the chair, and I was bending down to pick up the emerald to replace it on the third finger when a cautious knocking came from below.

That was the second or third time of knocking, and each time it was less cautious, and I knew it to come from the policeman on the beat, who would be wishing to have the primrose car put in its proper place, which was not on the King's high-road. I wondered if she had heard, but I could not see her face. I wondered if she heard me move. As I came to the door I switched out the light and the dawn pounced on her green hat, but she who wore it fought her battles carved in stone. She said something, I did not catch what, and I went downstairs and spoke with the policeman, who was an amiable middle-aged man of my acquaintance. 'My brother is with me,' I said, 'but he will be gone soon.' Shepherd's Market was creeping out into the dawn, draped and mysterious with the shadows of night. A window here and there was alight against the dark pile of Camelot House. The great car stood like a bruise against the passage of eternity, dawn fought for it, night draped it, and the silver stork flew unseen. The small noises of dawn stirred sharply in the night, and the lamps wore pale, tired faces. 'Summer's well on,' said the policeman.

I re-entered the sitting-room, saying impersonally: 'I'm afraid you must go, as . . .' The room was empty. The figure that had been carved in stone was wrapped in air. The disorder of the room lay jeering at me on the dim carpet of the dawn. It was all like a purposeless limbo stretched between the night and the day, the room, my life, hers, everything, the strong, the silly and the brave. The hundreds of books lay in soiled confusion on the floor, the wisdom of the world that has gone to the making of the soiled nothings that we are.

I was seized by a catholic anger against the woman. Through all the disenchantments of youth, despite the contagious impurities of life, in defiance of the crimes against love that we call love, I had kept romance for my ghostly companion. Romance was more than a silly lithe goddess coming down from a marble column. Romance was more than the licence to be shameless with clouded eyes. Romance did not steal through the fleshy portals of the heart, did not shiver at a Judas kiss, did not coil white trembling limbs into the puerile lusts of the mind. Romance was all that and was as much greater than that as a religion is greater than a church. To romance, which was the ultimate vision of commonsense, sex, as sex, was the most colossal bore that had ever distracted man from his heritage. And she would palm a facet of this colossal bore off on me! She would have me barter my ghostly companion for the fall of an emerald, she would invade my thoughts, perhaps my life, in exchange for a puny pleasure that needs love to exalt it above the matchless silliness of what, with an excessive zeal for scientific classification, is known to our civilisation as the sexual act.

I picked up the emerald from the floor, and it smiled in the palm of my hand.

In the dusk of the bedroom, she lay coiled on the bed. The hush of her breathing was no more than the trembling servant of the silence. Then she coughed a small cigarette cough. It was the usual cough, and gave me back my confidence. 'Iris Storm!' I said, but I wondered if I had spoken, the frail silence was so undisturbed. She was asleep.

Perhaps it was then that I realised that she was beautiful. She was asleep. Could any but the shape of beauty dare to wear that impertinence! She lay on her side, she lay anyhow. The green hat was gone.

'Iris!' I said. Her hair was thick and tawny, and it waved like music, and the night was tangled in the waves of her hair. It was like a boy's hair, swept back from the forehead, which was a wide, clear forehead, clean and brave and sensible as a boy's. Sensible, oh dear! The tawny cornstalks danced their formal dance on the one cheek that I could see, and the tip of a pierced ear played beneath them, like a mouse in a cornfield. Above her neck her hair died a very manly death, a more manly death than 'bobbed' hair was ever known to die, and so it comes about that Iris Storm was the first Englishwoman I ever saw with 'shingled' hair. This was in 1922.

I decided that I did not know what to do. I decided that that was just as well. 'I will play,' I thought, 'a waiting game,' and lit a cigarette. But in her tawny hair the night was tangled like a promise, and it smelled as grass might smell in a faëry land, and always about her there was that faint dry scent whose name I shall now never know. Her mouth drooped like a flower, and there was a little shiny bit in the valley between her cheek and her nose. To this I applied a little *Quelques Fleurs* talc powder on a handkerchief, that when she awoke she should not think so ill of herself as I did. Hers was a small, straight nose with an imperceptible curve, just as any straight line might have, and its tip quivered a little as she breathed. Her leather jacket *pour le sport*, that

31

had a high collar trimmed with some minks, was flung open, and over the breast of her dark dress five small red elephants were marching towards an unknown destination. Towards her feet her hat lay with my hat.

Gently, gently, gently as the phantom of myself, for was I not being better than myself? I would replace the emerald on the third finger of her right hand. I would, when hair that was not my own was pressed against my ear, and fingers that were not my own took the cigarette from my mouth, and teeth that were not mine bit my lip, and where the red elephants marched towards an unknown destination stirred breasts full of shadows, and a voice as clear and strong as daylight said: 'But enough of this hell!'

4

Of all that had once decorated the walls of my sitting-room there was left by the removers only a looking-glass in an ancient gold frame, above the fireplace. My mother had once given me an oil-painting, saying, 'This will do nicely for your flat,' but I in my pride had thought a looking-glass would offend the frame more judiciously.

She stood before that.

'What is the time?' she asked of her reflection, and I told her that it was ten minutes to six.

'Have you a comb?' she asked of her reflection, and luckily I had a comb which was not my comb. She looked at it and saw that it was so.

'Thank you,' she said to her reflection.

The light of the tawny hair mocked the clouded daylight, and when, with the palm of her hand on her forehead, she swept the comb from front to back, it flamed tiger-tawny and ate into my spirit. *Tiger, tiger, burning bright, in the forests of the night. . . .*

In the Upper Fifth at school there was a tall, cold-eyed blood called Dwight-Rankin—I think he died on Gallipoli— who used to sit at the desk just in front of mine. He was a man of the mode, wearing his fair hair plastered from front to back, and his neck was clean and unspotted as a girl's, and I would spend minutes wondering whether, if one touched the gold down in which his hair ended high above his neck one would feel hair or only skin. The back of her head affected me like that: it was just like Dwight-Rankin's, only dry, and tiger-tawny.

She tore the small comb through the dancing curls on each cheek, so that they trembled like voiceless bells. It is a commonplace about women, as assiduously remarked by brilliant feminine psychologists as women's 'caprice' and 'intuition', that every woman must now and then make a 'grimace of distaste' into a looking-glass. But she did not do that, nor need to. She was untouched, unsoiled, impregnable to the grubby, truthful hand of *lex femina*. She was like a tower of beauty in the morning of the world. The outlaw was above the law of afterwards, impervious and imperious. She was beautiful, grave, proud. How beautiful she was now! It was a sort of blasphemy in her to be so beautiful now, to stand in such ordered loveliness, to be neither shameful like a maiden nor shameless like a *mondaine*, nor show any fussy after-trill of womanhood, any dingy ember of desire. It was a sort of blasphemy in her, as it would be in a peacock to sing gracefully.

The silence got on my nerves, and I said something, any-thing. She looked over her shoulder at me, vaguely. She was the male of the species that is more fearless than mankind. I wondered what she was going to say.

'My hat, please,' she said. I appeared to have been holding it in my hand. With her left hand she crushed it on her head and kept her hand on the crown, looking at herself intently in the looking-glass. I was startled at her eyes in the looking-glass. They were cold blue stones, expressionless, caddish as a beast's.

Down, down, with two fingers of her left hand, she pulled the brim of the green hat over her left eyebrow. She said: 'I think I must have left my powder in the other room. Do you mind?' I brought her the case of white jade and the box of black onyx. She powdered, without interest.

'Good-bye,' she said. Her hand was held out, her eyes were full on mine, naked, expressionless. I felt that they were the heads of the nails under which she had nailed herself. It

33

would be a kindness to let her go quickly, a kindness which she would not have allowed me had I been a woman and she a man.

'Good-bye,' I said. And suddenly the hand that lay in mine pressed mine, and she gave a vague, brittle laugh.

'It seems a pity,' she said; and then the eyes in the shadow of the brim seemed to open wide, wide.

'You see?' she whispered. 'You see?'

But I could see nothing but her silhouette against the future days. I said: 'We have begun at the wrong end; but can't we work back?'

'Oh, no!' she whispered. 'It is not like that a bit. You don't understand. . . .'

Suddenly I said many things.

She seemed, her hand still in mine, to be absorbed in something just behind my right shoulder. There was such fear in her eyes that I cried sharply: 'What is it?'

'The beast,' said the lips of the eyes of fear. 'Just the beast. . . .'

The word I said was drowned in the din of a lorry that smashed through Whitehorse Street to Piccadilly. She took her hand gently from mine. 'There is a dream,' she said, 'and there is a beast.'

She smiled.

'That's all,' she said.

'I can understand regret,' I said, 'but——'

'Ah, we can understand, you and I! We are as old as sand . . . at this moment.'

'But, Iris Storm, regret seems like a scar on you!'

'Not regret,' she said, so calmly. 'Shame.' And she took my hand again, closely. 'You must forgive me. I couldn't have said that to any other man. My shame mustn't shame you, please! But you have a cold mind, you are disenchanted, you will understand. And oh, if one could be assoiled in human understanding! You see, I am not what you think. I am not of the women of your life. I am not the proud adventuress who touches men for pleasure, the silly lady who misbehaves for fun. I am the meanest of all, she who destroys her body because she must, she who hates the thing she is, she who loathes the thing she does. . . .' The breathless, pregnant voice seemed to fall to the floor, like a small bird with broken wings, and as it struggled upwards I said: 'You are like a boy after his first love.'

'Oh, if it was boyishness!' And she took from the pocket of her leather jacket a tube of gold, and she broke it into two pieces, and she stared moonstruck at the carmine tongue of the lip-salve.

'To be born a chaste woman,' she said to the carmine tongue, 'is good. I am in favour of chastity. I would die for purity, in theory.' She painted her mouth, staring moonstruck into the daylight. 'Yes, I would die for purity. I wouldn't mind dying anyhow, but it would be nice to die for purity. . . .'

I said thus and thus.

'Yes,' she said, not having heard a word of mine, 'it is not good to have a pagan body and a Chislehurst mind, as I have. It is hell for the body and terror for the mind. There are dreams, and there are beasts. The dreams walk glittering up and down the soiled loneliness of desire, the beasts prowl about the soiled loneliness of regret. Good-bye.'

'Then it must be "good-bye"?'

She looked at me with a strange, dark friendliness, and nodded.

'Because of shame,' she said. 'But if I were different, I would like you for my friend——'

To my interruption, which she did not hear, she said: 'I have only one lover. But I know that only because I always feel unfaithful to him. It would be good to be really bad, but I am not even that. I only misbehave. I will see you again, when I have found my only love. Or I will see you again when I am qualified to die for purity. I will let you know, so you can be there. God bless you, dear.'

And I said what I said, that He had, with Iris Storm.

She went very white. 'That shall be written down,' she whispered, 'as the prayer of the only man who ever shamed a woman of her shame.'

'My days of adventure, Iris Storm, are over. A few years ago it would have seemed nothing to me that you should disappear as you came, into the great hole of London. To experts in adventure that is, I think, the usual procedure. But now I would like a trace of you. You must not leave me, quite. If I may not see you again, mayn't I perhaps talk to you? Or, what is the main thing, feel that I could if I dared?'

She said she was in London now only on business that would last a few weeks, and lived always abroad. 'But this is the telephone-number,' she said, and I was looking round for paper and pencil when she said 'Here!' and her leather arm darted to the floor and came up with a book, and on the fly-leaf of the book she scrawled the number with her lip-stick.

High above the sharp noises of the young day I heard the scream of an electric-horn.

CHAPTER TWO   THE CAVALIER OF LOW CREATURES

I

And that, I think, is all that there really is about me, as a person in the tale. Of course, this first person singular will continue, and there'll no doubt be any amount of 'I this' and 'I that', but that is because of the nature of the work, and there's never, the way I see it, much more than a pen behind it. Hilary, however, and Guy de Travest are not of my mind about this. We have recently been talking about these affairs, and a sad enough talk they made, and my two friends, my two seniors, were reluctantly compelled, they said, to disagree with me about my lack of responsibility in the events to be related hereinafter.

To me, the way I see it, it looks as though certain things were decreed to happen and that, therefore, they did happen: they had it in their blood, these people, that certain things should happen to them, and I could no more contrive these things than they could evade them. But Hilary and Guy, murmuring together in that astonishing unison which can only be found in two Englishmen who disagree upon everything in the world but on the fact that conduct is three parts of life, are of opinion that my substitution of the word 'ptomaine' for 'septic' really affected the course of events. Had I, they say in effect, spoken the truth like a brave little man, there would have been a divorce and everyone would by now have been happy, as happiness goes. And then, too, they have something to say about those two red lights, those two rear-lamps of two cars sweeping into South Audley Street—had I told Iris, they say, about Gerald, those two red lights never would have been so close together. Oh, Guy, what a man is that! That latter-day thunder-god of dandies, that warrior of conduct, that man of cold eyes who never could give 'gratuitous information' about any one! Oh, Hilary, that friend of childhood!

Hilary and Guy, friends of the late Barty March, had known Gerald and Iris since their earliest childhood. But Gerald had no sooner grown up than, at the impulse of his furious nature, he had turned away from his friends, his people: he had dropped out, had cut away; and no one, it's not difficult to imagine, would want to intrude on that young man. But I was to find, after the coming of the lady of the green hat, that it wasn't only at the impulse of his furious nature that Gerald had, well, withered fiercely into solitude. In very truth that Gerald had been a hero-worshipper; and in very truth he had become, as his sister had said, a nothing without his hero. Very few things had ever mattered to Gerald Haveleur March; but those few things, one was to learn, had mattered far too much.

His sister was, as it's not impossible to have gathered, what is called *déclassée*—even for a March or a Portairley. And that was why I had heard nothing about her from Guy or Hilary, for while Guy never gave gratuitous information about anyone Hilary was held in thrall by that upside-down but virulent form of snobbery which will make of a man of property an extreme Liberal and a thorough-going die-hard disapprover of anyone who let his, Hilary's, caste down. Hilary, a sincerely good man, was an enemy of caste, he was an enemy of his own caste in particular, he did not believe in it; and yet, in the depths of that being where lurks a dragon that can ultimately defeat even the sincerity of a man of principle, Hilary believed in nothing else but caste.

And Iris, of course, had betrayed her caste to perfection. No one, you might say, could have done that more thoroughly than Iris. She had been malinspired to excess, she had reached Excelsior in the abyss. But she was ever completely not on her guard about what people might say or did say, she had an amazing, an enviable, snapped Hilary, talent for just not noticing things.

She had been quite surprised, Hilary told me recently, when once he had taxed her with being a renegade from her class. Genuinely surprised she was, Hilary says. It simply hadn't, she had told him, occurred to her in that light.

'Rushing about Europe like that,' Hilary had said, 'you let England down. You've no idea, Iris, how these young foreign blighters hold Englishwomen cheap.' Iris had maintained she had a very good idea about that. (But you simply had to disagree with Hilary. He was like that. And he said 'hm' all the time.) And you only had to travel on a liner to the East, she had said, to notice how British matrons reacted to foreign parts. As for Egypt! But she always did her best, she had said, to influence foreigners to a more lofty view of the gallantries of British matrons.

'People cut you,' Hilary had said, for that seemed to him an abominable thing, that she should have put herself into the position of being 'cut'; and she had admitted having noticed glaciers, but she had maintained that it was a far, far better thing to be cut by a county eye than to be killed by the boredom of a county tongue. 'I arose from the dead when I was twenty,' she had said. (Hilary, you understand, would provoke anyone.) 'Your class,' Hilary had snapped, and she had said she had never actually thought of herself as belonging to any class. Her class would be, she supposed, the landed gentry, same as Hilary's. She was proud, she had said, to belong to the same class as Hilary, and was very sorry indeed if she had hit him in the eye with her heel. But she hoped, she had said, that with him she had always been a lady.

That had annoyed Hilary very much indeed. But everything about any woman he liked would annoy Hilary very much indeed. Mr. Townshend was one of those Englishmen with an unlimited capacity for disapproving of any woman, whom he liked, who enjoyed being with other men as much as with himself; and an unlimited capacity for finding other reasons than that for his disapproval.

As for Gerald, Hilary had last known him as a 'dark diabolical schoolboy' with a disturbing capacity for threatening silences had an immense—'a corroding, almost,' Hilary said—admiration for Iris. But not long after Barty March's death—everyone had loved *that* drunkard!—he had quite lost sight of Gerald. Guy de Travest had been Gerald's colonel in the Grenadiers for some time during the war, but he never spoke but once of Gerald as a soldier—'young hell-fire idiot'—and never went near him while he lived above me in Shepherd's Market. 'Reminds me,' Guy said, 'too much of Barty left standing too long with the cork out.' And that was more or less what Hilary said, too. One must say this for the warriors of caste and conduct: they seldom try to improve any man.

This chapter has been called The Cavalier of Low Creatures because it is about Gerald, and therefore it is a short chapter, for what on earth is there to say about Gerald? It isn't at all a good description of him, but it is intended, if you please, more as a flourish, a naïve gesture. For you simply can't let Gerald stand without a flourish, without a something, anything. Besides, I liked him, and would like to do him a bit of good. He was, *sans* gesture, a zero with a scowl and a hat—and a hat. Certainly, he once wrote a novel, but who does not once write a novel? I liked Gerald, but I would not give him a line if he wasn't essential; and that is just what he is, essential, for these things simply couldn't have happened without Gerald. He hated his sister, he had not seen her for ten years, yet it turned out that he was the most important factor in her life. And, decidedly, her love for him was one of the most important factors in *her* life. I wonder if he knows. But he too, even he, grew up in the end. I can hear him now, through the twilight of East Chapel Street, his shoulder against the saloon-door of the inn. 'Give her my love,' he said. But you will hear him.

2

Sometimes I would see Gerald in the Café Royal. I would be dining, with Hilary maybe, and in the distance, cut as with a sharp knife in the tapestry of smoke and grubby faces, would be Gerald, darkly alone, a glass of whisky on the marble-top before him. One wouldn't attempt to join him, for it made Gerald shy, desperate, if anyone sat with him while drinking. He hated being 'messed about', did Gerald; and if you joined him he would presently mutter something about an appointment (Gerald with an appointment!), leave his drink unfinished and go and order one somewhere else; and as I understood he hadn't much money I did not like to drive him to that. Maybe, though, he was less shy with me than with anyone. 'I like you,' he once said—oh, darkly!

One never knew, as he sat there or as he strode about the streets, careless as a fakir impelled always towards a terrible and nameless penance, what he could be thinking of. Maybe he was thinking of nothing. Once I saw him come out of a Cinema Theatre with a look on his face as though he had been tortured. He always looked, you know, like something. You noticed him.

He had a grey suit. It was thin as paper, but still defiantly retained a little of that casual elegance which not even Gerald could wholly divorce from the combination of a good tailor and a lean Englishman. He never had but one other suit that I ever saw, a brown affair, but he bartered that with a boot-mender in Shepherd's Market in exchange for mending his shoes. And he had a hat. That was a hat. And never was Gerald seen wearing an overcoat, no matter whether it blew, rained, snowed or froze. See him any winter evening striding down Half-Moon Street in the biting rain, his thin grey suit blackening with it, the jacket held by one button with deep creases into his waist, the shapes of his knuckles stuck through his trouser pockets, that hat—there, but for the grace of God, went the most lovable man I ever met.

'Gerald—I say, Gerald! Why don't you wear a coat on a day like this? Gerald, aren't you an ass!'

'Coat?' Thoughtful he was always, and his dark, sunk eyes would pierce the pavement or the sky with unutterable contempt. 'Coat!' And he would repeat the word softly until, you understand, he had grasped the enormous idea, when he would say softly, savagely: 'What the hell d'you mean, "coat"?' and away he would go, towards that terrible and nameless penance of his.

Well, the flourish goes, the gesture is gone, to the limbo that yawns for all such vanities in the very second of their birth. The Cavalier of Low Creatures was never, to be sure, hailed as more than a zero. But, even as the ground is not the limit of a man's fall, as you may see in the picture with the trail of flame, so zero is not the limit of a man's nothingness; for what is that which is nothing but so completely nothing that it may not have even the mark of nothing? it is, to be sure, zero without the formative circle round it.

That solitary drunkard, that soiled ascetic! Those night-mare women, soft as the grass of Parnassus, marvellously

41

acquiescent, possible. Aphrodite, Ariadne, Anaïtis, white as marble, silent as marble, silent and acquiescent, possible, as only goddesses could be, the goddesses of soiled dreams, as no woman born of woman could ever be. . . .

And yet one might have been wrong in imagining the malcontents of the solitary drunkard's mind. God only knows, of course, with what nightmare fancies the man plagued himself. Boys have them, and grow out of them; men, at least, do not admit even to themselves that they have not grown out of them, men do not admit even to themselves that while they indulge in continence they may suddenly find themselves stumbling in the burning darkness among the vile rubbish-heaps of desire.

That women walked in all the delicious beauty of the un-attainable through Gerald's tortured mind, I know now. But I did not know it then, for never was a man so secret with another man as Gerald, never was a man so little given to discussing with another those inevitable matters of desire and concupiscence which only by being discussed can be seen in a proper and proportionate light. They should be aired, those secret silly things, that they may be seen for what they are. In the old days there was a god in a garden, and people would do their best to make pretty fancies out of their lusts, naming them to gods, satyrs, fawns, nymphs, sirens, sylphs; they, at least, got rid of them somehow. But now that we see them plainly for what they are, the nasty little enemies of our assault on nobility, a conspiracy founded by Saint Paul has smashed the god in the garden and hidden the pieces under the bed.

Gerald, who never spoke but he swore, was the cleanest-mouthed man I ever met with; while from his book one had gathered that there was one main idea in Gerald's mind; this was purity. It was to do with that one brilliant-childish romance of his that, about seven years before the coming of the green hat, I had first met Gerald. Then, for more than five years, I had not seen nor heard of him, had forgotten him, when one day a lean, dangerous hawk of a young man coming out of the Hammam Baths in Jermyn Street suddenly stopped me. I knew later that he must have been in an agony of shyness, but at the time he merely looked intensely furious. I, not recognising him, thought he was going to hit me, and gaped at him.

Bitterly and darkly he told me that someone had told him there was a flat to be let above me in Shepherd's Market. 'I'm staying here at the moment,' he muttered, looking indignantly at the Hammam Baths. Several minutes passed before I could place him, for he had been in uniform that first time, in that transfiguring long-waisted grey coat of the Brigade of Guards.

Gerald appeared suddenly, in the winter of 1915, at the office of Horton's *New Voice*. Now that Horton has left England on his adventure in un-individualism one does not hear much of *The New Voice*, but at that time and for long before *The New Voice* was, of course, a power, and Horton was a Power. Quite apart from Horton's personal quality you knew he was a Power because several of the greatest of the intelligent writers of our time kept on bitterly pointing out to their million readers what a futile man Horton was. Quite a number of the men whose names you can 'conjure with' now—it would be fun to meet that man who is always in the street conjuring with names!—had begun by writing for Horton's paper; but they had always gotten on his nerves by the time they had become the greatest of the intelligent writers of our time, and, since Horton was an honest man, he told them so, and he told them why, and he told them off, and they were furious. But the most inspired among the greatest of the intelligent writers of our time revenged themselves by republishing their *New Voice* stuff in book-form and omitting to mention *The New Voice* as the first medium of publication. That was discourteous of them.

We were correcting proofs when Gerald appeared. It was a Monday afternoon, and on Monday afternoons any of Horton's writers who wished could turn up and correct either his own or someone else's proofs and then go and have tea at the A.B.C. And Talk.

'Hello!' said Horton. 'He*llo*!'

'Defence of the Realm,' murmured Home.

We were not prepared for Gerald. We had, of course, seen

soldiers before; indeed, there was one in the room at the moment, the philosopher Home, who was to be killed a year or so later. But Gerald was a Figure, he was martial. The herald of the dominion of hell upon earth, that was Gerald. Take one small, frowsty room, the staff (Miss Veale) addressing wrappers at a desk by the window, Horton blue-pencilling at the other desk by the door, four of us sitting cramped round correcting proofs on bound annuals of *The New Voice* on our knees, smoking, muttering—enter six-foot-two of the Brigade of Guards with a face as dark as night and the nose of a hawk and the eyes of one who has seen Christ crucified in vain. The panoply of war sat superbly on Gerald. He looked a soldier in the real rather than in the technical sense of the word: he looked, you know, as though he had accepted death and was just living anyhow in the meanwhile. Ah, see him then! Not even Gerald's malevolent slackness in attire could make that long-waisted grey coat with the red-silk lining sit on him but imperially. Not Gerald's the common-or-garden chubby face of a Guards' subaltern. Gerald was no chap. He glowered at us.

'Eh,' he stammered. 'I say . . . I've been told that you people . . .'

'He's heard about us,' said Home sympathetically. 'Sit down, boy. On the floor, I'm afraid.'

Gerald began a fierce scowl at him—then grinned. Dear Gerald!

'Well?' smiled Horton. Always courteous was Horton, in manner.

'Heard,' muttered Gerald, 'that you didn't care what you published. . . .'

'Oh!' said Horton. 'Well, we don't care how good it is, if that's what you mean.'

You couldn't guess that Gerald was so shy that he could scarcely speak. You thought he stammered just because he stammered, not because he was so shy that he could scarcely get a word out. A man had no right to look like Gerald, an ensign of the fallen Prince of Light, and be shy; but that was always Gerald's trouble, he never was given the credit for being shy, he put himself between you and any sympathy with him, he made it clear that he didn't want your infernal sympathy. Just then, for instance, he looked as though he had strayed into *The New Voice* to send us all to blazes on general principles. And Horton looked as though he was quite prepared to go. Horton preferred bad-tempered men.

'There's this,' Gerald muttered, and lugged out an enormous typescript from the deep pocket of his grey coat. 'Novel,' he scowled at Horton. 'Thought perhaps . . .' and he planted the thing with a thump on Horton's desk. Horton grinned. Horton had had much too much to do with professional novelists to think that a novel by a subaltern of Grenadiers was necessarily unreadable. 'Bit long, isn't it?' he smiled.

'Long?' Gerald stammered. 'Of course it's long! Been writing it for four whole months. . . .'

'Ought to be good,' said Home gravely.

'It's *awful*,' grinned Gerald, 'but, you see . . .'

'Quite,' said Horton busily. 'Now, I'll . . .'

'Hello!' said Horton, for Gerald was not. Horton threw the typescript to me to read. Of course, it was mad. *The New Voice* published most of it, and then Heinemann's published it in the autumn of 1916 and ran it into three editions while people were still disentangling their eyes from the paper wrapper, which showed a woman with purple eyes crucifying a pleasant young man.

The Savage Device is opened before me as I write, and its opening lines are: 'The history of Felix Burton is the history of an ideal and a vision. They had nothing to do with one another except that the pursuit of the vision hardened him and blooded him for the attainment of the ideal. The ideal was aristocratic, in the sense that it was a striving after nobility in life: the vision was a contradiction, as scientific as it was mystic. The ideal was, of course, defeated: the vision, of course, defeated him. The ideal was purity: the vision had something to do with pain. . . .'

The 'vision', so far as one could see, had everything to do with pain; in fact it was pain, and the vision might or might not come afterwards. (And I detest that word 'mystic'.) The book was exciting and interesting because of a strange mixture of high romance, desperate villainy and an abysmal bitterness. The war came in, naturally. Gerald's hero had minority ideas about the war—letting the landed gentry down again! As for the pain . . . Young Burton's idea of it had not to do with pain as a fact, but as the most sublime among drugs. You know? 'In fact,' Gerald wrote, 'it is the only drug that cannot debase a man. It can kill him, but there are worse ways of dying than being killed.' It was full of quotations like that, but Gerald threw them at you with a dash sadly lacking in the originals. Young Burton was, of course, going to die in the war.

Young Burton, it appeared, had studied the major and minor tortures of crime and martyrdom. There was a long description of tortures, if you liked that kind of thing. I have seen Gerald's books on them, with illustrations . . . very interesting. Then young Burton had come across the old, old idea that after a certain limit of pain there is a definite state of bliss and definite and glorious visions of a real reality which men by ordinary are too sodden or too timorous to see. But poor old Gerald, try as he would, couldn't make *The Savage Device* a novel of ideas: it remained a novel of adventure, with an inhuman interest. Young Burton went everywhere in the world, having adventures, getting magnificently hurt—South Sea stuff—studying the effect of pain on men's minds. A Chinese bandit helped him to quite a number of visions.

Then he plucked Ava Foe from a 'dive' in San Francisco, she became Mrs. Burton, and then he had every opportunity for judging the visionary qualities of mental pain. That part was fiendishly well written, the hell that Ava Burton gave him. But young Burton's ideal of purity was, naturally enough, schoolboy stuff: fine in parts, but stuff. The only part of it that was good was that it was, somehow, purity. On the sexual side young Burton deserved almost all he got from his, one thought, unnecessarily callous young wife. In Ava Foe, I couldn't help thinking after the coming of the green hat, Gerald had let himself go about Iris. I realised then how he must first have worshipped and then hated his twin sister. What on earth, one wondered, could she have done to him to make him hate her like that? Ava wasn't in

46

the least like her, of course, but Ava might quite well have been like any sister to any brother who hated her. But this fierce, devilish, mediæval passion—why? Yet I should have guessed something of the reason after Iris had told me that young Burton was 'Boy', Gerald's hero of before the war. But it never occurred to me to connect Iris's casually dropped 'Boy' with the legendary Boy Fenwick of Careless-Days-Before-The-War fame. He will have his place, that dead Boy Fenwick. A deep place.

'Felix Burton's' idea of what a man should be to live nobly—he was full of those large strivings of Young Men which were in vogue in the Careless-Days-Before-The-War— seemed to take the form of wanting to found a new race of something like potent eunuchs. Young Burton was, of course, without the lusts of the body. Ava Foe wasn't. Nor did young Burton want any of your waste of time in graceful love-making; he wanted a sort of ruthless companionship, with occasional patches of mating; he did *not* want to pro-create gracefully, but with a sort of furious absent-minded-ness. Imagine Ava—Iris! Imagine Gerald himself, drawing the woman of his nightmares, that soft possible woman of lonely dreams, detesting her for destroying him . . . and for destroying Boy! One wondered, in reading, if Gerald had ever known a woman. The dark knight of purity . . . the fallen knight of purity, but how fallen!

3

I did not see Gerald whilst I was shaking the dust of Shep-herd's Market for ever off my feet, for he was still asleep. I left Shepherd's Market. The hearty-looking man and the thin wizened man who said 'Oi!' and the little bent old man with the bloodshot eyes gave me farewell.

That afternoon I snatched a few moments from the arranging of the new place, which was only round the corner, to go round and tell Gerald that his sister had been to see him on an Impulse. I had grown to feel responsible for Gerald: his solitude was somehow like a scar across one's own life, a rebuke.

I came upon him in our lane. I have forgotten to say that

47

Gerald, after a particularly hard spell of dipsomania, would go riding on a hack from the Mews nearby. He had a pair of fine polo breeches with which to do that, and with the fine polo breeches (Moss Bros.) went Barty March's riding-whip and the jacket of the old grey suit and that hat. A highwayman on an off day, that is what he looked like in the mean lane, passing the time of day with the little bent old man with the bloodshot eyes.

'You've been drinking,' said Gerald severely to me.

'Billy Goat's won the two-thirty,' wheezed the little bent old man. His hat was the captain of Gerald's hat.

One didn't, perhaps, look one's best in the middle of a removal. But Gerald, confound the man, looked positively healthy, taut, tempered, weathered. *Ach, le sale type anglais!* I told him that his sister had called. 'On an Impulse,' I said.

Gerald stared at me, his cigarette half-way to his mouth. 'Oh!' he said. 'Oh! . . .'

'Here's her telephone number,' I said. He didn't take the slip of paper I held out.

''Ere,' said the little bent old man, 'I'll give it 'im when he's better.' Gerald lowered his cigarette, scowling at me pathetically. No one else would have known it was 'pathetically.'

'Iris called hell!' he accused me. 'How you lie! What?'

'Honest to God, Gerald!'

He flipped away his cigarette and dug his free hand into his pocket as though it was a weapon. Those deep eyes scowled at me, but I wondered what they saw.

'That beast,' he whispered, 'Oh, that beast. . . .'

I left him.

And I did not see him again until the twelfth evening later. I wish I had. I ought to have been to see him, for I was in the habit of seeing Gerald, and during those twelve days he might, I think he would, have told me about the silly, shoddy thing that had happened, and I could have helped to make him see it as only a silly, shoddy thing. What made me feel responsible for Gerald was that his livid, unreasonable, childish contempt for all accepted things was not contempt at all, but fear, just plain fear. He was, I mean, so afraid of life that he simply couldn't exist but by pretending

48

to despise it. Piercing that tortured vanity, I felt that life was a huge hungry beast ready to maul Gerald if he so much as tried to placate it—by using, say, a little pumice-stone on his fingers. And one could never, after having seen through his furious *blague*, be rid of an acute sense of the shamefaced childishness in the man, a childishness beaten down, gone crooked, which could only do him a hurt if it was not watched. And one didn't, quite definitely didn't, want Gerald to be hurt more than he already hurt himself by just breathing.

But, whether it was because that involuntary whisper of his about his sister had sickened me even more than I had thought at the moment, or whether it was merely because I was too busy with arranging myself into the new place, I simply did not seem to have the time to look him up during those twelve days. I wish I had.

Nor, during those twelve days, would it have come very amiss to talk a little about Mrs. Storm. One would have liked to know just a little of the history of that shameless, shameful lady. After all, one didn't every day meet a woman with a pagan body and a Chislehurst mind. But naturally neither Guy nor Hilary were available during those twelve days, for that is a way friends have; Guy because he was down at Mace with the May-fly, and Hilary just because he was tiresome. Hilary, Guy wrote from Mace, was helping a Liberal to fight a musty by-election in some Staffordshire place. 'As if,' Guy wrote, 'a Liberal ever won, as if a Liberal could ever win without a pretty long start! and a handi-capper can never get a grip on anything in a Liberal to give him a start on—sticky little fellows they are, always sliding away somewhere. And as if it mattered whether a Liberal did or didn't win! He'll only get squashed with his own petard.' And, however it was, Hilary's Liberal didn't win, so maybe Guy was right. 'In ten years' time,' says Guy, 'Hilary will be the only Liberal left in Parliament, looking happier and younger and more sickening than ever.'

It was on the fifth morning after the coming and going of the green hat that I was on an instant afflicted with an impulse, and did on the same instant act upon it.

'Hello!' I said.

'Hello!' they said. They were a she.

'Could I speak to Mrs. Storm, please?'

'Who is that speaking, please?'

I quibbled quite in vain.

'I will put the name down in her little book,' said the she kindly.

'Thank you,' I tried not to say bitterly. To ring someone up on an impulse and then have your impulse perpetuated in a Little Book!

'Mrs. Storm is not in town,' said the she.

'Oh, I see,' I said. It is a detestable habit some people have of saying 'in town' or 'out of town'. What town? There can't, honestly, be any real harm in saying London. . . .

'Is there any message? I always take her messages.'

'Oh, no,' I said. 'Thank you very much. Good-b——'

'This is Mrs. Oden speaking.'

'Oh,' I said. Mrs. Oden?

'Yes?' said Mrs. Oden.

'Well, thank you very much,' I said. 'Good-b——'

'She never is, you know,' complained Mrs. Oden. Now that was a loquacious lady. I do not wish to be belittling anyone else, but I am sure that she talked more in the next few minutes than any other person of the same chest expansion in England. She seemed to have been suffering from silence all that morning until my ring. I learnt later that Mrs. Oden had once been Iris's governess, that there was always a floor reserved for Iris in her house in Montpellier Square, which house Mr. and Mrs. Oden owed entirely to Iris's generosity.

'She went off to Paris the other day,' complained Mrs. Oden, 'at a *moment's* notice. Here to-day and gone to-morrow. It is too bad of her, when we never see anything of her. She is too vague, I always tell her. I suppose she had made some arrangement with you, Mr. er, has forgotten to put you off, and now you are disappointed?'

'Oh,' I said. 'Yes, certainly.'

'Well, I expect her back any day, but how long she will stay this time I have not the faintest idea. Really it is too bad, she gets vaguer every year. And here has her aunt Lady Eve Chalice been wanting her address in Paris, and I have not the faintest idea of anything! What did you say the name was? Oh, yes, of course, I have it down. She will see it as *soon* as she returns, I promise you. Yes, yes. Good-bye, good-bye.'

It was five days later that there came to my hand a large box labelled from *Edouard Apel et Cie.*, *rue de la Paix*, *Paris* and stamped 'By Air'. Within the large box were several smaller flat boxes, and within these were reams upon reams of finest white notepaper, but good, manly stuff, stamped with my new address; and if that notepaper had its way I never would have another address, for there was enough in those small flat boxes to last a reasonably reticent man for all time. No note came with them. I searched. Then, across the top sheet of the third box that I opened, I found scrawled in pencil in an absurd, schoolgirl hand: 'That one day you may write to me to say that you have forgiven me for the only dignity I have left: the dignity of the . . .'

I could not make out that last word for several days. It was scrawled right across the foot of the sheet, a long squiggle with one eye looking out from the middle of it which might have been an a. At last I thought it was 'unaware'.

Much later Iris told me that it was 'unaware'. She said: 'I picked out the phrase from a book I was reading, and sent it to you like a flower.'

CHAPTER THREE   FOR PURITY!

The cavalier of low creatures dies hard; surviving even our gesture, he loiters dangerously in the tail of our eye, he awaits, with piratical calm, the final stroke; and only will he fade and be for ever gone, despised and distraught, before the face of him who bore the magic device For Purity, whose ghost was to be raised by Mr. Townshend over dinner on the twelfth night after the coming of the green hat. For, his wretched Liberal being at last retrieved from somewhere beneath the foot of the poll, that gentleman was again among us, saying 'hm'.

We have so far seen but the shadow of Mr. Townshend; now, at last, this shadow must emerge into the tale of the weak Marches as the person of Mr. Townshend of Magralt. He emerges, as becomes a man of property who believes in progress as though it were a pain, in a dinner-jacket, *le smoking,* a Tuxedo; of which the bow-tie is gathered together with that dexterous carelessness which is the affectation of elderly Englishmen who cannot put up with any affectations whatever. Now there is no known explanation for this pheno-menon of the sickly bow-tie among Englishmen of over forty years of age. That they are all blackguards, Mr. Shaw has assured us. But haven't they, God bless one's soul, eyes! It is not, of course, of the least importance whether a bow-tie falls straight or crooked, particularly on a grown-up man. It is not, after all, of the least importance whether one is clothed or naked. But one may, in passing, be permitted to wonder on the curious dispositions of the blind goddess Chance, whereby not once in a long lifetime, not even by one little bit of a fluke, will one of these elderly gentlemen ever tie a bow to fall even approximately right. They must, therefore, do it on purpose. But for what purpose? Let them, I say unto them, tie their bows carefully while the bow-tying is good, for voices from the Clyde are rising loud and every-where those snobs are dominant who affect that the shirt of democracy should be a dish-clout.

However, Mr. Townshend's shadow does not even yet

grow in substance without some difficulty. Between him and us, towards the dinner-hour, intrudes knife-like that deuce of cavaliers, he of the hat that Frederick the Great would have envied, for that wrecker of homes liked his hats soft and malleable, he liked to twist and torture them as though they were no more than men. In fine, Gerald made me late for dinner.

The clock of the Queen Street Post Office stood at three minutes before eight o'clock as I passed on my way to Hilary's house in Chesterfield Street. The roar of the marching hosts of Piccadilly was as though muted by the still evening air. The small straight streets of Mayfair lay as though musing between the setting of the sun and the rising of the theatre-curtain. Neat errand-boys, released for the day, kicked their heels about on the curbs. The drivers of sauntering taxi-cabs looked inquiringly, impersonally, into the faces of hurrying pedestrians. Limousines lounged softly by. Past me strode intently a tall raven-haired woman in a bright green wrap with a high sable collar, and moving frantically below were bright green shoes and bright green stockings that appalled the suave dignity of the evening light. These are not the only green properties we shall see in this tale, for women of the mode wore very much of green in the year 1922; although, of course, some women were not necessarily of the mode even when they wore green. Some women should not wear green. To such, their husbands should say: 'My dear, I can't help saying it again, but really I've never seen you look as well as when you're in black.'

It was from the Curzon Street corner, just by Jolley's the chemist, that I saw Gerald. He was across the road, against the entrance of the little tunnel that leads into Shepherd's Market, buying an evening-paper off a friend of ours, Mr. Auk, who used to have his stand just there.

I crossed towards Gerald. I would be a few minutes late for dinner, that was certain, but if ever I was punctual at Hilary's he never was dressed: a sense of conduct being the property of imperious men, who must disregard the servile virtue of punctuality.

53

I could not see Gerald's face as he stood on the curb glancing at his paper, the brim of that hat was so low over his right eye. Mr. Auk winked at me as I came up. 'Oiled, that's wot!' whispered Mr. Auk. Then a friend of his came by, and he and Mr. Auk retreated into the tunnel, where I vaguely thought that Mr. Auk seemed to be telling his friend something funny about Gerald. I never have passed the time of day with Mr. Auk since I found what it was that he thought so funny about Gerald that evening.

When I greeted Gerald he instantly looked up from the paper to me. I remember now that he seemed to watch my face for something, an expression, which he half-expected to see. But one notices those things only later on.

'I say, seen the evening-paper?'

'No. Why?'

The dark eyes haunted with abstraction, the thin hawk's nose, the fine, twisted, defiant mouth. . . .

'Why? How the hell do I know why!'

He crumpled his paper, thrust it under his arm and dug the released hand into his pocket. Thus was Gerald Haveleur March armed cap-a-pie against life. He had something on his mind, one could see that. But it would take hours to make Gerald confide anything.

'I say, have a drink?'

Now I wonder how many thousands of men are at this very moment putting that question to thousands of men; yet that, if nothing else, would have made that night significant in my life, for never before had the solitary asked me or, I think, any one to have a drink with him. Nor would he, as a rule, have a drink if you suggested it. And once, at a party I gave, he had some ginger-beer. But, even so, I had to say I couldn't, pleading that I would be too late for dinner. 'With Hilary,' I said, and he scowled absently in a way he had, and lounged up the road with me. Thoughtful he was always.

That was a curious, capacious evening. The Marches were gathered together that evening, they who were never let off anything. As Gerald lounged beside me the great primrose car with the menacing shining bonnet passed us

54

as silently as though Curzon Street was a carpet. It was empty but for a boyish chauffeur. Gerald, I suppose, did not know it, and I did not remark on it. I wondered if Iris had surprised Mrs. Oden by returning suddenly. Poor Mr. Oden. . . .

'What have you been doing with yourself lately, Gerald?'

'Doing?' His eyes pierced the pavement the other side of my shoulder, for tall was Gerald.

He grinned. . . .

'You'd never guess,' he grinned.

I did not like this grinning. It was unusual in Gerald. It was like a crooked mask on the fine dark face. There was by ordinary no grinning froth about Gerald . . . and, somehow, it crossed my mind that maybe Gerald was hard-up. I asked him, oh tentatively, if anything was 'up'.

'Up? The hell's up. O Jesu!' And he grinned. . . .

'Yes, but besides that—anything?' Not, you know, that I thought for one moment that anything really was 'up'. It was merely that I misliked that grinning.

I can see him this moment so clearly, the way he suddenly threw back his head and stared from under the brim of that hat as though into the heart of the heavens: the dark, defiant, hungry silhouette searching the heart of the above.

We were at the corner of East Chapel Street, where the great American pile of Sunderland House debases itself before the puny roofs of Mayfair: it loitered clumsily against the soft evening light, reluctant to yield to the grey embrace of London. . . .

'God!' sighed Gerald. Like a child, like a child . . . and like a fiend he suddenly laughed up at the veiled heavens. 'Imagine, you fool, just imagine the bloody degradation of being alive!'

But I will leave out Gerald's 'bloody's. One is tired of saying, hearing, reading that silly word. It is only chicken-food, after all, and does very well on the lips of the young ladies of the day, but there is no reason why grown-up people should use it.

'I like you,' he said, as only that devilish child could say it. 'You sit on your imagination as though it was an egg, and

55

a nice little chicken comes out. God, I wouldn't be you! Look at all the pretty eggs you'll hatch and not one have a chance to grow up into a splendid, lovely old hen that'll peck at the dung you call life. Why don't you write about fallen archangels? They're the only things worth writing about, fallen archangels. Phut to you, that's why I say. . . .'

I managed then, for the first time in our friendship, to suggest that if perhaps he was hard-up, well, phut to him. . . .

'Look here, that's not fair,' stammered Gerald. Shy himself, he made one want to sink into the ground with shyness. 'I mean, that's putting friendship to music, isn't it? What?'

'Oh, nonsense, Gerald! There's nothing so silly and mean as this reticence about money. . . .'

'God, but you've given me an idea! I'll tell you what I'll do for you, as you're late for dinner. I'll damn well lend you a fiver.'

'But, Gerald——'

'You talk too much,' Gerald stammered. 'I'd like to do you a bit of good. And I've still got to thank you for chloroforming me and lugging me off to that Home for Drunks, thanks very much. Now, am I going to lend you a fiver or am I going to make such a rough-house just here that all the police in London will come and arrest you for soliciting? I'll scream if you don't touch me!'

I was in a hurry. I had to take that fiver. I have that fiver still.

'I'll keep it for you,' I said. 'Damn you.'

'Yes, you keep it for me,' said Gerald thoughtfully. 'Nice, fivers are . . .' and then, savagely muttering 'Oh, hell!' he strode abruptly away down the slope of East Chapel Street, which leads into Shepherd's Market. Drunk or sober, you simply couldn't tell. You never knew that man was drunk until he was speechless. I was hurrying away when his voice held me—and a very clear boyish voice Gerald had, like a prefect's at school.

'I say, seen that sister of mine again? . . . You haven't?' He seemed to reflect profoundly. 'I say, if ever you do, give her my love. What? I say, don't forget. . . .'

'I won't forget,' I called back. 'Good-night, Gerald.' But

he had turned away, and the last I saw of him he was putting his shoulder against the saloon-door of The Leather Butler. I plunged across the road to Chesterfield Street, glad of the message I would certainly give to Gerald's sister. Maybe to-night, somehow. A furious conference of livid pink and purple monsters hung over Seamore Place, where the sun was sinking into Kensington Gardens.

2

'There was a cocktail for you,' said Hilary gloomily, 'but I drank it, in case it grew warm.' I thanked him politely for the idea. 'It wasn't an idea, really,' said Hilary gloomily. 'It was an impulse.'

It is not, therefore, impossible to understand how it came about that there were not a few people, youngish people, who considered Mr. Townshend to be a tiresome man. They said: 'He is very nice, but *frankly*, isn't he rather tiresome?' I supposed he was rather tiresome.

Hilary was a man of various ages; when nothing was going well with him, he would look no more than forty; when everything was going well with him, he would look about forty-five; when he was crossing a road, that is to say when he was thinking, he looked about fifty. The last was, I believe, his age.

Hilary was a man who had convinced himself and every-one else that he had neither use nor time for the flibberty-gibberties of life. He collected postage-stamps and had sat as Liberal Member for an Essex constituency for fifteen years. To be a Liberal was against every one of his prejudices, but to be a Conservative was against all his convictions. He thought of democracy as a drain-pipe through which the world must crawl for its health. He did not think the health of the world would ever be good. When travelling he looked porters sternly in the face and over-tipped them. His eyes were grey and gentle, and they were suspicious of being amused. I think that Hilary treasured a belief that his eyes were còld and ironic, as also that his face was of a stern cast. His face was long, and the features somehow muddled. It was a kind face.

57

Hilary is the last in direct line of the Townshends, who have held Magralt, a Tudor manor on the Essex coast, since a Townshend deserted to Henry Tudor on Bosworth Field. The Townshends of Magralt have always been soldiers, 'and that,' Guy, first and last a soldier, will say, 'is the only reason one can see why Hilary is a politician by profession and the foremost stamp-collector in Chesterfield Street by the sweat of his brow.' But one has to report that Hilary was once, before witnesses, perfectly beastly to an American gentleman who said that Blucher had arrived in time for the Battle of Waterloo.

But it was on the question of marriage that the two friends would indulge the sharpest difference of opinion; or rather, Hilary's wasn't an opinion, it was a lurking Silence.

'Suppose you die,' said Guy de Travest. 'You might. You are ten years older than me in years alone. You may receive your call to higher things at any moment. Look how I beat you at squash the other day! Let us suppose, then, that you are as good as dead. Unmarried, childless. You have done nothing. You are nothing. You leave nothing. Except, of course, what was left to you——'

'Less,' said Hilary.

'Your memory, then, goes down as that of a sickening philatelist. Whereas, had any one of your ancestors had a chance of a bit of war like ours, he would have died a Major-General!'

'A Field-Marshal, Guy. You forget that the Townshends have the reputation of having lost more of their soldiers' lives than any other service-family in England.' And so it would go on for ever, Guy contending that as Hilary was nothing in himself it was disloyal of him not to wed and bring forth direct heirs, while Hilary's attitude would be one of benevolently beckoning to the sombre heights of Cumberland, where sat the house of Curle-Townshend, heirs-apparent to Magralt and all its fiefs.

Anyone, as Hilary was once goaded into muttering, would have thought that Guy's own marriage was the happiest in the world; at worst, anyone might have thought that it was a happy marriage, as marriages go. Guy, it was

58

said, adored his wife. Guy, it was said, never spoke to his wife except in public and as he passed through her room in the morning towards his bath, when he said 'Good-morning.' It was Lady de Travest who volunteered this information. 'I do not see,' said Lady de Travest in her slow soft voice, 'why one should for ever conceal the fact that one's husband is cruel to one. It is nothing for one to be ashamed of, is it?' Moira de Travest was a quiet woman, with slow graces of movement, statuesque, exceedingly handsome in what you might call a public way, with a dark, restrained smile in the blue eyes under the hair that shone like black silver. Suddenly she would give a very loud laugh, and then her eyes would shine boyishly for a second. She had many intimate friends among women, and at times she was rather brilliant in a man-like way. Foreign Ambassadors liked to be with her. Mr. de Laszlo, M.V.O., painted her. Women novelists had tea with her. Twice a year she would say that a day must come when she must take a lover, but she gave one a profound sense that there was nothing in the world she could endure less. But, whatever it was that had gone wrong between those two ten years before, they had a son, a boy of sixteen, at Eton, and Guy de Travest would remain by his marriage without question of separation or divorce. That was cruel of him, Moira's friends said, but Guy was a very catholic gentleman, and he loved his son beyond all things. In the earlier pages of country house albums one might come on photographs of Guy and Moira arm-in-arm, yellow Viking and black silver. They did not seem to have aged at all since then, but maybe Lady de Travest was a little more statuesque and her eyes would shine more and more boyishly.

Hilary and Guy were friends. Inseparable, they were inimical. They agreed on nothing, nor had they one taste in common. But maybe it is in a similar tempering of a sense of conduct that Englishmen, regardless of all overt differences, will find their deepest friendships. Conduct was for Guy and Hilary one of three facts, the other two being birth and death. And it is they and their opposites who must finally make the storms of life. Warriors of conduct and enemies of conduct—there is the issue that has still to find its final battlefield. Hilary's Liberalism, in that issue, would come crashing about his heart; of his head he would take no account, for it is not by the head that one decides in ultimate moments. Guy, tall as a tree, Guy the latter-day 'thunder-god of dandies', would make a flaming figure, standing against the afterglow of the fires of an old religion called aristocracy. But Guy was far from being of those Tories, of whom Mr. Galsworthy has written with such cruel sympathy in *Fraternity* and *The Patrician*, who are obsessed by an illusion of their own exclusive right to national captaincy. Guy did not think that the hope for England or the world lay in himself or his caste. He was not a clever man; but his contempt for politics was born of a conviction that there was no hope of curing the diseases of life and society by anything that any body of men could do. Men individually must clean themselves within, questing for and grasping what cleanness there was in them. There was a frozen storm in Guy's eyes, and they were very clean. But, of course, he was not very clever.

Those two men are for me symbols of an England that I love. I am not sure that I can explain what that England is. I am not sure that I would like to explain it even to myself, as, maybe for the same reason, I would not like to read Jane Austen with a mental measure. I am not sure that there is such an England, that there ever was such an England. The soil, to be sure, is there, the clouds across the sun, the teasing humours of the island seasons: the halls, the parklands, the spacious rooms, they are there. But the figures that sweep across them—are these that we see, all? Are there no others, lost somewhere, calmly ready to show themselves—are these that we see, all? These healthy, high-busted women with muscles like those of minotaurs, these girls who are either stunned with health or pale with the common vapours of common dancing-halls, these stout, graceless ones here, those too slender, bloodless ones there, these things that have no voice between a shout and a whisper, these things that have yielded to democracy nothing but their dignity—are these that we see, all? These rather

60

caddish young men who have no vision between a pimply purity and vice, who are without the grace with which to adorn ignorance or the learning with which to make vulgarity tolerable, these peasant-minded noblewomen, these matrons who appear to have gained in youth what they have lost in dignity, these toiling dancers, these elderly gentlemen with their ungallant vices—are these that we see, all? Or was there never such an England? Were the parklands and the spacious rooms never peopled but by nincompoops let loose by wealth among the graces of learning and fashion? Was there never such an England as I myself once saw in the magic of a spring morning in London? It was no more than the passing picture of Guy de Travest walking by the sulky side of Piccadilly, as he must always do to pass between his house in Belgrave Square and his club in Saint James's Street, to which a few gentlemen will still absently resort. I saw Guy walking against the broken sunlight of the Green Park, and then I did not see Guy. It was as though from one step to another he had walked into a dimension wherein the desires of his heart melted his person into the England of his heart, and he was rendered invisible in the ambience of the Green Park and against the ancient landscape of Saint James's.

3

Hilary says that I was very quiet over dinner that night. He remarked it, he says, because it was so unusual. Hilary has an illusion common to Englishmen, that if a man can utter three consecutive sentences without breaking them up with 'eh', 'ah', 'hm', 'mm', and any other noises that may occur to him as fit and proper, he must be held to be talking too much.

How on earth, I was wondering, could I cast the name of Mrs. Storm before my host with even a tolerable hope of his more than grunting at it? For, of course, one never discussed women with Hilary. I believe he had been a member of several clubs once upon a time, but in these degenerate days he had finally withdrawn into the impenetrable fortress of the Marlborough: Guy and he agreeing that, since it was once said of a King of Spain that he had died of etiquette, they envied rather than cared to overlook their young friends in the exercise of the long lives assured to them.

'He will, if you provoke him,' Iris had said, absently enough. And, indeed, never but once had I ever heard Hilary expand at the mention of a woman's name, and that was when I had provoked him by defending her, the lady in question being one for whom he had a great regard but who had, as they say very aptly in the popular phrase, 'gone completely off the rails'. As regards Iris, in that case, it should be child's work.

Hilary says now that he was able, so soon as I mentioned her name, to account for my subdued air. Such, Hilary says, was the aftermath of Iris's effect on men. But all he said at the time was, snappy like, that he hadn't even known she was in London and would I have port or brandy or both, because I was detaining them at my side of the table? I said I was sorry and how amiable Mrs. Storm had been about him. 'And fancy,' I said, 'her being Gerald's twin sister!'

'Why "fancy"?'

Hilary was annoyed. Now why was Hilary annoyed? Why do men get annoyed?

'She is beautiful,' I said, 'she is good, she is——'

'It seems to me,' snapped Hilary, 'that they make a perfectly harmonious pair of twins. Hm.' And he lit a cigar and reflected profoundly on the flame of the match. Perhaps I had better leave out his 'hm's'.

'There's only one March,' he said, pushing a cup of coffee towards me as though he hated the sight of it, 'who has ever been any good, and that's the aunt, Eve Chalice, a dear old lady. Heavens above, the March blood! But they will be near their last gasp now, with young Gerald as the heir. . . .'

It just showed, you know, how much one ever knew about that young man. I had no idea he was heir to anything, let alone the bankrupt earldom. 'Ever since last July,' said Hilary, 'when his uncle, Barty's elder brother by a year, and his cousin thought they would do some fifth-rate mountain-

62

eering in Switzerland without a guide, and tried by mistake to climb the Jungfrau.' Hilary, I remember thinking, seemed very bitter about that mountaineering. You know, that bitterness of a calm, normal, reasonable air, with a slight flavour of old-world banter? He seemed to want to give the impression that he rather gloated than otherwise over the decline and fall of the house of Portairley. Gerald, as the nineteenth earl, Hilary seemed to want to say, served the house of Portairley right. If Hilary could only have seen his own kind grey eyes!

But that something, apart from the mere existence of the Marches, had annoyed him, was obvious; and presently I realised that the something was the fact that Iris had not let him know she was in London, but that he had heard of it from me, from anyone, in fact, but herself. I ought instantly to have guessed that was the matter, Hilary being one of those detached men who have no use for the flibberty-gibberties of life.

Gerald, one thought, would make about as pretty an Earl of Portairley and Axe as even the Marches could boast. 'But at least,' I suggested, 'he will have a little more money than he has now?'

'About,' said Hilary, 'minus five hundred a year. They can't even bribe anyone to take Portairley, and so the old gentleman has to live in a couple of rooms and pay the taxes on the property from what his creditors allow him. That old curse working, one would think. . . .'

There isn't really a great variety among these family curses. There appear to be no more than two schools of thought among the cursers, one which consigns the cursed to instant death, and the other to prolonged disgrace ending in damnation. The Portairleys' curse was of the second variety, and poor Gerald appeared to be in at the death for the damnation.

'Vaguely,' I said, 'I gather that Gerald and his sister had some quarrel in the distant past. But I happened to see Gerald as I came on here, and he seemed ready for a reconciliation. In that case, as Mrs. Storm seems to be wealthy . . .'

63

Certainly Hilary could surprise one. He exploded, in that quiet parliamentary way which is one of the loftiest dignities of a constitutional country: 'And thank the Lord she is! Imagine the shoddy life of an Iris—with neither money nor morals!'

Evidently, then, Hilary had a great regard for the lady of the green hat. You must remember that until this evening not so much as her name had passed between us. . . . 'He will, if you provoke him,' Iris had said. Well, hadn't I!

Hector Storm V.C. had, it seemed, left her every penny. Storm, steel, Sheffield. 'Fine boy, Storm,' said Hilary, pulling at a stiff grey thing which I forgot to mention he wore on his upper lip without, however, succeeding in looking anything but clean-shaven. 'Boy Fenwick left her all he had too, but she wouldn't, naturally, touch a penny of it. You would think the world was upside down when you came to inquire into the moral sense of an Iris! Strict as steel here, unbending as iron there—and then! She gave all Boy Fenwick's fortune over to old Aunt Fenwick, since when the old hag has called Iris every name out of the Apocrypha for her pains.'

'But, Hilary!' I said. Hilary says now that I was white in the face. 'But did you say Boy Fenwick? Boy . . . Fenwick?'

'Her first husband,' said Hilary; and he pushed his port-glass an inch or two up the polished surface of the table and stared at it. 'You couldn't,' he said, 'do better than young Fenwick. . . . Bit before your time, I suppose. . . .'

'I never dreamt,' I think I said, 'that Mrs. Storm had been the Mrs. Fenwick. . . .'

'Mrs. Storm,' smiled Hilary queerly to his port-glass, 'has been everything.'

But Boy Fenwick! And the shameless, shameful lady of the green hat as the tragic Mrs. Fenwick! So there was 'Felix Burton' and his ideal of purity! And there, plain as hate could make her, there was 'Ava Foe', and somewhere there was the reason for Gerald's mediæval hatred for his sister! Somewhere there, but exactly where? For no one knew less of Boy Fenwick's death than I did, that being a legend of 'a little before my time'. . . .

'I knew Iris,' Hilary was saying thoughtfully, playing with

64

the stem of his glass, 'when she was so high. They had a house in Cambridge Square then, and she used to go to that school in South Audley Street where they all go to. I'd see her walking along with her governess, a long little thing, all brown stockings and blue eyes. Hm. She was adorable.'

There was a pause . . . and suddenly he turned his face to me, that long thin grey-looking face with the kind, muddled features. And it was as though it had, suddenly, profoundly, lost all its inner calm. Hilary's outward calm, in spite of his detached air—'Mr. Townshend, the imperturbable champion of procedure'—was always rather like a Gruyère cheese, a sort of smooth surface with gaps. But this was different, this was as though a tap had been wrenched loose inside him, letting run a savage, hurt bewilderment which didn't quite reach his skin. 'And now,' he said softly, yet looking at me as though accusing *me* of something. 'And now! The last I heard of Iris was that she was seen night after night in a Russian cabaret in Vienna with an Italian Jew who is said to have made a fortune by exporting medicated champagne to America. There's the long little thing, all brown stockings and blue eyes. . . .'

'But,' I began, and decided that it was better not. But it was absurd, that 'night after night'. That wasn't, I knew, Iris Storm. Not 'night after night'. She might very possibly have sat one night in a Russian cabaret in Vienna with an Italian Jew who exported medicated champagne to America, but certainly not 'night after night'. Unless, that is, she had changed a great deal since then. After all, one couldn't be more unattractive than an Italian Jew who exported medicated champagne to America. No, really, that was too much.

'Your generation,' said Hilary thoughtfully, 'is a mess. Have some brandy.'

'It's absurd,' I said, 'to talk in "generations". Slack novelists do it to get easy effects. All generations are a mess. Thank you.'

'Your generation,' said Hilary thoughtfully, 'has more opportunities for being a mess than ours had. That's what I meant. And your children will have more opportunities than you have. There is a certain amount of horse-sense in the reluctance of many young fellows nowadays to having wives of their own. They're afraid of getting it in the neck from the results. For whereas you have motors and telephones and wireless with which to lose your sense of the stabilities, as you are losing them, they will have cheap aeroplanes as well. When you people nowadays begin to break loose there's no limit to your looseness. There was in my father's time. They couldn't get about so quickly. They couldn't grub about in so many cesspools at one time, rushing in a night between London and any vile paradise of the vulgarities like Deauville or the present Riviera. Even if they broke loose a little—the women, I mean—they generally had to make some compromise with the decencies simply because they had to live in the place, they couldn't make an appointment with a trunk-call to Paris and go and have a few days' "fun" there. But now if a woman has kicked through every restraint of caste and chastity there's the whole world open for her to play the mischief in, there's every invention in the world to help her indulge her intolerable little lusts. . . .'

I mastered an irrational impulse to try to defend Iris against the friend of her childhood. I would have liked to say that the little lusts were intolerable most of all to Iris. Hilary would almost have sympathised with that in Iris, for it would seem that the only vice a man of principle can understand is the vice of not enjoying what he has forfeited his principles to do. Hilary couldn't, obviously, forgive Iris for not having grown common and meretricious and, in the slim beastly sense, coarse, as the other 'rotten ladies' did. He couldn't, obviously, forgive her for the continued graciousness of her outward seeming, and of her inner seeming too, if one didn't know those things about her. He couldn't obviously, forgive her for being so indifferent to every distinction of class that she was equally indifferent, with the whole calm of her mind, to being 'declassed'. And he couldn't, obviously, forgive himself for still, God knew how, seeing in her the same qualities that he had seen in the long little thing, all brown stockings and blue eyes. If only Hilary had been a sentimentalist, and could have closed his

66

eyes against what he did not wish to see and could have opened his eyes to see all that he did wish to see! But Hilary was a realist with a backward-seeing eye. The Iris of long ago should have been dead, choked to death by this grown-up Iris—but, and there lay the perversity of this grown-up Iris who had kicked through every restraint of caste and chastity, if wasn't dead at all, she was still essentially the same Iris who had walked with her governess up South Audley Street. But, the devil, all these men! Yet there she was . . . profoundly *un*-different, profoundly as though untouched by any more soiling breath than that of the lightest passage of the years. It was, you might hear Hilary thinking, confoundedly unfair to all decent womanhood, Iris's immunity in the abyss. He should not like her—no, there should not be left anything about her for a decent man to like. The friend of Iris's childhood couldn't help a savage anger with her for retaining the interest of a clean, and otherwise quite balanced, mind. The friend of childhood liked the woman so deeply that, being a man of principle, he could see only her worst side. And then the man of principle would fall into the toils of the friend of childhood, and whilst the two antagonists were wrestling together they could see only the side of the woman that it made them the most wretched to see. The very fact that Hilary was deeply attached to Iris made him only her worst side. Many good men call that 'liking' a woman. Many good women call that 'idealism' in men.

4

It is curious how many irrelevant details will crowd back into the mind when one is trying to reconstruct only the main passage of an evening, which was throughout, now one looks back on it, as though directed to its inevitable end. I remember how, through one of the long silences common to our odd, antagonistic intimacy, I sat staring into my brandy-glass—those Gargantuan ones, Hilary had—and wondering at Hilary's, well, unsentimental sentimentality; and then I wondered what sort of a fight the man of principle would put up against the friend of childhood should Iris ever show the faintest inclination to take as her third husband Mr. Townshend of Magralt. The man of principle would lose . . . happily lose or unhappily, you could not tell, for no man can tell what odd happinesses, more secretly kept than crimes, another man will snatch from intimacy with a woman whom he would detest if he did not desire.

But through the silences of that evening there walked mainly the figure of the legend of Boy Fenwick, a boyish figure midst a babble of confused rumours and knowing silences. Yet I was so concerned not to appear, to that watchful and dangerous friend of childhood, too interested in Mrs. Storm, that the name of Boy Fenwick hung long on my lips before I was out with it. Oh, that name of Boy Fenwick! One knew it so well and so dimly, it would so often be just dropped into a conversation by some friend of his or some friend of a friend, just the name with a passing regret, to the perpetuation of his charm and his time. . . .

Many will, no doubt, remember the details of what must have been one among the minor sensations of that time better than I can pretend to. It happened during the summer of 1913, when I, having just left school, was enjoying a first taste of freedom up and down Switzerland, and was far from the long arm of even the Continental *Daily Mail*. Boy Fenwick was found, on the dawn of his wedding-night, lying in the courtyard of the Hôtel Vendôme in Deauville, dead of a broken collar-bone. He had fallen, it appeared, from his bedroom window on the third floor. His beautiful young wife (I collect the bits of rumour that came to me later) had been asleep, had suddenly awoken to a sharp feeling of solitude, had happened to look out at the dawn. . . .

Tests were made, and it was found that a man could, given certain conditions, have fallen out of that window. The hotel management suggested that a man could, given certain conditions, fall out of almost any window. Among the certain conditions suggested, tactfully, was champagne. That was, I believe, adopted, tactfully. Much, of course, must have been said and printed about the beautiful girl Mrs. Fenwick; and there was provided a little comic relief to the affair in the scarcely suppressed indignation of the illustrated

68

papers, for the beautiful Mrs. Fenwick had in some way prevailed on Sebastian Roeskin, the photographer in Dover Street, not to issue any of her photographs, and had shown a remarkable ingenuity in evading the street-camera. And, the tragedy happening at Deauville during the *Grande Semaine*—Deauville at that time was still in the first flush of its victory over Trouville—it was hushed up as quickly as possible.

Boy Fenwick had only that year come down from Oxford, and his memory was treasured by his many friends both there and in London. Indeed, to one who heard of him only when he had become legend, and when the first edition of a slim book of poetry by him, published posthumously with a charming introduction by P.L., had attained to a price only surpassed later by Rupert Brooke's memory, he appears to have been the most beloved of the beloved young men of that time. To youth of this decade, grown now a little impatient of the careless wise-seeming pastime of indulging 'sound' scepticisms or catholic idealisms, those youths of the days before the war must seem to have been the most gifted of God's creatures who ever walked this earth, always excepting the glory that was Greece. Several, to be sure, survive until this day, but nothing could be more unjust than to approach a man's youth in the light of the shadow that he casts in his early thirties. Yet they would verily seem, those few dead young men, to have a certain god-like quality of immortality, denied to the multitude that died with them and for whom cenotaphs and obelisks and memorials must do duty for memory: that they should retain the regret of their many friends is not remarkable, but it is odd, and pleasant, how they will ever and again loiter, gay and handsome and 'sound', in the imagination of those who never knew them. Boy Fenwick's name, now, would ever and again pass like a phantom of beauty and laughter across some conversation: so real, so dim. He had been notable, it seemed—and this is the only clear thing I had ever heard about him—for a certain catholic idealism that was almost an obsession with him. So, I was to think this night, thrusting from me the legend of Boy Fenwick, so it would seem. An idealist! Yes,

69

Boy Fenwick was an idealist. But would I had the debonair truculence of that puissant nobleman, the Earl of Birkenhead, who has dared to say, in an age given over to the new-rich snobbery of exalting plain, normal men: 'I do not like meek men.' I, had I that presence, would say: 'I do not like idealists.'

Yet it was not to be over this dinner with Hilary that I was to be given the full sum of the idealism of that handsome young god who, beloved of many, was the hero of one March and the fate of another. That was to come much later, on a night that was the sister of this night.

Mrs. Storm could have been no more than nineteen or twenty at the time of that tragedy at Deauville. And I suppose I must have remarked, probably apropos of nothing but Hilary's passing me the matches, how very terrible it must have been for a young girl, for Hilary passed, through one of those pregnant pauses which seem always to preface the cruelties of kind people, his Gargantuan brandy-glass round about his nose. 'And,' he said thoughtfully, 'rather more terrible for him, don't you think?'

'I suppose,' I said in all innocence, 'that he was tipsy or something, to fall out like that. . . .'

Hilary looked at me through his glass, for the rim reached his eyebrows as he sipped, in that way which is supposed, I believe, to make noisy Labour interruptors feel such fools as even a clown must despise.

'But, Hilary,' I couldn't help crying out, 'you're not implying that he threw himself out!'

Hilary, because I had given way to a moment's emphasis, gained instantly in leisured calm. 'Hm,' he said. Gently he put down his huge glass. 'Hm,' he said. He considered the stump of his cigar, and decided that it was not worth while relighting it. 'Hm,' he said, and took another from the box, pinching it. I passed him the matches. 'Hm,' he said. But not I to be provoked! I did to him what Mr. Beerbohm once so notably did to the late Mr. James Pethick in the Casino at Dieppe: I plied the spur of silence.

'Boy Fenwick,' said Hilary, lighting his cigar, 'was a young man of quality. I don't mean the word in the flashy

70

sense in which you use it in your stories. But of *quality*—in mind and spirit. And yet,' in a volume of white smoke he smothered the failing light of the match, 'he chucked himself out of that window.'

And, you know, just at that moment I saw him doing that, and Iris lying in bed . . .

Hilary was angry. The very thought of that buried tragedy seemed to wrench that inside tap a little looser, but still the savage, hurt bewilderment would not quite reach his skin.

'Of course,' I said, 'they just said it was an accident, then. . . .'

'Naturally,' murmured Hilary.

Naturally, Mrs. Boy Fenwick had not hurt her husband's name by saying publicly that he had died of his own will. 'And then,' said Hilary, 'you come to the upside-down morality of an Iris March, the part of her that's steel and iron and gold. She ruined herself, telling the truth.'

'But,' I said humbly, 'if you had preferred not to think of her as ruined, need you have believed that it was the truth?'

'Iris,' said Hilary, 'never lies. It bores her. One quite naturally gets into the habit of taking everything she says literally; for it always will be literally true, particularly if it's against herself. She hasn't, you see, a trace of the self-preservative instinct. Hm. Pity.'

Iris Fenwick couldn't, it seemed, endure for one moment the idea that his friends should think that Boy had fallen out in a moment of tipsy dizziness—Boy being well known to be a very light drinker, and Iris abominating drink, 'the very idea of drink,' Hilary said, 'as only the daughter of a drunkard and the sister of a drunkard can. If you ever get to know her at all well,' he suddenly smiled, 'you may be a little put out, in the natural satisfaction of your thirst, by seeing Iris look just a little, well, sulky. Unreasonable, yes. But they get unreasonable about drink, daughters or sisters or wives of drunkards.'

Mrs. Boy Fenwick had seemed to feel most deeply her responsibility to Boy's memory and to his friends' love for him. She simply had, it seemed, to safeguard the love they

71

had for him, by making it clear that he had died as he had lived. In disenchantment of an ideal—that, if Boy was to commit suicide at all, could be his only possible justification. His suicide, as apart from his death, naturally scarred his friends, but not so deeply when they knew that it was done in the despair of the disenchantment of an ideal. Boy's friends would understand that completely, Iris must have felt, for were they not Boy's friends? He was sensitive even to madness—they could, indeed they'd have to, think that. But that he was given something to rouse his sensitiveness and to overturn his balance—she had, Iris seemed to have felt, to tell his friends that, so that, in giving Iris all the blame that was her due, they should retain their memory of a Boy strong to the end in idealism. And they seemed, I gathered from Hilary, to have done that without stint. Hilary, too—for wasn't he a realist, that man? One could see them all at it, Boy's friends to Boy's widow—the dead adored youth in their minds, the still, pale, beautiful girl between them. She had to tell Gerald. You can imagine that. . . .

She had, Hilary said, a quite unearthly beauty just at that time, and was so still, so terribly *un*-young somewhere inside her. 'It was my fault,' she had said. She had been looking when he had thrown himself out of the window. He had just lit a cigarette, she said.

'That a girl of that age,' said Hilary, 'that a girl whose moral character, you can't help seeing, was . . . well, what it was, should be so impelled to tell the truth at her own expense, at the expense of her own ruin, at the expense of a queer brother's hatred, for that must have hurt her most of all, by a sense of honour that would make even the rigidity of a Guy look small, well——'

'But isn't that where, Hilary, there comes in that "caste" which you complain of her having always ignored?'

But Hilary wasn't going back on any of his words. A 'hm', and he was off, saying that it made him think there was something in the stale paradox that you never know the best about a woman until you know the worst. 'But, God in Heaven, what a worst!'

She had wanted, Hilary tried to explain—pathetically,

you can see, trying to make clear to himself the noble as well as the shady side of Iris—to keep permanent, even to reinforce, the love for Boy of Boy's friends by the idea that he had died untamed of his ideal. You could see her, Hilary said, meeting Gerald half-way on that. 'Boy died,' she had said, 'for purity.'

'Hilary! She said that!'

And that, you know, was all that she had said! Boy Fenwick had died 'for purity'. That was all.

'It seems,' I couldn't help thinking aloud, 'very sweeping. . . .'

It was, Hilary said grimly—and very pointed, in a girl not twenty!

'But!' I murmured.

Boy's friends, Hilary said, could naturally put only one construction on it. Naturally, Hilary said, 'For purity!' And Iris's friends could put no other. What, after all, didn't 'for purity' mean? It could mean, to all the decent people of the world, but one thing. . . .

Hilary looked at me in inquiry. I had made a noise. But I was so surprised. 'You don't mean,' I tried not to gasp, 'that you condemn her on that for Boy Fenwick's death!'

'One doesn't,' snapped Hilary, '"condemn" an Iris March, an Iris Fenwick, an Iris Storm. They stand condemned in themselves. They are outside the law by which we——'

'Hilary, as the Girondins were put by the Jacobins!'

'We're not perfect,' said Hilary quietly, 'but we're not *that*. What Iris was at nineteen or so—or before, evidently—she has been ever since.'

'What, as brave!'

'As loose. She made a gesture after Boy's death, a fine gesture—and then she set about proving how she had that in her to disenchant a Boy to his death. She had . . . "affairs". Not, you know, one long affair . . . but "affairs". Oh, quite openly. You've no doubt heard about some of them. And when four years later young Storm married her, against his people's wishes, she was no more than—well, what do you call those people? *Demi-mondaines?* And since Storm's death . . .'

73

'But!' I said, and also I said what it was in my mind to say, for are we sticks, are we stones, or are we human? It was Boy Fenwick I was thinking of, not of Iris's life later, although it seemed to me that Boy Fenwick had had a good deal to do with that too. I had begun by provoking Hilary. He had, with that appalling talent of his for appearing reasonable, provoked me. He could arouse all that was worst in a man, could Hilary. He had aroused all that was worst in me against that young purity hero. It seemed to me that it was, to say the least, rather hasty of a young man to die 'for purity' in connection with a girl of twenty. 'Hilary, in two thousand years we have discovered only one caddish way of getting to Heaven, and Boy Fenwick, like many "idealists", has taken it.'

'You probably don't realise,' said Hilary, oh reasonably, 'the depths of sudden despair—in decent people.'

'But I thought we were discussing human beings!' And, as regards human beings, one couldn't help thinking that a girl who had confessed that her lover had died 'for purity' was purer than the lover who had not been able to live for it. Boy Fenwick's death had an air of getting away with rather a good thing. He had destroyed the girl by exalting himself—for purity! How did boys come to have the infernal conceit of setting themselves up as connoisseurs of purity? And he had taken care to leave his corpse in such a position as best to foul the fountains of his young widow's womanhood. Sir Arthur Conan Doyle ought to speak to him about it.

'Words!' said Hilary. 'Words, words!'

'Well, we can't all,' I pleaded, 'talk by throwing ourselves out of windows. And I was brought up to believe that it was caddish to sneak on a woman, whether for purity or for humbug.'

'It was Iris,' said Hilary, 'who sneaked on herself.'

'Only because, Hilary, she didn't want the young man to waste such a fine suicide. She didn't want to do him out of the glory of dying for true-blue-manhood. At the age of twenty a girl is justified in having a belief in true-blue-manhood. But Mrs. Storm seems to have grown up since then.'

Hilary indulged me. I was young. 'Of course,' he said, 'the boy wasn't quite sane. Hm. But he loved Iris—you know, extravagantly—as Hector Storm did later. Iris isn't, it seems, one of those women you love a little. And Boy loved purity. And because, of course, the two simply didn't go together—the shock, man, of realising that, to a boy in love!—he went on his own way. And I don't think,' said Hilary, as though he was trying hard to be fair to one, 'that we should sneer at the things men die for—even that young madmen die for.'

In England, I reflected sulkily, you may not apply the faintest touch of reason to any of the accepted laws of life and death without being accused of sneering. The accusation is invaluable in puissance. It has made England what she is. It at once stops all argument, all nonsense, all sense, all thinking. So powerful is the effect that the one accused, thinking that perhaps he *was* sneering, at once checks his mind from further thought on that line. The word creates a vacuum. No one likes to be thought he is sneering—when he was merely, for a change, thinking. It is like being told you have no 'sense of humour'. It damns you completely, because it makes you damn yourself. And one of the reasons why there can never be a Marxist revolution in England is that the rebels will be told that they are sneering at the King. They will be abashed.

'Seldom,' said Hilary thoughtfully, 'have I known a man pull his weight less than you are doing this evening. Hm. I should try some brandy.'

75

CHAPTER FOUR   APHRODITE

I

One chapter can't reasonably be expected to bear the weight of that night. We have so far built but the groundwork of that night, and on that we have now to shape a peculiar edifice, according to the flimsy but saturnine manner of the third decade of the twentieth century; to which majority the twentieth century has attained, as more austere histories will tell you, only after the most unparalleled pains, reachings, belchings and bellowings; but we, taking a more private course, will be more circumspect in our derangements.

We have, so far that night, seen Gerald Haveleur March, by the way. We have seen his evening-paper; but we have not read it. (Nor had Hilary read his *Evening Standard*. He always 'glanced at it', he excused himself later on, as he was going to bed. As I did, if ever.) We have, also by the way, noted the presence in London of the car of the flying stork. We have dined, and had some brandy. We have talked of purity, and discovered an amiable dissonance in our views thereon. We would then, at about eleven o'clock, have by ordinary gone towards bed, for after dining with Hilary one somehow always went straightway to bed. That was why, Guy said cruelly, one dined with Hilary. The 'hm's' seemed to soothe the way thither. But that evening, however it came about, I did not feel that I would like to go straightway to bed. One has, I suppose, moods.

But I can't account plausibly for the fact that Hilary came with me to the Loyalty. Hilary did not go to night-clubs. His moods took a more exclusive course. He ignored night-clubs, and thought he was ignoring the whole of folly. Not so superior, I! Wherefore it passed that I discovered my mood to Hilary as we stood in the hall of his house, for Hilary was accompanying me to the door. Ross, red and silent and amiable, stood somewhere about with my hat. Where we stood, just without the door, the unusually warm June night smiled kindly on us. There is not much sky in London, but that little smiled on us with a faint load of stars, and somewhere behind the roofs there might be hanging a moon. There might? But there was such a pretty tilted silver boat among the chimneys of Curson House! From the small table in the hall Hilary had absently taken up the evening-paper, which was folded in that way which tells you in the Stop-Press News that Surrey had scored 263 for eight wickets. He held it in his hand with that air of one who has nothing left to do but read an evening-paper. Grey and thoughtful and kind, he stood there in the doorway of his tall sombre house, looking up at the faint stars on the ceiling of Chesterfield Street: his was just that contained air of loneliness that unmarried schoolmasters wear during their holidays. 'Hm,' he said. 'Nice night. . . .'

'Hilary, why don't you come with me? It won't probably be amusing, but we can always come away. . . .'

'Dancing,' he frowned. Hilary likes dancing, really. Only, not being exactly supreme among dancers, he never can understand how good dancers may like dancing so much that they will dance whenever they can. If Hilary had been a writer he would have put very witty and biting bits about dancing into his books. All writers have clumsy feet.

I made to assure him that he would find himself in the most polite company, for the Loyalty Club was notable as a relaxation for Government, diplomacy, and princes of the blood. He 'hm'd' viciously at that, but set out with me down Curzon Street and through the noisome shadows of Shepherd's Market. Gerald's light was on. But now that I was not there to turn it out, when would Gerald's light not be on?

Through the deep cavernous artery of Whitehorse Street we emerged on to Piccadilly, quiet as before the storm that would at any moment break on it from the theatres. Buses, their lights within revealing the seats, fled madly as though from a doomed city. Loitering taxi-cabs, attracted like moths to a flame by walking silk-hats, came near the curb, hung in doubt, loitered on.

I wondered whether she would be at the Loyalty. She might. I wondered whether she could have accepted the sacrifice of herself 'for purity' without question, without bitterness. She would—that 'Chislehurst mind'! Oh, yes,

77

she would have agreed with that idealist's harshest judgment—indeed, she had agreed with it so completely that she had plucked two words from her heart and given them to the world to whip her with. Boy Fenwick, you could see, had impressed himself like an anchorite's scourge on the souls of the twins. What was it she had said? 'It would be nice to die for purity.' Heavens, but wasn't she sickened of purity! That pitiful, pitiless moment in the bedroom of the Hôtel Vendôme! The messy kindergarten that men make of love, and call it 'romance', 'idealism'! Perhaps Judas was the first idealist—that desperate, exalted betrayal of the body to the soul. They are so certain about their souls, your carnal idealists! Soul, soul, soul! May their punishment be to meet their souls face to face in the afterworld! One could see that boy, a slim pyjama'd figure by the window, a silhouette of cold fire with the ruin of all mankind in his clean eyes, staring through the meretricious dawn of Deauville towards the goal to which he was exalted beyond reason by his disenchantment. He had loved Iris, madly. . . . But they do not love, those men! They torture, and are tortured. They take love as they might take a flower out of a garden, and they torture it because it does not thrive so well in the water of their tears as in the water of God's good sense. They do not love, those men, they stand in wonder before the power to love that is in them. And theirs the pleasure of a spurious conceit, theirs the pain of a spurious disenchantment. If that boy had loved, he would have turned towards the bed on which she lay, beaten, silenced, a child groping for sense, for pity, for any reasonable thing, and he would have tried to understand, and maybe he would have found the grace to understand, that in her, despite and because of the hungers of the body, there was that frightful humility to an unknown purpose which makes the limitless beauty of some women. But the boy had lit a cigarette. . . .

'Don't we cross?' muttered Hilary, and we crossed towards Jermyn Street, for the Loyalty Club lies in Pall Mall, to the end that, in immediate contact with the Royal Automobile Club, it may at least boast, as might occur to a student of Ruskin, a degree of eminence in the abyss.

One is, one can't help being, impelled by a sense of decorum to disavow at once any connection which may be fancied by worldly readers between the Loyalty Club and the Embassy Club. Such connection could not, of course, be fancied if the Loyalty were so well known as the Embassy; but the Loyalty is, or was—yes, was—the daughter of the Embassy, and although it is not yet so well known to the people of the town, who shall say that a daughter is not more of the mode than her mother? Even, life being what it is, in spite of the mother.

The Loyalty sprang from the Embassy, and it sprang in a polite direction, from Bond Street down the hill of Saint James's to Pall Mall, where it might lie over against Carlton House Terrace. It sprang because certain persons of *ton* had found that the Mother Society, while never ordered but with the most polite amenities, was growing perhaps just a little crowded with what-nots; had, by banding themselves in a body financial and social, founded the Loyalty; and were there assured of more freedom for the exercise of a reasonable exclusiveness since, the floor-space of the Loyalty being large enough to accommodate only one hundred and fifty dancers, the membership was strictly limited to one thousand and five hundred. Below were a swimming-bath and squash-courts, besides the more orthodox facilities; and while the whole place was appointed with the severest economy, if not with downright meanness, it is well known that those who spend more than a certain amount of money for supper, and see other people spending as much, will need no other assurance of being in surroundings of the first quality. That is a well-known French invention, of which England has only recently acquired the recipe.

The Loyalty Club can, however, claim no historical notice but in the person of the Chevalier Giulio di Risotto, its *directeur du restaurant*. We need not interrupt ourselves here to envy the salary at which the Chevalier was with difficulty persuaded to leave his retreat at Rapallo; but that he was worth it nobody can gainsay, for wheresoever Risotto went he took with him his invention. His invention he called *l'aristocracie internationale*; his name, you understand, for his people; they loved it.

A study of the lives of philosophers and statesmen will inform and ennoble the mind; but a sideways glance at such a phenomenon as the twentieth-century Risotto cannot help but make it supple. One of the menials of all time, he is one of the successes of ours; and a portent of the doom of aristocracy in England. Born of Machiavelli by Demoiselle Demi-monde, crafty, thin, pale, dry-shiny as shagreen, he had walked to fortune about every great restaurant in Europe, adding always, but with discrimination, to his order of *l'aristocracie internationale*; and to bankruptcy twice, of truly patrician magnificence, about the *baccara* tables of his less inspired but more cautious colleague, M. Cornuché of Cannes and Deauville. The 'creation' of the Loyalty Club must serve his biographers as the pinnacle of Risotto's career. *L'aristocracie internationale* was ultimately served at last. Not an American was left on Fifth Avenue, nor an Argentine in the Americas; while Australian fruit-farms deplored the absence of their masters, and Canada adored the *ton* of her peerless millionaires.

We had no sooner entered among the company than Hilary was for going at once: but Risotto having rewarded us with a sofa-table—for he and Hilary had, as the saying is, been boys together when Hilary had been attached to the Embassy in Paris and Risotto was ennobling patrons of the Ritz to *l'aristrocracie internationale*—he and I prevailed on Hilary to stay by ordering for him an angel-on-horseback, to which he was notably partial; while I, Risotto said, would have a haddock with a nice egg on it.

Hilary, like all middle-aged men who detest night-clubs, at once left me to dance with the first acquaintance he saw. This was Mrs. Ammon. Whereas I, in not dancing, was following an example set by many present. We, we watched our elders dance with each other's mothers, and for them the band on the balcony played with a sensibility approaching grief. There was no tune. But it is absurd, this querulous demand of young people for 'tunes'! Our fathers and our mothers have done with 'tunes'. Let there, our uncles say,

80

be a rhythm. Let there, say our aunts, be syncopation. There was a rhythm. There was syncopation. Grave, profound, unforgettable, there was a rhythm. It had a beat like the throbbing of an agonised heart lost in an artery of the Underground. Dolorous it was, yet phantasm of gaiety lay twined in it. They call this rhythm the Blues. It reminded you of past and passing things. It reminded you of the days when people over forty had still enough restraint not to crowd out every ballroom and night-club with their dancing in open formation, playfully aiming at each other's tonsils with their feet. It reminded you of the scent tangled in the hair of she with whom you had last danced to that rhythm. You saw the soft line of her face by your shoulder, the tender pocket behind her ear, the absorbed excursion of her breath through her nostrils, the dark eyebrow over which you would lightly pass the third finger of your left hand but that it would soil the tip of it. You mourned the presence of the dead. You mourned the memory of the living. They call this rhythm the Blues. It reminded you of regret. It reminded you of a small white face suddenly thrown back against your arm with a smile that disturbed the dance. It reminded you of the desire that pleasantly turns to dust when you are desired. It reminded you of things you had never done with women you had never met. You danced again at the Ambassadeurs at Cannes, with the masts of yachts drawn ebony-black between the tall windows and the pale blue night over the sea. The Lido lay like a temptation before your mind, and the songs of the gondoliers raved into the measure of whispering feet. The Spanish King brushed by you at San Sebastian, eating salted almonds, again you hesitated in the dance at Biarritz to listen to the roar of the Atlantic, and across a perfumed street in Seville you again saw the shiver of a mantilla through the cracked windows of a cabaret. You danced again beneath the vermilion moon of Algeria, between the American Bar and the pyramid-cypress tree. You danced again in the Bois in Paris, the trees like monstrous black pagodas against the night, the stars brilliant as sequins on an archangel's floating cloak, the magically white faces of women, the lights in the night making love to the

81

black shadows in their hair, their lips red as lobsters, their arm-pits clean as ivory, the men talking with facile gestures, the whole tapestry of the Château de Madrid like a painted fan against a summer night. They call this rhythm the Blues, which is short for a low state of vitality brought about by the action of life on the liver. O Baby, it's div*ine*!

That is what they say, our elders.

Astorias, *chef d'orchestre*, stood at rest by the edge of the balcony, his violin under his arm, his bow gently tapping the edge of a bowl of nameless ferns that hid his feet. His negligence is informed with depression, his poise leans on melancholy. The Blues, that man knows. He seems to wonder why he is there, why anyone is there, why everyone is there. No one can tell him, so he goes on doing nothing, lonely as a star in hell. He does not toil, nor spin, nor play his violin. From the crowded floor a woman, her face powdered brown, her mouth scarlet as the inside of a pomegranate in a tale by Oscar Wilde, beseeches him with an arm black-gloved to the shoulder to continue to play. He yields.

Nearby was a corner-table of eight young people. Maybe they would dance later on. Suddenly one of the girls would give a loud laugh, and then there would be silence. Of the four young men one looked as Richard of Gloucester might possibly have looked, a little bent, a little sinister, and pale, as though he had been reading a treatise on diseases far into the night before. They were four married couples, and they had all been boys and girls together, and they had a son and daughter apiece, and they all went to the same dentist. The women had white oval faces, small breasts, blue eyes, thin arms, no expression, no blood: literally, of course, not genealogically. One of them stared with wide blue eyes right into people's faces, and blinked vaguely. She was lovely. These eight young people were very happy. They ignored everything but themselves, in whom they were not very interested. Presently a prince of the blood joined them, there was a little stir for a minute or two, a little laughter, and then he rose to dance with the girl of the blind blue eyes. As she danced she stared thoughtfully at the glass dome of the ceiling. She looked bored with boredom.

There were many green dresses: jade-green, October green, rusty green, soft green, sea-green, dying green, any shade of green that would suit the expiring voices of formal women in a garden by Watteau. There were thirty-nine green dresses. There was a Jewess of the wrong sort in the wrong sort of green. She looked like a fat asparagus whose head had been dipped in dressing and then put in a warm place to dry. She dried in patches. A caravan of pearls crawled upwards from her bosom to her throat, and she said to Mr. Trehawke Tush, the novelist: 'The only decent cocktails you can get in Paris are at the Ritz Bar, but the people are so odd. My Archie wants to stand for Parliament. What do you think?' Mr. Trehawke Tush, portraits of whose pre-war face must be familiar to everyone, was the most successful of the younger novelists, and had earned from Miss Rebecca West the praise that he was 'the leader of the spats school of thought'. Mr. Trehawke Tush will go down to history as the originator of Pique as a profitable literary idea. He had hit on the discovery that English library subscribers will wholeheartedly bear with any racy and illegal relation between the sexes if the same is caused by Pique. He had observed that the whole purpose of a 'best-seller' is to justify a reasonable amount of adultery in the eyes of suburban matrons. He had observed that in no current English novel was there ever a mention of any woman having a lover because she wanted a lover: she always took a lover because something had upset her, as in real life she might take an aspirin. Mr. Trehawke Tush had then created Pique, and was spoken of as a 'brilliant feminine psychologist'. Since the rise of Mr. Trehawke Tush no reviewer will take any count of a writer as a 'brilliant feminine psychologist' unless he can explain the regrettable adultery of his leading female character by the word Pique. This will also persuade *Punch* reviewers to consider the tale wholesome. Mr. Trehawke Tush was up to all those dodges. He said: 'I have just finished a serial for *The Daily Sale*. I want to show up this kind of thing, the waste, the Indecency of it. All these girls. I thought the editor might take objection to certain passages, as there is some strong bedroom stuff in it, but he only asked me to change one thing. I had put "he kissed her where he would", and so I changed it to "as he would".'

In a corner far across the crowded room sat Venice Pollen, most sedately between her father and her mother. We waved, and decided that it was too crowded to dance; but we did not know, Venice and I, that we were met that night in darkness.

Observe Venice. We will always be found on Venice's side, and why? because she is a darling. Mark her now, and how the smoke about her clears, how clean she is, and so excited! For Venice! You know she is excited because she is so still, there between her hard father and her monstrous fat mother. Mark her there, a green flower with a mad golden head. And her eyes are blue, mad blue, and she is the queen of ten thousand freckles, of which she is very contemptuous, saying: 'Who wants freckles?' And she had a noble forehead which would crinkle when she did not catch what you said, and that was often enough, for she was always talking herself. 'Darling, darling, *darling*!' That is what she would say. And on her lion's-cub head was a tumult of short dusty-gold hair, which was by nature rebellious, so that she must ever and again be giving her head a fierce backward shake, as though that was going to do any good. Mark her there, so sedate between her hard father and her monstrous fat mother. Not sedate really, Venice! Yet she must be sedate now, for Venice, who by ordinary knew not fear, was as though fascinated by fear of her father, who was none other than Nathaniel Pollen, once of Manchester, but now of Hampshire and Berkeley Square, for was he not as rich as Crœsus would have been had Crœsus owned the half of the newspapers of England?

So there sat Venice, most excited-still, undoubtedly waiting for Napier. They were lovers, Napier and Venice, and in three days they would be married. Dark, shy, handsome Napier! Favourite of the gods, you might well call him, yet his was that rare, surprising quality which will keep a man poised in continual sunshine, which will never let him droop and laze in the certainty that his sins of omission and casual-

84

ness will be forgiven him. He was, to talk for a change of the things that matter, in the Foreign Office, and worked conscientiously hard at a career which would—'undoubtedly,' they said, 'undoubtedly'—in the course of time place Napier among the most honoured of the nation's servants; although he would—'undoubtedly', one can't help feeling, 'undoubtedly'—reach in the course of time the very same pinnacle if he did no work at all, for England and America are the only two countries left in the world wherein men's charm and good looks are really appreciated by men in the political, high financial, diplomatic, and educational spheres.

Our table faced the swing-doors across the room, and through the crowd of dancers one could see who passed in and out. There was a press of young men standing vaguely by the door, perhaps doubtful whether they should stay or go to return another day. A very haughty and flushed-looking lady, expensively dressed in a *dernier cri*, which she wore like armour, tramped past them, looked suspiciously into their bland faces, and out. She suspected they might be thinking she was going to more than powder her nose. They were, she was, who cared?

A voice rose above the saxophone at the table to the left of mine. It came from a heavy, drooping man with the eyes of a schoolboy, the smile of a genius, the gestures of a conqueror, and the face of a bully. He said: 'There are two things in England that not even God could afford to be truthful about: Himself and the Navy.' With the man of destiny was the most beautiful woman in Ireland (Ulster) and a dark woman with a high bust and flashing eye, who spoke Cockney with an American accent. Her father was a lord. She said: 'I am growing to detest London. There is nowhere to go and nothing to do when you get there.' The most beautiful woman in Ireland (Ulster) had hair as black as a raven's wing and two aquamarines for eyes, while the symmetry of her features appalled the epithet. She said: 'I took my little Juno out to tea with Fay Avalon to-day and she was so naughty on the handsome parquet floor, the mother's darling!'

85

Then things happened. Gerald happened. Gerald and Aphrodite. . . . Venice, Iris, Guy de Travest, Hugo Cypress, Napier, Colonel Duck, Gerald . . . if only one had a cinema for a moment! And there was also my Lady Pynte, with whom I should have been dancing. Where Mrs. Ammon went there also went Cornelia Pynte, and where Lady Pynte went there also went Angela Ammon. They were fine hearty women. And since Hilary was dancing with Mrs. Ammon I ought instantly to have begged the honour of taking the floor with Lady Pynte. There she sat, across the room, alone, a fine hearty woman. But, then, one goes to a night-club to think, to be alone, to be comfortable, to eat a haddock. Lady Pynte thought dancing Good Exercise, and she was taller than me, too. A fine woman. Once, as Hilary toiled by with Mrs. Ammon, he whispered fiercely over her shoulder: 'Why don't you dance with the old trout?' But I drowned discourtesy to Lady Pynte in wine, for it was a 'late night' at the Loyalty, which meant that you could drink wine until they took it from you. Lady Pynte was renowned as one of the five best women riders to hounds in the country. It was said that the foxes in the Whaddon Chase country ceased laughing when anyone said 'Pynte'! near them. But Lady Pynte also had her politics, and she headed Movements; while Angela Ammon was more of a literary turn. Lady Pynte liked young men to Do; Mrs. Ammon to Dare. Lady Pynte liked young men to be Healthy and Normal; Mrs. Ammon preferred them to be Original. Lady Pynte liked Boys to be Boys; Mrs. Ammon didn't mind if they were girls so long as they were Original. Lady Pynte insisted on Working For the Welfare of the People at Large and Not just Our Own Little Class, she played bridge with a bantering tongue and a Borgia heart, she maintained that the best place at which to buy shoes was Fortnum & Mason's, and if she saw you innocently taking the air of a sunny morning she would say: 'You look not at all well, my good young man. Why don't you take some Clean, Healthy exercise? You ought to be Riding.' That was why one maintained a defensive alliance with one's haddock rather than do the manly thing and dance with Lady Pynte. She would say one ought to be riding, and for four years I had hidden from Lady Pynte the fact that I did not know how to ride. I simply did not dare to confess to Lady Pynte that I could not ride. I had already tried to pave the way to that dénouement by confessing that I came from the lower classes, but she did not appear to think that any class could be so Low as that. She would show one round her stables, and one felt an awful fool standing there in the cold being expected to be intelligent about the various horses, whereas one could only mutter, 'Ah, good horse!' or 'Oh, there's a fine horse!' until one day I remembered what Peter Page, the critic, had once told me, that whenever he was shown a horse by a horse-lover he would instantly say 'What withers!' and thus create a sound and manly impression as a horse-fancier. But when I came out impressively with 'What withers!' I thought that Lady Pynte looked at me suspiciously, and Hilary, who was also fancying horses with us, told me later that it wasn't done to look a lady straight in the eye and say 'What withers!' Horses make life complicated, that is what it is.

Hugo Cypress, dancing by with his wife Shirley, called out: 'Ho, there! Seen the evening-paper? Friend of yours....'

'What?' I said. 'Hugo. . . .' But what on earth was this about the evening-paper? I was agitated—suddenly, I was very agitated indeed. There is something quite beastly about evening-papers, beastly and naked. . . .

Astorias stayed his men, and Hilary came back to the table. Gloomily he looked at the angel that was frozen to its horse. And he looked worried.

'Hilary, what's this I heard Hugo murmuring about the evening-paper?'

'Gerald,' said Hilary. 'Hm. . . .'

'But what, Hilary? Not serious, surely?'

'Oh, not serious,' Hilary grunted. 'Not serious. Hm. Just a nasty silly mess, I think. Didn't catch what. Hm. . . .'

I realised then that I had known all the time. That curious, hopeless grinning. . . . But, good Lord, what sort of a mess? Hilary didn't know. 'Something in the evening-paper,' he said. Hilary looked hurt, worried, and I had that jumpy feeling that I must do something at once. But what sort of a mess? A drunkard's row? What? Hilary didn't know, and I was just about to ask the waiter if he could find me an evening-paper when two figures by the door held my eye. And a third just behind them. . . .

'Kids!' murmured Hilary, with a sort of grudging smile. And they looked just that, for all their beauty—'kids'. One saw them playing together under a tree. A long while ago, they had played together under a tree. The favourite of the gods and the shameless, shameful lady. . . .

'Hm,' grumbled Hilary. 'Imitation. . . .'

But I knew, for I once had a friend who was a taxidermist. There were 396 white ermines round Iris. White and tawny and white. She was like a light, and you hadn't realised what an infernal dungeon the place was until the door had suddenly opened and she had come in, wrapped in cloth of soft snow. Boy's head, curly head, white and tiger-tawny. She was like a light, a sad, white light. I can't describe her but like that. Napier had been standing by the door, waiting for the dance to cease, so that he might join Venice. Then Iris had come in, grave, very unself-conscious. She didn't see Napier. He didn't see Iris. Her companion was Colonel Duck, M.F.H.

'God, that man!' sighed Hilary. Oh, Iris was hopeless! Why, of all men, Colonel Duck?

Napier made to walk away. Iris and Colonel Duck made to follow Risotto. Maybe one of the 396 white ermines just brushed Napier's sleeve. Maybe this, maybe that. 'Kids!' said Hilary. Napier had started round, looked blank: tall, slender, dark-haired, dark eyes always fevered with a fear of you could never tell what—they almost blinked now, you thought, at the light that Iris was, and she with her pools of eyes simply blazing with surprise and an unsure smile parting the painted mouth. 'Napier!' 'Iris!' As though, you know, someone with a soft 'There!' had turned a tap somewhere. They smiled completely. Well, they would, the old friends. Naturally. She wouldn't, I was sure, be calling him 'Naps', and she detesting abbreviations and the like.

The wrong sort of Jewess gave a short, audible outline of

Iris to Mr. Trehawke Tush. Hilary stared at her venomously. Then he stared across the room at Colonel Duck venomously. Colonel Duck stood behind Iris's white shoulder, a red dragon of a man, smiling relentlessly with his well-known geniality. Napier did not appear to see Colonel Duck, M.F.H. Napier and Iris were talking very quickly, laughing, maybe rather shyly. Then Astorias, refreshed, hurled his men against the conversation; bravely it held on for a second or two, then lay shuddering and shattered, and gone was Napier, gone Iris towards a table with Colonel Duck, whose red, relentless geniality showed no hint of the certain fact that the next time he was at that talkative club of his he would say that Napier Harpenden had been another of Iris Storm's 'affairs' and might quite well be again, Iris Storm being what she was. Notably good at all games and sports was Colonel Duck, M.F.H., and therefore tolerated with respect by decent men.

'I wonder if she knows anything about Gerald,' I was saying, when from her table across the room she seemed to be beckoning. To Hilary, not to me. She looked very serious. The emerald shone on the third finger of her right hand. She did not appear to see me. I felt bitter.

'Hm,' growled Hilary. He wanted to be persuaded to go. He wanted to go reluctantly. 'Hate that Duck man so,' he said pathetically.

'Go on, Hilary. She might know something. I'll get a paper.'

'Why, there's Guy!' said Hilary. 'Must have just come up from Mace. There, by the door. . . .'

The carpet of colours, on which the men were sprinkled like black smuts on a town garden, swayed between us and the doorway, but no crowd might hide that man, for he was tall as a tree and his crisp yellow hair glared like a menace above the intervening heads and his frozen blue eyes petrified smoke, noise, and distance. Hilary was standing, about to go towards Iris. He looked rather sheepish at being found by Guy at the Loyalty. Most unsmiling was Guy that night.

'Ross must have told him we were here,' I said. 'He'll have come about Gerald. . . .'

'This foul place!' Hilary snapped. 'You go downstairs with Guy, and I'll get Iris to rid herself of her fancy friend and bring her down. . . .'

2

And that was how, soon after midnight that night, I found myself for the first time in the car of the flying stork. For the first time. . . . Iris had dropped her boyish-looking chauffeur in the course of the evening, because, she said, she only liked driving at night, when the air blew clean and chill. She drove with assurance, that is to say, she drove as though her mind was not in the same world as the steering-wheel. The great bonnet swept round by the squat Palace and up the slope of Saint James's Street, which only by night may remember a little of the elegance it has long since forfeited by day.

'But that's not the point,' I remember saying. 'He won't care a button what anyone else is thinking about it. He'll just go mad at the humiliation in himself, he'll worry it, making a mountain of sordidness. . . .' I had told her that Gerald had sent her his love, and her eyes had lit up at that, and she had laughed, shyly. 'That's better,' she had said, and now she said: 'Yes, that's the point. He's proud, proud as Lucifer . . . and such a baby! Oh Gerald, you sensitive beast! I'm going abroad to-morrow, and he must either come with me or he must join me quickly, quickly. You'll persuade him, too, won't you?' I did not say that, if I knew Gerald, he would probably be in a state far beyond persuasion. But, I thought, there was no harm in trying to see him.

At first, when Guy had told me downstairs at the Loyalty, I had just laughed. It seemed so absurd, fantastic. Gerald had been arrested in Hyde Park for 'annoying women!' It was, you can see, unbelievable. How could Gerald 'annoy' a woman, Gerald who was so shy that he could never even speak to one? 'But there it is,' said Guy.

Perhaps it is because that was the last time I was ever at the Loyalty, but I remember the most irrelevant details and the vivid way each one of them seemed to impress some part of my mind. Guy and I stood in the deserted Bar. Through the open door at the far end came the clean, somehow biting tang of a marble swimming-bath: a faint splash now and then, a rustle of water: a boyish American voice calling sharp and loud: 'Dive, you Julie, dive and get it over! You've got no hips, kid, and you can't drown without hips. I want to go eat some food.' Then, I remember, Billy Swift walked intently past us, towards the Cloak-room. He comes to mind vividly because that was the last time I saw Billy Swift alive. His thin, lined, scarlet face glowed with the health-giving breezes that penetrate into corners of clubs and restaurants where men sit drinking brandy; his blue eyes always peered eagerly and kindly at you, as though he had something of the first importance to say. He said, very hoarsely: 'There's a boy up there dancing with two wooden legs. Good boy, I call him. Good-night.' And in a minute or two he repassed us, walking intently, his crimson grey-haired head, immaculate in every detail, sticking like an old fighting-bird's out of the wide astrakhan collar of the coat that he always wore against the midnight chill. Two months later he was found on the cliffs near Dover with that head beaten in, and someone was hanged. Billy Swift wouldn't have had him hanged. 'My fault,' he would have said hoarsely. 'My fault, chaps.'

'But there it is,' Guy said thoughtfully. 'Sickening, isn't it? Might appeal, of course. . . .'

'He'll not appeal,' I said. Imagine Gerald 'appealing' against a five-pound fine for 'indecently annoying' a woman in Hyde Park!

Guy always spoke low, he murmured in a chill voice, but you could always hear every word he said. Not that you didn't, after a while, know all his words by heart, for Guy's was one of those vocabularies that a classical education is supposed to have expanded. As he spoke he would always be looking at some point just above the crown of your head.

'Sorry about that boy,' he was saying thoughtfully. 'He's had no luck. And this Hyde Park business might happen to anyone nowadays. . . .' He looked down at me suddenly from that height of his, and I was, as always, surprised by the profound childishness which would suddenly sweep the ice out of the blue of those eyes.

'Beasts,' he went on, almost pathetically. 'But aren't they —those Park police? Arresting nice old clergymen, Privy Councillors, anyone, just because a poor old boy who's been brought up too well feels like having a word or two with a sickening woman. I mean, you need torpedo-netting around you to get round the Park in safety nowadays. Well, don't you? And now they plant poor young Gerald. I'm sure, aren't you, that these police put the women there on purpose as— what d'you call them?'

'*Agents provocateurs?*'

'Well, have it your own way. But I've been watching the police round about here lately, and of course they're mostly very good fellows, the best, but the police round the Park are quite a different lot. I'd like to kick them for the way they look those poor devils of women up and down as though they were dirt. I never thought much of the type of sneak who went for the Military Police during the war, and these fellows seem rather like that. Anything for an arrest and promotion.' He smiled faintly. Guy's eyes seemed always to get most frosty when he smiled. 'I once promoted some of them the wrong way for being inhuman. Inhuman, that's what these blighters get if you don't keep an eye on them. And these Park fellows seem somehow to have got spoilt since the war. I mean, it just looks like that to an outsider. Good Lord, you've got to have laws and to keep laws, but you needn't set a lot of dirty sneaks at the Bolshevik game of ruining gentlemen just for being silly old asses.'

I stared at the one black pearl that from time immemorial had stained Guy's shirt-front, which somehow seemed to fit him as no one else's ever could. Guy was easy to listen to, because you always knew what he would say and how he would say it. (He had an enormous reverence for any man of the smallest talent, any man 'who did things with his brain'.)

'I saw him for a minute this evening,' I said. 'He seemed rather queer, but he said nothing about it. . . .'

'But imagine the young devil! This business happened

92

one night last week, and he doesn't then come to see you about it—or even Hilary or me, because, of course, I'd have done all I could for him, for old Barty's sake as well as because he behaved himself in the war. I mean, this will almost kill old Eve Chalice when she sees it in the morning papers. It's her I'm sorry for, for she's always been fighting this sticky patch in the March brood—first her eldest brother, old Portairley, then her younger brother, Barty, then her niece Iris, and now young Gerald comes along to make the poor old dear cry her eyes out again. God, the vileness of it! Picking up odd women in parks. I haven't got a paper with me, but you ought to see the vile way they put down every beastly detail, and you can see as clear as anything that it was more bad luck and childishness on Gerald's part than anything else. But, good Lord, what's the matter with the man! I mean, one simply doesn't go into the Park for women! The accuser, or whatever you call them, was a woman called Spirit, and in evidence two plain-clothes men and a constable. I'm going to have an eye kept on Mrs. Spirit, just to see all's fair and square. I mean, it's beginning to look as though the law was the ass that St. George forgot to kill while he was showing off with that sickening dragon. This Mrs. Spirit said—wish I had a paper—that she was sitting on a bench waiting for her brother, when Gerald sat down beside her and made "indecent" proposals. Whereupon she was so shocked—and she a grown-up married woman, too— that she jumped up like a scalded cat and let out some sickening howls, and up come the police. Now you can't help thinking they were waiting behind a tree with old Spirit as a bait, can you? and caught young Gerald instead of a Dean.... They'd get more promotion, I shouldn't wonder, for a Dean. . . .'

And as Guy spoke I saw Gerald glancing at the evening-paper on the curb of Curzon Street, and I saw him suddenly throw back his head and laugh at the heavens. . . .

Gerald, Gerald! The despiser of the world caught by the meanest trap of the world's unrest. The worshipper of the hero who had died 'for purity' figuring in the filthy columns of the cheap Sunday Press as another peer's nephew gone wrong. Gerald, starved of life, Gerald who knew no woman, Gerald who wrote the tale of a man who had lived 'for purity' . . . and he had sat down beside a woman called Spirit on a bench in Hyde Park. Those nightmare women who rave in the minds of lonely men, soft women marvellously acquiescent, possible, the woman Aphrodite, goddess of love and beauty, silent as marble, but acquiescent . . . and Aphrodite had dwindled into Mrs. Spirit, who was sitting waiting for her brother in Hyde Park, and the law lurking nearby to give the Sunday papers 'copy'. And I saw Mr. Auk in an angle of the little tunnel, telling a friend of his something funny about Gerald. . . .

'It makes one just sick, Guy. Sick. . . .'

'Now look here,' Guy murmured, tapping my shoulder with one finger. 'Don't you waste any time being sick just now, but go round and see the young devil——'

'I'm going straight away.'

'Bright boy. And just . . . Oh, tell him it's all right and not to be an ass all his life. Tell him we're all on his side, and if there's going to be any being sick that we're all going to be sick together and in one corporate body, or words to that effect. Poor young devil. And I know he'll be feeling this, because I had a sort of eye on him in France, and he seemed as sensitive as a violin string——'

'And drink's made him worse now. He's almost certain to be nearly speechless to-night. But I'll see.'

'Lord, O Lord, what a mess Barty left behind him! But you see what I mean? All you've got to tell young Gerald is not to make a mountain of this in his mind, as it's the sort of thing that might happen to anyone who is ass enough to go into the Park at night without an escort, and you never know but they mightn't one night arrest the Bishop of London himself for saying "How do" to his aunt. . . .'

Now I have read in books about people 'sailing' into places, and I suppose Iris came into the deserted Bar like that. Hilary must have been just behind her, for I heard his voice, but I only saw Iris, and I remember how she seemed to hold the white ermine round her with one clenched hand, and how the great emerald shone like a green fly on the soft, soft white. And the tawny curls danced their formal dance on her cheeks as she came towards us, swiftly, oh swiftly, saying, in that suddenly strong, clear voice: 'Oh, Guy ... and friend of Gerald! Will you help me, dear friend? I want to go round to see Gerald, and Hilary says you still have the key of the house. I went hours ago, but could get no answer at the door. I wonder, would you come with me?'

'Iris,' said Guy sternly, and I remember the way she threw back her head to look at him, and I thought again of the queer, unconscious way she had of always meeting men on their own ground. 'Why don't you ever look up your old friends when you're in London, Iris? Or aren't we your old friends? Or is that fine representative English gentleman, Colonel Duck, your old friend? Answer me yes or no.'

'Oh, Guy!' she said softly, sadly. 'I wouldn't have you be a humbug. I wouldn't have you and Hilary be humbugs—you two, out of all the world.'

'But, honest, Iris, I'd like to see you. Ask Hilary. "Where's that girl got to!" I asks, and he says "hm", says he, if you see what I mean.'

'Whereas I, Guy, have learnt not to regret old friends. I've become an old woman on my travels, and one of the first things an old woman must learn is that the best way to keep old friends is not to see them, for then you can at least keep the illusion that they are friends ... which is, perhaps, a little different from being "old friends" ...'

'Iris, don't be so bitter!' snapped Hilary. That, I thought, came rather well from Hilary. Just at that moment a woman screamed from the swimming-bath, there was a resounding splash. Guy was saying: 'You'd better take Gerald away for a while, Iris.'

'If he'll only come,' she said, 'that's what I want to do. . . .'

I remember thinking just then that I mustn't forget to thank her for that beautiful notepaper, and also to ask her what was that last word in her note.

'I've got an idea,' Hilary was saying, in the specially detached voice he keeps for ideas, 'that now we *are* in this foul night-club we might as well do a bit of good. There's old Pollen upstairs, and we might . . . hm, well, perhaps not.'

'Perhaps not what, Hilary?'

'Hm. I was thinking of Eve seeing the things in to-morrow morning's papers. She only reads one wretched picture-paper, and that's Pollen's, so I thought, hm, that if we asked him not to . . .'

'Eve, the poor darling!' Iris whispered. We seemed to be in a desert, three shadows of men, three shadows of voices, and Iris, very white and alight. That is how I always remember her, alight.

'No good, Hilary,' Guy was murmuring. 'He won't, because it's what those fellows call News. And if you try you will only upset young Venice and make her perhaps feel she's in the other camp, rather the wrong camp for her, she might think, and just as she's marrying Naps. She's a good girl, loyal as anything to her father—and he's a good fellow enough, but he's got a queer complaint called Consistency. It's something you make money out of, I think. I know him very well, as I've blackballed him from three clubs. My God, ever seen the man's jaw?'

'She's lovely, I thought,' Iris said.

'Good girl, Venice. . . .'

'Hell . . .' said Iris suddenly, breathlessly.

'What?' Hilary jumped.

'Only . . . hell is raving with millionaires with jaws like Mr. Pollen's. I've dreamt, I know. People who snap "Yes" and "No" very brusquely and then stick to it, no matter what it is. This century likes them like that. Come along, my friend, come along!'

And in a trice Iris and I were walking up the long passage which connects the Loyalty Club to the pavement of Pall Mall. On one side it is hung (but this is two years ago) with glass cases laden with fine cut jades and ambers, while small blue and green figures of animal men, human animals, and bestial gods will delight the eyes of Egyptologists: on the other the faces of beautiful women and children will testify to the photographic art of Sebastian Roeskin of Dover Street. Iris walked swiftly, heroically, her eyes intent before her, impersonal, utterly unself-conscious. The glaring lights in the passage lit her swiftly-moving green-and-silver shoes, or were they sandals with high heels? and so intent were the flippant silver-flashing ankles, briskly striding on, as though chiming the never-to-be-known marching song of a lady who must always meet men on their own ground.

She said: 'You'll be wondering how I came to dine with a man like Victor Duck. Well, I've been wondering myself. Poor Victor Duck. He has taken to caddishness like a drug, and he goes on increasing the doses. It's almost fascinating to watch, just to see what inevitable things he will say next. And he said and did them all, every one, even to "Dear little girl" and to ordering a private room. But I said I never dined in private rooms on Fridays.'

There was a group of tall young men at the entrance, maybe waiting for their women from the Cloak-Room, maybe waiting for sirens to come to them from the night, maybe waiting for taxi-cabs, maybe only waiting for the next minute, as young men will. Admirably formal they looked, admirably toned to the dress-coats of Davies, the trousers of Anderson and Sheppard, the hats of Lock, the waistcoats of Hawes and Curtis, the ties of Budd. Handkerchiefs by Edouard and Butler. The glory to God. They looked furtively at Iris in the way that decent men will at a woman who is said to have had lovers, like cows at a bull. One of them said gloomily: 'Might go to the Albert Hall Ball.'

Pall Mall seemed wrought of stately marble palaces, and Iris said that the reason why so many English people seemed to prefer Paris to London was that English people saw Paris mostly at night, while if they could see enough of London by night they would never leave it. 'And the people!' she said. 'All these years I've spent abroad, and never met any people so good, so decent, as the English. Couldn't you sometimes kill people for the *quality* of their admiration? Oh, I've committed so many murders in foreign streets. . . .'

'But, if you like England . . . why are you going away? You're free. . . .'

'Ah,' she mocked, and, as we walked, a hand darted out

97

from her white cloak and touched my sleeve, and startled me very much. 'Wait till you're so free that you just daren't do what you like. Wait till you're so free that you can be here one minute and there another. Wait till you're so free that you can see the four walls of your freedom and the iron-barred door that will let you out into the open air of slavery, if only there was someone to open it. Ah, yes, freedom. . . .'

Then up the street of ghostly dandies we flew behind the silver stork, and the wind rushed down from Hampstead Heath and the wind ran out of Jermyn Street and jumped like a drunken man on the tawny cornstalks that were her hair, and waved them about and danced with them. But not she to notice, she who seemed to have a great talent for just not noticing things! She was silent, serious, intent. The light of an arc-lamp kissed the long slender legs into silver.

Once she turned to me, smiled, and looked away again. I wondered if she meant me to see that our friendship was in that smile. I hated her, I think, because she made me feel so incapable, unwise. As the stork, with scarcely a rustle of its wings, flew towards the Christian Science Chapel at the head of Half-Moon Street, she said: 'I'm tired. All day seeing lawyers and trustees, and then taking sweet old Eve all round and round Selfridge's because she had never been there before and someone had told her she could find everything she wanted there. And she was quite upset at being unfaithful to Harrod's. . . . And Gerald! Oh, but why couldn't they let Gerald alone! Just because, I suppose, the Marches are never let off anything. . . .'

'Here we are,' I said, and she pulled up beneath the lamp by The Leather Butler in East Chapel Street. From the footboard a lane of low houses and shops stretched in a vague, squalid line towards the open Market Place at one end and the darkness of the mews at the other; somehow like an etching in a clouded light by an uncertain hand. Bits of newspapers and torn placards, the nameless odours of yesterday's economies. The wind that came from Hampstead Heath could find no way into Shepherd's Market, and it lay still as a tramp sleeping. Cats watched us intently from the middle distance, and a striped cat leapt with a scream from

98

the shadow of the door of my old house. Gerald's light was on. 'What's that mean?' Iris whispered. She seemed to be frightened, and she said sharply: 'Why are you looking at me like that?'

'I was just thinking,' I told her, 'that if one could judge by appearances, which of course one must never do, in that white cloak in this mean lane you look as nearly an angel as this world could ever see.'

'Don't let's mock the angels. What does it mean, Gerald's light being on?'

'Only what it has always meant, that I must turn it out.'

'Ah, you've been very good to Gerald. . . .'

And I am glad that, just then, I said that I was very fond of Gerald.

Then we were on the narrow landing of my old flat, in the darkness. The musty stillness of that little old house brought six years of nights into my mind, and I wondered how people ever regretted their first youth, those intolerable uncertainties and enthusiasms that stare at you from the dead past like condemned gargoyles. The incapability of youth goes on long enough, Heaven knows, if not so long as the savagery of childishness. In the darkness I could feel the soft ermine of her cloak against me, and that faint dry scent whose name I shall now never know. She was very, very still, and I could not even hear her breathing.

'It is very kind of you to come with me,' she said suddenly, seriously. We were very still on that landing, and I drew back my arm where it touched her cloak. It was very soft, that cloak. 'I have thought of you, and decided that if you ever thought of me you had a right to think with dislike. . . .' She was talking smoothly, calmly, when suddenly her voice completely broke, into little bits. 'Oh!' she whispered. I was silent. She said quickly: 'To me there's something terribly indecent about humanity, all humanity. It's as though, in the whole lovely universe, humanity was cooped in this musty little house, talking vaguely of dislike, eternally talking of like and dislike, love and unlove, of doings and undoings, purposeless yet striving and savage. The other night I was motoring alone from Paris to Calais, and it seemed to me

99

that no law was strong enough, no crime was big enough, not even disloyalty, to stop us, when we had the chance of rising above the beastly limitation of living as we were born to live. Because we humans are not born to live, we are born to die. . . .'

'Something has happened to you to-night,' I said. She was a faint white shape in the darkness, and it seemed to me that that was as much of her as I should ever see; and I was right.

'No, nothing at all. Just a dream. But oh, failing the dream, how I would like a child!'

'A dream-child!'

'Ah, I've had those, a many! No, a real one. To be play-mates with . . .'

I said: 'I will go up first to-night and see how Gerald is. Will you wait here?'

'I'm tired and frightened,' she said faintly. 'Don't be long.'

I don't think I stayed up there more than a few seconds. I don't know. I switched out the light, and as I went down the dark narrow stairs I did not strike a match.

'Well?' she whispered from the darkness.

I don't know what I said. I suppose I must have said that he was in the same state as when she had seen him before. Then I pretended I had no matches left, and said I had better go down first while she held on to my shoulder. 'Then if you fall, I'll fall,' she complained, but I said I would not fall.

Stair by stair we slowly descended in the darkness. I wanted particularly to see Guy. There were certain things to be done, I supposed. My mind was vacant as a plate on which was drawn a confused picture that would, on looking closely, mean something horrible. There had been a stain on the wall, a great jagged dripping stain, and bits of hairs sticking to it.

'Oh, God, this drink!' she said frantically; then almost sobbed: 'What's that!' But it was only the telephone-bell from the hall downstairs, queerly strident and unrestrained in that still, musty little house. Brrr! Brrr! Brrr! . . . 'I never knew a telephone could be so shrill! Will it be someone for Gerald?'

'It will ring for ever if I don't answer it,' I said, opening the door into the lane. 'I'll follow you to the car.' I hoped it was Guy ringing up on the chance of catching us.

'Well?' his cold murmur came through the night. He said he would meet me at my door in ten minutes' time. 'What are you doing about Iris?' he asked me and I think I said: 'Nothing. What can I do?'

Iris was waiting by her car under the lamp. The car was like a great yellow beast with shining scales, and Iris, tall and gentle and white, the lovely princess of the tale who has enslaved the beast. Far above them towered the pile of Sunderland House, enchanted almost into dignity by the darkness. She looked at me gravely as I came, she seemed to crouch like a tired fairy into her white cloak. . . .

'You look very white,' she said.

'Now, Lady Pynte!' I made to mock her, and I suppose we laughed. Then she was at the wheel, sunk into the low seat, staring up at the darkness of the faint London stars. 'I'm tired,' she said again, and again I thought, what could I do? Then she did something to the dash-board with her left hand, and the engine hummed. I was on the curb, above her. Nearby a policeman was flashing his lamp on a door. I supposed one told the police. . . .

'Will you see Gerald in the morning?' the slightly husky voice just reached me. 'And tell him to follow me to Paris? I shall be at number — Avenue du Bois for a week or so, and then . . . Good-bye,' she said sharply, as though impatient with herself. 'Good-bye, dear. You've been very kind—to the twin Marches. Good-bye . . . perhaps for a long time. You have your work in England, and I'm the slave of freedom. Good-bye, my friend.'

I could not tell her just then. She lay aslant in the driving seat, and her tawny curls flamed in the light, and she looked sad and tired. I could not tell her, and as she took her hand from mine the great car leapt down the fat little slope of East Chapel Street to the end, turned in a blaze of light and colour, rushed up the parallel little street to Curzon Street.

I was at the corner where I had last seen Gerald putting his shoulder against the saloon-door of The Leather Butler;

and as Iris's car turned into Curzon Street a two-seater passed me swiftly, going the same way. I thought I heard a cry of 'Iris!' above the rustle of the two engines, and I thought I heard Iris's surprised voice, and the rear-lights of the two cars seemed to draw together, but I was not sure.

I crossed towards Queen Street, sure only that I wished to see Guy. From Jolley's corner I saw, far up, two red rear-lights twisting into South Audley Street, and then, from afar, came the scream of a Klaxon, the growl of a horn. I wondered who was in the two-seater, but at that moment the tall figure of Guy came towards me from my door, where a taxi had just dropped him. 'Sorry,' he murmured. 'Poor young devil. Only hope the other side won't disappoint him as much.'

'I couldn't tell her,' I said.

Guy smoked thoughtfully, looking over my head. 'I'll tell her,' he said, 'in the morning. Had an idea he might blow his brains out.'

CHAPTER FIVE   THE DARK LETTER

I

On a bitter afternoon in the last week of January of the year 1923 the writer found himself in the Place Vendôme in Paris.

Now here, in the Place Vendôme, is material ready to the hand of the as yet undiscovered chronicler of lofty frivolities: such, unfortunately, as am not I. But I can, at least, count up to fifty. There were forty-eight motor-cars in the Place Vendôme, and one coach-and-six.

The Place Vendôme is a paradox in grey stone. Spacious, noble, monumental, it is cast, even at the stranger's first glance, in an everlasting mould. The Place Vendôme is, without a doubt, one among the few things about which we may say with certainty: 'That will last.' And yet, monumental and everlasting though it is, what do we find in the Place Vendôme? Do we find therein the practice of the seven arts, the learning of the nine humanities, the study of any one among the august array of sciences, nay, the application of any one among the Ten Commandments? We do not. We find forty-eight motor-cars and one coach-and-six. We find that it is given over only to the frivolities of the trivial of two worlds and to every sort of 'high-minded depravity' that may occur to the enfeebled wits of the exquisite. We find, in other words, that the Place Vendôme is the centre of that floating population of a few thousand dressing-cases, sables and Cachets Faivre of which, under the lofty title of *l'aristocracie internationale*, the Chevalier Giulio di Risotto is the ultimate servitor. The Place Vendôme is, therefore, no place for a plain man, nor by any means a safe station for the man in the street: there are motor-cars kept in readiness to run them over.

Across the Place, from the rue de la Paix to the rue de Castiglione, dash for ever the nimble green Citroën taxi-cabs; whilst from the rue de Castiglione to the rue de la Paix will march the Renaults *de luxe* with scarlet wheels, passing in a fancy of cool brown eyes and the *poudre à la maréchale* of Bourbon days. Here and there among them, maybe, will flash the racing Bugattis of the dark young men, a *giggolo*, a *rastaqouère*, a 'racing-man'. They will come to no good.

And always the great column on which Napoleon stands rises to the clouds, but no one cares about that. All they care about are the forty-eight automobiles and one coach-and-six which stretch, in ordered array of two lines, from the foot of his column to the entrance of the Ritz. The shops are loaded with diamonds as large as carnations and with carnations as expensive as diamonds. The shop-keepers are very polite, and courteously do not mind how many you buy. Americans buy. Englishmen watch the Americans buying. Grand Dukes wait for the Englishmen to dare them to have a cocktail. A few Frenchmen are stationed at those strategic points where they can best be rude to the English and Americans. Then the English and Americans tip them. The women do not wear stays, and insist on their men shaving twice a day.

'Well, at last!' sighed my sister, as her car, colourless with dust, was added to the forty-eight. I had been in Europe for four months, had lately joined some friends at Cannes, had chanced on my sister there, and had motored back with her to Paris. We were foul with dust, numbed with cold, aching with tiredness, and this was because we had 'done' the six hundred odd miles from Cannes in two days and a few hours. The devil was in it if there was any reason why we should not have taken three days, or four, or five. But then, why do people say ''phone' for 'telephone'? Thus, they get an illusion of speed.

We went into the hotel. The long, narrow, crimson lounge was crowded with tea-drinkers. 'But what a crowd of women!' said my sister. But there were quite a few people in men's clothes. *Au Réception.*

'I-want-a-room-and-bathroom-please,' my sister said.

'*Madame?*' The dark-suited gentlemen of the *Réception* looked up from their desks at my sister, saw that her clothes were not bad and that she was in a hurry, and looked away again.

My sister repeated herself, in that dead and faintly
104

aggressive tone in which women ask for what is very probably going to be denied them. 'I wired,' she added. Liar.

I went towards the concierge's box. He was a nice man, and had a white imperial.

'Is Mrs. Storm staying in the hotel?'

'Sir?'

'Could you tell me if Mrs. Storm is——'

'No, sir, no, sir. Not at present, sir.'

'I thought that, as her car was outside. . . A yellow Hispano.'

'That is so, sir. *Parfaitement. L'Hispano jaune.*'

'But Mrs. Storm, you say, is not in the hotel?'

'No, sir. Not at present, sir.'

'Then, perhaps you may know, she has sold or lent her car to someone?'

'That is so, sir. Madame *a prêté l'Hispano. Merci, monsieur.*'

'You couldn't possibly give me any idea of Mrs. Storm's present address?'

'*Pardon, monsieur. . . . Timbre, monseigneur? De quinze centimes, un. Merci, monseigneur. L'automobile à huit heures moins quart? Parfaitement, monseigneur. . . .* I have no instructions, sir. That was the gentleman to whom madame has lent her motor. *Le duc de Valaucourt.*'

'Thank you. But Mrs. Storm, you say, is in Paris?'

'Sir? *Je suis sans instructions, monsieur. Madame?*'

'What is it, what is it?' asked my sister.

'Nothing,' I said. 'Got a room? Good. I am going to the Westminster, and I'll come at half-past eight, shall I, and take you out to dinner?'

'Yes, but not here. It's so crowded with minor royalties that you can't stand with your back to anyone except the orchestra. Larue?'

She had no sooner turned towards the lift than my name was cried in an agony of exultation. My sister says that my face as I started round was a face of fear.

'Only the other day,' cried Mr. Cherry-Marvel, exercising, with incredible perfection of gesture, his eyes, shoulders, hands, wrists, beautiful teeth, tie-pin and handkerchief, 'we were talking about you. . . .' But it was ever one of Mr.

Cherry-Marvel's many social charms that, the instant he saw you after an absence, he would make it his business to give you the impression that people had been interested in nothing else but you during your absence. Not, of course, that he stopped there; he had other things to say, too. 'Of course what I *really* must tell you first of all, is that Henri Daverelle, whom, of course, you know as well as I do, was saying to me only the other day, *à propos* of something which I am positive that you, with your sort of mind, will appreciate at its full value. . . .'

Cherry-Marvel was an artist enslaved by his art: he could not see you but he and you must instantly fall under its dominion; for it was an art too perfectly modulated to admit of hurry, it was an art too sensitive to admit of interruption. Indeed, a wicked little gleam would flash across his wicked old eyes if you so much as made to interrupt him. Pitiless to himself, he was only the less pitiless to you in so far as you were not himself; and, should you be a boor and leave him suddenly, you might hear the dry, clear voice dying in the distance, but dying hard, rising and falling to the fullest and most pregnant sense of each period; for his, you understand, was an art not of selection but of detail, and must always and continually be expending itself. . . .

'Ava Mainwaring, whom, of course, you know as well as I do, was saying to me only the other day, *à propos* of something which I am positive that you, with your sort of mind. . . .'

Essentially an aristocrat, in person dainty, neat, fastidious, Cherry-Marvel's art was essentially democratic, for it abhorred all limitation and exacted from him its complete display on every occasion, whether lofty, literary, or plebeian, which came before his relentlessly alert eyes; and you can hear, through the last sixty years of English social history, the rise and fall of Cherry-Marvel's voice, each word dropping on a stunned silence like a long-polished jewel. Eager, exquisite, always prepared, always with a handkerchief fluttering between his breast-pocket and the corner of his eye, you must imagine him against the tapestry of wasted time, a figure of ancient, æsthetic *dandysme*, on immaculate

106

lawns, in drawing-rooms, up and down terraces of palazzos, in clubs and cabarets. You might enter a spacious drawing-room in Rome, a museum in Naples, a friend's villa in Capri, you might stray from your boat in a South Sea lagoon into the smoking-room of the hotel, you might steal a moment from your companions to see the moonlight on the Pyramid. . . . Oh, you might be anywhere, and suddenly you would hear that voice, rising and falling, relentless, ageless, enchanting even lions to silence, with here and there a sudden, profound drawl on one word, any word, 'de-ar', and you would, fascinated, be compelled to face him—there, with full pale lips drawn wide apart, wicked blue eyes absorbed with cunning ecstasy in your stunned attention, the while, infinite as fate, he joined together the perfected pieces of his art with the word 'whereupon', which lounged from his tongue in a crescendo to a cry of sadic exaltation. And while you laughed at some elaborately phrased conceit, wondering how he had remembered the order of the words so well, he would watch the effect of his art with kind, cunning eyes, one wrist suspended in the air, his handkerchief fluttering towards the corner of his eye, in consummate politeness to show how he, too, by your laughter, was appreciating the full flavour of his art . . . 'whereupon Elsa, who, by the way, had really a very amusing experience in Venice last autumn, and one which I am positive that you, with your sort of mind . . .'

Now, if anyone could tell me where Iris was to be found, Cherry-Marvel was that man. Cherry-Marvel knew, of course, everybody, and he knew everything about everybody . . . 'of course it's absurd to suppose that Alice, with her intelligence, which I am positive makes its full appeal to you—it is absurd to suppose that Alice could for one *moment* have thought that her husband, whom of course you know as well as I do, would divorce her for going to Brighton with Cubby Tyrell, because, as I was pointing out to her sister only the other day, for one thing no decent man, and I am sure you will agree with me about this, would care to let it be known that his wife had ever gone to Brighton, and for another, and this, of course, is a Biblical detail which I am sure that you will grasp at once, Cubby Tyrell, who is a very intimate friend of mine, has been allowed, in spite of having been married twice, to remain a member of the Celibates Club. . . .'

At this time I hadn't the remotest idea as to where Iris was or how she did. I had not seen her since the night of her brother's death; and had been permitted to gather from Hilary that he knew as little as I did of her whereabouts. Secret she had always been in her absences, Hilary said, or, rather careless, but now she seemed positively in hiding.

She had, a few weeks after that terrible night, written me one long letter: from some place near Rome, from a draughty house, so she wrote, on a hill of strangled olives. There was no address on the notepaper, and this, she wrote, was because she did not want me or anyone to write to her. 'Please,' she added to that.

Her letter was presumably in answer to two of mine addressed to the care of Mrs. Oden of Montpellier Square, but she was at the pains to excuse it on the ground that she and I were tied together—'no, tied apart!'—by a bond, the existence of which I would never, never know. Well! It was, you can see, a feverish, mysterious letter; and made how much more mysterious by that almost illegible, pencilled scrawl! There were whole sentences on the first few pages which I could not make out at all, which I made almost blind guesses at, while at some I could not even contrive so much.

'It is your fault, my friend. You paved the road up which I raced in chase of the Blue Bird. Yours was the appointed dark finger in the darkness. May God forgive you, for I can't. I will try, but I think I can't. There is a waterfall of fire. . . .'

Sheets upon sheets of it, that letter is before me now, and still I am unable to decipher whole sentences from that maze of pencil-marks on the thin Italian paper. There was one that stared at me, shocked me, in the middle of the second page—'I may hate you'—but I could not, do what I would, make out the words above or below.

'. . . I am lonely beyond bearing, and afraid. I am so afraid. I wonder, will you understand? But if I bore you

108

take courage, for I will not bore you again. You are my friend, and this is my good-bye. Forgive me, dear, the arrogance of calling you my friend. But I am so afraid. *Et, satyr bien-aimé, j'ai raison. . . .*'

I could, you can understand, make neither head nor tail of it. She might hate—me! She might, heaven knew, be indifferent to me, but why, how, hate? And *satyr bien-aimé* was all very well, but it meant nothing.

On the later pages she seemed to have controlled her hand a little, but her mind, if one might judge, remained . . . well, was that, perhaps, the effect on a mind of a draughty house on a hill of strangled olives? 'I am lonely, but I have always been lonely since I was eighteen. Yes, I can trace my loneliness since then. It is a long time.'

This letter, you must remember, came only a month after Gerald's death. She wrote of that night, and here her haunted pencil was at its most firm, if that is saying anything. 'There I stood in the old, old darkness—how old darkness is, have you ever felt?—while you were upstairs in Gerald's room. And I listened, but I could not hear you moving, so I imagined you to be staring at Gerald from the door, as you and I did that night a million years ago, when, do you remember, you suddenly, strangely from your heart, made that defiant courtesy to my hand? And, do you know, I almost cried because of your kindness to that poor, helpless sweet. Oh, Hilary has told me about you, and you luring Gerald off to a Home, but all in vain, my poor Gerald. And then I heard you switch out the light, and down you came, slowly, slowly, more silent than the darkness, and when you spoke your voice was as old as the darkness. But you are very young really, else you couldn't be so defiantly, so imperiously, kind. And I remember wondering why you said you had no matches left, for before you went upstairs I had seen a box half-full in your hand, but I said to myself: 'He has forgotten, and he is wretched at his friend's weakness.' Ah, you should have told me about Gerald there and then, indeed you should! But you did not, for my unworthy comfort's sake. Dear, you have a fine touch for the affections—but cruel, that is what you were, cruel. You laid your foot down on the

109

soil of kindness, but where your foot fell there leapt up a dandelion . . . and in the heart of the dandelion a tiny little rose; but what, my friend, is one little rose surrounded to suffocation by a huge dandelion?'

Well! Puzzle this way, puzzle that way, I couldn't make a glimmer of sense out of that passage. I was pleased, of course, that she seemed to like me, but as to the rest. . . .

Guy, as he had told me he would, had been to see her early in the morning. He had—another friend of childhood—over-ruled Mrs. Oden, saying it would be better not to wake Iris and bring her downstairs at that hour, for could there be a better place than bed in which to receive bad news? Mrs. Oden knew him of old, he was Apollo Belvedere to Mrs. Oden. She had been desperately upset about his news, coming as it did on top of what she had read about Gerald in that morning's paper. Poor Mrs. Oden.

Iris was asleep—'Oh, as no man can ever know sleep!'—when she awoke dimly to a tall shape at the foot of the bed. ('As no man can ever know sleep!' That, too, puzzled one, as well it might.) Dark it was, the curtains drawn, 'and I remember them flapping peevishly because the door behind the tall shape was ajar. And I, scarcely awake, could think but of one thing, my awakening mind was hugging, in pain and joy, but one thing . . . and I called the shape at the foot of the bed by a certain name, a name which was not his name. He made no sign that he had heard the name which was not his name, and I am sure he instantly made himself forget it. For, as you know, Guy would defend a secret not only against the angels of God, but also against himself. "Guy!" I cried at last, and he seemed to smile faintly, like the handsome absent-minded god he is. "Yes, Guy," he said. "Sickening, isn't it?" Those high good looks of Guy's, that small poised head—frozen, tireless Guy! But that morning he was very gentle with me. . . .'

He had spoken for me, too, saying that I hadn't told her of Gerald's death at the time because she had looked so tired and sad. 'Poor Iris,' Guy had said, 'the men who don't know you very well care very much for your comfort, but the three young men who have known you best of all have not cared enough.' Guy had said that, and she lying in bed, stunned, staring, while he sat holding her hand, as he might be an elder brother and she a hurt baby.

'He knew, you see, that I loved Gerald, that Gerald was a part of me, although Gerald had spent ten years in pretending that he hated me. Do you think, my friend, that I would have let myself be crucified on Boy's death only for the sake of Boy's cruel relations and friends? Two people Gerald worshipped in the world, but always he would have sacrificed Iris to Boy, that was always the way of Gerald's heart. Above all things in this world I love the love that people have for each other, the real, immense, unquestioning, devouring, worshipful love that now and then I have seen in a girl for a boy, that now and then I have seen in a boy for a boy, that playmate love. It isn't of this world, that playmate love, it's of a larger world than ours, a better world, a world of dreams which aren't illusions but the very pillars of a better life. But in our world all dreams are illusions, and that is why the angels have crows-feet round their eyes, because they are peering to see why all dreams in our world should be illusions.

'But you can't, you see, get rid of the funny love between twins like Gerald and me just by the word "hate". Even Boy couldn't really upset that. There was something peculiarly *us* about Gerald and me, something of blood and bone peculiarly us which nothing but death could destroy. And so Mrs. Spirit was sent into Hyde Park that the thing that was us might be for ever destroyed.'

She had suddenly asked Guy, half-sitting on the bed beside her, what it was in the world he loved most, and he had said he was sorry to admit that he loved his son more than all the world. 'I could have killed him for jealousy, just then I could, he who had everything to have also that. You don't know the body-ache for a child, the ache that destroys a body . . . the lament for a child of love, a child of lovers. . . .

'He would be two and a half years old now, my son. Hector, you see, didn't know anything about his son, because he left me in a temper before even I was certain. And naturally when I was certain I wasn't going to be outdone in silliness by my own husband, and besides, I thought it would be mean to force him to come back if he didn't really want to come back, and so I didn't let him know. For men, I would have you know, might make an awful row and stamp away in a tearing jealous fit, and when they are away they might be as pleased as anything to have got away. You can never tell about men, especially when they are convinced that they are being genuine. But, of course, I knew he would rush back quickly enough when the baby came. Oh, I would see to that! And, my dear, the fun I would have all by myself, for Hector and I had always longed for a son, the fun I had thinking of the look on his face when one day he would get my wire in Ireland: "Arrival of Hector-not-so-proud. You come too." Can you imagine what he'd look like then, and he stern and handsome and all covered with V.C.'s and oddments, wasting his time chasing disgusting Sinn Feiners who wouldn't know a country of their own if they saw it. I had that wire all nicely written-out months beforehand, and I went and hid my ugliness in my old nurse's home near Peterboro' and stuck the wire with a pin over my bed, being superstitious, you see, and wanting a winner for once in a way. Well, and then—Oh, and then they killed Hector just in time, and when Hector-not-so-proud came along he thought, the poor sweet, that the proper way for a gentleman to arrive in the world was toes first to slow music, and so away he had to go again. . . .

'I have done with England, and England has done with me. But I don't think I shall be able to go and have tea with the Empress of China yet awhile, for just now I love England as I never before have loved it. The captains and the kings of England—clean eyes, long shadows, low voices . . . why, I must hover, held in running as in a nightmare. And from the distance, from these lands of loud shrill voices, I will hear the low, low voices that I had long since thought I had given up regretting. Indeed, I was quite sure I had given up regretting them. But I am regretting them now, like a baby. Good-bye, dear, and God bless you. And when you think of me think instead of your words "He has, with you," and you will have the sum of my pride in being liked by you.'

Often, during these past eight or nine months, that

scrawled writing would pass my mind, but as I could hit on no clue to her fantasies, and as I might never see her again, I had put Iris carefully away into that part of our minds wherein we keep fancies, images, regrets, the things that we will do one day, the things that we would like to do one day, the things that we will never do again . . . when, but a moment ago, the great yellow car had leapt from the Place Vendôme into the first place in my mind, and I would like, I thought, to learn from my friend Cherry-Marvel anything that might be learnt about Iris. But as I listened to him, the way he had said this and had done that and had heard the other, I wondered how I would ever get the chance to suggest so much as her name to him. . . . '*à propos* of something which I am positive that you, with your sort of mind. . . .'

We stood, for we had not yet had time to sit down, in the little reading-room of the Ritz that leads from the entrance-doors, while stern-faced Americans turned over the pages of *The New York Herald* on the long marble-topped table in the centre, and a woman or two sat here and there absorbed in waiting, and the dowager Lady Tekkleham's voice nearby was grimly suggesting to the Baron de Belus that he could not do better than let her drive him in her coach-and-six to dinner at her villa at Saint Germain-en-Laye.

Weighed down I was by the chill of my journey and my heavy coat, and weighed down, too, by the gloom of the early winter evening that was falling about us, so that my eyes, borne down by Cherry-Marvel's amenities, could scarcely make out the chairs and flowers and vases in the long courtyard through the windows; and suddenly I fell to wondering how it had come about that Iris, who loved her proud swift car, had lent it to a friend, but the instant I mentioned her name Cherry-Marvel's little eyes gleamed with fury at the interruption. I was abashed, yet I would try again, but . . . 'whereupon Auguste de Maupin, whom, of course, you know as well as I do . . .'

But at last I achieved the impossible, in inserting a wedge into the fabulous monologue, and then I murmured: 'Ill? But are you sure, Cherry? Mrs. Storm is ill?'

But illness appalled Cherry-Marvel, from illness he could

not help but turn away the neat, lined mask of his face, from illness his Florentine *dandysme* trembled away in the only unaristocratic emotion I have ever observed in Cherry-Marvel, the emotion of fear. 'Quiet we call Silence, the merest word of all!' For, appalled by illness though he might be, his art could always rise to a general view. . . . He had heard in a roundabout way that Iris had had a 'sort of minor operation——'

'But,' I said——

'Whereupon,' said Cherry-Marvel, his little eyes gleaming for a second with fury, 'what *I* said was, "Operations, where are thy stings?" for, as of course you know as well as I do, women are scarcely women without them, and I have not the faintest doubt that in Lesbos they suffered, if I may put it like this, from the impolite insistence of their womanhood even more than if there had been any men there, for as I was saying to Marc only the other day, *à propos* of the particular shade in which she had dyed her hair, men may come and men may go, but the moon, my dear boy, is always there. Now here, for instance, is Iris, quite one of the loveliest women I have ever seen, and one who, I am convinced, must be very fond of you with your sort of mind, here she has, I hear on the very best authority, fallen a victim to one of those mental derangements which seem, if I may put it like this, to be an irresistible incitement to polite surgery in quite another and more individual part of the person. But what I have always said about Iris is this, that I admire her so, and I am so positive that you also must, with your sort of mind, because she is one of the very few Englishwomen I have ever met who can, as I am sure you will agree with me, live abroad without becoming more and more English. . . .'

2

Paris rises in a cloud of chill darkness, the rain falls like whips of ice, the street-lamps loiter on vague, bitter errands, confused strings of light, a stealthy, idiot wind glories in being corrupted by corners. The platforms of the omnibuses are packed tight with small men whose overcoats are too short for them, the brims of their felt-hats too narrow, their trousers turned up too high, their eyes too dark, their faces too pale. The jargon of the traffic on the rue de Rivoli, as it squabbles for every step between the deserted pavement beneath the railings of the Tuileries and the reeking pavement under the long archway lit by impudent shop-lights falling on imitation jewellery, is multiplied an hundred-fold by the shrewish air into a noise that hurts like warm water on a chill hand.

The taxi, a clever little Citroën taxi, darted hither and thither among the squabbling hosts, and nimbly we capered across the dark face of the Louvre, nimbly over the Pont Royal and the river paved with broken darkness, and so down the slope into the rout of the Boulevard Raspail.

Maybe it is true that there are times when we can detest Paris more deeply than any other city. Other cities stare back calmly at our sudden hatreds, other cities grow more impersonal as we execrate them, while as for Paris, she is always personal, but when we are nervous and detest her for being Paris she becomes even more herself, she insists on being herself with a nerve-racking insistence, like a silly woman who, seeing she is getting on her man's nerves, gives a loud, nervous laugh and simpers: 'I can't help it, it's my nature to be like this. . . .'

Now why were the people yelling here, what was the matter? Millions of them there were, joined in some strife between the Bon Marché, the Hôtel Lutetia and the entrance of the Nord-Sud railway, while omnibuses and trams made strategic movements against each other, while *facteurs* in dirty blue, fabulously moustachioed, pushed carts about in all directions, irritating anyone they could, and a motionless *gendarme* or two played with his bâton, heedless, unheeded. The eager face of a young artist I knew, shadowed by a great black hat, artistic, anarchistic, strode out of the white mass of the Hôtel Lutetia and turned greedily towards Montparnasse. At last my clever little Citroën and I plunged into quieter wastes, lit here and there by the bastard glitter of a Cinema Theatre falling on posters livid with three colours, red, blue, and yellow.

That strange unstormy exquisite, Cherry-Marvel! That

115

most æsthetic creator of a monster more terrible than Frankenstein's, for it devoured the spirit of all who passed beside it! Why I should be worried about Iris I could not tell, indeed I was too tired to inquire, but worried I was despite Cherry-Marvel's so well-informed badinage about the white woman's burden, and the more worried too, as the taxi plunged into nameless darknesses beyond the Bal Bullier, towards the address of the nursing-home which Cherry-Marvel, that confidant at third-hand, had of course known.

Montparnasse lay somewhere behind, or to the east, or to the west. We were in unknown Paris, silent, ill-lit, fantastic Paris: silent but for a rending crash here, a jarring cry there. Cold as the devil it was now, as though because the prickly warmth of many lamps and shops was withdrawn. Carefully we traversed a broad avenue as yet scarcely paved, beneath the skeleton shapes of great tenement-houses. Ah, Paris, that we should have come to this, you and I! Paris, that we should have come together down to this! In how many moods you and I have passed the time of day and night together, we have sat in strange places and dared the most devilish shadows, we have wandered from the Rotonde to the crowning grubbiness of the Butte, we have raced in the Bois and up the Mont Valérien, we have laughed at painted boys and been reviled by painted women, we have danced, loved, gambled, drunk, and together we have been bored by the unmentionable and terrified by that which makes the eyes bright and the face white as a soiled handkerchief, while Mio Mi Marianne danced a *minuet du cœur* with a crimson garter and the moon fell across the french-windows of Berneval's house to be lost in the soft shadows of giant poppies. Paris, that we should now have come down to this, lost together in these nameless darknesses beyond even the low darkness of the Bal Bullier, that glory of another time than ours. . . .

And now we tore up a dark, endless boulevard, even as a shifty maggot in a pit of darkness. But surely this was the murderer's Paris, here lived the fathers and grandfathers of Apaches, here were born the daughters of the drinkers of blood and the sons of the mothers of crime. It stretched never-ending between lamps fixed at astronomical distances, and on each side tall naked trees thrashed the shadows of very high black walls. They hid from the world, the people of this boulevard of the high walls, and who shall say that they had no reason to hide? And then, do you know, a lion leapt out of the night, a huge lion that was black as sin and crouched for prey in the centre way between five lanes of darkness made even darker by confused strings of light. And as we breathed a prayer in thanks for our deliverance from the lion of darkness trams crawled near us and stayed a while, and tram, at the impulse of a vice peculiarly continental, was joined to tram and crawled away; while we, having regained our breath, came beneath the shadow of a terrible wall. It was the wall of a castle, a fortress, a something satanically majestic. This, I thought, is another of Carlyle's mistakes, this is no less than the Bastille skulking in these parts until such time as the Camelots du Roy shall have left the kindergarten and can crown the duc d'Orleans King of France. Far above our laboured passage glowed a long, long row of small windows faintly lit, and it seemed to me that they were striped with bars of iron. And there was a great gate of iron, and a black soldier with a beastly bayonet to his rifle, and an old woman with a great brown parcel under her arm, waiting. The clever little Citroën stopped. It is tired, I thought, and will go on later. . . .

'*Eh, numéro quarante-neuf, Boulevard Pierre Abel?*' the taxi-driver threw at me reproachfully, and I got out, and I stared up at the great fortress which towered above me like a beast with a row of unclean eyes about his forehead, and the rain whipped my face.

'*C'est une prison?*'

'*Mais oui, monsieur. Le Paradis.*'

The pavement was broad, of mud and asphalt. The prison towered on our right, filling the sky with darkness—but for those distant, terrible windows. The rain whipped down, stinging like little animals. Nearby one forlorn lamp lit the putrefying colours of the advertisements circling a *lavabo*. What, I wondered and wondered, could Iris be doing here? Facing me across the broad pavement of mud and asphalt

117

was a great gate which had once been brown, lit by a lamp on which had once been inscribed the number of the Nursing Home. Iris was here. Were we, then, always to meet in darkness, Iris and I? She was here, and perhaps, I thought, on the other side of her is a Morgue or an Asylum.

A yard or so from the great door there was let into the high wall a small door inscribed *Concierge*. I was startled at the clatter made by the bell. A nun stood in the dim doorway.

CHAPTER SIX   THE RED LIGHTS

1

The shape of her coif against the dim light was like some
legendary thing's head, and she was eating. I heard her.
That she was old and very stout was all I could see. I could
smell just a little, too. Poor Iris.

I asked if I might have news of Mrs. Storm.

'*Ah, la dame anglaise!*' She ate, but not finally. '*Madame
est assez bien, je crois. Mais pardon, monsieur. Je n'ai pas d'instructions à vous donner—*'

'But!' I pleaded. 'But——'

'*Je regrette, monsieur. C'est pas ma faute, vous savez. Pardon.*'

She was closing the door! Terse as you like. I was helpless.
'*Madame est assez bien, je crois!*' Dear Heaven, but didn't one
know those *assez biens*! Isn't there a company in Heaven
wholly recruited from those who have been *assez bien*, and
daily augmented by those who are *assez bien*!

I lifted up my voice.

'*Pardon, monsieur.*'

I lifted up my voice in vain. So I was active. She stared at
me, panting. I withdrew my first impression as to her being
a nun. She was no nun. She had a crucifix and a coif, but
she was no nun. She was a woman scorned. She said many
things and used many words which I did not understand. But
I didn't care. I somehow thought, you know, of Iris dying.

'I am here,' I said in effect, 'and here I stay until I can
speak to a doctor or a matron. I am sorry, but you have made
me anxious as to the lady's health.'

'*Mais je vous l'ai déjà dit, jeune homme! Madame est assez bien!*'

The ordinary dingy *concierge*'s lodge: a black stove, a table
covered with frayed red cloth, a chair, a stool, an indescrib-
able odour, a plate of food on the table—*bœuf bouilli*, which
is French for the salvaging of grey matter from liquid dungeons of onions, carrots and potatoes. I sat on the stool. It
was unbelievable that her coif had ever been white. Somehow my eyes were transfixed by the small wooden crucifix
which, like a dinghy on a choppy sea, rolled on her bosom
as she ate. I wondered how long I would have to wait. I

wondered if I could smoke. I wondered if this was one of those convent-nursing-homes. I wondered if one called a nun *madame* or *mademoiselle*. They were maidens presumably, so I supposed *mademoiselle*.

'*On peut fumer, mademoiselle?*'

I was wrong. She looked at me with contempt. '*C'est défendu, monsieur.*'

'*Merci, madame.*'

I wondered if she really could be a nun. I wondered if one could tip a nun. Out of sheer hatred one acquires a passion for tipping in France and Italy. Detestable it was on this detestable day to sit like this, being hated. I made a muttering noise and gave her a ten-franc note, and it was in a more amiable spirit that she went on with her salvaging. At last there were only two bits of carrot and an awful looking onion left to engage her attention, and I felt that one might perhaps converse.

I was right about her being no nun. She was a lay-sister, she said. And this place, she told me, was a convent-nursing-home. '*Nous avons ici,*' she was pleased to add, '*la clientèle européenne la plus chic.*'

Perhaps that was the worst stroke of that day, so far. Iris among a *clientèle européenne la plus chic.* . . . One saw the cosmopolitan divorcées, their secret illnesses and guileful pains, their nasty little coquetries and the way they would blackmail their lovers with their sufferings, and one felt the sticky night-club breath of all the silly, common harlotries of England, France, America. My poor ten-franc note must have seemed pathetic to this old lay-sister, who probably thought nothing of receiving a *mille* from an anxious Dago.

I had until then been trying not to wonder about Iris in the vile shadow of a prison. Suddenly I was furiously hot. What on earth was I doing here! Intruding where I was not wanted! I was about to go, to run, when the lay-sister was as though distracted from the last piece of carrot by the opening of a door in the back room. Frantically she hurried towards it. It would look too silly of me to run now. I could but ask, anyhow.

The lay-sister's voice, voluble, vindictive, explanatory.

Much good my ten francs had done! Then steps came towards me, into the lodge. 'Eh,' I said. How afraid one always is of the callous French doctors with their cynical eyes and purple beards. . . .

A man, bald, sharp-featured as a bird, in a rough brown great-coat, a tired-looking, an anxious-looking middle-aged —Englishman!

'Masters! Conrad Masters!'

'Well,' muttered that anxious-looking man. He looked just the same when he was playing bridge. He was always playing bridge, that man. And he said he hated playing bridge. That kind of man. 'Well? How are you?'

'Glad,' I said, 'glad it's no worse. Glad it's only you. I was afraid of a purple beard.'

'And how did you get here?' A man given to muttering, that. One could hear what he said or not just as one pleased. One couldn't, you understand, be afraid of Conrad Masters.

'Masters, the fight I've had with this Cerberus to see you!'

'Rules . . . must have rules, you know. . . .' A decidedly undecided man. Soft-speaking but not plausible, a combination peculiarly English. A man of nerves. Shifty without suavity . . . and then, suddenly, apt to bite your head off like a very captain of men: 'And how did you know Mrs. Storm was ill? Here?'

'Oh,' I said. 'Well. . . .' And I thought of many things. Of Conrad Masters, of 'Should a doctor tell?' of Cherry-Marvel, that confidant at third-hand, of Mrs. Conrad Masters. A dashing lady, that.

'Who but Cherry-Marvel told me!' said I.

'God in Heaven, that man!'

But Iris swept out of my mind her doctor's problematical indiscretions to his dashing wife. . . .

'Ill,' he muttered. 'Decidedly ill. . . . mm. . . .'

'I heard,' I said desperately, 'that she'd had a sort of operation——'

'There's been no operation!' snapped that captain of men. 'Simply maddens a man, the way these things get about. . . .'

'Well, I'm only repeating what I heard, Masters. And you

can't hope for secrecy once our friend gets hold of anything——'

'Who said anything about secrecy?' A dangerous, feline
muttering. 'I don't want secrecy. . . .'

Silence. Anxieties walked across it arm-in-arm with that
lank man's doubtful heat.

'I say, Masters, is she—is she very ill? But, of course, if
I'm intruding. . . .'

Those worried eyes were fixed on the feet stuck far out
from the chair on which he lay as though exhausted. The
lay-sister appeared to be pottering about in the next room.
'Thinking of Donna Guelãra, are you? Haven't much faith
in me and Martel-Bonnard, have you?' Faintly amused
those worried eyes looked to be. That was that man's way.
You would think he was being shifty with you when he
might be just laughing at you.

Some would speak well, very well, of Dr. Masters; whilst
others almost libellously, saying that, working as he did with
Eugene Martel-Bonnard, the surgeon, he couldn't be over-
scrupulous in advising profitable but unnecessary operations.
Martel-Bonnard's wife wore a famous pearl rope, of which
it was said that each pearl had been bought at the price of
a woman's life. But a brilliant surgeon's life, Martel-Bonnard
would say, is full of drawbacks. He charged accordingly. I
think that he and Mrs. Masters must have bullied Masters
every now and then—not that he wouldn't have looked
worried in the Elysian Fields. Between them, those three had
once made poor Anna Estella Guelãra very sorry she had ever
left Chile. She was quite well, Martel-Bonnard said she was
very ill, he almost killed her, then he saved her, and how he
hurt her! 'Naturally,' smiled Martel-Bonnard. 'Such things
hurt. But, my friend, she was—*pouf!*—but for me.' How
one would have liked to operate on that sleek little man,
unsuccessfully! He despised you if you differed from him,
operated on you if you were fool enough, and robbed you
according to a special system he had of discounting the
exchange. One hundred thousand francs, poor Anna
Estella's life had cost her that time. And pain, such as falls
only to the lot of women!

'But, Masters, it's surely not as bad a case as that!'

'Mm . . . not as bad? Well . . . different shall we say?'

'But that was an internal operation! You just said——'

'Quite. That's why it's different. . . .'

Talking with Conrad Masters was like playing a game in which he who made out the most of the other's words scored the most points. . . . But Iris alone here, in this obscure place as full of crucifixes as a cemetery!

'I'm sorry,' I said, rising from the stool. 'I'm intruding. . . .'

'You're all right,' he mumbled. 'So you heard about it from that *femme fatale*, did you? Damn that man! Bla, bla, bla!'

Those worried but faintly amused eyes were on me. 'Been hearing quite a lot about you lately. Nurses would have your *dossier* complete by now if they could understand English. You seem to have put your foot in it somewhere. Rather sorry for you if . . .'

This bantering . . . medical bantering! Only doctors dare do it. 'Well, how are we to-day?' But by paying close attention to the game I had scored one point. She was delirious. So far, delirious. Then . . . 'if'!

'Masters,' I said, 'are you telling me that she is dying?'

'Mm . . .' he muttered impatiently, and as he jumped up from his chair the rough brown great-coat seemed to fill the dingy lodge. It smelt of England, that coat. And, protruding from it, that sharp, naked, weary face with the worried eyes. . . .

'Look here, Masters——'

'Here you are,' he muttered. I could not understand why he muttered 'Here you are' until I found a cigarette in one hand and one of those wretched spirit-lighters in the other. A man without conviction even in his ability to strike a match. . . .

'Known her for years,' he muttered towards his feet. 'At Deauville that year . . . terrible for her. Poor child. . . .'

'Masters, you said Donna Guelãra might die. You know you did. But she didn't, did she?'

He looked at me sharply. 'If only she'd help herself, lift a finger to help herself! That's what beats a man. Doesn't lift one finger, she doesn't.'

'Oh!' I said, trying to look reasonable. But I couldn't, for the life of me, accommodate myself to the idea of Iris dying. 'I suppose this is the crisis, is it, Masters?'

The rough great-coat gave one vindictive flounce, filled the room. 'Crisis! The way you people talk of crisis this and crisis that! Hear a word once and stick to it through life! "When does the crisis pass?" There is no "crisis" in most of these infernal things. Malaria, pneumonia, a few others—yes, crisis, know where you are. But in these things the patient just continues ill, two, three, four weeks, might live, might not. Lysis, not crisis. Crisis!'

'Sorry. Lysis. . . .'

'Oh, here!' He suddenly began fumbling in an ancient pocket-book, from which he extracted a small folded piece of paper. 'Might interest you,' he muttered.

Scrawled in pencil across the slip of paper were what looked like two names. That indecipherable scrawl! At last I made out the two names: Hilary's and mine.

'She said, should either of these two happen somehow to hear I am ill and call, just be nice to them, please. Her very words. . . .'

'Oh!' I said. And I went on staring at the slip of paper. It was a rather grubby slip of paper. And those two scrawled names were like a faint cry of loneliness.

'Known her for years,' Masters was muttering. 'Nice! First tells me not to tell anyone, then to be "nice" to you two. . . .'

I gave him back the slip of paper. I don't know why, and now I wish I hadn't. I would like to have it now, beside that fiver. 'Nice, fivers are. . . .' Thoughtful Iris! She knew her friends, she did. Lying lonely here . . . and having an after-thought about Hilary—and me! 'If they should somehow happen to hear and call.' Poor Guy hadn't a mention. She wasn't for putting any strain on Guy's lawfulness. But why lawfulness? I looked at Conrad Masters.

'Septic poisoning,' said Masters. 'That's the trouble.'

That meant very little to me, for never was a man so ill-informed about such things. 'But,' I said doubtfully to those gentle-worried eyes, and he murmured:

124

'Sure you're not thinking of ptomaine poisoning? Not that that isn't quite enough to be going on with. . . .'

'Pain,' I said. 'Good Lord, pain. . . .' All I could think of was pain, pain, pain. One can almost feel the stabs of someone's pain. Worst of all, one can mentally hear the faint screams of a voice just recognisable. Conrad Masters, the sight of him, reminded me vividly of Anna Estella's pain. Once, from a waiting-room, I had heard her screaming. 'Pain?' I said.

'Oh, no . . . no.' He weighed the matter. 'Nothing to speak of. Just keep still, that's the main thing. Very still, for weeks and weeks. Long business, you know. But what worries a man is that she doesn't try to help herself at all. Letting herself go . . . can't tell whether consciously or not, but somewhere inside her just not caring. I've been sharp with her. . . . Nice business for me, isn't it? Good Lord, nice! If only she'd take a pull, pull herself together . . . someone just give her mind a jab somehow. No good talking, of course. If she won't, she won't. Lies there, you know, just not caring. . . .' He was drawing on a fur-lined glove, and it was to that he spoke; almost, one thought, shyly. A curious, complex gentleman. 'She's said once or twice she'd like to see you and . . . well, learn you a thing or two. Some stuff about roses and dandelions. You seem to have made a *gaffe* somewhere, and it's quite on her mind to tell you about it. Hope I'm not giving anything away . . . but might do her good just to see you, feel you're round about. You can't tell. We'll see how she is to-morrow. Extraordinary, I've found it, the way a woman will wake up for a second from days of delirium for no other purpose than to feel lonely. . . . Not awake now, though. Ill, this evening. Can't really, you see, be iller if she tried. It will be good news, really good news, if she is alive in the morning. That's as much as I can say. Sorry. . . . Well, I must snatch some dinner. . . .'

We were outside. The rain had ceased, it was much warmer. The Masters's Renault, sleek and shining black but for the scarlet wheels, dwarfed my taxi.

Septic poisoning. I began to remember a little about that.

I remembered two words which seemed very like 'septic poisoning' in reports of trials of wretched women who had 'operated'. Surely, Masters couldn't . . . she had, after all, trusted me—'be nice to him'—and I must at once think the worst thing. Oh God, how foul a thing a man's mind is, how foul! But, Iris, dear Iris, why is one able to think of these awful things in connection with you!

'There's always hope, you know,' Masters was muttering. 'Pity you kept your taxi. I could have dropped you. And Donna Guelãra didn't die, did she?'

But how Anna Estella had desired to live! 'Die, me!' she had later screamed with laughter.

Iris had trusted me. 'Be nice to him'—her very words. And I had thought that . . .

'Masters, you won't mind my coming round again? Perhaps to-night?'

'Sleep here, if you like,' he smiled. 'I'll be coming myself for a second, about midnight. Wife's got a party. Like to come? Rather good bridge. Well, please yourself. . . .'

2

I agreed with my sister that it was abominably rude of her younger brother to be nearly an hour late to take her out to dinner, especially as she had been ready for at least twenty minutes. She was furious. I said: 'There is a new dance place open. I heard about it from a friend of mine, Mr. Cherry-Marvel. You will meet him, he is charming. This new place is called *La Plume de Ma Tante*. It has only been open three nights, so it will be very modish for another two. There is a nightingale there.'

'One cannot dance to a nightingale.'

'But why are you so exclusive?'

'It is cruel and beastly to keep a nightingale caged.'

'Dear, it takes a woman who once had a passion for aigrettes and who loves eating lobsters to be so sensitive. But there is probably baser music to supplement this nightingale. There are, in fact, five lovely niggers. The place is called *La Plume de Ma Tante* so that English people may know exactly where they stand.'

'You are so funny to-night, but would you mind not polishing your shoes on my dress? This is a very terrible taxi, and I think men are monstrous. If you were taking any woman but your sister out to dinner you would have chosen the taxi with discretion.'

'Rudolf and Raymonde are the dancers. I do not want to go to The Pen of My Aunt, but for your sake I would go anywhere. After dinner.'

She was pleased, loving to dance. We walked up the pavement of the rue Royale to the quiet doors of Larue. She said: 'I love Rudolf and Raymonde. I saw them dancing at Monte Carlo, and they say American women give him platinum watches from Cartier and that he was a footman in San Francisco, or was that Rudolf Valentino?'

I said: 'I say, do you know anything about septic poisoning?'

'Really, how callous you are! Do I know anything about it! But I had it!'

'No!' One's sister!

'But of course I had it! It is amazing when one's own brother is quite unaware that one has been through endless pain and torture.'

'Not pain and torture,' I said. 'A little bird told me.'

'But I am not responsible for your feathered friends! I was as good as dead, that's all I know.'

'But, my dear, that was when you were having a baby! I was in Vienna.'

'So you said. But, of course, it came on after I had a baby. One does not get septic poisoning for nothing. I nearly died, I can tell you.'

'*Vestiaire, monsieur?*'

'. . . Oh, I see. A baby. After that. . . .'

'I have never been so hungry in my life,' my sister said, 'and you talk to me of septic poisoning. I suppose you think you will destroy my appetite and therefore the bill will be less. I will begin with caviare.'

'Septic poisoning,' I said, 'did not kill you, that is the point. You cannot imagine how glad I am. Let us eat caviare.'

127

La Plume de Ma Tante. Bright green walls splashed with vermilion. A platform at one end, whereon five blackamoors perspired. At the other, a naked woman. She was without hips, according to the fashion for women. Her arms were twined above her head, and raised on the tip of her fingers was a bowl of green malachite from which pink water splashed into a white alabaster basin at her feet. Many English people were present. They would be going to the Riviera, then they would be coming back from the Riviera. Colonel Duck was there, with the quality. Colonel Duck was, no doubt, just returned from some notably swift exploits on the Cresta Run. But he never was so talkative about his outdoor activities. Cherry-Marvel was there, with a great big woman and a nice-looking boy with the hands of a housemaid who was a famous boxer. There was the usual group of Argentines, very well dressed indeed. They talked about *le polo*. All over the room elderly women were dancing with young men of both sexes. Mio Mi Marianne was there, sitting alone, but I might not speak with her because I was with my sister. A *demi-mondaine* will feel insulted if you speak with her when you are with your sister. Two years before Mio Mi Marianne had one night tied a silk handkerchief round her wrist, and it became the fashion for women to tie silk handkerchiefs round their wrists. Then Mio Mi Marianne tied a silk handkerchief round her throat, and that became the fashion. She thought of these things while smoking opium. She sat alone, staring into a glass of Vichy Water. A young American polo-player called Blister went up to her table, and maybe he asked her to dance, but she just looked at him and he went away again. Her eyes were intent on an opium-dream, and she was very happy in the arms of the infinite. Mio Mi Marianne will be found one day lying on the Aubusson carpet of her drawing-room. There will be a hole in the carpet where her cigarette has died out.

A blackamoor beat a warning roll on his drum, the dancers left the floor, the lights dwindled and awoke again in swaying shadows of blue and carmine. A heavily-built young man with the face of a murderer danced a tango with a lovely young girl with short golden curls. Then he threw her on the floor, and picked her up again. Rudolf and Raymonde. He did it beautifully. An American woman called the Duchess of Malvern threw Rudolf a pink carnation. The Baron de Belus said harshly: 'That is a white carnation really, but it is blushing at the fuss that women make of Dagoes.' In a cage clamped to the bright green wall near us was a dumb nightingale. It kept pecking at the floor of its cage, looking at nothing and nobody. I left my sister in Cherry-Marvel's care. I said to her that he could dance, and next day she was furious.

4

The burning eyes of the Renault made the grim Boulevard Pierre Abel almost hospitable. That was a conscientious man, Conrad Masters. How glad I was of him at that moment! What had he said about Iris? something about his having known her for years, something about 'that year at Deauville . . . terrible for her'. That would mean, then, that Masters had been there during the Boy Fenwick tragedy. Iris, poor Iris! Such punishments . . . for what crimes? What crimes deserved such punishments? Iris, poor Iris! But she wouldn't mind dying, not she. That was the trouble, Masters had said. But no doubt she knew best. . . .

The Paradis prison was a pit of blackness in the night. The dim lights behind the iron-barred windows were out, and it was impossible not to wonder if they slept up there in their iron cages, the wicked, the foolish, the betrayed. Perhaps the nightingale in its cage did not care. Perhaps those up there did not care, and slept like angels. But the wrongly accused would not sleep, that was certain. Does innocence wrongly accused profit anyone except a very wise man or a very good man, except a man who cares nothing for the opinion of this world or one who cares only for the love of the next? I said to the taxi-driver: 'Hell can know no torment like the agony of an innocent in a cage,' and when he had carefully examined his tip he agreed with me.

Gently as I could, I rang the bell, praying that the old woman would not be angry with me.

'*Aha!*' she chuckled. '*Aha! Monsieur-toujours-de-l'audace! Mais entrez, monsieur, entrez!* The doctor is just this moment arrived. Truly he is a good man, this Dr. Mastaire—but our French doctors, you should see! They come for a moment, they go, and she lives or she dies, what do they care as long as they are paid? But this English doctor, he does not know how to make money easily. Madame his wife was this moment telephoning that he should go home quickly, for they are awaiting him for *le bridge. Ah, cet bridge, bridge, bridge!*'

'But you see how anxious I am! Have you heard anything since I last saw you?'

'To have heard nothing, young man, is to have heard good news. But sit down, the doctor himself will tell you in one moment——' That demoniac bell! It clanged through the place. Perhaps of all the nations in the world the French alone are capable of fixing the loudest possible bell to a nursing-home. The fat old woman grinned vindictively at me. We had been enemies, now we were allies against the intruder. 'Bah!' she said, and opened the door. From where I stood I could not see who was without, but I could hear a voice: low, hesitating, in very correct French, in Foreign Office French. . . .

'Napier!'

We stared at each other in the most profound surprise and confusion. Napier, favourite of the gods, shy, sensitive, fine . . . just here, just now, facing me in the obscure silence of the Paris night!

'This is funny,' Napier made to smile. 'What?'

Napier Harpenden and I had known each other well, as 'well' goes, for years, but never before had we been alone together. But once, some years ago, I had seen him in a curious moment. Late one night I was walking down a villainous alley near the East India Docks when through a lighted window I was astonished to see Napier's white, thin, fine face and those dark fevered eyes. He was talking earnestly to an old man and a very pretty young girl who was crying, and I felt ashamed to have seen him, for that is how Napier affected one, you were hurt at the idea of hurting him. I had wondered often what he could have been doing there, what

130

secret good work he was at. He was a strange, secret, saintly youth, a favourite of the gods who never once relied on the favouritism of gods or men. . . .

He still stood outside, a serious slack shape in a tweed overcoat. He masked, behind that faint, deprecating smile of his, more than the mere confusion of surprise. He would very much rather it had not been me he had met just there. Napier and I were friends only because all our friends were mutual. We hadn't ever found, tried to find, any common ground for friendship. Sincerely, I was very sorry to be there. Napier had that effect on one.

'Venice is waiting in the taxi,' he said. Whenever Napier and I met he would instantly speak of Venice. This was to show me that he knew Venice and I were great friends and that, if he and I weren't great friends, that must somehow be his fault. How could you help liking a man like that? The courtesy of that favourite of the gods went so much deeper than anyone else's: let it one day go a little deeper, and you felt that it might have gone a little too deep, down, down to self-destruction.

I said I had arrived in Paris only that afternoon, and had heard, by chance, that Mrs. Storm was ill. My presence there seemed, you can see, to require a more definite explanation than any he might think fit to give me. One felt, with Napier, uncomfortably familiar to be asking after Iris in this obscure place at this late hour. He and Iris had been 'kids'. Then I thought, comically, of the two scrawled names on the grubby slip of paper. Well, I seemed to have rights too. More rights than Napier, really. Conrad Masters had no instructions to be nice to Napier. Poor Napier. . . .

'But,' he said, slowly, slowly, 'surely she's better by now? I only just called on the off-chance . . . really wanted air after the train journey more than anything else. Surely . . . what?'

I stared at him. What to say? You see, the sudden, white way he was staring at me made me feel terribly canny of anything I might say. Besides, one treated Napier *differently*.

'Better?' I repeated. 'Well. . . .'

'But, look here,' he said, protested. . . . It was dark, there between the dim lodge and the night. Why on earth didn't

131

the man come in? 'Venice and I are going south to-morrow, and I just thought I'd inquire—but, look here, I never dreamt that she . . .'

I at last grasped the fact that he had known she was ill. He was the only one among us who had known she was ill. One kid had known that the other kid was ill . . . and had waited until, on his way south, he could conveniently come round and inquire. Well!

'You had better come in, hadn't you?' I said. I simply couldn't say slap-out that Iris was ill nearly to death. You couldn't say things like that to those dark, troubled eyes. You protected Napier from your own impulses, always. A favourite not of the gods alone. . . .

But he still stood there in the darkness, staring at me very strangely and scowling in that funny, attractive way he had. Whenever I think of Napier I can see that Napier scowl and I can hear that involuntary 'what?' he would tack on to questions.

'Look here, something's the matter.' His voice trembled absurdly. . . . 'Something serious. What?'

'She's very ill,' I think I said.

'Very!' he snapped. 'What? You mean . . . really ill? What?'

'I think so,' I said. 'Yes.'

I looked into the room, avoiding those eyes. The lay-sister, a pair of horn spectacles on her nose, and without a sign of interest in us, was mending the heel of a black woollen stocking, one end of which lay coiled in a black tin-box. I couldn't somehow look at Napier just then. That, you see, was the first hint I had of the thing, and though it was no more than a hint, it tore at one. The look in Napier's eyes, I mean. The man's heart was in his eyes. . . .

'Look here,' he said sharply, 'I don't understand this. What? I mean, I'd no idea it was . . .'

'I don't know anything,' I said, 'except just that she's ill.' We stared at each other.

'As ill,' I said, 'as can be.'

'Oh,' he said. His eyes on me, not seeing me, he pushed past me through the doorway. And when I saw his face

132

again, I was appalled. It was lost, abandoned, terribly unaware of everything but fear, it was enchanted by fear. He simply didn't *care* but about one thing. . . .

'Haven't seen her,' he said, and scowled at me. Not that he had, at that moment, the faintest idea who I was.

'Here, a cigarette,' I said.

He stared at it in his fingers. He crushed it. . . .

'Haven't seen her for nearly a year,' he said in a rush, and stopped abruptly, seemed to realise me, scowled. 'I say, what is it? Pneumonia or something? What?'

I fumbled. I wasn't, I said, certain. Had only seen the doctor for a moment. Something inside, I thought, had gone wrong. . . .

I was immensely lost in all this. He had known she was ill—but not seriously ill, nor of what! I grabbed at one certain point of behaviour for myself. One had to. I was, anyhow, going to make no mischief. Like Guy, I would give no 'gratuitous information' of any sort. For better or for worse, I wouldn't. News of septic poisoning was obviously not for Napier, not for anyone—except for the two names on the grubby slip of paper. This septic poisoning seemed to mean only one of two things, a child or not a child. That was most utterly Iris's business. Iris the desirous—for a child. 'To be playmates with.' And I wondered, just then, if it had been another Hector-not-so-proud. 'Like to have a winner once. . . .' I kept on hearing that slightly husky voice saying little things.

'What I mean to say is,' Napier said, with sudden astounding calm, 'that this is perfectly idiotic. What? You see, I hadn't the faintest idea. . . .'

But when, deceived by the calm of his voice, I looked at him, I found it better to look away again at the frowsty old lay-sister sewing away at her stocking. It was mean to look at him, he was too naked. I realised how masked we always are, how this is a world of masked men, how we are masked all day long, even on the most trivial occasions. Then I felt his hands suddenly tight around my arm. And tighter. Now what?

'I'm awfully sorry,' I said idiotically.

'Look here—I say, for God's sake! You see, I don't understand. What? She wrote to me weeks ago that she was going
to be just slightly ill, and now . . .'

The fingers dropped from my arm. 'Hell!' he muttered.
'Oh, hell! What?' He hadn't the faintest idea of what he was
saying. I wished to God he had, I didn't want to listen to
him, I hated listening to him, it was like spying on the man.
Spying on Tristram wandering in the forest raving with love
for Yseult. But what could I do? How leave him like this?
How let him return to Venice like this? Good Lord, and
Venice waiting in the taxi! If she saw him like this. . . .
Good Lord, was the man mad to have brought Venice with
him! Here, to see Iris! The misty impulses of a man of
honour . . . do nothing behind his wife's back. After, you
know, having done everything. But . . . Good Lord, if Venice
grew tired of waiting in the taxi and came and found Napier
like this, like a demented knight in a story! Venice of the
lion's cub head, the mischievous, loyal eyes, dear Venice!
adoring and adorable Venice! Napier's wife. . . .

And, at that moment, I saw Venice again at the Loyalty,
that night ten months ago, happily waiting for Napier,
whose wife she would be in three days. 'Darling, darling,
darling!' That night of Gerald's death! And then for the first
time I remembered the cry of 'Iris!' in the night, and the
two red rear-lights swerving into South Audley Street, and
I understood how it was that Iris in her letter had called me
her 'destroyer' . . . her 'destroyer' with love, for no lover
could have passed her way that night had I told her about
Gerald. And Napier had passed her way, Napier whom
she had seen that night for the first time in many years,
Napier her ancient friend. 'There were two roads leading
from a certain tree. . . .' And the two roads had come
together in the darkness of that night, in the darkness of
cruelly blind chance, and now they had come together again
in the darkness of this night, while Venice waited outside. . . .

I couldn't, you can see, not do anything just then. I
couldn't let this love-lost man be found by Venice in her
husband's shoes. Napier and Venice, the happy lovers. . . .
I was on Venice's side. For Venice! Always, I was for Venice.

One likes so few people, but one likes those few very, very much. This love-lost man must be woken up, must *behave*. Of course he must behave! Venice, for Venice! How dared he have done this to Venice? Marrying her on the third day from that night. . . .

I asked him where he was staying, and when he said 'the Meurice,' I told him that if he would go now I could ring him up when I had seen the doctor. 'It's no good waiting here,' I said. 'I know the doctor.'

He stared at me with the immense, the devastating, dignity of the utterly careless. I bitterly wanted to wake him up, to make him see the thing he had done, the beastly thing. For Venice! 'It's no good,' I said cruelly, 'keeping Venice waiting for ever. . . .'

He scowled at me, or at something just behind my shoulder. 'I'm going to see Iris,' he said.

It was quite definite, he was going to see Iris. It would probably, I supposed, do Iris all the good in the world to see Napier on this critical night. Napier and Iris. It might make her care whether she lived or died . . . but why shouldn't she die? Venice would condemn her to die. Iris was the foe. Why shouldn't she die? You can't do things like that, and not die. Stealing like a little thief into the garden of Venice, and stealing away like a little thief . . . to bear Napier's child, unknown to Napier. . . .

'Hell!' he muttered. I stared at him, at those burning, broken eyes. . . .

'Hell!' he said. 'Oh, God, what hell! What? If you only knew. . . .'

'I don't want to know,' I snapped. Well, did one want to know? But he didn't hear, didn't care, didn't see. Being with him, you can see, was exactly like eavesdropping. Why, if Venice came in and saw this love-lost man . . . her Napier, her darling, like this, with burning broken eyes. But there are some things that can't happen! You couldn't take Napier from Venice. And how quickly, how poignantly, Venice, if she saw him like this, would know the difference between his easy, smiling love for her and this . . . damnable madness.

But in the dark taxi she wouldn't see his face, and I was

just about to try again to get him away when he said fiercely:
'It's not as though I don't know anything about it. Or do
you think Iris is a liar? What?'

'Napier, you really must pull yourself together——'

'No, but anyone would think I was a most fearful cad.
What?'

And he scowled, in that Napier way of his that made one
want to forgive him everything. 'I mean, not coming before,
seeing she's so ill . . . waiting all this time, and coming just
now. Why, she wrote to me four weeks ago, saying she was
going to be just slightly ill and have a rest for a week or two,
so of course—— Oh, look here, here's the letter, you'll see
for yourself——'

'But I don't want to see for myself. Steady, man! I quite
understand. Of course you couldn't know. . . .'

'No, but look here, you'll see. . . .'

Feverishly he began fumbling in his inside-pockets,
pulling out papers, a pocket-book, passports. . . .

Venice could be very still. I imagined her in the doorway,
looking at Napier in this state. She would be very still, and
in her stillness she would be destroyed. Venice was jealous,
so jealous and possessive. 'Got to be with Napier,' she had
pleaded to me once. 'You don't know what he's thinking
about half the time, and he doesn't know what he's doing
the other half.'

Some of the papers dropped to the floor, and I picked
them up and thrust them into his gaping pocket. The old
nun smiled at me over her spectacles, and then looked at
Napier and tapped her forehead. But you could see she liked
the looks of Napier. '*Quelle belle silhouette!*' she grinned. I
don't believe that Napier to this day knows there was anyone
but our two selves in that lodge.

He waved a white thing covered with scrawled pencil-
marks, and beside it I somehow saw that letter from a
draughty house on a hill of strangled olives. But between the
two came the vision of Venice destroyed.

'I don't want to read it, Napier. I quite understand. What
on earth does it matter whether you knew or not, so long as
you know now?'

'Thinks a lot of you,' he said darkly. 'Told me, last time I saw her. . . .'

He passed a hand over his mouth. I said: 'But . . .'

'Beastly,' he said, looking at me with enormous, dark surprise. 'That's what I feel. Beastly. As though my skin was a dirty shirt. Ever get that? I mean, here she's dying, and I . . . God, how one gets to know oneself! What? But I'd like you to see. I mean, since it's you. She thinks a lot of you, I know she does. Thinks you're nice. Funny how she says that, 'nice'. What? But what's she want to lie for? Iris never lies. Never. That's what beats me. I mean, why, to me? What? Go on, you'll see. . . .'

Crumpled the letter was, but he had, in a sort of way, smoothed it out. I stared at it. I had to, for he was watching me with those ruined, pleading eyes. The greyhound unleashed. . . .

'She's dying.' I heard his voice from miles away. 'You can't tell me! She's dying. . . .'

'She won't die,' I said firmly, glad to look up from the letter. And, you know, I was quite certain at that moment that she wouldn't die. The beloved of the favourite of the gods wouldn't die. The favourites of the gods are not let off so easily. Oh, she wouldn't die! It would be too easy to die. 'The Marches are never let off anything. . . .'

I stared at the crumpled-looking thing in my hand. I didn't read it. The poor devil was only showing me the thing because, at that lost moment, he was starving for understanding, for anyone's understanding, after these ten months of silence, of Venice-Napier-Iris silence. . . .

I couldn't, merely from the wretched fact of staring at the thing blankly, avoid the first few lines of that schoolgirl scrawl. 'Napier, I have to go to a nursing-home for a few weeks' rest. Napier, dear Napier! I've tried not to write, you know I have, just as we promised, but as we are never to meet again I'd like you to pray——'

That is all I read, and there I stood, staring at that crumpled letter like an idiot. 'As we are never to meet again. . . .'

Figures moved, I could see them, hear them, their cries,

laughter, silences. Their silences. Napier, Venice, Iris. They had come together, blindly, desperately. By chance—but it is written in vinegar that there is no such thing as chance. And I, why, I had been appointed, a silly finger of fate, to make 'chance' more sure! They had come together, those three, propelled to each other from darkness for darkness's sake. The weak of the weak, the strong in chains. Always that is the way of things, and for no reason at all except life's most damnable unfairness, which is for ever saying: the weak shall be made weaker, the strong shall be destroyed. Venice was strong, strong as gold, in loyalty and love. Incorruptible, golden Venice! Salute to Venice! So, said the Prince of Darkness, she must be destroyed, and to destroy her in the most efficient and painful way Napier must see Iris, unseen since girlhood, a grown-up Napier must see a grown-up Iris, a youth curiously sensible to the pitiful must suddenly see an Iris wrapped in tragedy and scandal, a helpless, hopeless, unhappy woman—the favourite of the gods and the poor shameless, shameful lady! And it was arranged, the destruction of Venice, to begin with a sudden, surprised cry of 'Iris!' in the night, and then, behold! two cars would sweep through the silent streets into the heart of the dark forest of London, even to Napier's small toy house in Brompton Square. Oh, how clearly one could see them, hear them, those friends of long ago. Clear to see they were, fumbling with their lives in the darkness of all life, most emphatically not talking of love, most emphatically being old friends. Clear to see, those two, Napier and Iris, the ancient friends. Maybe, to make chance more sure and flesh more weak, which is a jesting habit of the fallen archangel's, they had been in love long ago and had been unhappy and had parted. The queer death of Boy Fenwick would have come between a boy and girl love, and across the wide gulf that separates a young man of consequence from a lady of pleasure they would not have seen each other for a long time. 'There were two roads leading from a certain tree.' And one might hear Napier that night, not this love-lost thing, but the favourite of the gods, happy on the wings of an ancient friendship, pulling at Iris's arm to

138

persuade her out of her car: 'Iris, come in for a moment.
Oh, come along, Iris! I know how fond you are of a nice
glass of cold water, and I have some of the most superior
cold water in London. What? And we'll never have another
chance to talk again. . . .' And Iris, Iris of the lament for a
child! Iris had lit a flame and was like to be burnt to death
in the cold fires of that flame. Iris had lit a flame, and the
flames that Iris lit seemed quenchable only by death. Boy
and Iris. Hector and Iris. Napier and Iris. But Napier could
not die, favoured of the gods. Iris could not die, 'for the
Marches are never let off anything', and so it would be the
younger brother of Hector-not-so-proud who must die,
who must have died, thoughtfully trying to tempt his mother
into the carelessness of death.

The lay-sister had gone into the other room, which must
have been a sort of kitchen, and Napier had taken her chair.
He sat there, shadowed with whiteness, scowling into the
black tin-box.

'I see,' I said. 'Of course. . . .' I made him take the letter
back, and suddenly he looked up at me intently. He'd find
out something, he would.

'She is dying, isn't she? You're certain yourself, aren't
you? What?'

'The doctor should be in in a moment, and you can ask
him. No, I don't think she's dying. My sister had the same
sort of thing, and she's dancing at the moment——'

'Same sort of—what thing, then? What?'

A *gaffe*, a *faux pas*, a bloomer! He scowled up at me,
blackly intent. . . .

'Ptomaine poisoning,' I said.

'Oh God!' he said. 'Oh, God! What? Poison. . . .'

He stared at the letter which I had put into his hand. He
turned it about, and seemed to think profoundly. 'You see,'
he muttered, 'it's all wrong, this. All wrong. What?'

I wasn't cast for a moralist. What I said, very uncomfortably, was: 'Well. . . .'

'All this messing about,' Napier scowled at the letter. Then
he looked at me, darkly, helplessly.

'Get let in for things,' he said.

'Difficult,' I said. 'I know . . .'

'God, isn't it! Difficult. . . . What? I mean, when you want to be . . . well, when you want to live clean. We promised, oh God, yes! not to write, never to meet. . . . Must live clean, you see. What? There isn't, when you come to think of it, any other way *to* live. . . .'

'Guy says that. . . .'

'Guy? Yes, but . . . need guts like Guy's, don't you? What? Look here,' he suddenly waved the letter at me, 'will you go out and keep Venice company for a moment? I mean, see what she's doing? And I'll see the doctor fellow and make him let me see Iris for a moment. Promise wiped out by approach of death. . . . What? I mean, lonely for her here. . . . Told me, last time I saw her that she was lonely. Hurts, loneliness. What? And then I find her in this hole. . . .'

He thrust the letter into his gaping coat-pocket. I could see it there, that pencilled scrawl. Letters, letters, letters like radium-bombs, left lying about for years, then bursting. What fools men were, keeping letters . . . travelling about with them, sticking them into their coat-pockets. Suppose Venice saw that letter . . . just a few lines of it. Whether Iris lived or died . . . suppose Venice saw just a few lines of that letter. For Venice. . . .

'Napier,' I said.

He stared at me, extraordinarily handsome at that moment, and I remember thinking just then of what is always said, that women are not very attracted by good-looking men. But what is always said must be wrong.

'I say,' he said, 'got a cigarette? What?'

'Napier,' I said, 'give me that letter. . . .'

'Or,' I said, 'have two matches to your cigarette. . . .'

A tiny smile fluttered round the thin quivering lips. 'There's no end to it,' he whispered, 'is there? Once you begin. The nasty precautions. . . .'

He struck a match, and the flame lit the ruin in his dark, fevered eyes. 'You can't,' he said, 'have anything cleaner than love. You can't. This love, anyway. Clean . . . clean as the Virgin Mary. And then . . . you're dogged by dirt. You think fine things, fine sacrifices . . . and you're dirty as all Sodom and Gommorah. All this nastiness round a thing, all this messing about. . . .'

It was as the letter burnt in his hand and fluttered, just like a hurt crow, to the floor, while he watched it with intent seriousness, that I heard a step by the door in the other room. To see Conrad Masters alone, I hurried towards it. There he was, tired, worried-looking, his sharp features sticking like a great bird's out of that rough brown coat.

'Bad,' he muttered. 'Can't do more. She's conscious, too. And doesn't give a damn. Not a damn. I told her you were here, and she said "Nice" to that, but didn't seem to think you were worth living for. Need a miracle now. . . . "Nice"!'

'But, good God,' I said, 'we've got a miracle here! He's a bit mad, but miracle is his second name. . . .'

'And what's his first?' Masters snapped.

'Harpenden. . . .'

'First name, Christian name,' said Masters wearily. 'Napier, by any chance?'

'You're right,' said Masters. A decidedly undecided man? Why, he radiated resolution: and a lean sort of mirth. 'Never know your luck,' he said. 'Not in this world. . . .' I just managed to catch him by the coat as he plunged towards the other room, in which one could make out the tail of Napier's coat. 'Masters,' I whispered, 'I went and told him it was ptomaine poisoning. . . .'

'Good,' said Masters. Those gentle worried eyes with the faintly amused look. 'That's all right,' he smiled. 'Young ass.'

There sat Napier, a lost man. . . .

'Come along,' Masters jabbed at him. 'Come along, man! Waive introduction. Life and death. . . .'

Napier jumped up. Masters looked almost fresh and boyish beside him. A captain of men, that was Conrad Masters.

'I say,' Napier said. . . .

'Look here,' said Masters, 'I'm taking you in to cheer her up. Might make all the difference. Just might. . . .'

Napier tried to smile. Oh, he tried.

'But, doctor,' he said. 'Is she . . . going?'

'She wants to go, that's the trouble. Anyone would think,' snapped that captain of men, 'that I was committing a felony in trying to keep her alive. By the way she looks at me. You've got to cheer her up, Mr. eh . . .'

'Captain Harpenden,' I said.

'You've got to make her care whether she lives or dies. That's your business, Captain Harpenden. I'll give you five minutes to do it in. . . .'

Napier looked from him to me. He scowled immensely.

'I'll go out to Venice,' I said, but I don't suppose that Napier, passing me, heard a word. Conrad Masters stayed a second. Gone was the captain of men. He looked terribly worried. . . .

'I say, want to play bridge?'

'Bridge!' I said. 'Bridge? Bridge!'

He looked terribly worried. . . .

'Well, my wife wants—Oh, wait till I'm back! I'll drop you, anyway.' And he was off, his brown coat flouncing peevishly. Through the open door I could see Napier, his coat open, everything about him open, standing in what looked like a wide courtyard. . . .

'*Mais quelle belle silhouette!*' chattered the old nun. '*Le vrai type brun anglais. Mais c'est naturel qu'il soit fou avec ces yeux là. . . .*'

Napier and Conrad Masters walked across the courtyard towards a tall red-looking building. Its door was pointed like a church door, and windows here and there were alight. Through one of them a nun was looking at me. On the sill outside the largest window of all, which was not alight, stood a pineapple and some grapes on a plate.

5

After that chill, stuffy lodge the night was like a kiss. The dark shapes of Masters's Renault and Napier's taxi faced each other, their dimmed lamps lighting only the darkness. The chauffeur of the Renault looked to be asleep at the wheel. I hoped Venice was asleep, too. The driver of the taxi was nowhere to be seen, and stealthily I was approaching the dark shape of the taxi, mentally communicating to

Venice that it would be only decent of her to be asleep, when the taxi-driver emerged from the malodorous shape of the *lavabo*. '*Elle dort, je crois,*' the fool shouted at the top of his voice, and I bolted into the capacious Renault.

'Sorry to wake you,' came the mutter of Conrad Masters from the open door. 'Where are you staying?'

Through the front window I saw the door of the taxi close. Napier would tell Venice he had seen me, and she would be surprised I had not spoken with her. 'You were asleep,' Napier would say, but she would still be surprised. . . .

'Look here,' Masters said persuasively, one foot on the footboard, 'why not come to my place for a while? Come along, it won't kill you. A night-hawk like you. My wife has a party of some sort. Dancing, bridge, Parisian-Americans. . . .'

Dancing, bridge, Parisian-Americans! The end of a perfect day. . . .

'It's another form of septic poisoning,' I pleaded. 'Take me to the Westminster, Masters, and let me sleep. And you'd better get a room there as well and spend the night in peace. . . .'

The taxi in front of us bumped and rattled away. Masters muttered wearily: 'Well, I will probably have to take a hand if you don't. Most of 'em dance, but I left three bridge maniacs stranded to come on here. They stay up to all hours, the blighters. . . .'

Smoothly the Renault picked its way among the pits and chasms of the fearful boulevards of outer Paris. 'Their last chance of ever being mended,' Masters muttered, 'went when the Germans lost the war. . . .'

'All right,' I said sulkily, 'I'll come. Bridge, dancing, Parisian-Americans. . . . What a monstrous life you lead, Masters. But what about that miracle?'

'Can't tell,' he muttered. 'Can't tell. Seemed bucked up a bit, of course. Took notice, recognised him, and that's something. But you can't tell. . . .'

'She'll live,' I said.

'I'm glad you're so certain,' snapped the captain of men.

'I'm so little certain that I put that young man on his honour to look round again to-morrow afternoon.'

'On his honour!' I said. 'On his honour?'

'What's the matter with his honour? Looks all right to me. . . .'

'But he's going South in the morning!'

'He musn't go!' snapped Masters. 'That'll be your job. We must give her one more chance . . . one more *piqûre*. It's essential that he shouldn't go to-morrow. You must prevent him.'

'I'll try,' I said. 'But . . .'

'But surely he won't *want* to go!'

'Oh, *he* won't want to go . . .'

Masters stared at me thoughtfully. 'Um,' he said. 'Um.'

'Of course,' I said, 'you never know. . . .'

'Well,' said Masters, 'now she's seen him once she'll expect to see him again. It's only natural.'

'Of course,' I said. 'Naturally. . . .'

Smoothly ran the Renault with the scarlet wheels. The black lion found in us no little Citroën, cowered before us, slunk back into the jungle of nameless boulevards. Montparnasse showed lights to hold us, faces in cafés, singing groups of young men, little flashing women with lots of hair like dyed haloes. Artists. Swiftly we fled through the darkness, the stillness, the deep shadows of the phantom fortress of the Faubourg Saint-Germain, away we went from the *ancien régime*, the *haute noblesse*, across the river to the *nouveau régime*, the *noblesse*, down the stately slope of the Avenue Hoche into the sweet valley of the Parc Monceau, where lived the dashing Mrs. Conrad Masters, with bridge, dancing, Parisian-Americans. . . .

'You can't,' that man muttered, 'expect her to be reasonable. . . .'

'No,' I said, 'I suppose not. . . .'

'Nice!' snapped Masters. 'Good God, "nice"!'

CHAPTER SEVEN   FOR VENICE!

I

Fat white clouds hurried over the pale blue roof of the rue
de la Paix. Spring, the first day before the first day of spring,
the day that is not spring but is as a voice of spring crying
in the wilderness of the chilly heavens: 'Here is spring, and
lo! these are the clouds of winter fleeing before her, white
as polar bears, and as stupid. Enjoy, enjoy *le printemps*!'
Anxious the fat white clouds seemed, most anxious, hurrying
from the vanities of the rue de la Paix towards the Cathedral
of Our Lady, that they might pray, the poor clouds who
know not that the pagan gods are dead, the poor clouds,
who love the winter, against the return of Persephone from
the arms of Plutus. The stormy brittle sunlight, eager to
play with the pearls and diamonds of Van Cleef, Lacloche
and Cartier, aye, and of Tecla also, chided away the fat
white clouds, and now the sun would play with one window
of the rue de la Paix, now with another, mortifying one,
teasing another, but all in a very handsome way.

Early the next morning it was when I found myself
looking upon these mighty diversions, but I had so much
rather been asleep. My bedroom looked down on these
things, but unfortunately not from a great height, for they
are not tall, the hotels of Paris; and men are sent round the
streets of Paris first thing in the morning, to the end that
people may not fail to be aware of the beauty of shuttered
shops, some of these men being directed to push along
enormous tin barrels with which to make a *carmagnole* of
dust, whilst others are placed on ancient taxi-cabs with
especially adjusted gears and magnified horn-power. There
is no peace in the world, that is what it is. There is no peace
in Paris.

I lay in bed, staring through the lace curtains. What had
happened, what were the alarums and excursions of that
grey day yesterday, which had leapt at me from the darkness
as I made to return to England after four months of pleasant wandering? Iris was ill unto death, Napier was enchanted. . . .

145

Men, some in shirt-sleeves, were taking down the heavy, grey, burglar-proof shutters of the shops opposite. Set in the small windows above the shops, the modistes' assistants seemed to be talking and talking. Some had hats in their nimble hands, some other things. It is pleasant, maybe it is the only pleasant pastime that does not ever pall, to see and not be seen. And now the shop windows began one and all to glitter in the stormy brittle sunlight which transmuted the pearls and diamonds on yellow velvet into celestial jewels fit to adorn the crown of the word *printemps*, than which there is not a more beautiful word in all the languages of the world. In the great window of *Edouard Apel et Cie.*, whence in the long ago had come to this person such polite but manly notepaper, stood richly white and coloured papers, boxes of lacquer, ebony, and cedarwood, flaming quills and great cut-glass bottles for ink, and many another device to make one realise how pleasant writing must be for those who do not have to write. Before a shop not far from Tecla's, which displayed the most charming baubles of all and completely deceived the sun, two short dark Semitic men and a lanky Semitic youth were having some difficulty with their shutters. The shutters did not look new, far from new, but maybe, I thought, a new burglar-proof arrangement has been wrought on them, and that would be causing the difficulty. The traffic had as yet but caressed the rue de la Paix, and through the open window one might hear the rising anger of the two short Semitic men with the lanky Semitic youth, an anger which seemed to call for and to attain a cuneiform language. Then a fourth man, also in shirt-sleeves, came out of the shop, a patriarchal mountain of a man with a great black beard and a mighty nose, who might that very moment have come from a breakfast of dates in a tent over against Ur of the Chaldees, and instantly I knew him for what he was, a millionaire. Many were the race-horses he owned, and often you would see him at Longchamps, talking to a beautiful woman in a deep voice about himself, for that was a vain and terrible man, and the worst of it was that he was always right about everything, whether it was a horse, a jewel, a woman, an antique, or the

146

fall of a card. With one look of his eye he scattered the two short Semites and the lanky Semitic youth, who were his two brothers and his son, who were also millionaires, and in a thrice he had those shutters off that window, and lo! there, royally alone against terraces of dingy green velvet, sat a brown Buddha with what looked like the largest emerald in the world in the middle of his forehead, but maybe it was only the second largest. The last time I had been in Paris there had been a golden chair in that window, golden arms and legs and back and sit-piece and all, and so it was no wonder that that man owned race-horses and said 'Banquo!' to half-a-million francs while yawning, and rightly, for he always won, as I know to my cost. And one night he had come into the rooms at Cannes with a great ruby on his finger. Only he would, of course, but apart from the ethics of the thing it was an amazing ruby, crimson as blood and clear as a glass of Burgundy. 'But what a stone!' cried Billee Ponthéveque, a *cocotte* who sat at the table losing all the money that she earned by breaking every Commandment but one, for she adored her father and mother and never failed to put aside for them as much as she gave in tips to the *croupiers*; but she never saw her parents, she would say, because of a funny idea they had that it was bad for her health to take cocaine on an empty stomach. 'Yes, it is flawless,' said the deep voice of that terrible man, shouting 'Banquo!' as an afterthought to some poor devil who thought he was going to get away unchallenged with fifty thousand francs. 'You can have it, child. Here you are.' But Billee Ponthéveque had always a sense of the proprieties, and so, as the saying is among the vulgar, she damned his blasted cheek for offering her so valuable a present in public, but he said that made no matter, for it was just because the ruby was flawless that it was quite valueless. 'If only it had the smallest flaw,' he boomed, 'it would be beyond price, for anyone can counterfeit a flawless ruby so that no expert can tell it from the original. . . .'

'*De la part de Madame Arpenden*,' said a voice, and after the passage of curses and cat-calls which are peculiar to the telephones of Paris, I heard Venice's voice.

147

'Venice! Venice!'

'That will do,' she said. 'Oh, that will do from you, thanks very much. Naps told me he saw you last night in that odd place, but did I see you?'

'You were asleep, Venice! But I am so glad to hear your voice after all these months, you wouldn't believe how glad. Venice, how are you?'

'I can't tell you now, I have to buy things. Listen, child, will you give me lunch to-day? Naps is busy for lunch. Listen, you must give me lunch to-day. I hate Paris.'

'But Napier told me you were going South to-day!'

'Oh, Naps is mad!' A boyish voice, a very boyish voice Venice had, even on a telephone in Paris. 'Not dangerously mad, but just mad. I never knew such a silly, one can't ever arrange anything beforehand with him. We are going by the evening train now, though we had everything booked for the one this morning. Listen, are you going to give me lunch? Oh that's a dear. About one, here at the Meurice...'

'Venice!' I called, but she was gone, and I could see her striding intently through the sombre halls of the Meurice, lovely Venice, like sunlight, just like English sunlight. And keeping my mind to sunlight, and avoiding all thoughts of death and dark enchantment, I said to myself that I would stay in Paris now that I was in Paris, rather than return to London, for over London lay a memorable fog, so said the Continental *Daily Mail*, as also it said Hats Off To France, the guileless thing. . . .

'*De la part du Docteur Mastaire*,' said the telephone this time, and there was that captain of men muttering, as he had promised he would in return for my playing bridge till all hours for his sake, that there was little change in Iris, but what little was for the better rather than for the worse. 'But don't go thinking,' said he sharply enough, 'that she's nearly out of the wood yet, because she isn't. And, by the way, she seems to want to see you, but remember that you'll do her the worst turn you can if you let that boy leave Paris to-day.'

'Yes, but,' I said, but I spoke only to the roar of the

148

Parisian scene, and I thought: 'Oh, well! He isn't going till the evening, anyhow.' And, still keeping my mind from dwelling on death and dark enchantments, I renewed my decision to stay in Paris a while, no matter how bitterly my sister might inveigh against me for letting her return to England unaccompanied. By now the rue de la Paix was languishing brilliantly in the stormy sunlight, and from my bath I could glimpse the cars lounging up and down and women walking swiftly by, intent on errands of the greatest importance and looking as attractive as only women can look when they are not thinking of men, while Englishmen and Americans walked seriously towards the chairs on the boulevards that they had read about in Nash's Magazine. Then my sister's car passed by towards the Place de l'Opéra, and she sitting forward with an air of moment, the ferrule of her parasol poised above the shoulder of the chauffeur, poor Mr. Hebblethwaite, who hated the French so! 'I will tell her,' I said, 'that I am regrettably detained in Paris owing to the call of my art, my Work, for I have just thought of a tale about a man who would not dance with his wife, and would you have me, I will put to her frankly, write a tale like that in a London fog?'

And it was while debating with myself over this silly fancy about a man who would not dance with his wife, for some good reason that I would no doubt hit upon in due course, and while congratulating myself that I had throughout the morning successfully avoided thinking of any of my friends' troubles, that I passed through the soft-carpeted and sombre halls of the Meurice, towards Venice, towards Venice, where she sat in a deep chair behind a paper, while in deep chairs all around sat people drinking cocktails and talking in low voices. All people talk in low voices when in the Meurice, and that, I dare venture to say, is one of the amenities peculiar to the Meurice among the hotels of all the world; but that is as it may be.

2

Venice was in high looks that day, Venice was all of a glitter, and that was because, she said at first, of this and that. But

149

we had no sooner passed through the glass doors into the restaurant than she said, she almost cried, that something marvellous had happened just a moment before. 'What do you think?' she dared me to guess, and when I said that I thought I would have some oysters she said she was too excited to eat anything, but might she have some ham and a glass of lager beer?

Venice hadn't met my sister but once or twice, but they had met again that morning in some shop or other, 'and I was complaining bitterly,' said Venice, 'about Napier, how he made a perfect jumble of everything by never knowing his own mind for two minutes running, and how we couldn't now find any sleepers in to-night's train—when she offered to lend us her car to take us to Monte Carlo! She couldn't bear the sight of it, she said, for another week at least, and that gives us plenty of time to get there and send it back, doesn't it? Now fancy your having a sister like that!'

'And how is Napier?' I asked. 'I only saw him for a moment. . . .'

'I can tell you,' said Venice in a sudden sombre moment, 'that I'm not a bit sorry to be leaving Paris as quick as quick. Naps has been working awfully hard lately, and here we come away for a holiday and the first thing he does is to go off the deep end about this old friend of his being ill.'

'Well, she is rather ill,' I said.

'Yes, I'm awfully sorry, really I am. I've never met her, but I saw her once, one night at the Loyalty just before my——'

'Yes, I remember, Venice.'

'And I thought she was the most lovely woman I'd ever seen, and rather sad-looking, which made her lovelier than ever. She'd be sad, I suppose, because of her two husbands and the things people say about her; for they do say some things, don't they?'

'*They! They*, Venice, will say anything. . . .'

'Yes, of course, but you know what I mean. And Naps, you see, can't bear anyone to be ill and miserable, and I'm sure he's got an idea that Mrs. Storm is lonely up there, but really, I think, he might consider himself a little, don't you?

And so I ordered the car at three o'clock this afternoon, and off we'll go. He'll be surprised when he gets here. . . .'

'Yes,' I said, 'I suppose he will.'

'Well,' said Venice, sticking out that Pollen jaw, 'there's no use in hanging about Paris, is there? And so I sent him a message to the Embassy, where he's been all morning, to come as soon as he could and not worry about getting "sleepers". And as I've already had his things packed we can start off as soon as he's here, which will be while we're at coffee, I shouldn't wonder.' That Pollen jaw! What, I wondered, was Venice thinking of when she stuck out that Pollen jaw like that? Maybe she had been disturbed by Napier's white-thunder looks when they got back to the hotel last night, and was wanting to get him to herself and normal as quickly as she could—and Provence, Oh Provence! It is not every day that a girl can motor through Provence with her lover. Venice's love was like a solid marble monument, and I said to myself that one should respect illness but also one should respect love, and so I held my peace.

Napier had not come by the time we had finished luncheon, and as we took two deep chairs in the corner of the lounge, where we would have coffee, Venice asked me if I knew anything about the psychology of men as regards children. When I had picked myself up I said that I would reserve my defence, laughing heartily the while, but now there was a cloud of thought over Venice's mad-blue eyes, and she was ever so serious, a fat cigarette tortured between her full, pale, dry lips. Venice, you know, said she hated the taste of lip-salve; but, with no idea at all of ever doubting Venice's word, one had noticed that it was only since her marriage that she had grown to hate it so consistently, and so it might be that Napier had made a face after kissing her one day, for it is the affectation of Englishmen to be tiresome about cosmetics, and if they are not tiresome about cosmetics they cannot be the right sort.

'Sugar?' I asked, and she nodded intently, her mad-blue eyes absorbed on a point of the thick carpet.

'How,' I said, 'you will love Provence!'

'Listen,' she said sharply. Wise those eyes were now, and

151

steady as stars in a cavern, looking into me as though judging me, balancing life.

'Well?' I said, to get it over. But what could she know?

She made herself look unimportant. 'Oh, it's only,' she said, 'that I can't have a baby.' And she looked at me with a frantic smile, and because every second of her twenty-one years seemed to me to be in that frantic smile I did not know what on earth to say, saying: 'You have probably been to some silly doctor——'

'I haven't!' she whispered, so fiercely that an old gentleman nearby almost spilled his coffee.

'Hush, Venice!'

'But I haven't been to any doctor——'

'Well, then,' said I wisely, 'in that case, of course, I don't see——'

'Oh, you don't!' she whispered with her fine, savage impatience. 'I tell you, my child, that I can't—I just feel that I can't, in my bones I feel it, that I'll never, never, never!' And she put a cloud of smoke between us to make her smile look plausible, but through the smoke her eyes looked as though they were holding back a pain.

'Venice, darling,' I pleaded, 'I'm not old enough to deal with an emergency like this. What you need is a man of Hilary's years to turn you over and smack you and tell you that as long as you're such a child you don't deserve to have one——'

'I'm so miserable,' she said.

'But it's absurd, Venice! I mean, it's just nerves, you can't possibly know——'

'Do you actually think,' she grabbed a cigarette fiercely from my case, 'that I've got to go to some dud doctor and have him poking about all over me before I know what's *me*! Of course I can know, and I do know, and it's a shame, and I daren't tell Napier. . . .'

'You better hadn't, on such insufficient evidence. I know what I'd do.'

'Darling, darling, *darling*! Tell me, do men love children? Really, really, I mean? Would Napier hate it if he knew that I was as barren as that old fig-tree——'

'Venice, how dare you let your nerves get the better of you like this! I've only got to be away from England for four months, and I find you in this silly state!'

'Oh, but answer my questions! Why is everyone so *awful* these days! You see, I never know what's going on in Napier's mind, never! Do you think I would if he loved me?'

'"If?"' I said. '"If", Venice?' Was I now to defend Napier's love for Venice? And then I found that she was looking at me with wide-open, motherly, amused eyes.

'You don't actually think,' she almost laughed, 'that I ever thought that Napier loved me?'

'Well, I have thought so,' I bravely admitted. 'Certainly I have. It is quite usual.'

'But isn't my gentleman friend stupid!' she suddenly giggled. 'Of course, I know he loves me—as much as he can ever love anyone. But that's all, don't you see. . . .'

She stared at the wounded end of her poor cigarette, and lit another from my case, as that was handy. The number of cigarettes that girl smoked, and how she tortured them!

'You see,' she said, knitting together her golden eyebrows so that I should see, 'Napier can't love like other people— me, for instance, and perhaps you, though I'd have my doubts about you. I suppose people are born like that, and you've got to take it or leave it. Napier loves just as much as he can—which means that he's willing, oh anxious, to do anything in the world for you—but you're never quite sure what he's thinking about while he's doing it. See what I mean?'

'I try hard, Venice.'

'Yes. And so, you see, you've always got a feeling that he's keeping something back in himself, something rather important, if you see what I mean, something you can't get a grip on but that's there to *be* gripped, that Napier would like to be gripped, if you see what I mean——'

'I'll tell you what I see, Venice. I've seen it before, and so I recognise it——'

'But I don't want to hear about your fancy friends! I want to talk about myself.'

'The matter is, Venice, that any woman in love with a

reserved man will pass her spare time in ascribing stormy villainies to his secret nature, whereas generally the poor devil is——'

'Stormy villainies,' said Venice quietly, 'is good.'

'Women,' I said largely, cursing myself, 'are always making themselves miserable about what they don't see in a man, as though what they did see wasn't quite enough.'

The full dry lips ravaged the cigarette for a while. Then they said, thoughtfully: 'The other night we were dining at Fay Avalon's, just a very few of us, and when someone said that Mrs. Storm was a nymphomaniac Napier went as white as death——'

'And what did the other guests do, Venice? It's the least Napier could have done, as she's an old friend of his.'

'Of course,' said Venice very calmly, looking into her cup as though for more coffee, 'I don't know her, or anything about her, except just what people say. And I'd never have known that Naps even knew her if I hadn't seen him speak to her that night at the Loyalty. That was the night her brother died, wasn't it? Napier had never mentioned her name before—nor since, if it comes to that, until last night, when he seemed so upset about her that after a while I upped and said he could go and take a room at the nursing-home if he liked——'

'Wasn't that rather harsh, Venice? After all, he's known her a very long time, and it upsets anyone to see an old friend very ill.'

'Oh, I know, I know!' she said eagerly. 'You mustn't think I was jealous, but I suppose it just got on my nerves a bit, seeing that he'd never spoken about her before. And that's why, you see,' she showed all her very white teeth in an utterly insincere smile, 'I'm rather wretched about this idea of not having any children. Do listen, *please* listen! Oh, why is everyone so tiresome! I'm not talking about Mrs. Storm now, but about the Mrs. Storms of life. You see, they've got a lot more to give a chap than anyone like me has—I mean to say, they know *how* to bring everything out of a man, how to make him a lover and all that—a real lover, I mean, a fire-and-ice, pits-and-mountains, sunlight-and-

154

shadows, nice-and-nasty sort of lover, whereas people like Napier and me are just the same with each other as millions of other people, the men being pretty good duds at loving and the women even worse duds at being loved, if you see what I mean. Oh, I know! A man might be a just come-here-girl-oh-darling lover with one woman and then be a marvellous lover with another, just because, you see, she'd know how to make him be. Of course, with their experience . . .'

I sat there in that deep armchair, subdued by the thought of the awful helplessness of men and women to understand one another, and of the terrible thing it would be for some of them if ever they did understand one another, and how many opportunities the devil is always being given of making plunder out of decent people. Here was Venice groping blindly in the corridors of her love, looking for the one golden key which she couldn't find among the treasures there displayed. For there were treasures there. Venice was quite certain, marvellously certain she was, that Napier loved her as much as he could ever love anyone. Oh, but her love was quite big enough to cope with that nonsense of Napier's! And, since the love of a good woman for a man is a compliment to all men, maybe I looked at her with understanding, for she gave me a sudden sharp smile, and said, quite calmly: 'And so, you see, if I don't have a baby soon I'll bust.'

'Darling, darling, *darling*!' a low voice mocked behind us so that we started, and there above our deep chairs stood Napier, and I remember how he gave me one quick clear look, not in the least a conspiratorial look, but just a clear look, as though the last time he had seen me we had both faced a great danger; and between two men there can be no bond so faint and yet so binding as that which is forged of an understanding which is unmentionable between them; you may not like the bond, as I most sincerely did not like it, for it was Venice who was my friend, but there it is, a bond of invisible wire that cuts at the wrists of the mind.

Napier looked composed, but always the fever lurked in the dark eyes, always the dark eyes looked as though they were suffering from what neither you nor he could tell. That greyhound, sensitive and doubtful and poised . . . for flight!

155

And he somehow looked queerly festive in that sombre, conventional hall, with his faded I Zingari tie and the brown Shetland waistcoat which was for the most part unbuttoned.

'Oh, Naps, such a wonder!' cried Venice on the instant, and I saw what one is so apt to see after an intimate talk with a woman, that one has only been talking to a mood. Venice was in an instant as I had always seen her with Napier, impetuous, imperious, gay. 'What do you think, Naps! I have got a car, a lovely car, swift and shining, and a man called Hebblethwaite for chauffeur. Now what do you think of that?'

'I think,' said Napier gravely, smiling at me, 'that it must be an English car. And what do you intend doing about it? Driving in the Bois? What?'

'Driving in the Bois! Am I mad! My child, it's his sister's car, and she has lent it to us, and we are going South in it, that is what we are going to do. And I ordered Mr. Hebble-thwaite at three, and I've had all your things packed, and I've settled the bill, so we can go right away.'

Napier stared at her—he was sitting now—and it was as though he had put his hand to his mouth and placed a smile there. It was a very charming, helpless smile. I said something to the effect that I must go now, but no one was taking any notice of me. Venice was saying, in a voice tangled with confusion, impatience, a sort of gaiety: 'But, Naps, you don't mean to say you want to stay still another night in this foul Paris, when we might be in the sun!'

Napier scowled, the smile still on his mouth. 'Of course, I don't *want*, but——'

'Oh, but Naps, I'd like to go straight away, right away, as the Yankees say! And I thought we might have tea at Fontainebleau and I'd show you the place where I was at school. . . .'

'Now look here,' Napier scowled, touching her knee with one finger, 'I can't quite do that, Venice. You see, I made a sort of promise to that doctor fellow that I would go and sit with Iris just for a while this afternoon——'

'Oh, I see,' said Venice. 'Well, in that case. . . .'

'Give her an idea—that's what the doctor fellow said—

that some of her friends care whether she lives or dies, for anyone would be rather lonely up there. What? I went round for a minute this morning just to inquire, but I didn't see her, as they said that——'

'I thought you were at the Embassy this morning,' Venice said, in a very natural voice: and she crushed out her cigarette on the marble top of the table, and she picked up her vanity-case.

'Yes, so I was,' Napier scowled, 'but I just went round there for a minute——'

'Oo, what a long way to go for a minute!' sighed Venice. 'When one can always telephone. . . .' And she rose from her chair. Somehow an immense new dignity had suddenly come on Venice. Napier rose, facing her, smiling under his scowl, as though she had made a joke. I rose, saying that I must be going. . . .

'As a matter of fact,' said Venice brightly, 'as I knew you were so worried about her I rang up that place this morning, and they told me she was *assez bien*, if you see what I mean. . . .'

'Venice, that was kind!' Napier smiled with his whole thin, fine face, and I thought how glad I was that he didn't know what had caused Iris's illness, for would he then have smiled gratefully at Venice for inquiring after her? And he said, as though happy in her understanding: 'I mean, we can start off first thing in the morning, can't we? What? It's rotten luck, cutting in on your holiday like this, but— well, friendship has duties. . . .'

'But of course I understand, Naps!' And Venice turned at me, smiling as though to show me what sort of a man that Napier was. As though she didn't understand! As though she didn't know the duties of friendship! She said to Napier, with a fine air of business settled: 'Well, I'll just go upstairs now and tell Mary to unpack some things again. And I do so hope, Naps,' she said with a fine large smile, 'that your friend won't die, for then how will I manage a man who has nothing left to live for?' And Venice turned to me, and her hand was in mine, and we were saying good-bye, when Napier said briskly:

'Come on, then. We'll go now. Might as well, now the car's there. . . .'

'But, Naps!' Venice turned on him, stared wide at him. . . .

'Oh, come on,' said Napier, as though eaten by impatience.

'But!' she pleaded desperately. 'But, Naps, I don't really want to go now a bit if you would rather stay until to-morrow. . . .'

'I don't want to stay,' said Napier, quite reasonably, but he turned away as he spoke. One saw the set white profile. 'Come along, Venice. There's been enough talk about this already. . . .'

'But, Naps,' said Venice bitterly, 'it's wrong of you to go now, if she needs you. You know it's wrong and naughty, what you're doing. Naps dear, I'd very much rather not go now if you don't mind——'

'Well, you'll jolly well have to go now, if at all,' Napier tore at her so sharply that she stared at him dumbly for a full second, and then she made a white smile, half to him, half to me. 'Silly baby,' she said. 'Such a silly baby. . . .' And she was again about to say good-bye to the unwilling spectator when Napier broke in, to me, beginning with astonishing grimness and ending quite conversationally: 'I say, if you should happen to see Iris in the course of the next few days, you might tell her I couldn't stop, and'—here the grimness suddenly ended—'say good-bye from me. Will you? What?'

I said of course I would, and then he took Venice's arm to lead her away. But Venice dragged, her eyes intent on the carpet, and when she suddenly looked round at me I saw that her eyes were brimming with tears.

'Men!' she smiled. 'Men!'

'Men!' mocked Napier, but he smiled, too. 'What?'

'But don't you think it's a shame!' she bitterly appealed to me. 'There's Mrs. Storm very ill and expecting to see Napier, all lonely up there, and here Naps puts me in the beastly position of a wife who——'

But I was thinking that the shame of it lay in the dis-advantage at which a woman always is with a man whom she loves more than she feels he loves her, the disadvantage of never knowing how far she may use an artificial pride, for there is no real pride in a heart in love, without upsetting the apple-cart.

'Nonsense, Venice,' Napier was saying, and it was his mildness, his calmness, that was so astonishing now. It was as though the man had suddenly found peace: as though love-lost Tristram raving in the wilderness had, in a sudden flash, realised that he was trying God too far. . . .

'Nonsense, Venice,' he scowled, still holding her arm. 'She isn't beginning to expect me and she never did. I just turned up by chance. . . .' He turned to me with that clear, not conspiratorial, look in his eyes. 'You will say good-bye from me, won't you?'

'Of course,' I said. 'I may be seeing her to-day.'

'Yes, just say good-bye,' said Napier, and as he and I shook hands Venice laughed nervously: 'Dear, how serious! I can't bear good-byes. . . .' And so she shook my hand without saying good-bye, saying instead: 'You have been a darling to let me bore you with my nonsense, and I hope you'll pray that it keeps fine for us in your sister's car. See you in London soon. . . .'

And away they went, Napier and Venice, he still holding her arm just above the elbow, she still appearing to drag a little, across the now deserted and darkening lounge to the glass doors, which a small boy opened to them. But the small boy must hold it open, for they stood in the doorway a short while, as it might be they were arguing, and through the gloom of the afternoon I could see Napier's set white profile, drawn in ivory it might have been, and the way he seemed to be smiling grimly into Venice's upturned face, and I could see the way Venice's face suddenly lit right up with a smile, just like a garden with the sun after rain. Now what could he have said to make her smile so, or had he said just any little thing, which her love, most princely alchemist, had straightway transmuted into a golden word?

He has said farewell to his love, I said to myself, and now, if love has left any honour at all in him, he must convince himself that there never was any love to say adieu to, for even so much would be a disloyalty to Venice. He has

159

renounced his love, I thought to myself, as a man of honour should do, but he knows that a man of honour is not worthy the name unless he can also convince himself that there never was any love to renounce, for that would make him feel martyred for his wife's sake, and that would be a treachery to Venice. . . .

And, smoking one more cigarette in the calm security of the darkening, deserted lounge, while a waiter or two began laying the small tables roundabout for tea, I seemed to understand Napier as he were myself, and he the most different man from me that could well be found. Looking at the thing full and square, you might say that Napier had done a caddish thing; in fact, that was what you had to say, looking at the thing full and square; but it is a mistake to look at everything full and square, and it is too easy to dismiss people's actions as 'caddish' and the like, for such are no more than words coined to save people from wearing their minds with undue thinking, and tiresome people will go on and on using them with a great show of conviction, in the very same way that they will put down a book by Mr. Shaw or Maître Anatole France and say: 'Look at Dickens!'

Now Napier had suddenly come upon a queer sort of peace following on a second's cruel decision not to go and see Iris again, a very cruel decision, I thought, and she no doubt expecting every moment to see his face in the clouds all about her. 'How like a man,' I could hear a feminine voice, 'first to stain what he thinks his "honour" by taking a mistress, and then to retrieve his idiotic "honour" by hurting his mistress!' But, maybe, how could one tell? maybe Napier had suddenly realised, in the very moment that Venice spoke, that if he went to sit with Iris even once more he might fall right down into the pit of dark enchantment and he might send all life but that which he found in Iris to the deuce and nevermore return to Venice, to whom he was held by every one of those principles that are born in the blood of a Napier, a Hilary, a Guy de Travest. And I wondered what I would have done had my life been so weighted and tangled with people's emotions as Napier's must always have been, and what, I wondered, would I have

160

done had I, in Napier's place, been as unaware of myself until a fiercely revealing moment three nights before my marriage to my betrothed? The answer to that was very easy, and it was by the measure of the ease with which it came that I could judge of Napier's struggle with himself to keep his pledge to Venice, for never were two men so different as Napier and me. I, I would have broken my troth, that is what I would have done, and I would have broken away from any other thing that stood in the way of my passion, I would have fled father, friends, career, honour, everything, at the call of the enchanted voice whispering of better dreams. *There are better dreams!* For so I remembered a phrase in a book telling of the love of a lady of the sea for a mortal man: *There are better dreams.* . . .

A waiter, no doubt wishing for something to do, asked me if I would take tea, but I thanked him, saying I would rather not, for it was not yet half-past three, and saying to myself: 'In every man there is always unfolding a dream of things that never were and never can be, since life will always be what it is and men and women will always be what they are, and so we will always go on, men of high fancies and low flights, and the higher the fancy is the lower the flight will be, as it is written in the Scriptures concerning vanity. And maybe Napier had had his dream when he was very young, and then the world came along and told him that his dream was very silly, and so he did not dream any more, until one night he was appalled to hear calling him a playmate's voice, but a playmate's voice torn with the wonder of life and the sadness of living, whispering to him: *There are better dreams*. And he listened, and he was lost, and then he found himself again in renunciation, as so many Englishmen will always be doing, for it is as true as any generalisation can be to say of Englishmen that they will often only find themselves when they have lost themselves.'

I could see Napier during those two days and two nights before his marriage, I could see him casting his mind this way and that way, to find that each way lay dishonour, on Venice's side dishonour with cruelty, and on Iris's side dishonour with whatever happiness can go with dishonour

161

to a man such as Napier; and that, I thought, would be very little, for can a man of honour embark on any dishonourable adventure without first of all taking every care and precaution that neither he nor his companion shall enjoy the fruits of it? But that, I thought to myself, is a woman's thought, surely I am not becoming effeminate!

And you could see Napier scowling as he beat his mind to know what a man should do, for you might be sure that Iris had not tried to persuade him, she would have loved him and left him, putting the seal of her kiss on his lips and the seal of her voice on his ears, telling him only to do what he thought was right. So Napier would be beating his mind, always driving from him the phantom of a compromise, a fair enough phantom, that: how he would go to Venice and tell her that it had happened to him, born vile, to do thus and thus, and would she please forget him, for forgive him she could not? But that was just what Venice would do, proudly and imperiously she would forgive him, and then he would have to confess the real truth, which was not that he had held Iris in his arms, but that he loved Iris with his body and soul as he never could love Venice, that he loved Iris and Iris loved him as though they had drunk a love-philtre together, and in that way he did not love Venice . . . but Venice, unfortunately, did love him in that very same way, and you could see Napier just quailing before the cruelty of telling Venice that, after all, he did not love her. And you could see him marrying Venice, thinking the while that maybe the best could be made of a wretched business if Iris and he kept to the promise they had sworn together, never to meet again. And they had kept to it very stoutly, the Iris who had plucked the device For Purity from her heart had kept to her promise, and Napier would have kept to his promise for ever and a day but for the chance of illness in the obscure silence of the Paris night; and so it had come to pass that he must see Iris yet once again, and Iris maybe thinking that she was seeing her lover in a dream, she who had nothing to live for and did not care one farthing if she lived or died. But that dream, said Conrad Masters later, saved her life, that dream was the angel appointed to save

162

Iris from death, for that time. How wise was Iris, how wise, she who knew that the Marches were never let off anything. For even the angels were against her.

But it was to Conrad Masters that I had first to break the news of Napier's—well, from Masters's point of view, desertion while on duty. And very whole-heartedly did that man swear, the telephone simply throbbing with his pregnant mutter; but I, thinking there could be little profit in arguing at this time of day that the whole thing wasn't and never had been any of my business, merely suggested: would it be any sort of idea for me to see her for a minute?

'You!'

'But your instructions!' I pointed out. 'Whereas, if I may say so, you have so far been so "nice" to me that I have lost five hundred francs at bridge on your behalf.' That is what I was driven to saying, but I doubt if he heard me, the telephones of Paris being very well adapted for selective hearing, for all he said was that he was due at the Boulevard Pierre Abel in half an hour, and he would pick me up on the way if I liked. If I liked! As though, Heavens above, there was one single thing in all this wretched business about which one might say, with any hope of being attended to, 'If I liked, this,' or 'If I liked, that. . . .'

I

Twilight was spreading her cloak as we passed from the lodge into the flagged yard. Several windows of the tall red building were already alight, and on the sill outside the largest window of all, which was not alight, stood a pineapple and some grapes on a plate.

Within, the feet fell chill on the chequered flags of the hall; and this, by its size, should have been a spacious-seeming hall, but that was not the way it impressed one. There was one of those bamboo hat-stands with a strip of looking-glass running up the middle of it, but I followed my companion's example in not leaving more than my hat, for that was a chilly place. Through a great oaken double-door on our right came murmurings of a religious nature and every now and then a woman's manlike voice raised, no doubt, in exhortation. Conrad Masters explained that some of the nuns would be at their devotions whenever they could manage, their religious observances being so deranged by night-duty and this and the other. 'But why,' I thought to ask, 'is Mrs. Storm here, for don't you as a rule immure your patients in the Avenue Malakoff?'

'She wished it,' said Conrad Masters sharply. 'She has a God.'

And thereupon he left me, to see another patient he had there, but I had not waited more than a few minutes in the waiting-room, which had that intangible odour of old cloth and illness, when I was called upstairs by an old stern nun, hard and silent as a rock, and I remember wondering:

'Good my God, if this should be Iris's day-nurse, Oh poor Iris!'

The stairway we ascended was handsome and wide, of polished oak, the most dignified stairway you could well imagine in a nursing-home. It swept in a noble curve to a broad passage, also of oak, as, no doubt, was only fit and proper in a nursing-home patronised by *une clientèle européenne la plus chic*. But maybe it was a little too dignified, I thought, it was sombre; and the old stern nun who was my

164

guide did not seek to relieve the atmosphere, giving me a massive black shoulder and to my question no more than a stern whisper, which was no more and no less than a shout of disapproval: '*Assez bien, monsieur, assez bien. Nous nous confions en Dieu.*'

The chill, the gloom, the nun, the air of religious prostration, to which I am lamentably ill-accustomed, had quite killed my spirit, else, as I did my best quietly to follow her up the long, dark, uncarpeted passage, I had put it to her that to trust in God is very well but must He be trusted at such little expense, for in these oaken passages they had no more than a jet or two of gas-light, and wasn't it also reasonable to suppose that the patients behind the doors, each inscribed with a Saint's name, would lie the more comfortably for a strip of carpet along the passages? From below, as though from the bowels of the earth in labour, one might still faintly hear the murmurings of a religious nature and the woman's manlike voice raised, no doubt, in exhortation; but I supposed the patients would not be minding that for they would be Catholics, and I wondered if Iris was a Catholic, but nowadays that is the last thing one ever learns about anybody, whether they are Catholic, Anglican, Jew, or what they are. . . .

As we came by a certain door, not far from which a gas-jet flamed an ailing yellow, it was opened from within and I saw before me the sweetest face that I ever saw in my life, and I knew that her God had been good to Iris.

'*Sœur Virginie,*' said the stern old nun, and I am glad to say I never saw *her* again. Sister Virginie, looking up at me with a grave smile, for she was very little, greeted me by my name, and do you know that I said: 'Sister Virginie, had I only met you last night I would have slept much better than I did.'

She had altogether such a neat and tidy look, an inner look as well as an outer look, that you must be sceptical indeed not to believe at once that if ever there was a nurse to soothe away death here she was before you, her hands folded over her wooden crucifix, smiling up at you as though you were a gentle friend. Her face was oval and so white, but

165

white in a different way, a soft clear way, and it was only when I came to think back on this sweet lady that I realised that of course this would be so because Sister Virginie never had used powder and such things, and that must also be why she had the lips of a girl, although what I could see of the dark brown eyes under the nun's coif showed the understanding of more than forty years.

'You see, I know your name,' she said. She did not need to whisper. 'Madame has a great regard for you, I must tell you. Now, you must not talk when you go in. She will look, look. But you must not say one word. She will see you are there, and it will make her content that her friend has thought of her.'

The oak door behind her was just ajar, and within I could see a faint pink glow, as it might be of a deeply-shaded light far in the room. Across the door, just above Sister Virginie's coif, for she was very little, was painted in faded black lettering the name of a Saint, but what the Saint was I could not make out, and the only other time I called there I forgot to look.

'Now, remember,' Sister Virginie was saying, 'you must not say one word in there. She will look, that is all. But how she looks, as though she is listening to the choir of angels!'

'Sister Virginie,' I said, 'do you promise me that she will not die?'

And Sister Virginie smiled up at me with a gaiety that I have only seen on the still faces of women in old French books.

'To-day we have thought she will not die,' she said, 'for last night we gave her a *piqûre du cœur*. . . .'

2

I wish I could describe that room in which I saw Iris lying, for it was such a strange room to find in a nursing-home, and you would not have been surprised to find the like in one of the hotels in the Faubourg Saint-Germain. But the truth is that I never yet was sure of the appointments of any room I might find myself in, except maybe that it was large

166

or small, that it was panelled or papered or distempered, and whether or not you walked on a carpet, a strip of oil-cloth or a parquet floor.

It seemed to me that I must walk a long way to the bed near the window. It was a great four-poster bed, and it had a very tall head, of carved oak. There seemed to be but dark wood in that strange sick-room, and the perfume of wood. Beneath my careful feet was a narrow strip of drugget slanting from the door across to the bed, but on all sides of this strip the floor shone vast and brown in the dim light of a shaded lamp that stood on the heavy oak mantelpiece.

Never was one so little conscious of the odours of a sick-room, but, although I wouldn't swear to it, there might have been the faint tang of furniture-polish, and maybe, as I stole nearby the great wide bed by the large window, that was the scent of Napier's roses, which spread their heads from a *carafe* on a small table near the foot of the bed. Sitting against the *carafe* was a large white doll with her head asleep among Napier's roses and a red silk handkerchief tied around her wrist. Ah, Mio Mi Marianne, unrepentant Magdalen, even the toys of your sisters heed your dominion! It was dark by the bed, for the light from the lamp did not reach nearly so far. The blind was not more than half-lowered down the large window, and across the courtyard I could just see the light within the lodge and, on the sill outside, the shape of a pineapple and some grapes on a plate.

The tall oak panel at the head cast a black shadow over the darkness of the bed, and at first I could no more than make out the shape of Iris's head. I could hear the faint hush of her breathing. Boy's head, curly head, white and tiger-tawny. But gone now the tawny pride of the tiger, gone the curls. Very tidily brushed her hair was, tidily swept back from the forehead, tidily lying on each cheek. It would be damp, I thought, to lie so flat. Her head lay like a dark flower on the pillow.

She was asleep, I thought, and I was going away, very well content to have heard the faint but regular hush of her breathing. She had fallen asleep, I thought, even as Sister Virginie had left her, and could there be better news than

167

that she was asleep, breathing like a child? Then how frightened I was, just as I was about to steal away, to see her eyes wide open, staring up at me. Dark as her hair were her eyes, and almost as big as her head. I was in terror, real damp terror, lest she should be taking me for Napier. I did not know what to do, and her great dark eyes staring up at me. It would be like a stab from the mists about her to be thinking it was her lover who had come and to realise that it was me. Then I was happy to see that there was understanding in the dark, still eyes, she was not taking me for Napier, she was not dreaming. She was hurt, her eyes said. And, because I might not speak, I just touched her cheek with my hand, and the hair on her cheek was chill and damp. But her eyes seemed to wish to be saying something. She was hurt, her eyes said, but more than that I could not understand, and so I bent down nearer to her face. The skin was like thin grey paper over her shoulder-blades, her lips were chapped, and they drooped.

'Dying. . . .'

I shook my head sternly. Her lips were so dry and rough, and now I saw through a mist what I had not seen before, that her eyes were stricken with fear. That is what her eyes had wished me to understand, that now she was terrified of dying. That was what her dream had done, that was what last night's *piqûre du cœur* had done. I turned to go away. But her eyes, dark and stricken, seemed to flutter, then they seemed to look at the roses on the small table. What is it, I thought, what is it she wants, and her eyes fluttering like that? Beside the white skirts of the doll whose head was asleep among Napier's roses lay the great emerald and a small tortoise-shell comb. I thought of the tawny formal curls trembling like voiceless bells before the looking-glass in my flat above the mean lane, and when I took up the small comb there might have been a smile on the tiny grey face, like the shadow of a candle's flicker. I passed the small comb through her hair, and it passed so easily through the straight damp hair, and then at last her eyes were closed and I went away as quickly as I could. Sister Virginie stood a little way up the passage, but for reasons of my own I did not wait for her to approach where I stood under the ailing yellow flame of the gas-jet, but went towards the darkness where she was.

'Were you good?' she asked me, and I think I said that I had tried to be good. 'But, Sister Virginie, she is afraid! She is terrified!'

'Then she is being good, too,' the nun smiled. 'She has been too little afraid of dying, and then it was we who were afraid.' She looked at me very seriously, and seemed to purse her lips. I knew what she was going to ask, and I did not know where to look. 'Do you know, monsieur, if we will be allowed to give her another *piqûre du cœur*? Madame has been very unhappy, and it is good to have happy dreams. . . .'

I do not remember what I said, but Sister Virginie said magnificently: 'Then I will lie to her for the time being,' and when she had gone I stood at the head of the oaken stairway, thinking how I would like to be very alone for a minute or two. Now and then a nun would pass softly but quickly along the passage behind me, she would seem to be sliding along, and then there came a firmer step, and out of the tail of my eye I saw that man's great brown coat ballooning towards me.

'Well as can be expected,' he muttered gloomily. I looked at him. 'Better, really,' he muttered gloomily. 'Ready?'

We went down the oaken stairway, treading on our toes. There was a sickly whisper of incense in the air, and I found that I had a headache.

'But I wish to blazes,' growled that man, 'that you hadn't let that boy go. You could have stopped him. . . .'

'No,' I said, 'I couldn't. Besides, I didn't want to.'

'Mm. Well, how did you find her? Wasted, isn't she?'

'Masters,' I said, 'she is lying there terrified!' For that was all I could think about, that and the feel on my fingers of the damp, chill hair that had no waves in it now.

Masters said: 'And a very good thing for her she is terrified. Keep her bucked up, that will. But I wish to blazes. . . .'

'Yes, I heard you,' I said, fumbling with the latch of the great doors.

'Women!' snapped Masters. 'Here, let me.'

169

'I don't suppose,' I said, 'that there are many worse sights than a helpless woman afraid. . . .'

'You get used to it,' said Masters gloomily, but I was thinking that Napier would not have been at all used to it, and that he had been very wise in his good-bye, for as sure as anything I was that Venice could not have afforded to let Iris have even one more *piqûre du cœur.* . . .

'You don't look so well yourself,' said Masters.

'Growing-pains, Masters. One is always growing up, at other people's expense. . . .'

3

I was not to see her again for a while. That man said: 'You did her no good the other day. The reverse. She has something on her mind she wants to say to you, and she can't, and it worries her. Naturally. . . .'

'Your instructions,' I said. 'She will be angry with you, Masters.'

'When she is well,' snapped that captain of men, 'she may burst, if I may say so. And so I'll tell her. But in the meanwhile you will have to wait ten days. Or more.'

It was more, quite a while more, and when I went again into the oak-room of the Saint whose name I forgot to look at Iris met me with accusing eyes. She did not turn her head, she just gave me a sideways, accusing look. Turnings of head were discouraged, she must lie very still, oh for a long time, for that, it seems, is the way of septic poisoning. And Masters had said to me in the passage outside: 'If she as much as moves a finger, God help you!'

'You should not be in Paris,' she whispered, not without vehemence. 'And why are you laughing, please?'

'Why, at your voice! I do believe, Iris, that it's stronger than you at last.'

'Yes, but you should not be in Paris, that I'm sure of. You have waited to see me,' she complained bitterly, but I protested that never was such nonsense, for why in the name of common-sense would I wait to see her? 'But, Iris, the very night I arrived in Paris I had an idea for a tale, and I thought I would stay in Paris to write it.'

'You must tell it to me. Oh, at once. Oh, please. . . .' And the voice expired. And we waited. 'I can't laugh,' she said bitterly, 'because it hurts. Everything hurts. . . .'

'Iris,' I said, 'I am so sorry. . . .'

'Yes.' She gave me a long sideways look.

'Yes,' she said. 'But please to tell me your tale. What is it about? What is it called?'

'No, Iris, I mustn't tell it to you. It was indiscreet of me to mention it, and you only just returned from the valley of death. It is a terrible story. Everyone dies. It is about a man who would not dance with his wife.'

'Yes, but . . . Oh, why wouldn't he dance with his wife? What a silly man! You do get some beastly ideas, I do think. . . .'

'Please, Iris, be still and good! That man said he would fire me out for two pins.' So grey she looked, frail beyond frailty, in the gay afternoon light. It was the fifteenth afternoon of February, as I remember well.

Never moving her head, only her eyes vivid with restless insurgent life, she whispered defiantly: 'As long as I lie quiet like this no one can do anything to me or . . . fire you out or anything. You just . . . stay where you are. Be brave, child. . . .'

Now there were queer, funny things in the great eyes of the still head. They were childish, too, and I laughed at them, but she would not laugh, because it hurt her.

We sat in silence, not to tire her. She lay flat on her back, her head on a pillow which was so low as to be only a pillow by courtesy. Her eyes would be fixed on the ceiling, and then she would look sideways at me, and that was when I seemed to see queer, funny things in her eyes. They were as though glistening with bits of things . . . fear, pride, a sort of childish glee, a sort of childish naughtiness, a sort of childish shamefacedness. It was as though she was terrified of her new toy, and very proud of it, too—her returning life. And then the shamefacedness, an almost guilty look, as though she had just cheated someone out of something in a funny way. Not that she hadn't been very clever either, her look seemed to say. And somehow I was made a fellow-conspirator in all this . . . in the terror, pride, glee, mischief, shamefacedness with which

171

she was deliciously playing with her new toy, returning life.

She said suddenly, in an enormous voice which she had obviously been husbanding for the purpose: 'No one wants me. . . .' And I think, but I am not sure, that she would have giggled if she could.

'Iris, you'll have Masters in here if you go shouting like that.'

'He didn't want me, even. . . .'

'Who didn't? Masters didn't?'

'No. God.'

'Oh, I see,' I said.

She panted breathlessly, eager to be talking: 'I made my application, all . . . all in order. Forms all filled in and everything. But . . . Oh, they weren't impressed. Not a bit, they weren't——'

'Oi, you're talking too much, Iris!'

'Oi to you. Listen. . . . The old man said to me: "Well, young woman, and what do you want?" I wasn't afraid, not a bit. Had all my forms ready and everything. . . . "What do I want, Father?" says I. "Why, I'm as good as dead, that's what I am. Doctor's face all of a blur, nurse's face all of a blur, temperature 106—why, I *am* dead, if it comes to that!" "Nonsense," says God. "Never saw a woman more alive in all my life. Ho, Gabriel! Expel this woman!" "Yes, but!" I said. "I want to die, I do, I do!" "In that case," says He, "death will be a great disappointment to you. We want none of your sort here, young woman. Ho, Michael, Gabriel! Eject this sinner. She's still alive. . . ."'

After a long pause I found those great eyes looking at me very seriously. She whispered: 'Owe it to you. I mean, life. Thank you.'

'Iris, to me! My dear, what rot!'

'Not rot at all. If you hadn't been kind enough to come round again that night to . . . inquire, he'd have called and found only that old nun there and she would have said . . . *assez bien*, and away he'd have gone. And me, too. . . . See?

'*And,*' she said, 'that ptomaine poisoning. You dear, you dear! Oh, how I like you when you're not looking! Genius, I call that. And when . . . Masters told me, I laughed so they had to give me morphia. Darling, these *piqûres*! I got holes all over me. . . .'

'*Piqûre du cœur*,' I let slip.

'*Piqûre du* what?'

'Nothing,' I said.

'You're laughing at me,' she whispered, 'that's what you're doing. I'm going to close my eyes now for five minutes. But don't go. Don't go. . . .'

It was the fifteenth afternoon of February, as I remember well, and Mademoiselle Printemps was dancing in the sunlight that fell in a shower of gold on the window-sill, on which now stood three nectarines and a large pear on a plate. But the blind was drawn so that she could dance only in a bright splash across the little mountain which, I ventured to suppose, was made by Iris's toes. In the shade of the room stood the small table, and on the small table the doll with the red silk handkerchief round her wrist sat sleeping beneath tall sprays of mimosa, sprays of bright yellow powdered with fresh gold. . . .

'Yes,' I heard her voice, faint, faint, and when I looked round from the mimosa to her I saw that her eyes had followed mine to a garden in the South.

'Iris, I was to say good-bye. . . .'

'I know,' she said gravely; and she smiled. 'I heard him. . . .'

'You heard him, Iris?'

'Dreams, clouds, mists. Faces, phantoms, fates, words. Yes, I heard him. . . .' And she smiled, with every bit of her eyes, as though to reassure me. 'That's quite all right,' she said.

'Iris, I'm so sorry,' I said. 'Do you . . . promise that that's quite all right?'

She was looking at me with a smile. . . .

'Promise,' she suddenly sobbed, and her eyes were streaming with tears. I was terrified.

'Lie here,' she sobbed, 'like a mummy . . . no inside left, nothing left . . . thinking and thinking and thinking . . . trying to lie to myself right and left, north and south . . . can't have what I want, so must make up stories . . . and you sit there stiff as a pole saying "Promise" . . . call yourself a friend. . . . You don't know how ill I've been!'

173

'I do, I do, Iris! For pity's sake! If that man comes in and finds you like th——'

'And you think I'm awful,' she whispered helplessly. She stared at me. 'You think I'm awful,' she said quite calmly.

'Iris,' I said, 'I like you. Of course, if I didn't . . .'

'Of course,' she said, 'he doesn't know. . . .'

'Of course,' I said.

'And he'll never know. . . .'

'Good,' I said.

'As for me,' she whispered . . .

On her forehead there were little beads of wet. I wiped them off with my handkerchief, and she said: 'My nose, too, please. Had my hair waved . . . but it never stays when you're not well. Got to be well to have curly hair. . . .'

'And, Iris, if you don't have it cut soon it will be as long as a woman's hair.'

'As for me,' she whispered, 'all this effort wasted . . . no playmate, no nothing. Masters warned me, too. . . . Dead as dead, the poor darling was. . . .' Slowly, slowly, tears were crawling down the tiny grey cheeks. Hastily I wiped them away, hearing a step outside. 'Nothing, nothing . . .' she kept on whispering with closed eyes, and I barely had time to whisk away a tear from her eyelash as the door opened.

'Well?' that man muttered. 'Killed her yet?'

'I think she's asleep,' I whispered. 'Ssh. . . .'

'Stuff!' snapped Masters. 'She's been crying. Out you go.'

Suddenly Iris said in that enormous, preserved voice: 'I have not been crying.'

Masters, whose great brown coat filled the whole side of the bed, so that I was nowhere, looked down at her like a worried bird. . . .'

'I'd like,' she pleaded, 'to say good-bye . . . to this gentleman, if you would kindly . . . get out of the way for a minute. . . .' And when I bent over the wasted hand, from which the emerald-ring now hung like a hoop, she said: 'Ah, that defiant courtesy! Thank you, my dear. And good-bye for ever as ever is, for I don't suppose I shall ever come back to England again . . . nevermore, nevermore. And,' she whispered, 'I will keep my promise. . . .'

CHAPTER NINE   TALKING OF HATS

That was on the fifteenth afternoon of February, as I remember well.

Now those who are sensitive to any extreme condition of our climate will not have forgotten that towards the end of July of the year 1923 there was a week or ten days when the heat in London was so oppressive that frequent complaints were made at the confectioners and Soda Fountains on the ground that their ices were warm: nor were the nights less uncomfortable—'uncomfortable,' that is, to quote from a gentleman who wrote to *The Times* about it, 'in a country so unprepared for any extreme of temperature that, if I do not seem too fanciful, on a cold winter's day there is nothing warm but the drinking-water and on a hot summer's day nothing cool but the sun.' Of course he did seem too fanciful, but, however that may be, the nights were certainly stifling, and one in particular I remember very well.

It was towards eleven o'clock, and Hilary, Guy and I, having sat long over dinner upstairs at the Café Royal, were returning towards our homes down Piccadilly, walking as slowly as we might for the prodigious heat. We had, however, barely touched the corner of Saint James's Street when Guy ceased even to pretend that he was walking, and said: 'Just a moment, will you, while I go into White's to see if Napier's there, to remind him about dinner to-morrow night.' But Guy never in his life looked less like running, and Hilary said: 'The idea of eating in this weather! Hm. And what is this party, Guy?'

'Children's party,' said Guy, whose frozen blue eyes might conceivably have made one feel cool had one only been tall enough to be able to look into them . . . and just at that moment, as Guy turned away, and the three of us facing down towards the Palace, Napier came swiftly down the steps of White's, about ten yards down. At the curb a taxi was waiting, its door swung open.

'Naps! Napier!' Guy called, thinking to catch him with as little exertion as possible in that stifling heat. But Napier, swift as a shadow, that greyhound of a Napier, was already in the taxi, the door was slammed-to, and round it swept by the Devonshire Club to turn northwards up the slope to Piccadilly.

'Drat the boy!' said Guy, as we made to cross the road. 'Catch him on the rebound as we cross. . . .' But when, as the three of us stood by the island under the arc-lamp, the taxi rushed past us with screaming gears, he made no effort to hail Napier.

'Well?' Hilary grunted, as the taxi tore up Albemarle Street.

'Oh, ring him up,' said Guy shortly, and in silence we walked towards Hyde Park Corner.

I only knew from Guy's look that he had seen her in the light that fell through the open window of the passing cab. She had seemed to be in a black dress and her head wrapped in a tight silver turban, and I had almost gasped not only with the surprise of seeing her at all, but the small face in that second of light had seemed so dazzling. 'Naturally,' I thought. 'She's happy. . . .'

Hilary hadn't, of course, seen her, for he was always at his most thoughtful when crossing the street. Nor had those two in the cab seen us, I was certain: they were talking too eagerly. Guy, Hilary and I walked on in silence, as slowly as we might for the heat. Maybe, I thought, Guy did not know I had seen her. As for himself, he never gave away gratuitous information about other people. And Guy loved Napier like his younger brother.

We were passing by the great gates of Devonshire House that now more becomingly adorn the Green Park when Hilary muttered 'Bed-time' and left us, crossing towards Half-Moon Street. I found myself walking on with Guy, despite the economy in walking I might have made by going with Hilary, for my flat also lay in that direction. But I might cut up Down Street. Guy said, as though for some minutes past he had been giving his whole mind to the matter: 'Not bad weather, really, if one was dressed for it. . . .'

'If!' I said.

'Of course,' said Guy, 'these infernal stiff shirts. . . .'

'Quite,' I said.

'Although,' said Guy, 'I think they're cooler than those sickening soft things. . . .'

'I'm wearing one,' I said.

'I said what I said,' said Guy.

Once upon a time, as he had stood at the foot of her bed in a dim room, Iris had called him by a name that was not his name. 'But Guy would defend a secret not only against the angels of God but also against himself.' Yes, Iris, yes . . . but was it necessary, Iris, to remind him of it? For Napier was Guy de Travest's friend, and as dear to him as a younger brother.

'To swim,' Guy murmured from deep reflection, 'would be very pleasant just now. Very pleasant indeed.'

'Yes. But where? I'm not for the Loyalty, in water debauched by face-powder. . . .'

'I thought,' Guy murmured, 'that I would swim at the Bath Club this afternoon. I get ideas, quick as you like. But everyone else had also been thinking on the same lines, so you can imagine the crowd. A man there told me that the best way to get in was to pick on the fattest man in the water and as he came out slip into the hole he'd made. But I couldn't even see the water. . . .'

Tall as a tree, his hat swinging lazily in his hand near his thigh, he lounged on. . . .

'Sickening,' he murmured.

Bus after bus, laden with the people from the theatres, thundered past us and up and down the switchback, embracing us with waves of heat so that one's very skin felt like a sticky garment. . . .

'Yes,' I said.

'London's all right,' said Guy thoughtfully, 'as London. . . . .'

'Of course,' I said, 'as London. . . .'

The wide sweep of Hyde Park Corner lay ahead of us like a bright handkerchief in the night. The buses trumpeted across it and around it and down it and up it, but one and all looked as snails beside Bus No. 16, which is beyond compare the fastest bus in London, making the voyage from Grosvenor Place to Hamilton Place and back again at a speed to astonish the eye of man.

The din that night makes in closing its doors on London was as though muted by the still, stifling air, and I envied the lofty calm of the Duke of Wellington where he rides for ever amid his pleasaunce of small trees. The lights of Constitution Hill glowed like fire-flies between the leafy valley of the Green Park and the dark gardens of His Majesty the King.

'Trouble about London is,' said Guy thoughtfully, 'that people are always expecting it to be Paris or Rome or some other place. Always wanting something else, people are. . . .'

'Anything,' I agreed, 'so long as it's not their own. . . .'

'That's about it,' Guy murmured. 'Sickening. . . .'

We thought about that for a while.

'Guy, one almost might go down to some part of the river. Near Maidenhead. Now. And swim.'

'Haven't been to Maidenhead,' Guy reflected deeply, 'well, it must be ten years. Difficult, isn't it, to realise it's almost ten years since that war started? I haven't been—let me see—not since the night that poor boy got himself drowned. . . .'

'Only an hour or so by car,' I said, 'and you can relive your youth.'

A smile flickered across the stern, small profile. 'A long time to waste to relive a wasted youth. What about a game of squash instead? Make us enjoy a drink. Come along.'

And so it came to pass that we bathed quite differently than in the river by playing squash-racquets by electric-light. Guy has a court in the basement of his house, and when he beats you, which is always, he says: 'Sickening.'

'Where,' I asked, when we had bathed sufficiently and were enjoying long tumblers of the stuff that such good jokes are made from, whilst from upstairs came the faint notes of a piano and a thing they call a saxophone, for Lady de Travest was 'throwing' a small party; 'where are we dining to-morrow night? And, now I come to think of it, why this sudden children's party?'

Guy had happened on Venice playing tennis the other day, when she had said she was feeling perhaps a little depressed. 'The heat,' she had said. . . .

'Whereupon,' said Guy, imitating Cherry-Marvel, 'it came to me as not a bad idea if we had a party for the child. Real good girl, Venice. Hope that young man of mine will find someone only half so good. . . .'

'Yes,' I said.

'Be a sort of family party, I thought. Hugo and Shirley, Napier and Venice, some clean and wholesome young woman I'll find for you, while I, thank the Lord, will be odd man out. But as to *where* we should dine . . .'

'In this heat. . . .'

'God, yes, too hot for dancing. Just listen to them upstairs! Even the ceiling's sweating. . . .'

The faint, slow lilt of the tango, pleasantest of all dances but one that is so seldom danced in London because nobody in London can dance it, which seems a pity. . . .

'Might almost dine here,' Guy murmured, 'if Moira doesn't want the place. And we might, now you've suggested it, and if it's still so hot, go and bathe somewhere afterwards instead of sitting up in some stuffy place till all hours. See how we feel about it, and if Venice would enjoy that. . . .'

'Imagine Venice not enjoying that!'

'Well, we'll see,' said Guy, but more seriously now. 'If we do, it will mean no cocktails before dinner, no more than a glass of wine apiece over dinner, and not a thimbleful after. I'm not going to have that river play any more tricks on my friends, I can tell you.'

'And decency, Guy, will be more than served, for there's no moon and the nights are pitch-black. . . .'

'That's right,' said Guy thoughtfully, and then, as he saw me to the door, he said thoughtfully: 'By the way, you any idea if Venice has ever met Iris?'

'I don't think so,' I said. 'But I'm not sure. . . .'

There is never any harm in saying one isn't sure. One should never be sure, conversationally.

'I just had an idea,' Guy murmured, looking out over the heavy trees of the great square, 'that Iris might conceivably be passing through London, as I heard from Eve Chalice to-day that old Portairley was lying near death. The last Portairley, dear, dear.'

'Gerald won't be sorry to have missed his turn, I've no doubt.'

'Poor young devil! But what I was thinking of was, just in case Iris is in London, that we might get her for the third woman to-morrow night. . . .'

'Oh,' I said. 'I see. . . .'

'You'd quite like that, wouldn't you?'

'Oh, I'd like it!'

'Just had an idea,' Guy murmured vaguely, 'that she and Venice might meet, if they haven't already met, and see how they like each other. That is, if Iris is in London. Different types . . . you never know. Tell Iris, if by any chance you hear anything of her to-morrow. My idea, tell her. . . .'

'All right, if she should give me a ring. Good-night, Guy.'

'Good-night, boy. Sorry about the squash. Sickening. My idea, tell her.'

As I looked back from that wide corner of Belgrave Square which sweeps suavely up to Hyde Park Corner, I could see the very tall figure of the friend of his friends still framed against the lighted doorway. Across the four open windows above him figures passed slowly.

But what, what in the world, could suddenly have happened to Iris, she whom I had last seen, whom I had last heard, saying she would nevermore return to England, promising . . .? And one realised, in wondering that with so deep a bewilderment, how very literally one would take Iris's word, how completely one had believed in her promise, as one would have believed in any promise made by that Iris March who, as Hilary had reluctantly to confess, did not lie. But now . . . nevermore, nevermore!

And as I let myself into my flat, I found myself picturing Guy de Travest and Iris face to face in a place where no people were, Guy and Iris completely alone with each other and God. And it was Guy whom I heard speaking, Guy's low cold voice telling Iris of certain things, how he had been shocked that dim morning to hear her whisper a name like a kiss, a name that was already pledged to another, and how, when he had long since forgotten her whispering of that name, he had chanced on a night to see her no further than the span of that name apart from him who bore it, and how he couldn't but think that she was committing the one unpardonable crime of stealing a man from his wife, like a mean little thief in the night. And I could imagine Iris in her tight silver turban, like a star it would be in that lonely place where she faced Guy, and her tiger-tawny curls dancing formally on each small cheek, and all about her that dazzling brilliance which will suddenly enwrap a very fair woman in a black dress, whilst the blood would be clean emptied from her small grave face as she listened to the judgment of the slender giant with the cold eyes and the quiet, so quiet, savage voice. They were of the same people, Guy and Iris, of the same blood, of the same landscape, and you couldn't help but wonder how she would face his judgment, she who had for so long outlawed herself, she who so profoundly impressed you as not caring the tremor of an eyelash for the laws of her fathers. Would she, faced by the warrior of conduct, still not care, or would she be ashamed and afraid, would she be as though seeing England, her England, the very soil of her England, turning from her in contempt? I simply could not tell what she would feel, so little did I know of the nature of that shameless, shameful lady. And that was again the thought that came to me the very next night to the one I am telling of, whilst I sat beside her in her car, and we in the van of the children's party's raid on the river. A torment of heat lay over England that July night, but that is not why we who sped through the countryside will remember it.

She was driving, and when I dropped a word into the silence of our drive, for Iris and I were at enmity now—for Venice!—a curious smile seemed to devour the white profile, to devour it quite: a very witch of a smile that was, I thought, and more than adequate to meet my word, for the word I had dropped was what the raven quoth: 'Nevermore!'

But as she smiled so, she drove that menacing bonnet ever more furiously along the road to Maidenhead, so that corners perished like midgets before our head-lights and Hugo and Shirley, who sat behind, murmured against her driving, saying that it would be bad for their reputation as a happily-married couple to be found dead on the road to Maidenhead. 'A friend of mine,' yelled Hugo, 'was asked to resign from Buck's for being found dead on the Maidenhead road. . . .'

But Iris drove faster and ever faster, and suddenly I realised that the rare devouring smile that was like my enemy on her face was new to me who had never before seen Iris smile happily.

2

I have gone too far ahead in the tale of the last March, letting myself be beguiled from a narrator's duties by the reckless flight of the silver stork through the quiet country-side. But from the night of the children's party I can only go back by saying that she was wearing that night not her silver turban but a green hat, yea, a green hat, of a sort of felt, and bravely worn; and who but I had bought that green hat for her that very day, she having said to me after luncheon that she needed a green hat *pour le sport*. I understood that the *sport* would be under even warmer skies than ours, for in three days' time, she said, she would be on board ship for Rio de Janeiro, and she did not need to tell me that she would not be voyaging unaccompanied. That was a fell lady for whom I bought a green hat that day.

Nothing easier than a green hat, it appears, can well be bought. Like a flash of summer lightning, that is how a green hat is bought. Says the lady to the shop: 'Greeting, sir. I will have a green hat *pour le sport*, similar in every way to the green hats I have bought here every year since the death of Dr. Crippen.'

'Very good, madam. That will be so much, madam. On your account, madam?'

'Oh, no! My friend will pay. Farewell.'

We spoke very little over the luncheon we took together.

It was a stifling day, and what, anyhow, was there to say? Very far from my business was it to speak of broken promises unless spoken to, and very far from her thoughts did any question of broken promises seem. Oh, but that was a fell lady who luncheoned with me on that sweltering day!

We sat picking at green olives and salads and bits of toast, we drank those long iced drinks full of vegetable matter which, apparently, one must drink so that one may feel the heat more poignantly than before, we had nothing in particular to say. Early that morning she had rung me up, a calm, happy voice, demanding from me not the smallest expression of surprise at her presence in London; although, of course, one did make a show of being surprised, for she couldn't possibly know that I had seen her in that cab, and, I thought, she never would know. The Marches would be let off that, anyhow.

But Iris, over that luncheon, did not appear to remark that I had nothing in particular to say. And, what with the heat and with that, I suppose I grew more and more annoyed, for there isn't, I suppose, anything in the world more irritating than to be angry with a woman and she not notice it at all. Of course many women will appear not to notice it, but you can see that that is put on; but this Iris just, I'll swear it, did not notice anything.

Nor, I thought, did she have a very healthy appetite for one not long since recovered from a serious illness, the way she picked at bits of things here and there; but she excused herself to Charles, who came up to protest against the dishonour she did his food, on the ground that she never did eat with her meals.

And then there was a moment when I asked, from a large silence which seemed to her maddeningly natural, I just asked paternally, since it is always easier to be paternal than to be fraternal: 'Happy, Iris?'

She was buttering a piece of *toast Melba* about half an inch square. My question stayed her knife. She stared intently towards the doors of the restaurant for a long second, and then she said, frankly, gravely, calmly, not at all intensely, but with unutterable conviction: 'Unbearably.'

183

Then she went on buttering her piece of *toast Melba*, and I could do what I liked about it.

Now I must say this for the Iris who sat with her profile to me that day, that she was a more lovely Iris even than the one I had known. But as to how she was more lovely, that I do not know; nor, if I knew, could I describe it but by using the word 'ethereal', to be immediately followed by the word 'unearthly', for it is a convention not to be broken lightly that a woman who has not long since recovered from a long illness must look 'ethereal' and 'unearthly'. But she didn't, I think, look either of those two things. She seemed, I mean to say, more lovely than ever just because she was more earthy. She looked, I fancy I mean, in love—her skin, that is to say, looked as though she who wore it was in love. Yes, her skin did. I fancy it must have been that. A beautiful woman in love and loved seems, in however unaware a moment, to glow with an earthy beauty. When writers say that 'Gloria was looking very spiritual that morning' what they really mean—of course, this is all theory—is that Gloria was looking more earthy that morning, that in her eyes there was the afterglow of love's delight. A beautiful woman neglected or unloved appeals, of course, more to the chivalrous sense in men, for men will stand more of a chance of a sad woman being interested in them; but the very skin of a woman who is coiled in love seems to have a jewel-like quality, and her mind is like a temptation one wants to touch.

'And,' I said, fascinated for some reason by the faint, faint golden down on her arm, 'you're quite well and strong now?'

'Of course,' she said, 'not so strong as all that. But strong enough. . . .'

'Oh, dear! Strong enough for what, Iris?'

'Everything,' she said, shrouding a boiled cherry in whipped cream. 'Must get fat,' she explained as an afterthought.

Now there were two red camellias painted on the left side of the crown of her hat—women at that time didn't wear bowler hats, or, as they prefer to call them, *cloche* hats—which was of the same colour as the sun, of straw, and with a narrow stiff brim. The two red camellias looked just as waxen and artificial as two real red camellias would look, and so it must have cost a power of money, that hat. She would have flown like the wind to Reboux in Paris, saying to herself: 'I am in love. I must have a hat,' and so she had bought that hat. As for her dress that stifling day, you would have called it blue if you hadn't seen that no colour made by hands could compare with the blue of those grave eyes, and it was of that fine texture which is finer than the texture of silk of China, if such a thing can be, and here and there upon its lower parts were worked large white arabesques in what looked to an uninformed eye like wool, but surely it could not be the fleece of the lamb that Iris was wearing that day?

'And did Guy,' she asked, 'say anything when you three saw me in that cab last night?'

'Oh!' I said.

She had very suddenly turned to me, so that at last I must look full into the eyes that blazed so incredibly blue from the shadow of the yellow hat ... and I, I could not meet those eyes! I stared instead at the emerald on the third finger of her right hand, and how white and frail that hand looked, so weak, so frail, when you thought of it as belonging to those deep, compelling, unscrupulous eyes.

'Well?' It was her voice, faint, slightly husky; yet it rose above the roar of London and was lost in the clouds that pass over a strange, unknown land.

'Personally,' I said, 'I liked your silver turban very much.'

'Dear, that was not a turban!'

'Turban is a pretty word, Iris. And suitable, too. . . .'

'Turkey, polygamy?'

'Just a boyish fancy.'

'And Guy? You haven't told me?'

'But, Iris, he never, as you know, gives away gratuitous information. He just asked me to ask you to dine to-night, as I have done. "My idea, tell her," he said. In fact, he repeated that. And you're coming?'

'Why, of course!' she said absently, so absently.

'But why do you ask about Guy, Iris? I fancied you didn't care what anyone thought.'

185

Throughout that passage her face had been turned to mine, but only now could I muster the courage to raise my eyes from the third finger of her right hand, to see that her face was as though turned to a mask of white stone with two amethysts for eyes. It was a mask, that face, and those were the eyes of a mask. Yet it was far from a mask of concealment, it was the mask of herself, of her very self, of the self that was, in some remote part of her being, really herself. And again I couldn't help thinking of her as of someone who had strayed into our world from a strange land unknown to us, a land where lived a race of men and women who were calmly awaiting their inheritance of our world when we should have annihilated one another in our endless squabbles about honour, morality, nationality. Strong were the people of that land, stronger than the gold they despised but used, deterred by not qualm nor fear, strong and undefeatable. And just like that was the white mask of this beautiful woman, strong and undefeatable. It knew not truth nor lying, not honour nor dishonour, not loyalty nor treachery, not good nor evil: it was profoundly itself, a mask of the morning of this world when men needed not to confuse their minds with laws with which to confuse their neighbours, a mask of the evening of this world when men shall have at last made passions their servants and can enter into their full inheritance. . . .

'I don't,' she said at last from a remote distance, the amethysts absorbed in the air between us. 'I don't.' And then she smiled faintly, but even so much was enough to change the amethysts into eyes. 'I don't,' she said very huskily. 'But I just asked. . . .'

'Iris,' I said, my mind charged with that mask, 'you have us all at a great disadvantage. . . .'

Slowly, thoughtfully, she made a circle of air with a small golden tube that had a crimson tongue, and then she passed the golden tube through the circle's heart. She was thinking.

CHAPTER TEN THE FALL OF THE EMERALD

I

As I think of that wretched night of the children's party
there will be two pictures that cross my mind. The first, of a
group of brightly coloured people, for we were in white
flannels and the women in those mad, barbaric colours
which fashion, goaded on by Chanel and gallantly led by
Captain Molyneux, has lately flung as a challenge to our
dark civilisation, around a table lit by the cameo flames
rising from eight tall cast candlesticks by Paul Lamarie; and
I remember that in the still air of Guy's great, bare dining-
room those cameo flames never flickered even so much, they
might have been flowers of light cut out of the stifling heat.

The second picture is of a darkness. A darkness torn here
and there by the sudden flame of a match which drove the
stars trembling back into the invisible and joined to groping
eyes the silky soft blackness of the water. The black night
pinned round the world with stars, shouts, laughter, splash-
ings, an empty boat, silence, shrieks, a whisper from the
black face of the water, and so home. Total losses: one
stocking and one emerald. 'I'm so glad, so glad,' she whispered, just before going to sleep against my shoulder, for
it was Hugo Cypress who was riding the stork home-
ward.

But I have said that whilst we were on our way riverwards,
and I sitting beside Iris as she hurled us headlong through
the still night, we stood at enmity, she and I—for Venice!
And yet, so far as I could make out, there was not a soul but
myself out of that party, Guy, Napier, Venice, Hugo,
Shirley, Iris, who seemed in the least degree uncomfortable.
Those people had been, throughout dinner and afterwards,
completely and supremely normal. For all you knew, I
mean, they might have been having fun. There weren't any
undercurrents. Not even what you would call any undercurrents. Those people were quite calmly themselves, they
just *behaved* as themselves in that confoundedly unassailable
way which is peculiar to the people of this small island: as
though, to be sure, they weren't giving away anything of a

187

personal nature even to themselves. You can't help seeing why Napoleon found these people so detestable.

And it was all, you couldn't help feeling, so mean, such a humbug of a thing. I suppose, of course, that I was the only one besides Iris and Napier who knew of their departure together in three days' time. 'I have always wanted,' she had said to me, 'to go to Rio, and then across the continent. One can't *talk* in Europe, it's got so stuffy now. But I always thought I would keep the Americas until my fate should be fulfilled.' Yet, I was quite certain, everyone at the table must have known that something was wrong, else why was that fell, beautiful lady there at all? For Guy, in the ordinary way, wouldn't, it simply wasn't in Guy's nature to be able to, ask Iris Storm to the same dinner with the young wives of his two young friends, his *protégés* almost, Napier and Hugo. And if he had asked Iris to-night, knowing that she wouldn't funk coming—though the real reason why she had come was that Iris simply did not attach any importance to such things, 'and besides,' she had said, 'I want to see dear Hugo again, and as a married man'—it was just because he wanted Iris to realise the scene on which she was intruding so wickedly. It is such catholic cruelty as Guy's that, by always lopping off the rotten limb, has kept the heritage of so many English houses almost, despite the common talk of the day, unimpaired. To-night he was wanting Iris to see that her old friends, her old playmates, Hugo and Napier, had grown up differently from her—better or worse, that wasn't Guy's point, but *differently*—that while she had lived according to her nature they had lived according to their country, they and their young wives, Shirley and Venice. Not the most prejudiced eye, Guy knew, could but see that they made a fine, harmonious, clean four. Youth was there, and simplicity, and friendship, and love, too. And Guy had dared Iris to come to the children's party merely to say to her, with her eyes: 'See, Iris, here are four people, two by two, happily paired, friends and lovers, husbands and wives. See, Iris, and let them be. One of these men you may be able to introduce to the magic mysteries of love more completely than his young wife ever can. But see, Iris, how much you deprive him of, how utterly you deprive her! You have put yourself outside this long ago, you never can be of this again. See, Iris, how happy they are, and young, and clean, and earnest to do right: most earnest to do right, Iris, despite the most damnable enchantments. And as they are so you might have been with Boy Fenwick, but you chose differently. Iris March, the death of Boy Fenwick puts you out of court. See, Iris, and for God's sake let these children be!'

But that catholic Guy had not seen that beautiful white mask between the tawny formal curls and the two amethysts for eyes. I have told him since that had he seen that mask he would have foreseen the little profit he might expect to derive for his friends from Iris's presence at that dinner. I have told him how it was in my mind that night that nothing could move Iris, because it was as though in winning Napier she was winning the thirty years' war of her life. The shameless lady had at last lopped off the limb that was called the shameful lady; and so she had come again out of the darkness to Napier, she had come again as the enchanted voice whispering of better dreams, and not all Guy's Englishry could hold Napier now from following that enchanted whisper across the seas, that Iris March might at last come to fulfil her fate.

And yet, by the perfection of their normality over dinner, it might have been this person, me, who was being treacherous to his friends by fancying disloyalties among them! Shirley, for instance. Shirley, little sister to George Tarlyon, was of the same age as Venice, they had been at Heathfield together, they had always been together, and where Venice led there Shirley followed, and what Venice saw that Shirley saw, and where Venice raged there Shirley raged. And Venice was raging now. Oh, she must be raging frantically! Yet Shirley never once, as they say, 'let on' about her state of mind. She was just Shirley all the time, sweet in a small way, sarcastic in a large way, Shirley of the brown eyes and unbreakable spirit, pretty Shirley. Maybe she was behaving a little better than was her general wont, for Shirley was so well-bred that she never practised what you would call

189

deportment, but that was the only way the strain of that evening seemed to affect *her*. . . .

Exactly at what point, one wondered that evening, did behaviour become hypocrisy? For instance, Guy. There he sat, that knight of old beliefs, at our head, very gay in white flannels and a brilliant Fair Isle sweater, for all the world as though it was not already stifling enough, for all the world as though two people at his table hadn't offended him on the one essential point of conduct by which Guy de Travest knew friends from strangers: never to give way to what you want to do, if honour tells you that you may not do it.

And Napier, that love-lost man! Love-lost, that man? Let me tell of a moment after dinner when Venice suddenly, tremendously, helplessly, cried to Iris: 'Oh, dear Jesu, aren't you lovely!' And Napier, at that moment gaiety itself, came suddenly between them, an arm round each of their shoulders. 'Why, of course she is, Venice! I tell you, I was particular about my friends when I was young. . . .' It wasn't, of course, voluntary, he was not thinking, Napier couldn't think and then be a hypocrite: it was just the natural, normal sort of nonsense that happens. He had, at that moment, forgotten what he would have to tell Venice, to-morrow or the day after, of the love-philtre. And the child Venice! Venice, that very queen of hypocrites! Charming she was to Iris, just the tiniest bit deferential, as a girl of one-and-twenty might well be, but seldom is, to a woman of thirty. And yet Venice, ever since that afternoon in Paris, had been, I knew, eating her heart fretting about Napier, fearful and jealous and racked by what she could not see of his heart, tremulous with terror and suspicion of that legendary playmate, that Iris March of long ago. And how she hated the idea of Iris, I knew well, how she hated the thing she thought Iris was—and wasn't Iris just that!—with all the uncompromising savagery of her heart! Venice, Oh Venice! And once, over dinner, she whispered to me: 'I like Mrs. Storm.'

I don't know, of course, but I suppose that in saying nothing one said quite enough to that.

'I do really,' Venice insisted, but not with enough vehemence for one to be able to fix on that as evidence of her insincerity. 'She gives you a sense of . . . well, completeness, if you see what I mean?'

'Oh, quite,' I said. 'Completeness, certainly. . . .'

'Not like Shirley and me, you see,' she said thoughtfully.

'Yes, I can just see that, Venice.'

'Mrs. Storm,' said Venice gravely, 'gives one a sense of being a lady from herself, in her own right, if you see what I mean. Whereas Shirley and me——'

'Shirley and I.'

'Shirley and I, dear, and nearly everyone we know are ladies just because our mothers were, and that kind of thing. I'd trust Mrs. Storm. . . .'

And so I was to tell Iris that Venice trusted her! And then, according to the Scriptures as written by Venice, Iris would feel such a cad that she wouldn't, after all, be able to bring herself to steal away her husband. She would repent, Iris would, on being told that Venice trusted her, and she would go back again into the nasty darkness of outlawry, leaving decent people to the safe enjoyment of their husbands. Dear Venice, I am afraid my telling Iris that wouldn't have quite that effect, she just wouldn't notice, Venice, that I had spoken; for such a plot might do exceeding well in a novel, whence you have no doubt derived it, but in life, Venice, your Iris March isn't to be deterred from her chase of the Blue Bird by being trusted. If only life was a movie, Venice, you would only have to let Iris know that you trusted her, and away she would slink, weeping.

But imagine that Venice, an eagle in her eyrie, desperately beating her wings to hide the sun from the eyes of her mate! Oh, but Venice acted superbly! Not, of course, that there wasn't provided a very handsome peg on which to hang the acting. The bathing idea came as a boon and a blessing to all the company. You could talk about an idea like that, and no harm done. Guy chivalrously gave me the credit for it, and I was acclaimed by Shirley and Venice as something they have in America called, so Venice swore on oath, a 'he-man'. But Shirley thought it was very silly of Guy to go and spoil the whole picnic by insisting on bathing-costumes. Shirley thought that at length. So did Venice.

'I mean, on a hearty picnic like this!' said Shirley helplessly. And Venice said it was absurd to go digging about among bathing-costumes on a nice, warm, pitch-black night. One's chemise, said Shirley, would do ever so well. One's chemise, said Venice, had done very well before. And one wouldn't, said Shirley indignantly, really need the chemise afterwards, just to come home with. Not in this heat, said Venice, and they appealed to Iris, but Iris protested that she must be neutral, because she was not going to bathe; but she would have thought, she said, that a dry shift was always preferable, when possible.

'Not going to bathe!' cried Venice. 'Not going to—Oh, you must bathe! Of course you're going to bathe! Oi, you'll spoil the whole party!'

It was after dinner, and Hugo was doing a few card-tricks with champagne-glasses, the idea being, Hugo said, to settle our digestions after one of the best dinners that had ever left him with an appetite.

'Of course she'll bathe!' said Hugo. 'I've known the girl all my life, and I'll answer for her. She'll bathe. Leave her to me. Silly, not bathing.'

'She's rather common, your friend,' Shirley sighed to Guy.

'Sickening. Can't not bathe, really, on a night like this.'

'Seems to me,' Napier scowled, 'that she will have to bathe. Tell me if I'm wrong. What?'

'Listen,' Iris pleaded.

'Coming here,' said Shirley indignantly, 'and not bathing!'

'I am terrified,' said Iris desperately. 'Terrified of masses of water. Once, in the Black Sea of all places, I got cramp, and ever since . . .'

'If you only knew,' sighed Hugo, 'how cold all that leaves us! You'll swim, girl. Good for you. Make your coat shine. Give you back your lost youth.'

'Hugo, don't be so tactless!' cried Shirley.

'The girl's right,' Guy closed the discussion. 'She's only been out of bed about a month. . . .'

'But I haven't been near mine for longer than that!' cried Shirley inevitably, and it was just at that moment, under cover of it, that I touched the ice-cold hand. That was the only sign until we reached the river that Venice's married life had tumbled like a house of cards about her heart, that and her 'trusting' Iris.

Venice was saying: 'And didn't we just have some trouble with you, Mrs. Storm, when you were ill in Paris! Naps white in the face thinking you were going to die, me green in the face thinking my holiday would be spoilt if you did, this he-man here purple in the face telling me to be reasonable. . . .'

'But you were in bed for ages, weren't you?' said Shirley sympathetically. 'What was it? Some foul plague?'

'Ptomaine poisoning,' said Napier, and as I was giving Venice a light with which to torture yet another cigarette my hand happened to touch hers. 'In this heat!' said I.

'Shut up, you fool!' she whispered desperately, and then she tried not to smile frantically, whispering: 'Darling, darling, *darling*! My one friend. . . .'

'Venice, they're never any real good, friends. They can't *do* anything. . . .'

'I know. Oh, I know. Oh God, I know! . . . Mrs. Storm, what a divine lip-stick! May I see? May I use?'

Baby.

2

Thus, the children's party. . . .

Their engines no louder than a whisper through the quiet noises of the night, and swift as arrows with flaming eyes, two touring-cars, a primrose and a blue, passed through the villages riverwards. The good people slept on undisturbed, as why should they not, for a motor-car will disturb the amenities of a village by night less than a wheel-barrow. Maybe through the crack of a blind flashed a startling light on a sleepless pillow. Maybe a distant scream, as of a great sea-bird, stirred a boy to dream of vain, polite, perishable delights. Maybe a cow stared thoughtfully at the strange, swift, whirring insects with the livid eyes and the cruel screams. Here and there the lamps shone on the buttons of a policeman, stockstill in a doorway. There was no air but the wind of our passage, warm, heavy with dust and dry grasses. 'Rain, rain!' breathed England in her sleep. And there was no rain, nor breath of rain, nor yet that damp, oppressive foretaste of a thunderstorm to come, only a torment of heat over the land and around the land the un-clouded darkness pinned with faint stars. A myriad flies withstood the stork, were appalled, died. Wrapped in silence, armed with light, we fled beneath the suns of the night like battle-chariots rushing to the assault of the strong-hold of the gods. Iris had gone mad.

I thought of Mr. Polly disturbed in his sleep, twenty years ago, on a Sussex hay-rick by the roar of a racing-car. Mr. Polly could have slept undisturbed for us. One hundred and twenty horses drew us, shadows of nothing from nothing to nothing beneath the impersonal stare of the stars. Look away from the stars, lovers of the world's delights, for they are the destroyers of the world's delights with their dreams of grander things. To listen to great music, to adore God in vast solitudes, to kneel before the face of beauty, to pass through the quiet land like an arrow with flaming eyes, swifter than your thoughts: such and the like, according to each our nature, are the captains of the world's delights, so keep your eyes from the stars, that destroy our delights with their dreams of grander things.

Silence marches with the thoughts in your mind. Maybe a word or two will drop, hesitate in the wind, fight with the dying hosts of midgets, perish on the road. Small flying things brush by your face, and a dry unsweet scent, as though England is sleeping with her windows closed.

The green hat was somewhere beside me, it fell and rolled about my feet, she murmured: 'Leave it.' To the warm wind fell the honour of the dance, and with the tawny cornstalks the wind stepped a wide-flung dance. Why does your hair dance so, Iris March, like a halo possessed of devils? Why this, why that, Iris March?

In the glass of the wind-screen we might now and then see the faint reflection of Guy's lamps behind us. Nay, once or twice his bonnet nosed up beside Iris, just beside her elbow. But the stork cried hoarsely, flew on.

Again, silent as the rustle of a woman's dress walking in a dark garden, Guy's shining bonnet menaced the tail of our eye, and Guy himself, alone in front, yellow-haired, grim, fair herald of a fighting pageant in his brilliant Fair Isle sweater, and now the face of Venice, leaning forward to Guy's shoulder, excited, exhorting. Venice, for Venice! She would pass the lady of the dancing hair, would Venice. But the stork cried hoarsely, flew on.

We wrestled. Silent as phantoms, we wrestled. One hundred and twenty horses, a winged Mercury and a stork wrestled for the dominion of nothing on the Reading road.

There was a corner, proud and saturnine from many fell triumphs. The stork screamed a taunt, flew on.

'Ho!' gasped Hugo, chattering, from behind. 'Steady, girl! Shirley's frightened. . . .'

'Let him pass, Iris!' cried I. A little scared, a woman driving, you never know, might lose her head, boy's head, curly head, white and tiger-tawny, but too white, too intent, too infernally reckless. . . .

'Iris, Iris!'

'Can do seventy-five if you like,' cried the lips of the dancing hair.

'Let him pass, Iris!'

'Pass? Am I mad! As soon let happiness pass! See, the stars are laughing. . . .'

'Iris, Iris!'

'Let him pass, Iris! Damn you, it won't hold the road!'

'Why, the road's fainting with joy! Can do seventy-six if you like. But not more. . . .'

A new road, recently laid down to soften the passage of footlight-favourites to the reaches of Taplow and Maidenhead, wide, deserted of houses. Meadows swept each side into the desert darkness. Iris, perhaps remembering Mr. Polly, perhaps thinking Mr. Polly had slept long enough, kicked open the exhaust. That lends another mile an hour to speed. Another sixty horses gave answer behind, then fell snarling back towards London. 'Seventy-one, Iris!'

195

'Ow!' she breathed. 'Accelerator burning foot. Ow! Hell!'

'Maidenhead!' screamed Shirley.

'To the right, Iris!'

And so we came into the yard of Quindle's. Still, sleeping, shuttered, Quindle's hostelry was a rebuke to the flaming lights which made a festival of the desert scene. Then Guy's car swung in, poor winged Mercury. Shows one, don't you know, how much gods are worth. . . .

'Sickening, Iris. You had me properly beat that time.'

'But how my foot burns, Guy!'

'Look!' said Venice. 'Hist!'

A man in shirt-sleeves was come out of the hotel. He stared at us, rubbed his eyes, stared at us.

'Ho!' called Major Cypress. 'Ho, there! Is that Quindle's speaking?'

The man in shirt-sleeves came through the flame of the lamps. An amiable man, he looked.

'Now remember,' whispered Shirley at large, 'no matter how beastly they are to us, we are going to bathe. Let everyone speak at once. That will baffle him.'

'Evening,' said the man in shirt-sleeves. 'Bit late, isn't it?'

'Not one yet,' said Hugo. 'I say, we want to bathe.'

'Can't have no rooms,' said the man in shirt-sleeves. 'Hotel's full.'

'But we don't want no rooms!' Venice pleaded. 'We only want to bathe. . . .'

'Bar's closed,' said the man in shirt-sleeves.

'Serve you right,' said Hugo. 'But we'll give you a drink if you want one. Here you are. Beer or champagne?'

'I want to bathe,' Shirley pleaded.

'Can't bathe 'ere,' said the man in shirt-sleeves.

'You don't know about us,' said Venice severely. 'We can bathe anywhere.'

'Against the lor, miss.'

'That will be all right about the law.' A sudden voice, a calm voice, a cold, chill murmur. It fell from heights like a douche. The man in shirt-sleeves tried not to have to look up all the way to Guy's face. Too tall was Guy, in that light. Guy smiled down at the man in shirt-sleeves.

'Hot night,' Guy murmured. 'Very hot. My children, all these. . . .'

'Ho,' said the man in shirt-sleeves. ''Ot or cold, it's against the lor, that's wot.'

'Don't you worry your head about the law,' said Guy. 'But what you might do, now, would be to get us some towels. We forgot towels. . . .'

'Against the lor, anyhow,' said the man in shirt-sleeves.

'I do wish you'd say something else just once,' snapped Shirley.

Iris, a white face, gardenia-white, mocking hair, a barbaric scarf about her throat, her hat a splash of black against the frail fancy that was her dress, standing a little away, staring at the stars. 'A light,' she murmured. 'A light!' Then Napier was beside her, lighting her cigarette, lighting also the curious, still smile on his acolyte's face, an enchanted smile, the smile of a man drowned in a magic pool. The collar of his white shirt was unbuttoned, the dark hair sleek in the glow of the flaming lights. . . .

'Naps, give me a light too.'

'Here you are, Venice,' said Hugo.

'Oh, it's gone out! Naps, a light!'

'Sorry, Venice. . . .'

Guy seemed to be shaking hands with the man in shirt-sleeves.

'Get you some towels,' said he, moving off.

Hugo whispered: 'One law for the rich, one for the poor. Dear me!'

'Sickening. But we may as well take advantage of what's left of it. Getting a bit mouldy, that law.'

'Come on, Hugo. God, it's dark! Which way is it? We must find a boat. . . .'

'Naps, this way! No, down here . . . but hang on to my arm! Soon find a boat. . . .'

'You can't have no boat!' called the man in shirt-sleeves.

'You get those towels,' said Hugo severely. 'The way you talk!'

'Please, your arm,' Iris begged me, husky voice. 'Foot hurts. And isn't it dark!'

'Here you are!' came Venice's clear boy's voice from the pit of darkness ahead, beneath us.

We faltered, blind as bats, down the slope of a landing-stage.

'Matches, please!' Shirley's voice. Oh, trust Shirley and Venice to have the affair well in hand! The pit of darkness ahead was bitten by tiny flames. 'Oh, look out, Naps! Ow, God damn you!'

'Naps, you might wipe your feet on your own wife, would you?'

There were uncertainties, holes, fissures of splintered wood. The tiny flames in the pit ahead were like lance-points thrusting the darkness deeper into the eyes.

Iris and I marched slowly as the smoke of our cigarettes in the breathless night. She leaned on my arm, completely. 'Foot hurts.' I wished she wouldn't. I almost said, 'don't.' Her touch confounded, confused. She was tangible, until she touched you. She was finite, until she touched you. She was a woman, until she touched you. Then she became woman, and you water. She became a breath of womanhood clothed in the soft, delicious mystery of the flesh. Touching her, you touched all desire. She was impersonal and infinite, like all desire. She was indifferent to all but her desire, like all desire. She was a breath carved in flesh, like all desire. She was the flower of the plant of all desire. Desire is the name of the plant that Lilith sowed, and every now and then it puts out the flower that in the choir of flowers is the paramour of the mandrake.

'You are very silent, Iris. . . .'

'Yes . . . yes? Sometimes. . . . I don't know, but it's as though the stars make me nervous, sometimes. They're so hopeless. They sneer, I can't help thinking. But are we going right?'

The darkness ahead stirred with tiny flames and exultant voices. Venice and Shirley!

'I say, lovely boat!' cried Shirley.

'Where, Shirley?' I called.

'Between you and me,' Iris whispered, 'I wouldn't mind sitting. Foot hurts. . . .'

'Come straight on. Don't go right or left. River.'

'It's not a boat at all!' cried Venice. 'It's a lovely motor-canoe. Oh, chaps!'

'Ssh!' Guy's voice.

Who cared? Not Shirley. 'And cushions! And steering-wheel! And everything. . . .'

'Naps, this way! Here you are! Isn't it a beauty?'

'Hope no one gets drowned,' Iris whispered.

'Everyone's cold sober.'

'But weeds and cramp and things. . . .'

'And currents,' came Guy's murmur from somewhere just above our heads. 'But it's safe as houses as long as we keep in a line between this bank and the other. Had inquiries made to-day.'

'Sensible Guy!'

'Best way to mend things is to stop them, Iris.'

Our eyes pricked by the wicked little match-lights, we could just make out at our feet the shape of a long motor-canoe and, at one end of it, a jumble of figures. They seemed to be fighting, those figures, bent this way and that in heroic attitudes. The canoe twisted and rocked frantically on its moorings. Fierce whispers, wicked words. . . .

'Steady a moment,' said Guy, just beside us. But they weren't steadying any moments, Venice and Shirley and Hugo, whilst Napier helped them by getting in their way. They were up to something, those frantic figures.

'Steady, I said!' said Guy sharply. That learnt them. Someone in the boat lit a match, and the water shone like black silk. I saw Napier's white face looking towards us, white face, dark eyes. Love-lost, dreaming. . . .

'Now look here,' said Guy gently. 'Just leave those sickening ropes alone. You Venice, you!'

'But, Guy! We must get——'

'Must nothing. It's not our boat, Venice, and I never break more than one law a night.'

'But—Oh, damn the man!'

'Honest to God, Venice. Now, Shirley, behave yourself! We'll sit in the wretched boat, but no more. And the river just here is safe. . . .'

'Look here,' said Hugo. 'What about this for an idea? The women have one end of the boat and we the other?'

'And no matches to——'

'But where's Iris?'

'Here,' came her voice, as though from the water. 'In the middle of the boat. Very comfortable. Many cushions. I'll take care of the boat while you swim. . . .'

'Isn't she kind, our fast friend! I say, no matches to be struck until someone gives the word! My figure's good, but even Reville doesn't think it's perfect. . . .'

'And better hand all your nasty bits of jewellery and watches to Iris.'

''Ere's towels,' said a miserable voice.

The canoe rocked beneath us. At our end soft things dropped to our feet, got in the way. Never was so dark and still a night. It was a relief taking off even the white flannels.

'Any swimming to be done,' said Guy, 'to be done in a straight line between this and the other bank. First man or woman who disobeys gets a crack on the head (a) from the bridge over there and (b) from me.'

'This wing's getting a bit crowded,' sighed Hugo. 'It's a blessing we're not French and haven't nice warm under-clothes as well.'

The glow of her cigarette lit Iris's mouth and eyes. . . .

'I got one foot in the water,' she said at large.

'Taking the edge off our bathing!' Dear Hugo. . . .

'Now, wot's all this about bathing?' said a Voice.

'Police! Puss, puss!'

'Didn't I tell 'em!' panted the man in shirt-sleeves. 'Didn't I! Told 'em it was against the lor.'

'Look here!' cried Venice from the pit of darkness. 'Don't you put that bull's-eye this way, else God knows what you won't see!'

'And he'll never go back to his wife again,' sang Shirley. 'I know men.'

'You ain't allowed to swim here,' said the Voice tremendously. 'Are they, Bill? Out of it, now!'

'I do wish,' Hugo said violently, 'that perfect strangers

200

wouldn't force themselves on us like this. Anyone would think we were at a Royal Garden Party!'

The canoe rocked frantically. 'Damn you, Guy!' said Napier. The constable turned his bull's-eye to where he thought Guy's face would be, then flashed it a foot higher.

'About this law,' murmured Guy.

'Now, sir,' said the Voice, rather pathetically I thought. 'I don't want to have no trouble.'

'The very word! I was just going to ask you if it would be troubling you too much to ask you to run up to your house to lend us some towels. It really would be very kind of you. Our friend here hasn't brought us quite enough. . . .'

Splash!

'Look 'ere,' began the Voice desperately.

'Don't look, constable! Be strong. Use your will-power. Women are but idle vanities.'

'Oo!' gurgled Venice. 'If you only knew how lovely it was! Come on, everybody. Oh, it's so warm!'

'Now remember, Venice—in a straight line between the banks.'

'That's right, sir,' said the voice.

'You and your banks!' sighed Shirley. Splash! 'Ow, it's freezing!'

'An' it's not their boat!' pleaded the man in shirt-sleeves. 'They got no right in that boat. It's Lord Lamorna's, that is.'

'Good Lord, Johnny's! And he's kept it hidden from us!' Splash! 'Where are you, Venice? Shirley?'

'Napier, be careful!' cried Iris, laughed Iris. . . .

'Are you gentlemen saying as you're friends of Lord Lamorna's? asked the voice.

'Friends!' said Hugo. 'I won't know him. We served together in Romano's Riflemen, but now he'll be jolly lucky if we don't scuttle his boat. Owes me a fiver. Good-bye.'

The river was warm, soft, quiet. Most un-English were the waters of the Thames that night, most Italianate. Never before had one understood the verity of that phrase 'on the bosom of the waters'.

From several yards away I could see the long shape of

the motor-canoe. How Lamorna's creditors would like to hear of that canoe! Hugo would blackmail him for his fiver. Dear Hugo. Suddenly the glow of Iris's cigarette stabbed the darkness, and maybe that was her shadow there, and that the one foot in the water. . . .

'Who's that?' she gasped.

I was anchored to her ankle. My hand could have gone twice round it.

'Take care of them,' she whispered. 'Dear, take care of them. Keep your eyes on that Venice child. She's reckless. Quick, and catch them up. I rely on you somehow——'

'You mustn't, Iris. I am enemy to Iris Storm.'

'Oh, friends and enemies! One relies on what people are in themselves, no matter what circumstances may make them feel.'

'And circumstances, Iris—do they make a woman so heartless?'

'Heartless! That's a large word, rather. Heartless? But maybe I am tired of being unhappy. So maybe I walked into a garden and built a high wall round it. Oh, may be, may be! Dear friend, go after them now. I am nervous, they're so young. By their voices, they seem to have gone very far. . . .'

But from the water the voices seemed to come from within a foot of one's ear. They must, I thought, be straight ahead, towards the opposite bank. Swiftly a whisper cut the water near me, past me. 'Young slacker!' came Guy's murmur. But I, not for exercise was I on the bosom of the waters that night. I lazed, listening to the voices ahead, sharp and clear across the water. Dimly, softly, clammy-cold, a weed would brush one. The stars were like the lance-points of a mighty host marching down to the chastisement of the world. But the darkness baffled them, whilst I floated into the heart of it, I loitered.

'Mind your head on this quay here, Venice! Venice! Hello, where's Venice?'

'Here. I say, what's this place?'

'Oh my pretty dears, why isn't one always in the water! I say, what's this wooden thing?'

'Looks like a landing-stage to me. What? I say, Hugo, what's this place? What?'

'Am I a graduate of Maidenhead, asking me? But let's try the place, anyway.'

'I've heard there's a River-Night-Club arrangement about here. Very exclusive.'

'We know. Excludes all who can't crowd in. Come on. Me for wine.'

I found them, having almost broken my shins against a wooden affair, lying grouped on what Shirley said was unmistakably 'a sweep of velvet sward'. Venice, it seemed, was exploring. You couldn't see your hand before your face. But you didn't want to.

'Funny,' sighed Hugo, 'if chap, just any chap, probably quite a nice chap, but timid chap, wakes from sleep to see Venice looking in on him. Mermaid theory. . . .'

'Wot's this?' snapped a voice. 'You're trespassing.'

'What did you think we were doing?' Napier asked mildly. 'Playing dominoes?'

'Tell us what this place is,' said Shirley severely, 'and perhaps we may let you go.'

'Gawd, don't you know The River Club!'

'I knew it was,' said Hugo proudly, 'as soon as I picked up a bus-ticket scented with Bacardie Rum——'

'But where's Venice?' cried Shirley sharply. 'Venice, Oh!'

The darkness stirred, and from the river-edge Napier called on the name of Venice.

'All right, all right! Here I am.'

'Venice!' cried Guy sharply. 'Keep straight ahead towards that canoe.'

'I'll swear,' said Napier, 'her voice came a good way from the left. What?'

'From the right, and what to you,' said Hugo.

'From the left,' said Napier, and there was a faint splash and a faint rustle from the water.

'Now, Shirley,' said Guy, 'I'll drown you if you go playing any fancy tricks. Come along, let's race back.'

'Naps, found her?'

'Oh, she's only playing the fool!' came Napier's voice. 'Heard her a moment ago. It's all right.'

I think that Guy and Hugo and Shirley must have deflected rather to one side, for although I was the poorest swimmer of the four I arrived first at the boat. My sight in the darkness was not helped by bumping my head against the gunwale.

'Iris! Iris?'

'Hello, where's Iris? What? God, it's dark. . . .'

'But haven't you found Venice?'

'Oh, she's playing the fool! Missed her. . . .' We held on to the gunwale, panting. 'God, man, where's Iris? What? I say, Iris!'

'She must have got out to stretch her legs,' I said.

'Yes—God, look!' panted Napier. 'What the devil! What?'

Hugo's voice, Shirley's, Guy's. . . .

Napier and I were in the canoe. Iris's white dress lay anyhow over the cushions in the middle, over the watches and rings. I stumbled over her shoes.

'Oh!' sobbed Shirley. 'Something's happened!'

'Naps, what is it?' snapped Guy from the water.

'Iris—I say, she must have changed her mind and gone in!'

'Stuff, changed her mind! Gone in after Venice, you mean!'

'Iris! Iris!' Hugo called. We all called.

'But where's Venice?' Shirley screamed just as Napier plunged in again.

'Iris! Venice! Iris!'

'For God's sake, Naps, take care!' snapped Guy. 'Don't go under that bridge.'

'Iris! Venice! Venice!'

Shirley was sobbing. In the pitch darkness. . . .

'Hugo,' said Guy, 'you and I together, for that bridge. Here, this way. . . . Naps, Naps! Come back, you fool!'

'Help. . . .'

'God, who's that! Iris? Venice?'

'Help . . . here, to the right. . . .' An exhausted whisper from the pit of the water.

'It's Iris,' said Guy. 'Where are you, Iris? Here, I'm in the water. Hold on.'

'Quick . . . tired. . . .'

'But where's Venice?' screamed Shirley.

'All right, Iris has got her. . . .'

Iris's whisper: 'Call Napier back. Oh dear . . .'

'Naps! Naps!'

'All right, coming.'

'Hang on, Hugo!' said Guy from the water. 'Iris coming. Pull, you fool. I've got Venice.'

'Please, my foot. . . .'

'Hugo, don't capsize the bloody boat!' sobbed Shirley. 'Naps, here they are! Guy, give me Venice at once! Venice!'

'All right, Guy.' Was that Venice's voice? 'I can manage. . . .'

'You've managed quite enough, you have!' said Hugo. 'You all right, Iris?'

Iris was lying panting somewhere in the canoe. Mostly on our flannels, I thought. But you couldn't see a thing. We were on the quay, Hugo, Guy, and I. Then Napier came. A silent, phantom presence.

'Don't strike a match, anyone,' Iris whispered. 'I'm in my chemise . . . what's left of it. . . .'

A sob, a jumble, a cry: 'Oh God, Oh God! I'm so glad to be back!'

'Little donkey!' said Guy. 'All right now, Venice?'

'Hugo,' Iris called, very huskily, 'where's that champagne? Venice would like. Child, must you breathe your last down my neck?'

'You saved me!' sobbed Venice. 'Yes, you did!'

'Ssh!'

'Ow, I was frightened!'

'Like a mouse in the water. Poor Venice. . . .'

'Here's another towel, Mrs. Storm,' said Shirley brusquely. Shirley would be a little jealous now of Venice liking Iris. . . .

'Listen!' cried Venice into the night. 'This woman saved me. Saved my life, she did! "Oi!" said I, and there she was, quick as quick. . . .'

205

'But, Venice, you're sitting on my only other stocking, and I've only got two!'

'Pop!' said the champagne.

'Have mine, please do! Like barefoot. Jimmy, I got such a bump on the head.'

'How?' Guy asked dangerously.

'Against the bridge, please. . . .'

'That's only bump (a),' said Hugo kindly. 'There's still bump (b) coming to you, if I heard aright.'

'You did,' said Guy.

'You leave her alone!' snapped Shirley.

'Venice!' Napier's voice, a white, still voice. He was kneeling, beside me, peering into the canoe. 'All right now, Venice?'

'Yes, Naps.' A shy, uncertain voice that was. She was afraid. 'You must thank Mrs. Storm for that. . . .'

Napier did not call on Iris's name. Hugo chattered to cover the silence. I thought I heard Guy mutter something between his teeth. During the next few minutes Hugo's dexterity with the champagne was a great relief. Dear Hugo.

'Venice!' said Guy beside me, chill, queerly harsh. 'Your health, Venice! You'll need a good deal, if you go playing any more tricks like that.'

Shirley was saying: 'Here's another towel, Mrs. Storm. Do have my stockings, please. . . .'

'Oh . . . no, it's quite all right, really. Please, really. But would you mind seeing if my shoes are anywhere there, by the steering-wheel thing?'

Formal, like the voices of women in a drawing-room.

Iris called to me for a cigarette. It was her right hand to which I gave it. It seemed very naked, that right hand. 'Your ring, Iris?'

'In the Thames,' she whispered. 'Fallen for ever! Not a word. . . .'

Venice was explaining to the darkness, gulping lavishly at her champagne: 'Thought I'd go for a swim and not just paddle about. Thought I'd be clever. Thought you were fools. Thought I'd thought right. Thought I'd—anyhow, I caught my head crack (a) on that bridge. And then I didn't want to let out a yell about nothing and look a silly ass. Heard you calling me, but thought I'd better keep my breath for swimming. Began swimming, and got a weed like a wrestler's torso round me. Head hurt, like hell it did. Thinks I, now for a yell, but began kicking instead——'

'You would!'

'Wait. And my head hurt. And I was frightened to death. And I prayed like fury. Naps! Where's Naps? I missed you. And when I wanted to yell all I could let out was a miaow. And Mrs. Storm—well, Iris, as she saved my life, cries out: "Oi, what's that? Who? Where?" And before you could say knife, and just as I was succumbing to a watery grave, she was saving my life, quick as you like. Quick, terse stuff. She could swim us all off our feet, she could. . . .'

'Get very easily tired,' Iris said.

'Iris!' Napier's voice, sharp. 'You dressed? What? Risky for you, messing about, after your illness.'

'I'm almost ready, Napier.' Impatient, Iris's voice was, I thought.

'Naps, get a rug from the car. She's shivering.'

'Please!' Iris whispered, frantically, desperately. 'For pity's sake, please not!'

Silence. . . .

As we collected round the two motor-cars, Guy, fiddling about with his starting-arrangements, seemed, I thought, to be saying something. But he was only swearing.

At the back of the Hispano Iris went to sleep against my shoulder. She spoke in her sleep: 'You will find me quite light on you, as I haven't got a chemise. They say it is very smart, to be chemiseless. Already I feel less of an outlaw from society. She did it on purpose.'

'Iris!'

'She did. Half on purpose. I know she did. The pet! Oh, dear . . .'

'But, Iris, why?'

'Because, dear. So that I should like her . . .'

'Oh! Well, do you?'

'Yes. Oh, yes.'

'Well?'
'I'm sorry if my hair is tickling your face.'
'Well, now you like her, does it make any difference?'
'No. Oh, no.'
'Oh!'
'Good-night.'

THE LAST CHAPTER   SAINT GEORGE FOR ENGLAND!

I

Now as I come to that last night of all, a night that was as though set on a stage by a cunning but reckless craftsman of the drama, and as I look every way I may at the happenings that were staged on the platform of that night, I do sincerely thank my stars that it is no novel I have set my hand to but a faithful chronicle of events. For it would seem that the novelist, so he is an honest man and loves his craft, must work always under a great disadvantage in his earnest wish to tell of life truthfully; since, as the old, old saying is, he never can dare to be so improbable as life. He may, to be sure, be as dingy as life, according to the mode of the day, or he may even achieve the impossible and be more dingy than life, also according to the mode of the day, but to be as improbable as life will be as far beyond the honest novelist's courage as it must be against the temper of his craft; for should his characters have to 'break out', should the novelist be so far gallant as to concede something to the profligate melodrama of life, his people may only 'break out' along lines which the art of their creator has laid out and made inevitable for them; whereas you and I know that living men will do queer things which are desperately alien from what we had thought their possibilities—nay, impossibilities—to be, living men will defy the whole art of characterisation in the twinkling of an eye and destroy every canon of art in a throb of a desire: so that we may make no count or chart of the queer, dark sides of our fellows, nor put any limit, of art, psychology, romance or decency, to the impossibilities which are, within the trembling of a leaf, possible to men and women.

It is not often that I see Venice nowadays, for she lives for the most part with her father in the country, but now and again she will ask me to luncheon in her house in Upper Brook Street, or maybe I will call there on a sudden and find her sitting alone with an unopened book. We do not ever talk of that night, nor of the two chief players of that night, but the other day it came about that I found her sitting absorbed in the shadows of a dying fire, and I some-how said: 'Waiting, Venice, waiting!'

She was crouched like a child in the gloom of a Dorothy chair, and as I sat in another nearby a friendly flame darted through the twilight and made toys of her eyes. They were looking at me with every appearance of deep reflection, but now it was a woman who was looking out at me from Venice's eyes, and the woman seemed to smile, and she said: 'He is in India, with Bruce's expedition. He will be coming home soon.'

And then for the first time we spoke of that tempestuous night in July, the night but one after the children's party. But of course I did not tell Venice all, particularly about the last part, according to the promise sworn between Sir Maurice Harpenden, Hilary and me.

My clock was about to strike nine o'clock, as I very well remember for I had nothing to do but stare at it, when the telephone-bell beat it, may I say, by a short head, and Iris's voice said:

'Is that you?'

'And who should it be,' I said, 'but me? I am so glad you rang up, Iris.'

'Oh, you are lonely!'

They shout on the telephone, people do, so that one cannot always hear them very, very well. But this fell lady's slightly husky voice was considerate and clear.

'But fancy,' she said, 'finding you at home now, and all the world at dinner or the play! Dear, are you, too, a social outcast? I am so sorry you have had to dine alone.'

'Iris, you should have brought up the friends of your childhood to a better understanding of the arts of peace. I was to have dined with Hilary to-night, and because of my engagement with him I did not go to a dinner where I was to sit beside a woman who has studied the Yogi philosophies and was divorced last year in New York with nine co-respondents, the tenth being disqualified on the ground that he was a black man weighing seventeen stone in his boots. And then Ross rings me up at half-past seven to say that Hilary has been called to the country!'

'Yes, I knew you had been put off for dinner. I was so shocked.'

'Thank you. But, Iris, you knew?'

'Oh, I know everything! But listen, I am ringing you up to ask you a plain question, and I would like, please, a plain answer. Does it mean anything to you that I am leaving England to-morrow at dawn?'

'You depress me, Iris Storm.'

'But I, oh I am so gay!'

'Yes, that is what depresses me. My friends are wretched, but you are gay! Iris, we are all of us miserable sinners, but you are a very captain of wickedness. Iris, you are a wrecker of homes, and you say you are gay! I am not being flippant. I have dined alone.'

'Dear, I understand. I do respect your disapproval, you must believe me, or else I would answer that we begin to die when we are born, that all comes from God and goes to the devil, and so what does anything matter? But listen, O father and brother of disapproval, would you like to see me before I leave England to-morrow at dawn?'

'Yes,' I said, 'I would.'

'"See" me, I said, not "murder" me!'

'But, Iris, I can qualify nothing to-night!'

'My idea is to take you into the country to-night. We go *à deux*. We go into a darkness. My friend, there is a sun-dial in a certain garden, and it is written that you and I shall stand by that sun-dial before we part to meet nevermore.'

'Iris, your voice is laughing, but you are not laughing. What does that mean?'

'But I am afraid! I am laughing with fear. . . .'

'And we are driving into the country to escape your fear?'

'Oh, but that hurts! I was never before accused of being a coward. . . .'

'Iris, I'm sorry.'

'Sir Maurice Harpenden knows me better than you do, my friend. Ah, he is very clever, is Sir Maurice! But you will see. We are driving into the country, let me tell you, to meet my fear. And when we meet it I shall not mock, nor tremble, nor quail, but I shall be a very Saint George for steadfastness. That is the programme, so far. And you, will you be my esquire?'

'You speak of darkness, of sun-dials, of fear, of Sir Maurice Harpenden, whom I do not know, of Saint George of Cappadocia, whom, alas, one sees only too little of these days. I think that you, too, must have dined alone. And you have gone mad. Else why must we drive into the country?'

'But we go to keep high company to-night, that's why! Are you afraid of *that*? The captains and the kings of the countryside are our adversaries. Sweet, you and I shall stand arrayed against the warriors of conduct.'

'Not I, Iris! I am for conduct.'

'You lie, dear. You are for love! Oh, why do you lie?'

'Because one must be reasonable, Iris.'

'Oh, because this, because that, because of the persecution of men, the savagery of beasts, the malice of gods! Free me of your becauses! Lies, all lies! One must be truthful, there is no other law, all other laws are lies. We are educated by lies, we live with lies, we worship lies, we fight for lies, we die bearded with lies. God made men out of clay, and countries out of mud, and what can the son of a marriage between clay and mud be but Master Lie? Oh, let us have just one look at the Demoiselle Truth!'

'Unfortunately, Iris, that demoiselle shows a different figure to all of us. Now I may like her with a trivial ankle, tawny hair, boyish breasts, but another may like her with golden hair and spacious loins, as Rubens painted women——'

'I will say this for you, that when you insult one you do it with kindness. It is kind of you to have described me as your idea of the demoiselle. I am proud of my breasts, because they are so beautiful. Life is generally so rude to a woman's breasts, but it has only kissed mine——'

'Iris, you are shocking the girl at the exchange!'

'No, no, Miss Dell has prepared her for anything! But you haven't yet said if you will be my esquire into the country? Why are you so silent?'

'But, Iris, I don't understand a word of this!'

'Sweet, do we need to wait on your understanding! Chivalry?'

212

'Away with that from me to you! You always chose the man's part.'

'Gallantry?'

'But I shall be gallant to another in being ungallant to you!'

'Friendship?'

'You are driving me very hard, Iris. I do not want to say what is in my mind.'

'Can you stand there with your lips to the receiver, which I hope your servants keep clean for you, and tell me you are not my friend? Can you stand there facing me across Queen Street, Curzon Street, Hertford Street, Hamilton Place, Hyde Park Corner and Knightsbridge, and tell me that you are not my friend? I am sitting here on the edge of the bed, in the next room is Mrs. Oden trying to pretend she is not listening to every word I say, all round me are trunks and boxes, about me is a leather jacket with a collar of a few minks, and on my head is one green hat. Are you not my friend? Answer me! Answer me, I say! Dear, a woman must have one friend! It is usual.'

'But the emerald is gone, Iris! So you are not the Iris I knew. You were Iris Storm, you are Iris March, and I never have met Iris March.'

'The emerald was wise. There's a *galanterie* in jewels unknown to men, I see that. So you won't come for a drive with me? Our last?'

'I never said that, Iris!'

'Ah, I have frightened him! Well, I will come round for you in five minutes. How are you dressed? In black and white? Maybe I would have preferred you in something less formal, in something more——'

'Enough of *pour le sport*, Iris! Oh, enough, enough!'

2

And so we were again, again and for the last time, in that swift motor-car, wrapped in the gentle silences of the night. The oppression of the heat was gone since the rains of yesterday, but even yet London could not quite rouse itself from the stupor of the past tropical week. And to-night the flight of the stork did not torment the hosts of the midgets, 'for,' said Iris from the shadow of her green hat, 'there is no hurry, no hurry at all.'

A clock in the High Street of Kensington was at a little after half-past nine o'clock. The wide sweep of road towards Olympia was quiet with the gentle traffic of no-man's-hour, for such is a little after half-past nine o'clock. I said: 'I do wish you would tell me what all this is about.'

'It begins a long time ago, it is a long story. Having to do with the loves of babes, the wisdom of sucklings, and the sins of the fathers. And the sins of the fathers. But I will tell you more when we come to Harrod's.'

'But we passed Harrod's long ago!'

'There is another. You will see. Patience.'

Through Hammersmith and Chiswick, by Ranelagh and Roehampton, we sped into the veiled countryside. The glow of London was a yellow arch in the night behind. We passed the last omnibus on its last journey to a far-flung corner of the town.

'But,' I pleaded, 'I don't even know where we are going to!'

'Why, to Sutton Marle! Didn't I tell you? It's not far. . . .'

'But I don't know Sir Maurice! Really, Iris, how dare you let me in for this?'

'It is all right, dear, you are expected. I said to Hilary, not an hour ago on the telephone: "I am not for Sutton Marle unless I may bring my one friend."'

'Well, I never heard such cheek! And why, Iris, am I your one friend?'

'Because once upon a time you shamed me of my shame. Because you did not hold me cheap. Because romance dies hard in you. Because, dear, I rather like you. And that is why I told Hilary that you were my friend and that I would not dare Sutton Marle without you, adding that as he had put you off for dinner it would be something for you to do.'

'Iris, you are laughing all the time, you who told me you were afraid!'

She glanced at me just then, and that second's smile is like a wound on my memory. A car screamed and passed u

and she cried through the disordered air: 'I am afraid, but of course I am gay, too! Haven't I waited twelve years for my inheritance!'

The flame of the lights on the road ahead made a wall of blackness on each side of us. I was like a child in this blackness, and it seemed to me that her voice was the voice of the night. I did not know what to say. I said: 'Iris, that girl will die without Napier.'

Minutes later, she said: 'If people died of love I must have risen from the dead to be driving this car now!'

'Indeed, Iris, how can I argue about love against your experience!'

'My friend, you can't shame me! For I am shame itself come to life. Yes, I have lit many small fires to quench one large fire. I have been unsuccessful. Thank God, thank God for that! And now let the one large fire burn, with a boy and a girl of eighteen for fuel. Nothing else matters.'

'My dear, so much else matters! Restraints, nobilities, decencies, sacrifices!'

We passed slowly through a village High Street, hailed and mocked good-naturedly by a group of men emerging from an inn.

She said: 'In the ancient love-tales and the songs of the Jongleurs we read of maidens sacrificed on the altar of circumstance. I was a maiden, even I, once upon a time. Dear, I am afraid you must take my word for that. And I, a maid, was sacrificed to the vulgar ambitions of a Sir Maurice. So let us not talk of sacrifice. It makes me sick with anger.'

Not fast, not slow, the Hispano-Suiza swept through Surrey. Then she said sharply: 'But if Venice had had a child!'

I could not see her face, for her hat and the darkness were between us. But ever so faintly I could see her mouth, and her lips were parted, as though she was praying. I wondered if she was praying, to whom she could be praying. 'She has a God,' had said that captain of men.

'And why did you say that so bitterly, Iris?'

'Was I bitter? Oh, that's a sin, to think of that angel and to be bitter.'

'Angel? Did you say angel?'

'I said angel,' she said, and no other answer had I but from the stork crying dolorously to warn corners of our flight.

'If Venice,' she said reasonably, 'had had a child, I would have called to Napier in vain. We can't know the beginning and end of honour, nor what it is, nor what it will do, nor what will debauch it, nor what will make it unbending as iron. Let us say I have debauched Napier's honour. Oh, let us say anything! We don't stand on words on ultimate nights like these. Honour is like a little child, let us say, and like a little child it may be led away by a shining toy, and in this case I am the shining toy. But had Venice had a child I might have shone like Aldebaran and called Napier in vain. And that would have been right and just. We must all give way before children, always, always. Oh, if people had always done that, what miseries wouldn't the world have been spared! Those whose dreams are clean must give way to children, for babies will carry clean dreams further than the wisest of old men, and slowly the world will rise above the age of smoke and savagery. . . .'

'But it's absurd, Iris! What chance has the girl had of having a child yet!'

'But I am not pretending to play fair! Or did you think I was? I awoke from my illness, and I awoke suddenly to life. Awaking, I took my chance as it came. And quickly, quickly, for fear of giving Venice a longer chance. And it's because I haven't played fair that I am going to Sir Maurice's house now.'

'Oh!' I said. 'Good God! Let me out of this car, Iris! I will walk back to London.'

'Napier doesn't know. Napier would be frantic if he knew. Napier is dining with Venice to-night. They would both be frantic if they knew I had taken Sir Maurice's challenge and gone down to Sutton Marle. But I must go, to make unfairness a little less unfair. I must let Sir Maurice have his last joy of me. Besides, there is a fascination in letting men tell the truth to one. There is a fascination in wondering if it will ever be the truth. But look! Oh, look! There is Harrod's!'

The car had pulled up on the brow of a small hill. The

lights searched across the road into an unhedged field. Iris pointed along the flame of light.

'There is Harrod's,' she said gravely.

'But where is Harrod's? I see a field and what looks like a giant oak.'

'That is Harrod's. Not an oak, but an ash. It is very old, and smells of fairies and moonlight.'

There were once two roads that led away from a certain tree. . . .

The tree, a solitary giant of enormous girth, stood perhaps twenty yards from the road. Its trunk dammed the far-flung eyes of the car, and in the light its leaves were made of silver, and you fancied that, had there been a breath of wind, it had spoken from its ancient wisdom, of which this night stood so sorely in need; but never a whisper stirred the countryside.

'Iris, doesn't that make your passions look . . . silly?'

She took my hand, and lifted it, and dropped it. I do not know why she did that. Her face was hidden. It seemed to me that a long time passed before she spoke, and I seemed to think of many things.

'If there was a moon,' she said at last, 'a little way behind Harrod's you would see a small hill, and on the hill you would see a white house. That is where Gerald and I were born. Perhaps Gerald knows why now. That is one of the many things Napier and I have to talk out in the solitudes, why all we men and women are born. There must be a reason. Across the fields this way is Sutton Marle, where Napier was born. We used to play beneath this tree, Gerald, Boy, Napier and I. Boy was older than us, and bossed us. So there was a revolt, and then we made two camps, Boy and Gerald, Napier and I. Sometimes Aunt Eve, who took care of Gerald and me when mother died, would take us all up to London, and we would have tea at Harrod's. Napier and I loved Harrod's, because we at once got lost there. And so we called this tree Harrod's, because we were happy here, too. We were twelve then. Later on they discouraged our being together. Aunt Eve didn't want me to be made miserable when I grew up by not being allowed to marry Napier, for she knew that I didn't come into Sir Maurice's plans. Poor Maurice, I've

217

crashed into them now, haven't I! Father got poorer, we sold this house, and went to live in Cambridge Square. Napier was not allowed to see me any more, but we managed to meet somehow. Gerald helped, Aunt Eve helped, Boy helped. That was when Boy first loved me, he said later, because of my determination not to lose Napier. But Sir Maurice won. I was stronger than Napier, but I was not so strong as Sir Maurice. He wanted Napier to marry a rich girl, and Iris March was only the daughter of the younger branch of a bankrupt house. One day, when I was eighteen, I got a wire from Napier to meet him here at Harrod's that afternoon. I borrowed the money for a taxi—bit from Boy, bit from Hilary—and here Napier was, white, desperate. In a general clean-up before going up to Oxford he had promised his father never to see me again. "I like Iris," Sir Maurice had said, "but she comes of rotten stock." I don't think we had ever realised before that we were in love. I suppose I grew up in that one second. But Napier was still a boy of eighteen, while I was suddenly as old as the Queen of Hearts. I told him I loved him. Dear, I have known many men, I have married two, but I have only told one that I loved him, and he was a boy. Poor Napier, so torn, white, distracted. Afraid of my love, which seemed to him almost unholy, afraid of his father, who seemed to him almost holy. England, my England! His father was strong in Napier, and the Harpendens were strong in him. They were stronger than me at eighteen, and they were stronger than the sweet memories of Harrod's. I said to Napier then, just over there where the lights fall by that trunk, I said, eighteen to eighteen: "Napier, I think I have a body that burns for love. Napier, I shall burn it with love, but I never will say 'I love you' to any man but you, because it never will be true." And what I said at eighteen is true now at thirty, I have never said I loved him to any man but Napier, for it hasn't been true. I have given myself, in disdain, in desire, with disgust, with delight, but I have kept to that silly, childish boast of mine. I say that to my shame, but now shame is a weed under my foot. I married because my body was hungry for love and born to love and must love. And I

218

thought I would destroy my body with love's delight, but all I did was to destroy a good man. Hector Storm went off to Ireland and died because one night in my sleep I whispered Napier's name. Or perhaps I had whispered it many nights. I told him that he was being jealous of a ghost, but he wouldn't believe. Now all those things are passed. The nymph unloosened her girdle to desire, and now she has unloosened it to her only love. One grows out of everything, even desire: and then one can love. Look, Harrod's is smiling, all silver and smiling! Here Sir Maurice sacrificed me twelve years ago. To-night I have to say to him: "This is what you have done, Maurice—the unhappiness of Venice, the unhappiness of your son, and twelve years of hell for me. Are you content?" Oh God, it's been hell, these twelve years! If you had kissed hell, as I have kissed hell, if you had sacrificed to hell, as I have sacrificed my body to hell, you would know what I mean. But now I can't grudge Maurice the final satisfaction of telling me what he thinks of me. Dear, it matters so little what men like Maurice think of one. They worship all that is despicable, they despise all that is really good. From the beginning of time this world has been wounded by the manliness of fools. Oh, let Maurice have his say to-night! And mighty Guy. And my sweet Hilary! Let them have their say. I can only answer them with love. How could I answer them but with love? But I can silence them with love! Love, love, love! A glorious word, a matchless word! But isn't it? Love, love! I am in love, I glory in love, I will die in love! Love, my sweet, love, love! To be in love as I am in love is to be in heaven before hell was made. I am in love!'

The car rushed on, up a wide slope that curved handsomely so that the light played on meadows and startled the beasts of the fields.

'And you are so sure, Iris, that these three men, who have known you all your life and one of whom has loved you with all his heart ever since he saw you walk down South Audley Street, all brown stockings and blue eyes—you are so sure, Iris, that nothing they can say will touch you?'

The lights swept over great lodge-gates standing wide

open before a curving avenue of tall trees. We passed beneath them, showering gold on their trunks. The drive shone like a yellow carpet beneath our lights.

'I tell you,' Iris whispered, 'I shall be a very Saint George for steadfastness!'

The stork fled up the curving avenue of Sutton Marle. It seemed, to me, to crouch with fear beneath the noble line of trees. They stood above us like towers. I was afraid.

'This is the lion's den, Iris!'

'Well, I have killed lions, and tigers too, in twelve years' wanderings through hell.'

'But this is the den of the king of lions, Iris! This is the den of the lion of England!'

'Love smiles at lions. Love can never be a clown, but a lion can wear an ass's skin. Darling. I'm no good at natural history, but I have studied history.'

'You couldn't mock it so unless you loved it very deeply. You are like a child, dear Iris, daring her father and mother. These trees——'

'But I laugh at the trees of Sutton Marle! I always did, I never could play with them, not even believe in them. I tell you there is no tree but Harrod's, my servant, and my master, and my playmate tree, Harrod's. Oh, how Harrod's hates Sir Maurice! It makes me afraid, to think how Harrod's hates Maurice Harpenden. Let him beware as he walks beneath it!'

Then the trees parted from above us and we came into an open place where stood a fountain, and round the fountain we swept a circle and came before the doors of a long white manor house. De Travest's car stood there. As we drew up beside it the doors of the white house opened and a fat old man stood at the head of the steps. His hair was like his house, quite white.

'Truble, we will go round by the garden,' Iris said.

The fat old butler looked very gravely down at Iris. She was like a small knight at the foot of the broad steps, he a kindly old dragon up above. Oh, he looked so grave!

Iris said to me: 'Mr. Truble is my oldest friend. He is a very nice man. Truble, what have you to say to that?'

'Sir Maurice did not expect you, Miss Iris.'

'How, Truble! Sir Maurice knew I was coming!'

'But he did not think you would come, Miss Iris. But his lordship expected you. The gentlemen are in the library.'

'His lordship, Truble, does me too much honour in thinking I can keep my word. . . . Truble, my dear!'

I had been looking round me when that sudden cry shook me like the cry of a bird in pain. The fat old butler was weeping, there was not a doubt of it. There at the head of the broad steps, quite motionless, a broad black shape under his white hair. Iris had him by the shoulder, was shaking him, her hat like a toy against that black shape.

'Truble,' she said, so huskily, 'that I should ever have made you cry! My dear, my dear!'

'Sir,' the old man appealed to me down below with a funnily out-flung hand. 'I never was so ashamed of myself in my life! But it came on me all of a sudden hearing Miss Iris say, here at the doors of Sutton Marle, in a voice as hard as that ash she was always in love with, that about his lordship doing her too much honour about her keeping her word. I held Miss Iris in my arms, sir, when she wasn't above a year old, and now—I'm sure I beg your pardon, sir. And yours, Miss Iris. I'm sure I don't know what's come over me to-night. . . .'

One leather arm had the old man by the shoulder. Iris's face seemed painted white.

'Truble,' she said, so huskily, 'I am so sorry to have upset you. You have been faithful to me, Truble, for thirty years, and now, I suppose, you mustn't love me any more. You don't love me any more, Truble!'

'Miss Iris, Miss Iris! There's no good comes from loving, I see that!'

'Then, Truble, I here and now do release you from giving me a thought ever again. Adieu, Truble.'

Her face painted white, her eyes absorbed in what they did not see, she came down to where I stood. 'Come,' she said, expressionless. She could make her words into pieces of iron, and I did not dare to look at the motionless old man at the head of the steps. We skirted the house in silence. I supposed we were on a lawn. The rains of yesterday had not softened the drought, the grass was hard as stone under the feet. I said: 'Iris, you are moved already—you who were not to be moved by anything that was said!'

I felt her fingers tightening round my arm. Hers were strong white fingers. 'I hadn't bargained for Truble. He should have been in bed by now. Often in moments of self-hatred and contempt I have taken a little heart from that old man's devotion. And he would always send me wishes on my birthday. No, I hadn't bargained for Truble. . . . Look!'

'Why, they are playing bridge!'

'And, dear, how grimly! See, Hilary is looking quite young, he must have a bad hand. And Guy Apollo Belvedere —Oh, he's thinking!—and then he plays the wrong card! Ah, poor Guy! He always did treat his trumps as though they were tulips, with too much respect. And Sir Maurice! Now, dear heart, what do you think of Sir Maurice? Isn't he the handsome soldier!'

'Oh, handsome! Napier with a gay sinner's face. . . .'

'Judge him for me! Oh, do! Here we are, conspirators, whispering. Now, judge me, first, Mr. Townshend of Magralt.'

'Iris, must I! Can I? I can't!'

'Of course you must, can, will! Speak without thinking. It is only thus that truth is made.'

'He is a good man. His goodness is supported by his principles, his kindness is rebuked by his prejudices. He is not a weak man, but he is the weakest man in that room. He has loved but one woman in his life, and she has crucified his heart on a hundred carnal Calvarys. But he still loves her, and that is why he is the weakest man in that room.'

'And you, satyr, you are the cruellest man I ever met in my life! But judge me, secondly, my lord Viscount de Travest.'

'He is the elder brother of honour. He is that rarest of men, a schoolboy who has grown out of his schooldays but remains, by strength of will, a schoolboy. He prefers to be that. He never did an unworthy thing, and has thought less mean ones than most people. Like all decent Englishmen, he is like a woman: he knows everything without ever having

222

been taught anything. He has a profound sense of obedience, therefore he is a good commander. He never thinks when he is alone, lest thoughts should undermine his sense of obedience and paralyse his habit of command. One day a thought will strike him, and instantly he will cease to be the captain of his soul. He is the only man in England who actually believes in obeying the King.'

'Oh, how horrified the King would be! And of Sir Maurice, enemy to Iris March, what have you to say? Besides the fact that he is the cleverest man in that room. Oh, he is clever, that Maurice! It was he who had old Truble waiting for me. Judge me that man!'

'But I don't know him, Iris!'

'His face is there, man—the proconsular features, the cunning Norman nose, the smile—Oh, my God, the smile! And you won't, my friend, take my opinion of him?'

'Iris, how can you ask me to do that! We can't take any woman's opinion of any man. They find evil in good men, they overlook the vices of cads. . . .'

'Oh, Maurice is not good, not bad! Only immemorially infantile, like all successful men. . . .'

Where we stood now the lawn was damp and velvet-soft, the air whispered of flowers. The light that fell across the lawn from the three tall french-windows reached almost to our feet. It was a long, oak-panelled, scholarly room in which the three men sat, towards one side, about a card-table. They were absorbed in their game, silent figures of black and white. Yes, the fine profile of Sir Maurice seemed apt to smile. Iris murmured: 'We will wait for them to finish their game.'

As my hand moved to throw away a cigarette I touched a cold stone, and I saw that we were standing by a sun-dial. Iris was looking at me, and clearest of all the happenings of that night I remember that long moment of Iris's looking, and how, as I looked into her eyes, her beauty seemed to enwrap itself with the whisper of the flowers and enter into my being, so that I cared not for right nor wrong. My hand rested on the sun-dial. She laid her hand on mine, and her hand was colder than the sun-dial.

3

Sir Maurice received me very kindly. I had thought, seeing him at the card-table, that he was a tall man; but he was small, slight, taut; very ready to smile. He offered me a cigar, which I was very pleased to take. Iris said she would not smoke just yet. No one sat down, but everyone seemed at their ease. It was as though Iris and I were paying an evening call. Hilary apologised to me about dinner. I forgave him. Somehow, suddenly, I found myself absorbed by Guy and Hilary. I found that Iris was alone. It was as though her green hat stamped her aloneness with a light. How bright that green hat looked in that scholarly room, like a green flower, like a green flame! Iris stood by the card-table, on which the cards were scattered face-upwards.

'Good of you to come, Iris,' the General said. He smiled very easily. He was one of those young old men who are very old when you look close. He was charming.

Iris looked up from the cards across the room to Hilary. Her eyes were untroubled and clear, she was very still, and her lips were silken red. She said: 'Hilary asked me. So I came.'

'It was my idea, Iris,' Sir Maurice said, and he smiled. He was fidgeting with a black ebony paper-knife. 'My idea entirely. Hilary was against it. Very glad you brought our young friend. Sit down, Iris. We are all of the world here, we are civilised people. Let's talk about this like civilised people.'

Iris did not sit down. Maybe someone sat down, but I don't remember. Iris picked up the ace of clubs from the table and looked at it thoughtfully.

'That was really why I came, Maurice. Because it must have been your idea. You are a very clever man. It was thoughtful of you to give me a chance of saying good-bye to Truble.' She looked up from the ace of clubs to Guy with her untroubled eyes. She had not once looked at Sir Maurice. 'Guy, what have you to say to me? I think you have wanted to say something to me for a long time. It would have been cowardly to leave England for good without giving you the chance.'

'Iris,' said Hilary sharply, 'Guy has always been very kind about you. Hm. Much kinder than I've been.'

224

'Yes, dear,' she smiled so suddenly at Hilary. That was a surprising, complete smile. It excluded us all, it excluded even Iris and Hilary, it excluded everyone but the friend of childhood and a long little thing, all brown stockings and blue eyes. That was a true smile. 'Hm,' said Hilary.

Sir Maurice put a whisky-and-soda into my hand, but I do not remember tasting it. The slight, poised old gentleman's smile troubled me. His was too fine a face to smile like that. He had clever, darting eyes. I felt that Iris was making an effort to keep her eyes from him. And I felt that the two enemies were each terrified of the other.

Guy spoke for the first time, he murmured: 'It was brave of you to come, Iris. I don't know much about using words, but I think it was noble of you to come. I don't know any other woman who would have even thought of accepting Maurice's invitation. But we, your friends, have never compared you to other women. In some things to their disadvantage. We have always admired your pluck. But we have admired your candour and honesty even more. That is why this sickening business baffles us so. Maurice and I just thought it might be fair both to us and to you if we were to try to clear it up a little.' And then Guy snapped: 'I'm damned if I want to hate you, Iris.'

Iris broke the back of the ace of clubs and dropped it among the others on the green cloth, where it lay cruelly curled.

'Steady, Iris, steady!' said Sir Maurice. And he tried with the black ebony paper-knife to straighten out the ace of clubs. And he smiled. But Iris looked at Guy, and she seemed very tall.

'Iris,' Hilary said gently, 'we loved you too much as a child not to be able to hate the woman who has gone out of her way to kill every memory of that child. . . .'

'That's it, Iris,' Guy murmured, restrained, amiable. 'You see, as a child and as a girl you were very much in our hearts. Much more than any other child and girl has ever been. I don't know why. And in spite of all the things you've done we've always . . . well, we've always kept one side of us which was yours for the asking. I mean, Iris, we couldn't

225

believe in you as a . . . well, as a decent woman, but we've just stayed fond of you. Even when we've had to hear your name being pitched about by vile women and ghastly cads. Until now. But now. . . .'

'A moment, Guy!' The clever, darting eyes, the neat figure, the iron-grey hair, waving just a little. He smiled. He waved the black ebony paper-knife at Iris as though she was a naughty girl. He knew Iris inside-out, did Sir Maurice. She wasn't all bad, not she. Iris looked at him for the first time, and the clear untroubled look seemed now to be fixed stonily. I wondered if she was afraid. The General spoke quickly, brittle-bright: 'Guy has just said, Iris, that we've known you all your life. But there's more than that, much more. That's why I wanted you to come here to-night. I wanted to show you us, Iris. This isn't an ordinary elope-ment, Napier's and yours. It's a stab in the back——'

'Maurice, am I stabbing you in the back by coming here?'

'You were always a strange, unfrightened girl, Iris. But the stab in the back is made. It's stabbing us, your people, in the back. Venice's people aren't in this as we are. But that isn't what I want to tell you. Is it, Guy? And I've no inten-tion of trying to beg Napier from you. I'm not even yet old enough to beg favours from a woman. No, it seems settled about you and Napier, as he told me this morning. And I tell you, Iris, it wasn't my son who spoke to me this morning. It was an enchanted boy——'

'We are both of us enchanted, Maurice.' And Iris smiled. Her lips looked very red, silken red.

'Very good, very good! Well, you go to-morrow. That's fixed. But I just wanted to show you us, Iris. I think you have forgotten us on your travels. You are of us. I think you have forgotten that. And you are stabbing us in the back. I'm not talking of Napier now as my son, my only son. Am I, Guy? Hilary? I've taken great pride in the boy's career. I haven't married again for his sake—but let all that go. I'm talking of Napier now just as one of us here, the us that you belong to, of the England that we stand for. We, Iris— you and us—we aren't made only of flesh-and-blood. There's a little devil of slackness who stands waiting for any

226

of us who thinks he or she is only made of flesh-and-blood. We are made of air, too—this air, Iris, that we are breathing now. We are made of this air, you and us. We were born in it, our fathers and mothers were born in it. Guy, Hilary, I, you, Napier, we were all of us born within a hundred miles of this room, Guy at Mace, Hilary at Magralt, Napier and I here at Sutton Marle, and you not two miles away across the fields. We are of this soil, Iris, of this air, of this England which is still our England. My God, we haven't much left, but we still have this. That is all I have to say, Iris. I just wanted to show you us, because I thought you must have forgotten us. You have decided, Iris, that you will break into our lives, and break up our lives. Why, Iris? What sort of hell is your ambition in the next world? Tell me that.'

'No, Maurice!' said Hilary sharply. 'Keep to this world.'

Cold as stones were Iris's eyes on Sir Maurice. She hated him beyond words or looks. 'Don't let's talk of hell, Maurice,' she whispered. 'It would shock even you if I were to tell you how much I know about it. I am leaving hell behind at last. And do you know, Maurice, that hell looks at me with your face? But I am leaving it behind now.'

'Listen, Iris. Just this one question.' Those clever, darting eyes were curiously, strangely kind. I could not understand Sir Maurice. It was as though he loved, feared, hated, indulged Iris. He waved the black ebony paper-knife at her. 'Now I am a man of the world, Iris. Unlike Napier, as you know. And what sort of a woman are you? Tell me that. I have known many bad women. I have liked some. I have liked you, Iris. You know that. But this isn't badness. Damn it, girl, this is evil! There aren't any words in English to describe what we think of a woman who comes wantonly between a man and his wife, a man and his career. I'm not saying anything of your having come between Napier and me. He looked at me this morning as though he hated me. But leave me out. You are smashing a man's career and you have stolen a man from his wife. What sort of a woman are you, Iris? Tell us that.'

'Maurice!' And Iris smiled, and those very white teeth bit the moment into two pieces with their smile and dropped the pieces into limbo. 'You are a baby sometimes, Maurice. You never dream of asking a woman "what sort of a woman are you?" so long as she keeps to the laws made by men. But the first time you see a woman being a woman, you are surprised.'

'But what we don't understand,' Guy murmured amiably, 'is how you've come by an entirely different set of ideas from ours. I mean . . . well, ideas about loyalty and treachery and things like that. You see, Iris, we've suddenly found to-day that we simply don't begin to understand you. Isn't that so, Hilary? I mean, we just don't seem to think in the same sickening language.'

'Exactly,' Sir Maurice rapped out. With the black ebony paper-knife. 'That's it exactly, Iris. You see, this isn't just your business and Napier's business. This concerns *us*. This stabs at the roots of our life, Iris. But you and I don't seem to think in the same language. I think in English.'

Iris whispered, with eyes of stone: 'Unfortunately, I think in English, too. . . .'

'Oh, come, Iris!' Guy murmured.

'If she didn't think in English,' I said, 'would she be here?' Sir Maurice started. I was surprised, too.

'That's true,' said he. 'Quite true, boy. Yes.' And he smiled. I wished he wouldn't smile.

'In that case,' Guy murmured, 'all I can say is, Iris, that yours must be a very odd dialect of English. I mean, in yours there doesn't seem to be any distinction between words which—well, they mean rather a lot to us. We've never even learned how to spell most of them, they're so inevitably part of our lives, or should be. I'm not sure to this day if there's an s in decency. One's born knowing them. . . .'

'Guy, I've had twelve years' unhappiness. You talk to me of those words we are born knowing. I have had twelve years' unhappiness through not being able to forget those words.'

'Unhappiness!' Sir Maurice rapped out. 'Oh, come, child! You seem to have done exactly as you pleased all these years. I'm not saying you haven't had bad luck—we're all sorry about that. But if you have been unhappy can you blame anyone but yourself?'

228

Iris's face was very stern as she looked at Sir Maurice. I could not have thought that a beautiful woman could look so stern. And she made not one gesture of womanhood. She could have made but one, and asserted her right to live according to her womanhood. But that would have seemed to her to be playing not fair. She must meet men on their own ground always, always, and she must keep herself on their own ground without showing the effort she made. She would advantage herself neither with her womanhood nor her beauty. She seemed to look for a long time at Sir Maurice. Her lips were silken red, and I thought just then that to kiss them would be to kiss the infinite.

'Yes, Maurice. I can put the blame on three words.'

The General threw the paper-knife on to a small table, where it fell with a crash. 'Weakness? Wickedness? Wantonness?'

'The three words I was thinking of make Sir Maurice Harpenden.'

Then, curiously, Sir Maurice darted a look at Hilary, as though to see how he stood with Hilary. Hilary was white. He said: 'I've told you, Maurice, that you're not free from blame. You've been too damned imperious with these children.'

'All this,' Guy murmured, 'has got me beat, I'm afraid.'

'It hasn't got you beat at all, Guy,' snapped Hilary. White he was. 'Maurice, years ago, didn't realise that in our time we are not our children's masters. Their ideas are not ours, their ambitions are not ours. And there's no reason why they should be, since ours have sent all Europe to the devil.'

Then Iris's voice slashed the room like a sharp knife: 'Maurice, did you understand what I said? I am here to-night that you should understand what you have done.'

'My dear Iris!' said Sir Maurice, again picking up the paper-knife. One saw why he had been so successful a soldier. He could evade any issue. 'Boy and girl love!' he said helplessly to Guy. He looked at me. 'Boy and girl love!' he said helplessly.

'You mustn't despise it, Maurice,' Iris suddenly smiled,

and I had a fancy that her smile was one of protecting a child from a man's good-sense. 'It won't do to despise that boy and girl love, Maurice. It has lasted nearly all my life so far. And it will last me until I die.' She looked at Guy, and as soon as she looked away from the General the clear, untroubled, boyish look came back into those enormous eyes. 'Napier and I were in love at eighteen, Guy. Napier and I have always been in love. But Sir Maurice had other ideas for Napier, and this is the result of them. I am sorry, Guy, but I am also human.'

'Love!' rapped out Sir Maurice. He was not smiling now.

'Love!' Iris whispered. 'Love, Maurice! You daren't look into my eyes and say you doubt my love for Napier. You daren't say that my love is not the only thing in this room that is made in the image of God. You talk to me of your England. I despise your England, I despise the us that is us. We are shams with patrician faces and peasant minds. We are built of lies, Maurice, and we toil for the rewards of worms. You would have Napier toil for a worm's reward, you are sorry I have broken Napier's career in the Foreign Office. Maurice, I am glad. To you, it seems a worthy thing for a good man to make a success in the nasty arena of national strifes and international jealousies. To me, a world which thinks of itself in terms of puny, squalid, bickering little nations and not as one glorious field for the crusade of mankind is a world in which to succeed is the highest indignity that can befall a good man, it is a world in which good men are shut up like gods in a lavatory. Maurice, there are better things, nobler things, cleaner things, than can be found in any career that will glorify a man's name or nationality. You thought to bully me with our traditions. You are right, they are mine as well as yours. May God forgive you the sins committed in their name! And may He forgive me for ever having believed in them. . . .'

With one darting stride Sir Maurice had his hand sharply on her shoulder, that leather shoulder. And at that moment, when she had seemed at her strongest, her eyes seemed to flutter from his unsmiling face. Her eyes were flooded with gentleness, and they seemed to flutter, to want to fly from

230

that stern, handsome face. Yet Sir Maurice's eyes were curiously kind. Perhaps that was why she had suddenly wilted. She hated him so, and his eyes were curiously kind. That was a clever man, Sir Maurice. Then, in a second, with an effort she superbly hid from our eyes, she was calm again. Always she must meet a man on his own ground.

'Iris,' Sir Maurice said quietly, his hand on her shoulder, 'I am sorry I caused you unhappiness when you were a child. I admit I wanted a different alliance for Napier. And you must admit, child, that the March blood is not a very encouraging prospect for a father. But I am sincerely sorry I was unkind to you. But you must see, Iris, that yours was an unusual case. You were mature at eighteen, but I could realise neither that nor the depth of your feelings. Really, child, you mustn't blame me too much. We can't always tell when a boy and girl friendship is serious——'

'Maurice, why do you lie? I didn't think you would lie to-night. You knew very well that it was serious. That was why you made Napier promise never to see me again. And your son kept his promise.'

'But why didn't you come and tell me about it frankly, Iris? I had other plans for Napier, yes, but apart from that I was always your friend. You should have come and told me about it——'

'Oh, I was proud then! As I am not proud now. . . .'

'What!' We started at the odd snap in Guy's voice. 'What, Iris?' And he laughed, desperately, helplessly. Guy! 'Iris, that's the first lie I've ever known pass your lips. Why, you're as proud as an archangel!' We stared at him, somehow staggered by him, as he suddenly strode forward, the fair, slender giant. 'Just a moment, Maurice,' said he, and bent down and kissed Iris's cheek.

'Oh!'

This moment I can hear that despairing cry. 'Oh!'

And then she tried to catch back her cry, she sobbed: 'Judas!'

Guy had caught her as she started back from him like a frightened animal. 'Judas nothing,' he murmured. Her face streamed with tears. Guy held her, his eyes strangely sad.

231

'Judas nothing, my Iris,' he murmured. 'You've won, girl. Go away and play at your lovely game of love. You've got me again, as you had when you were a child. I must say I like someone who really loves and really hates. I'm proud of you, Iris.'

Somehow, somehow, as Guy held her, Iris's eyes looked through the mist towards me, and I moved my lips to make two words: Saint George. Somewhere in the mist she smiled. . . .

She whispered: 'Unfair, unfair, unfair! Guy, to kiss me like that, sweet, forgiving Guy! Oh, unfair, unfair, unfair! And I was so sure I wouldn't cry to-night. . . .'

Sir Maurice was fidgeting with the black ebony paper-knife. Hilary said 'hm' and blew his nose. It was very funny now that it was Sir Maurice who seemed to be alone. I was glad. Iris had at last been forced to retreat from that proud battlefield on which she met men on their own ground. She had made her one gesture of womanhood; and now it was Sir Maurice who stood alone. Clever Guy. He was looking towards the General, smiling. . . .

'Maurice,' he smiled, 'the girl's right. You were rather a sickening ass. . . .'

'My dear Guy,' said the General with a tremendous helplessness; and he smiled. 'How on earth was I to know then that a boy and gir——'

'Oh, phut!' Guy smiled like a boy. 'You don't catch me interfering with any of my boy's friendships, I can tell you. Not that I've ever really thought about these things before. One just goes driving along never giving these things a thought until one day we all go off the deep end just because we never have given them a thought, I fancy Hilary's right about this father and child business. I mean, people have been having sons, I suppose, since the year one, and the relation between them is still a mess. In this century, for instance, all we people have been bucking no end about being brotherly with our sons, as though being a fat-headed brother was any good if you don't understand what the cub is driving at. I just thought of that this very moment. For instance, my boy told me the other day that Kipling wrote true-blue miracles calculated to increase the blood-pressure in men who were too old to fight. I gave him a thrashing with the gloves for his infernal cheek, especially as he must have got it out of some book, for the boy hasn't what you could call a brain, which is just as well, for it will keep him from going over to Labour. But, after all, our cubs can't make more of a mess of everything than we and our fathers have done. That's the point to hang on to.'

'Good God, man!' snapped Hilary. 'I've been saying that to you for twenty years, and you've——'

'That's right, Hilary,' Guy grinned. 'But you've got a way of saying things. . . .'

Iris was looking from one to the other of us. It was as though she was in a dream, looking at faces in a dream. Soft she was now, soft and white and small. And her eyes were clouds of blue mist. She stared at Sir Maurice, who stood fidgeting with the paper-knife. 'Maurice,' she whispered, 'good-bye.'

Sharply he looked up from the paper-knife. He flipped the paper-knife on to the card-table. Then I saw that Sir Maurice hated his ancient enemy.

'Good-bye, Iris,' he said. 'But you must not expect me to wish you happiness. You have taken from me my only son.'

'Maurice,' she said desperately, 'isn't that special pleading? Haven't you any pity, any understanding, of what I have been through?'

'Understanding! Yes, I have understanding, Iris. But I can't let it stretch across the wide gulf that should separate you from my son.'

'But you made the gulf, Maurice! You, you!' She seemed passionately to want his understanding now!

'I!' cried Sir Maurice. 'Good God, woman, I merely parted a boy and a girl. But you could have found each other again—if you hadn't been you! *I* made the gulf! Iris, did I murder Boy Fenwick?'

'Maurice, you take that back!'

'Hilary, never mind.' It was a faint, husky whisper. 'Just don't mind, Hilary.' She was staring at Sir Maurice as at a snake. She was calm. 'Did you say murder, Sir Maurice? Murder?'

Sir Maurice made the most helpless gesture. He looked very old. 'I apologise, Iris, I apologise! I take it back completely. I was carried away. I apologise, child. Of course, murder was much too strong——'

'Too strong?' Guy echoed softly. 'If you ask me, sir, it was so damned strong that it's a wonder to me that it hasn't blown us all out of the house.'

'I have apologised, Guy!' snapped Sir Maurice.

Iris was looking at me. She seemed lost in some thought, she was very still. Her lips said: 'Dear, take me away.'

Sir Maurice darted for his paper-knife, fumbled among the cards for it, got it, rapped out: 'Just one moment, Iris. I didn't mean to say that. You must see that. I apologise sincerely.'

'I cannot hear your apology, Maurice. Because of that gulf.'

'I never thought of saying that,' Guy murmured. 'Damn!'

'Just a moment, just a moment!' the General waved the paper-knife fretfully. 'Ever since Napier came to see me this morning I have been thinking of these things. I saw Venice this afternoon. She is mad, I think, or enchanted. She believes in your love for Napier. I can only see the helpless ruin you have made of my son. And you say you love him! Let's forget if we can all the other men you have "loved". Just take this one fact. Not two years after parting from Napier for good, which you say broke your heart, you marry Boy Fenwick. And when Boy Fenwick died you yourself said he had died "for purity". What did that mean if not that even before you married him . . . you yourself, I say, said that he had died "for purity"!'

'For hell, sir! That was why Boy Fenwick died!'

'Napier!' There was a long, long silence. 'Napier!' Iris whispered frantically. 'My darling, why are you here!'

'To get you. . . .' Napier's voice trembled pitifully. He controlled it by whispering. 'To get you from these . . . men!'

'Steady, Naps!' Guy murmured. 'We began the evening by bucking about being civilised.'

Again, as in the obscure silence of the Paris night, the white face, the lost eyes . . . facing us from the middle french-window.

'Napier!' Iris pleaded. She seemed to be pleading against something which only she could see in those two dark ruins of eyes. And they made ruins of us all, those eyes, but saw only one of us. And behind his shoulder, in the garden, pale, wide-eyed, steady as a judgment, stood Venice. . . .

'Good God, man!' Sir Maurice rapped out. 'Why bring Venice into this!'

'He didn't. I came.' And Venice smiled in a sort of way.

Napier said in a scarcely audible voice: 'Let Venice alone. I think she is my only friend.' As he stepped into the room Iris made a step towards him, two, three. Her eyes were dilated, beseeching. But never once, since the shock of his first words had turned us to the windows, had he taken his eyes from his father. The dark, fevered, lost eyes. He was passing Iris. She snatched at his arm, pulled at him. 'Napier, don't, don't. Napier, please, my sweet! Venice, for pity's sake stop him! You don't *know* what he's going to say!'

The thin white fingers of the so naked right hand were buried round the black-covered arm, holding him in his stride; but still Napier looked only at his father. His face was so white that we all looked red and swollen. But Sir Maurice was not put out by his son's fixed stare. He had his black ebony paper-knife.

'Well, Naps? What does this mean?'

Iris cried: 'Napier!' Then she turned passionately to Venice. 'Don't you see, Venice! He doesn't know what he's saying!'

'It means, sir,' Napier said quietly, 'that if you weren't my father I would call you a cad.'

'Don't!' Hilary snapped. 'Hm. Run away now, all of you. Together or separate. Just run away.'

Iris pulled at Napier's arm. He did not see her. He said very quietly, his voice imperceptibly trembling: 'Venice and I called after dinner at Montpellier Square. Venice wished to say good-bye to Iris. What is between Iris and Venice is their business. They make me feel a lout, they make you

235

look like . . . We found Mrs. Oden upset. She said Iris had come here, and . . .' His voice broke, and he passed a hand over his mouth as though to steady it. He scowled.

Venice, still by the window, was wearing a leather-coat like Iris's, but it looked much newer and lighter. She had her hands dug deep into the pockets. Iris cried: 'Venice, for pity's sake help me make Napier come away! Oh, you don't understand! He's no idea what he's saying!'

For the first time Napier took his eyes from his father. His mouth twitched funnily, and he scowled. 'Yes, I have, Iris. But I want to clear up this business once and for all. It's gone on long enough, this—this Boy Fenwick business. What?'

'But, Napier, you promised!'

He scowled. 'I don't care, Iris. I'm awfully tired of all these pretences. It can't . . . it can't go on, this slandering of you. It can't. I can't bear it. And the first thing I hear as I come into this room is my father chucking that slime at you——'

'Napier, don't you see that it's me you hurt, not them! You hurt me deeply, Napier. Listen to me, my dear, listen!'

But Napier seemed able to hear nothing, to see no one but his father. Again he put his hand to his mouth to stop it twitching. Venice, a flame in a leather jacket, suddenly threw an arm round Iris. 'Darling, darling, *darling*! How dared you come here! But how dared you! Oh!' she stamped her foot, 'these beasts of men, these beasts, beasts!'

'Venice,' Guy murmured, 'take these two children of yours away at once. Go along now.'

Napier started at Guy's voice. He had admired and worshipped Guy always. Guy smiled faintly, helplessly, was about to say something when Napier said bitterly: 'Guy, I know it wasn't your idea to bring Iris down here and throw that mud at her. I know that——'

'It was mine,' Sir Maurice rapped out. With the paper-knife. 'And it's over now. You may go, Napier. I am asking you to go, boy! And you, Iris March. You and I, Napier, must part from to-night. For some time, at least. You will prefer that, too. You have every right to be angry with me,

236

according to your lights. I gambled—for your future, boy—
and I have lost. I am not sorry to have tried. I am sorry to
have lost. Now you may be as angry as you like—but go!'

Napier's voice trembled: 'Before I go, sir, I'd like to
say——'

'Naps, enough of this!' Guy snapped. 'The more we talk
the worse we make it. Go along, for God's sake.'

Napier shouted: 'I will not go!'

And in the deep, startled silence that must always follow
a shout in an English house, he said, livid quiet, to his father:
'I've ceased to be a boy of eighteen, sir. And I've ceased to
want to be any of the things you seem to admire. This last
year it has seemed to me that not one of the things that have
made my life as you directed it have any reality. You've only
got to think once and the whole ghastly pretence of a life
like mine drops to the ground. And I've been trying lately
to understand the point of view that makes men admirable
in your eyes, sir—and I can't get near it. It seems to mean
sacrificing all the things that are worth while to all the
things that aren't worth while. You sacrificed Iris for what
you call my future, my career. Weigh Iris on one side and
on the other my future, my career, now that I am thirty!
You sacrificed my happiness to the ghastly vanity of making
our name something in this world. You call that 'working
for my future', sir. And I call it the cruel sort of humbug
which has dragged God knows how many decent people
into a beastly, futile unhappiness. Here I am at thirty, a
nothing without even the excuse of being a happy nothing, a
nothing liked by other nothings and successful among other
nothings, a nothing wrapped round by the putrefying little
rules of the gentlemanly tradition. And, my God, they are
putrefying, and I bless the England that has at last found
us out. And if they hadn't been putrefying, sir, and if we
hadn't been going rotten with them, you couldn't have
taken advantage of the fact that Iris never funked anything
in her life to bring her down here and drag her through the
slime——'

'Napier, you must allow me at least the quality of patience.
My one desire, boy, was to protect your happiness. I do not

237

take what you say in the least seriously, for it isn't you speaking but Iris with your voice. You are enchanted——'

'And I should jolly well think he was enchanted!' cried the boy that was Venice, her arm round Iris. A warrior was Venice then, and her leather jacket like a shining breast-plate. 'And I'm enchanted, too—and if you really want to know what's the matter with the whole lot of you, you're all enchanted—by the love of Napier and Iris. I'd stuff all our marriage-laws down a drain-pipe rather than keep them apart for another minute. And I think you must be mad and bad not to see the loveliness of a love like Iris's—and after all this time she's beaten you all in the end, and I'm glad, so glad, so glad!'

'Maurice,' said Hilary gravely, 'you are getting more like God every moment. You're in a minority of one.'

Napier stood in the middle of the room, looking from one to the other of us, scowling, seeing no one, hearing nothing. He was a man lost in an obsession, trying to find his way out. His back was to Iris. Some great man, Balzac maybe, has said that women do not love with their eyes, but there was a blinding love in her eyes, and her lips trembled, tried to smile at the lost thing that Napier was. Only she seemed to know the obsession in which Napier wandered, and she just managed to say: 'Come, Napier. Come. . . .'

Napier turned to her vaguely, seemed about to go with her, then pulled himself round to his father again: 'Before I go, sir, I'd like to tell you—I'd like to say that—that it was a foul thing to do to throw Fenwick at Iris——'

'Napier,' Sir Maurice said quietly, 'I have apologised for that——'

'But have you apologised for us all, sir?' Napier seemed at last to awake from his obsession. He looked happy at that moment. 'Have you apologised for the opinion we've all had of Iris for ten years? Because all these slanders about her go back to——'

'Napier, my Napier, you please mustn't!'

'Iris, I must put this right! You've never had enough respect for yourself——'

'But I have now, dear! Let me . . . keep it. . . .'

238

Napier seemed to appeal to Guy. There was a curious understanding in Guy's look. He said: 'Go on, Naps, let's have it all now. What's this about Fenwick?'

'Guy, don't encourage him!' Iris cried passionately. Venice held her tight. Iris looked at me once just then, and I think that is the last time she ever saw me.

Napier seemed to appeal to Guy: 'Iris has always put her friends before herself. And the only time in her life she ever told a lie we all rushed to believe her. And that's why Iris and I never saw each other after Fenwick's death until three nights before I married Venice. I wasn't to know then that I was marrying an angel, and so I couldn't tell her what had happened to me and Iris. Iris told me about Fenwick that night. I made her. You see, until then I'd never wanted to see her, because the Iris that Boy had killed himself for wasn't the Iris I'd loved as a boy——'

'But she is now, Napier,' Iris whispered bitterly. 'Why can't you let be, why can't you!' ⋅

'Because,' Napier flashed, 'I love you, and I'm damn well going to have these people respect you as I do. . . . That lie Iris spread about the reason for Boy's death was because she didn't care what happened to .her. She just didn't care. But she wanted people to think as well of Boy as people can of a suicide. She wanted Gerald to keep his little tin-god hero. And she had it all her own way because the doctor at the hotel in Deauville was a friend of hers and let nothing out. She just didn't care what people thought of her, and so she said that Boy had died "for purity". That might mean anything, and so of course we all took it to mean the worst thing as regards Iris. Oh, she knew we would. Well, so Boy did die "for purity". He was mad with love for Iris, and from the moment she had to give me up he pestered her to marry him. Then one day she surprised him by saying she would. I suppose she surprised him by giving way in the end, and instead of the cad saying he couldn't, he took her while he had the chance. He——'

'Napier!'

'He had syphilis when he married her, and went mad when he realised what he had done. That's all. There's

239

your Boy Fenwick. There's Iris, that's Iris!' He turned to her blindly. She was staring, so thoughtfully, at the carpet. 'Come, Iris. We'll go now. And we'll begin again from the time you and I said good-bye under Harrod's.'

'You've taken from me,' the husky voice whispered to the carpet, 'the only gracious thing I ever did in my life. Yes, let's go.'

They were going in silence. Iris had one foot in the garden when across the silence darted the neat figure of Sir Maurice. He touched her shoulder. 'Iris,' he said. She looked round at him with huge, sleep-walking eyes.

'Iris,' Sir Maurice said. He was holding out his hand.

'I can't,' she whispered. 'I've hated you so bitterly, so long. I can't. Maurice, please don't ask me.'

'I do ask you, Iris. I beg it from you. You are good.'

Iris's eyes were as though transfixed over the taut old gentleman's shoulder. Iris's eyes were on Venice. Napier had touched Venice's hand, and somehow as he had made to kiss her cheek she had started back frantically . . . and had instantly smiled . . . brightly. Iris's eyes seemed to dilate. Then she took Sir Maurice's hand. 'Thank you, Maurice. But it is Venice who is good. Venice is good. Good-bye.'

They went silently. For a second the green hat flamed in the mist of the light that fell on the lawn, and then the green hat was gone. I stared out into the garden.

I remember a 'hm' just at the very moment when behind me there was a thud of someone falling, and Guy's murmur: 'Hand me that brandy, Maurice.'

Venice sat very erect in a great leather armchair. Her eyes were closed.

Sir Maurice darted about. He waved at me that black ebony paper-knife. He smiled that ancient smile. 'Boy, we shouldn't make hard-and-fast rules for anyone but ourselves. And not even for ourselves. Leads to no good. . . .'

'She's all right,' Guy murmured to Hilary. De Travest was one of those men who always know how to deal with any physical emergency. He knew tricks. . . .

'Poor child, poor child!' sighed Sir Maurice.

'She's all right now,' said Hilary. He was very white and

young-looking, Hilary. Oh, the hm's that dropped from Hilary that night!

It was Guy's face that Venice saw when she opened her eyes. Suddenly, she was crimson.

'Your first words should be,' Guy smiled, '"Where am I?" I may or may not tell you.'

'Guy, where am I?' She was crimson, like a child found out.

'With your friends, Venice, who love you. And Napier has gone.'

'But he hasn't!' she screamed, and caught her scream to her mouth with the palm of her hand. We followed her terrified eyes to see Napier where we had first seen him that night. He stared at Venice. And just at that moment the silence was shattered by the roar of the Hispano. That shattering roar held us all still bewildered. From beneath the trees of Sutton Marle it swept on us like the roar of a thousand rifles.

'That car's gone mad!' rose to my lips.

I saw Venice bite the back of her hand, staring at Napier. The roar of the car had held him at the open window. As he came in Guy spoke savagely. 'Napier, what the hell does this mean? Can't you see what you're doing to Venice?'

Napier said wearily, and he tried to smile, his eyes on Venice: 'All right, Guy. I thought Venice was my friend. I was wrong——'

'Naps,' rapped out Sir Maurice, 'what does this mean!'

As Napier approached near to Venice she jumped up from her chair and started away from him.

'Napier, I don't understand!' she tried not to sob. 'Why have you come back? Napier!'

He said wearily: 'Why didn't you tell me, Venice? I can't understand. God knows I've no opinion of myself left, but I'm not such a pitiful blackguard as——'

'But what is it, Naps!' And she bit the back of her hand. 'I don't know what you're talking about! Why are you looking at me like that?'

'You told Iris, but not me, in case it might interfere with my happiness! My God, Venice, what do you think I am,

241

not to have told me! Do you think I can leave you when you are with a child of mine! Iris said she had promised you not to tell me, but she broke down at the last moment——'

'But it's a lie!' Venice screamed. 'It's a bloody lie! I never told her anything! It's not true! Oh God, it's not true!'

What was said then, what was done, how they looked, I can't remember. I remember only that as Venice sobbed the roar of the car seemed to lessen. The stork had passed from under the trees of Sutton Marle. I think Napier was holding Venice, she was sobbing as though with a breaking heart. 'She's sent you back,' she sobbed. 'The beast, the beast! She's sent you back to show she loved you more than I do. . . .'

Sir Maurice darted across at me, rapped me on the shoulder with the paper-knife.

'Boy, what was that you said about that car going mad?'

I stared at him. I hadn't the faintest idea what I had meant. The distant roar still filled the room like a menace. 'I don't know,' I said. 'Sounds mad. . . .'

'Come along,' the old gentleman rapped out, and darted through the window. I have a confused picture of Guy towering over Napier and Venice with a brimming glass in his hand, of Hilary staring whitely after us. Like a young lover, I see Hilary at that moment. I caught the General up as he was starting-off Guy's car.

'After her, boy. After her. Feel sick, her going like that. Feel sick.'

'Can't catch her in this car, sir.'

'We'll see. Try, anyway. Must catch her. Must beg her forgiveness.' He looked at me as the car started off. He was smiling. Those clever darting eyes were wet. Then Hilary, hatless like ourselves, jumped on to the footboard and into the back.

'What's this, Maurice?'

'After her, man. Iris suddenly thrown her hand in. Listen to that hell's own racket!'

Sir Maurice rushed that ancient Rolls break-neck up the winding drive. From the distance came that menacing roar. 'Can do seventy-six if you like,' I heard the husky whisper above the roar, I saw the dancing tawny curls through the darkness, boy's head, curly head, white and tiger-tawny. . . .

'Can't catch her in this,' I cried again.

Hilary was leaning forward from behind, his chin by my shoulder. He whispered through the rushing air: 'Afraid of her happiness in the end. You beat her, Maurice. You beat her, you and your mouldy old England. And your son wasn't worthy of her love. Good God, he cared whether we respected her or not! She wasn't enough for him as she was. Maurice, it's on your head, all this. She'll be in despair. You've got to catch her.'

We swept headlong round a corner. We were on the crown of the several small slopes that I remembered ascending from Harrod's to Sutton Marle.

'There!' yelled Sir Maurice. And he laughed like an excited boy. 'We'll catch her yet.'

Far down the slope, winding, killing the darkness, rushed the lights of the Hispano. Sir Maurice kept his thumb on the button of the electric-horn, and we drove headlong down that slope with a wild cry of warning to Iris.

'She can't hear!' I yelled.

'Go on, let her know we're here!' yelled Hilary.

The General's silver hair waved frantically in the wind. He was driving like a madman. He was smiling. The two great lights ahead lit the country-side. Then they seemed to shorten, and Harrod's stood like a pillar of light against the darkness. The silver leaves, the giant trunk . . . in the lights of Iris's car. The stork screamed hoarsely, once, twice, thrice. . . .

'Iris!' Hilary sobbed. 'Stop her, man! Stop her! Not that——'

'Iris, not that!' Sir Maurice whispered. 'Child, not that!'

I was blind, sick. There was a tearing crash, a tongue of fire among the leaves of Harrod's. Our car had stopped. 'Iris!' Sir Maurice whispered. 'Iris!' Once again the great tree was lit by a shivering light, then from the darkness there came a grinding, moaning noise as of a great beast in pain. I stood beside Sir Maurice on the road. At the angle at which we had stopped our lights did not fall on the throbbing wreck. He was staring into the darkness.

'But that death!' Hilary stammered. 'That death!'

My foot touched something on the grass beside the road, and I picked up the green hat.

Sir Maurice said hoarsely: 'Chose the only way to make it look like an accident to those two children. . . .'

'Here's her hat,' I muttered, and as Sir Maurice turned to it his face was puckered like a child's.

Suddenly the moaning of the wrecked car ceased, and in the silence Hilary walked into the darkness about the great tree.

The end of the romance called The Green Hat.

THE STORY OF MY LIFE

Ellen Terry

Ellen Terry (1847–1928) was the most magical figure of the Victorian stage, and her enchanting memoirs were described by Ian McKellen recently on Radio 3 as 'the best theatrical autobiography I've ever read.' She wrote these memoirs in 1908, at the end of her main stage career, though her last stage appearance was in 1925. She tells her story very simply and unaffectedly, beginning with her childhood as a travelling player (she first appeared on stage at the age of nine), her ill-fated marriage to the painter G.F. Watts when she was sixteen, her return to the stage and to a series of triumphant successes in London and New York, particularly during her time at the Lyceum with Henry Irving. Her wry and humorous self-portrait is matched by vivid sketches of the great actors and actresses she worked with, and her character study of Irving himself, spendthrift and prodigious in all he did, is in itself enough to ensure the book's place among the classics of the theatre.

240pp, 216 x 135mm, ISBN 0 85115 204 X

THE HOLE IN THE WALL

Arthur Morrison

The Hole in the Wall is one of the most gripping adventure stories ever written. From its unforgetable opening – 'My grandfather was a publican and a sinner, as you will see. His public house was the Hole in the Wall, on the river's edge at Wapping; and his sins – all of them that I know of – are recorded in these pages' – it is a book that you genuinely cannot put down. Stephen Kemp goes to live with his mysterious grandfather after his mother's death, and is gradually drawn into the seedy world which Captain Nat Kemp inhabits, but of which he is determined Stephen shall not become part. Morrison brilliantly conveys the child's sharp observation of all that goes on around him, and builds up a portrait of the East End he himself may have known as a boy; and against this background of dockside life, he unfolds his story in masterly fashion.

179pp, 216 x 135mm, ISBN 0 85115 205 8

THE MONKEY'S PAW

W.W. Jacobs

W.W. Jacobs was at the height of his powers when this volume was first published in 1902, under the title *The Lady of the Barge*. It shows to perfection his skills in thumbnail characterisation and his flawless timing. He could turn these skills to widely differing ends, from the broad comedy of his tales of life aboard Thames barges or in the rural peace of Claybury, to the spine-chilling tragedy of *The Monkey's Paw*. This story, together with *The Well*, has that gothic atmosphere of horror familiar to readers of M.R. James. But where other stories of the supernatural rely on elaborate trappings, Jacobs is economical and direct; a dozen pages are sufficient for him to create the atmosphere, set the plot in motion and bring it to its eerie conclusion. A writer who in one volume can range from a masterly ghost story such as *The Monkey's Paw* to sketches worthy of P.G. Wodehouse – who once described himself as a disciple of W.W. Jacobs – deserves a place on any reader's bookshelf.

W.W. Jacobs (1870–1943) was one of the leading popular writers of the 1890s, the golden age of the short story. Of *Light Freights* (also available in Bookmasters 0 85115 202 3) Michael Sadlier wrote 'His economy of language, his perpetual understatement, his refusal himself to be the joker but the suggestion in a rapid exchange of conversation of the ludicrous catastrophes which have overtaken them – these are qualities in a writer granted only to a master of his craft.'

160pp, 216 x 135mm, ISBN 0 85115 216 3

BRIEF LIVES

John Aubrey

John Aubrey's *Brief Lives*, those racy portraits of the great figures of 17th-century England, stand alongside Pepys's diary as a vivid evocation of the period; in recent years they have been brought memorably to life on television and in the theatre by Roy Dotrice. Yet Aubrey never actually completed his project, nor did he ever manage to put even a single life into logical order. All we have are the raw materials, his jumbled, confused notebooks. Added to this, his language and spelling are often obscure for the reader of today, and it is therefore surprising that there has never been a 'complete' edition in modern spelling. Richard Barber provides just this, reproducing as closely as possible what Aubrey wrote, modernising the spelling and paraphrasing obsolete words, in a version that will allow many new readers to enjoy this vivid and eccentric masterpiece.

John Aubrey was born in 1626, the son of a Wiltshire squire. He never completed his education at Oxford or at the Middle Temple, and when he inherited the family estate at the age of 26 he fought a losing struggle with his father's debts. He finally went bankrupt in the 1670s, and led a sociable, rootless existence at the houses of friends, pursuing the antiquarian studies which had always obsessed him. He published only one book in his lifetime, suitable entitled *Miscellanies*, and died in 1697, leaving a mass of notes and manuscripts, among them the material for *Brief Lives*.

332pp, 216 x 135mm, ISBN 0 85115 206 6

THE YELLOW BOOK

The Yellow Book is the most famous of the literary magazines of the 1890s, summing up the mood of those years, when aesthetics became a subject for fierce debate, satirized by *Punch* and by W.S. Gilbert, and as fiercely defended by the artists and writers who formed the new movement. *The Yellow Book*, in its brief three years of existence, came in for more than its fair share of denunciation and derision, particularly for its illustrations by Aubrey Beardsley. Fraser Harrison's selection allows us to find out what all the fuss was about, and he contributes an introduction on the history of the magazine and its social and artistic context. His essay and the selection of contents, by authors and artists who are now deservedly famous, show that *The Yellow Book* was not merely a *succes de scandale*, but still has much to offer us today.

288pp, 216 x 135mm, ISBN 0 85115 207 4